CALL TO ARMS

The *U.S.S. Virginia*—the first in the most technologically advanced new class of U.S. attack submarines—sets sail, even as the Navy's high-tech submarine program falls under attack from a Congress that believes it unneeded. But a threat no one anticipated is gliding silently through dangerous waters. A rogue Kilo-class submarine built by a shadowy and powerful ally has become the latest weapon in al Qaeda's terrorist arsenal. The submarine's brutal strikes have created an explosive hostage situation in the Pacific . . . and have left hundreds of people dead.

This new and stealthy terrorist threat must be eliminated before more innocent lives are lost. But the officers, crew, and Navy SEALs aboard the *Virginia* will face more than they anticipated in the turbulent waters of the South China Sea—as one untried American sub races toward an explosive confrontation with an old, cunning, and ruthless enemy.

Other *Silent Service* Titles
by H. Jay Riker

SEAWOLF CLASS
LOS ANGELES CLASS
GRAYBACK CLASS

THE
SILENT
SERVICE

VIRGINIA CLASS

H. JAY RIKER

AVON BOOKS

An Imprint of HarperCollinsPublishers

This is a work of fiction. Names, characters, places, and incidents are products of the author's imagination or are used fictitiously and are not to be construed as real. Any resemblance to actual events, locales, organizations, or persons, living or dead, is entirely coincidental.

AVON BOOKS
An Imprint of HarperCollins*Publishers*
10 East 53rd Street
New York, New York 10022-5299

Copyright © 2004 by Bill Fawcett and Associates
ISBN 0-06-052438-3

First Avon Books paperback printing: May 2004

Avon Trademark Reg. U.S. Pat. Off. and in Other Countries, Marca Registrada, Hecho en U.S.A.

HarperCollins® is a registered trademark of HarperCollins Publishers Inc.

Printed in the U.S.A.

10 9 8 7 6 5 4 3 2 1

For Nina,
my love and my inspiration,
no matter how rough the seas

THE
SILENT
SERVICE
VIRGINIA CLASS

PROLOGUE

Tuesday, 15 March 2005

PLA Base, Small Dragon Island
Spratly Islands
South China Sea
1500 hours, Zulu −8

Captain Jian Jie Deng looked up from the paper he was reading and scowled. "I must repeat, General. I do not like this . . . this arrangement. We can gain nothing from an alliance with these people . . . and we could lose so much."

General Han Do Liu shrugged, his broad face empty of emotion. "You do not have to like it, Captain. But you *will* follow orders."

"Of course . . . of course. But one is permitted to wonder if someone back home hasn't taken leave of all reason. These orders are nothing less than insane!"

"Captain Jian! You go too far!"

Jian looked away, letting his gaze rest on the rolling

swell of the ocean below. The two men sat in Han's sparse and utilitarian office, at the north corner of a drab, industrial-style building constructed atop a wave-washed coral atoll. Just visible through the large windows, the main reason for the base rose from the azure water—a huge, flat-roofed enclosure covering the artificial harbor blasted out of solid coral and rock. The bright red flag of the People's Republic fluttered in the sea breeze from a mast above the heliport above the sheltered enclosure.

Only two vessels were visible at the moment outside the shelter—a pair of ancient Hainan-class patrol vessels patrolling the waters. Jian's command, his brand-new command, was still back at Darien. He'd made the trip out to Small Dragon on board one of those Hainans in order to be specially briefed.

According to this plan, the operation wouldn't even begin until next year. Certain things had to happen with China's new allies first. In his opinion, though, the mission for which he was now being briefed went far beyond the merely daring and deep into the realm of errant, even willful stupidity.

He looked again at the paper. They were calling it *Yangshandian*—Operation Ocean-Lightning. He wondered, though, who would be struck by that lightning— the enemies of the People's Republic? Or the People's Republic herself?

To refuse those orders, however, was tantamount to resigning in disgrace from the PLA Navy. It would be suicide, so far as his professional career was concerned, and might even hurt his uncle's standing within the Party. Jian Jiasuo, his father's brother, was a forty-year survivor of Party politics and Jian's patron, the man who'd won for him his chance at attending both the Nanjing Naval Command and Staff College and the Qingdao Submarine Academy. Even the elder Jian wouldn't be able to save a nephew who point-blank refused orders, and he might be disgraced himself.

And Captain Jian would be lucky if the life of his naval career was the only life he lost.

"I apologize," he told General Han at last. "Our duty always is to carry out the will of the People, as expressed by the guiding principles and experience of our superiors." General Han was nearly twice Jian's age, a senior PLA officer with *very* high connections within the Party. Jian would be unwise to show his true feelings here. Within the military of the People's Republic of China, the People's Liberation Army served as the parent organization of all the military services, including the navy. Han was his direct superior and held the power to relieve him on the spot.

The PLAN, the PLA Navy, Jian thought with just a touch of bitterness, was going to have to carve out a separate and equal place for itself within the military hierarchy if it was ever to have the freedom and the respect the navies of other countries enjoyed.

But this was hardly the time to discuss or even think about the bureaucratic insanities that still riddled his nation's government and the people's military service. He would have to maintain his silence and soldier on . . . hoping, perhaps, to lessen the damage any unusually shortsighted policies inflicted on the PLA Navy by the gerontocracy back in Beijing.

It seemed as though the general was reading Jian's mind. "I understand your concern, Captain. We have set foot on a perilous path."

"It could mean war with the United States," Jian told him. "*Real* war, not the skirmishing off Taiwan two years ago."

"I remind you that the People's Republic is not Iraq or Afghanistan. Our American opponents might go to war with a backward, third-world military dictatorship for harboring terrorists . . . but they would not dare bully the People's Republic. That would be true insanity."

"As you say, sir." Privately, though, Jian had resolved to talk to his uncle, as soon as he could establish some means of guaranteeing private communications.

Jian was no coward. If unfolding fate threw him into combat with the Americans, he would fight them, and fight bravely, drawing on every bit of his considerable skill, talent, and training to defeat them . . . or to cause as much destruction to their forces as he could before they dragged him down.

But Jian was also a patriot. When he saw the Beijing government or the military bureaucracy thundering headlong on a course of national suicide, he had to act.

For now, though, he would bide his time. "You are, of course, absolutely right, General," he said.

Tuesday, 15 March 2005

Assembly Building
Submarine Yard, Electric Boat Division
Groton, Connecticut
1553 hours EST

"You're aware, of course, Commander, that I am completely opposed to this . . . this tax dollar-guzzling hole in the water?"

Tom Garrett glanced at the man beside him, wondering if Blakeslee was deliberately trying to push his buttons, or if it simply was the man's acid attitude. How, he wondered, could such an *unpleasant* man be a successful politician? Damn this asinine babysitting duty, anyway. There were better uses of a boat captain's time.

The two of them were walking through the mammoth assembly building above the New Groton ways, Garrett in his blue uniform with its three bright gold stripes like rings at the ends of his jacket's cuffs, Congressman Blakeslee in a conservative gray suit. Both men, however, as per shipyard regulations, wore bright yellow construction helmets against the possibility of tools or other deadly objects dropping from overhead. Above them, like a huge tapered cigar, the pressure hull of the submarine yard's premier construction project hung suspended from overhead cranes.

"Oh, yes, Congressman," he replied with as easy a smile as he could muster. He had to speak loudly to be heard above the whine of machinery, the sharp clang and clatter of metal on metal. "I've been well briefed."

"I damn well imagine you have." John Blakeslee, the honorable representative of the twenty-third District of his state, placed his hands on his hips and stared up at the smooth and gently rounded cliff of metal hanging above them. The flare of an arc welder dazzled and sparked just above the shroud masking the eight-bladed screw at the cigar shape's aft tip. "The Cold War is over," he said after a moment more. "We don't need these monsters any longer. The tax dollars are better spent elsewhere."

It must be tough, Garrett thought with a suppressed smile, to be a member of both the House Armed Services and Appropriations Committee *and* the Congressional Military Appropriations Oversight Committee. Blakeslee's double-barreled quals made him an extraordinarily powerful figure within the government but must also leave him a bit scattered in his job focus at times.

"With respect, sir," Garrett said carefully, "that's not an opinion shared by everyone on your appropriations committee." *And thank God for that,* he added, keeping the thought well concealed.

"What are you talking about, Captain? The Cold War was over when the Berlin Wall came down."

"I didn't mean that, sir," Garrett replied. "I meant about not needing these beasts or the money being better used elsewhere. The *Virginia* is going to pull her own weight, believe me."

"Oh, really? And I say it's about time we found that peace dividend everyone's been talking about for the past sixteen years! Submarines are damned expensive toys, Captain, and they're toys we can now do without."

Garrett had heard the sentiment before, had argued against it more than once.

"Congressman, the peace dividend wasn't leftover money in the national budget. It was forty-some years of *peace*."

"Indeed?" Blakeslee snorted. "Our veterans of Vietnam, Korea, and the Gulf Wars would be most interested in that sentiment."

The man, Garrett decided, was definitely testing him, pushing him to get a reaction. No man could be that obtuse, even if he *was* a politician.

"Peace between us and the other superpowers, Congressman. Somehow we made it through the fifties, the sixties, the seventies, the eighties . . . and not once did either side in the Cold War fire a nuclear missile. Not once was an American—or Russian—city incinerated. We fought wars, yes, sir—Korea, Vietnam—but we were never in a shooting war with the Russians or the Chinese. And part of the reason, a damned big part of the reason, I'll add, was the technology we put into military programs, including submarines. Technology is expensive, but the payoff was that we managed to balance things in such a way that we didn't turn our planet into a radioactive desert."

"Obviously we stand on different sides of the issue," Blakeslee said. "There are different ways of looking at history, you know. Different interpretations. But . . . even granting that you're right, my point is that we don't need attack submarines like this one any longer. The Navy can and should make do with the Los Angeles–class subs, gradually phasing them out as they reach the end of their operational service. We should never have built even one *Seawolf* . . . and certainly not the *Virginia*."

"Sir, did you ever hear the expression penny-wise, pound-foolish?"

The corners of Blakeslee's mouth twitched, and Garrett couldn't tell if it was a frown or a suppressed smile. "Don't overstep yourself, Commander. You do not want me as an enemy, believe me."

"The last time I checked, Congressman, you and I were on the same side. We both care for the peace and security of this country. And for the health of the armed forces."

"You're right, Commander, of course." He sighed. "Forgive me. Perhaps it was I who overstepped the bounds of propriety. But the tangle of budget and military appropriations is something of a Gordian knot . . . a very frustrating one. If there's a sword with which to cut the puppy, I have not yet been able to find it." He stopped suddenly and pointed. "What the hell is that?"

"The command center module," Garrett said, following Blakeslee's gaze. Amid a flurry of activity on the scaffolding, something like a huge, squat tin can was being lowered into place within the pressure hull. "Most of *Virginia*'s compartments are being assembled separately, each in one piece. Then we lower them in—or 'snap them on,' as we say—to cushioned mounting points on board. The system is called MID-S, for 'modular isolated deck structures.' With each compartment riding its own set of cushioned mounts, it helps make for a *very* quiet boat."

"A very expensive boat, Captain. Who's going to hear you out there? The Iranians? The Lithuanians?"

"The Chinese are a possibility, sir. And a very real threat."

Blakeslee snorted again. That snort, Garrett decided, was a standard-issue part of Blakeslee's debating armamentarium.

"Your part in the Taiwan incident two years ago has not been forgotten," Blakeslee said. "If anything, I should think you, of all people, would understand that the Chinese are no longer a credible naval threat."

"Who suggested that, Congressman? Beijing has no interest in becoming a global naval power, but with eight thousand and some miles of convoluted coastline, they're very interested in becoming *the* regional power to be reckoned with. They remember the Battle of the Taiwan Strait as well as we do, sir, and they have a long memory."

In May of 2003, Garrett had been in command of the SSN *Seawolf,* the first-in-her-class demo model of a whole range of new submarine technologies. Tensions had heated sharply, as they did, periodically, over the island of Taiwan and its independence—as the Republic of China—from the Communist mainland, the People's Republic of China. An attempt by the People's Republic to cow Taiwan into accepting Beijing's rule had escalated. Taiwan had been bombarded—not for the first time—by missiles fired from the mainland, and the PRC's fleet of submarines had moved to block the Formosa Strait.

The naval action that followed between the People's

Republic forces and the U.S. Seventh Fleet had ended
with the sinking of all but three of Beijing's attack submarines, including a deadly, nuclear-powered, Russian-
built *Akula* and the sinking of a Luda-class destroyer.
Referred to now as the Battle of the Taiwan Strait, the
conflict had been played down by both Washington
and Beijing. The PRC had its own reasons for mini-
mizing its loss of face over the undeclared miniwar,
and Washington, still involved in both Afghanistan
and the Gulf, hadn't wanted to encourage the idea either at home or abroad that America was a bully, picking on rogue regimes around the world.

Garrett had often thought that he would have done
it differently; letting the whole world know that the
United States had stopped the Chinese threat with a
single carrier battlegroup and the USS *Seawolf* ought
to make hostile governments from Havana to Tripoli
to Pyongyang think twice about testing American re-
solve or capabilities.

But Garrett was a sub driver, not a maker of foreign
or military policy. His opinion didn't count, nor was it
permitted a public airing.

"China is no threat to us," Blakeslee told him, "or
to our interests abroad. They learned their lesson two
years ago, and it's in our best interests to treat them as
a prospective ally and business partner. Sinking someone else's submarines is not recommended if you wish
to do business with them."

Garrett thought it politic not to point out that the
PRC had fired first with its bombardment of an American ally or to mention that the U.S. had lost a ship of
its own in that conflict, the USS *Jarrett*.

"Governments change, Congressman. Foreign policies change. In my experience, it's best to be ready."

"I quite agree, Commander. But this boondoggle's

contribution to American readiness is completely unproven, even speculative. It's simply the Navy's way of getting around the fact that Congress curtailed the Seawolf program. Not on *my* watch, sir!"

Garrett's jaw and fists clenched as he bit off a reply. Damn it, what did Blakeslee want with him, anyway? Admiral Logan had ordered him to accompany Blakeslee on his tour of the Electric Boat yards—a simple enough request, given that various Washington bureaucrats frequently came up here for tours of one sort or another, and someone needed to guide them around. Garrett was beginning to wonder what he'd done to warrant a punishment detail.

Blakeslee was right in one way, of course. The *Virginia* was an ongoing set of compromises in a long and ugly war over the Navy's dwindling budget.

The Navy's planners had foreseen the need for a fleet of 80 attack submarines, beginning with 39 original Los Angeles–class subs and 23 improved L.A. boats. These 62 SSNs had a planned operational life of thirty-three years; the lead boat, the *Los Angeles,* had been launched in 1974, and unless her service life was extended, she would be pulled from the fleet in another two years. Eleven of the older, "straight" L.A. boats had been decommissioned in the nineties for various reasons. One more, the *Memphis,* had been turned into a research platform, bringing the total down to fifty.

Worse, those fifty attack subs represented aging technology . . . and in the superscience world of undersea combat, technology did not age well. The transfer of the *Memphis* to Navy R&D had been prompted by congressional criticism that the Navy was not pursuing advanced technology for its submarine forces, and the improved L.A. submarines were a partial answer . . . but not a complete one. When the Walker spy-family scandal had broken in the eighties, the Navy realized that the Soviets would very soon possess submarines as stealthy and as deadly as even the improved L.A. boats.

So the Seawolf project had been born, emerging from design studies in the midseventies, but refined and given shape under the impetus of the Soviet submarine threat of the eighties. Originally planned as the Navy's "submarine of the twenty-first century," *Seawolf* would be far quieter than the Los Angeles attack boats. Faster, stealthier in every way, and carrying a mammoth arsenal of torpedoes and Tomahawk missiles, *Seawolf* had been intended to counter high-tech Soviet submarines—especially the sleek and deadly *Akula*, the so-called Walker-class boat designed using the secrets sold to Moscow by the Walkers. Thirty Seawolf-class attack subs were planned.

Then, with astonishing suddenness, the Soviet empire had collapsed, and much of Moscow's vaunted military was revealed to be a rotting shell. Somehow, the need for an eighty-boat fleet hadn't seemed quite so urgent, especially in light of the fast-rising price tag for the *Seawolf*. Already incredibly expensive when she was originally designed—in the seventies, cost estimates had run to about $1.3 billion per unit—cost overruns and redesigns swiftly sent that estimate soaring. At $4 billion per sub, the *Seawolf* was indeed a "golden fish."

And so, in August of 1990, after a four-month review, Seawolf procurement was reduced to twelve units. A new attack submarine—then called *Centurion,* because now *it* would be the "submarine of the new century"—was proposed as a complement for the twelve-boat Seawolf fleet, aiming for a total submarine force of fifty-five boats. The Defense Acquisition Board had ordered that the new boat cost less than a billion dollars per unit.

By that time, *Seawolf* was at ground zero in a raging controversy between the Defense Department, Congress, and the White House. In January of 1992, the Department of Defense had announced that only one Seawolf would be built. In a backhanded twist of politics, President Clinton—usually no friend of the military—had promised to raise the number from one to three as a bit of political palm-greasing to the state of Connecticut, where the Seawolfs would be constructed. More than one observer had noted the irony of a Democratic president resurrecting a military project a Republican president had wanted cancelled.

And so the Seawolf project would end with three units—the *Seawolf* herself, launched in 1995, followed by the *Connecticut* in 1997 and the *Jimmy Carter* in 2003. The Navy had long since shifted its full attention to *Centurion*, which was now referred to as the NSSN, or "New SSN" project. By 1998, the NSSN had been named *Virginia*, yet another bit of political baksheesh. Connecticut was the location of one submarine builder, the Electric Boat Division of General Dynamics, but Virginia was the other, with the yards at Newport News.

But political gestures or no, the budgets battles were continuing. By 2000, the NSSN program had been cut to twelve funded units, with one to be launched per year beginning in 2004. By 2005, the number had been cut to four, with the lead boat scheduled for launching in 2006. The Navy ultimately still wanted thirty Virginia-class subs, but the way things had been going with Congress and the military budget-snippers lately, that number seemed most unlikely.

"You know, Congressman," Garrett said carefully, "the Navy has done its share of budget-busting, I admit, but it seems to me that the Navy Department and Congress are too often sabotaging each other. Remember the about-face you guys pulled on us over Newport News?"

Originally, the *Virginia* was supposed to have been assembled entirely at Electric Boat here at New London in Connecticut, a decision that would have closed the submarine yards at Newport News, Virginia. That move, it was estimated, would have trimmed quite a bit from the Navy's appropriations budget and helped meet congressional demands to cut costs and close bases. Congress, however, had stepped in and ordered the Navy to use both Electric Boat and Newport News. Shipyard workers in the sovereign state of Virginia voted, and they would vote for the congressmen who kept them employed.

"Well, son, yes, I do. But it worked out okay, didn't it?"

"After a fashion, Congressman. After a lopsided and very expensive fashion."

Eventually, the Navy had encouraged both yards to participate in the building of all Virginia-class boats. Newport News built the bow, stern, sail, crew compartments, auxiliary machinery, and weapons handling spaces of each boat; Electric Boat built the pressure hull, command and control compartments, engine room, and the main propulsion unit raft. Both yards would construct the nuclear reactors. They would then be pieced together, two at Electric Boat, two at Newport News.

At least, that was what the gouge was *this* week.

"You know and I know, Captain," Blakeslee went on, "that this whole process has been politicized to an incredible extent. And you're right. It's not efficient, and we do get in each other's way. I'm here, though, because I can't help but wonder if we can't just cut across the whole mess . . . Alexander's solution to the Gordian knot, right?" He made a chopping motion with his hand. "*Ffft!* Done."

"And put all the shipyard workers out of business?"

"They would keep working on the Los Angeles SSNs. Damn it, Commander, every one of the fancy electronic doodads on both the *Seawolf* and the *Virginia* could have been retrofitted into the L.A. boats, and for a fraction of the cost!"

"If someone could just justify to me why we need this damned thing," Blakeslee said, gesturing at the *Virginia*'s hull overhead. "You know and I know, America's biggest concern today is the goddamn al Qaeda. Terrorists don't have submarines and they don't have merchant fleets. They don't even have a navy. There is no power in the world today to match our surface navy. We are the undisputed masters of the world's sea lanes. Why, I ask you, do we need the Virginia program?"

Garrett gave Blakeslee a sidelong look. Was it possible the man was trying to goad him into opening up?

He took a deep breath. "Congressman, I'm sure you've seen more briefings and papers on the *Virginia* than I have. *Virginia* is the answer to Congress's original demands—that the Navy build a submarine utilizing the latest technology, capable of extended littoral operations, with the ability both to conduct missile bombardment of inland targets and to support special operations force insertions along any coast.

"*Virginia* possesses twelve vertical launch tubes for Tomahawk TLAM cruise missiles, letting her hit targets 1,600 miles from the ocean, and that means some-

thing like 80 to 90 percent of the world's land surface
is within her reach. She has four torpedo tubes that can
handle Mark 48 ADCAP torpedoes, with a range of
seven miles, or Harpoon antiship missiles with a range
of eighty miles or better. She has facilities on board for
SEALs or Marine Recon personnel, which she can put
ashore anywhere in the world through a nine-man
lockout trunk. She is as quiet as the *Seawolf*, which
means she's ten times quieter than an improved L.A.
boat . . . and that's in spite of being considerably
smaller than *Seawolf*. Standard engineering doctrine
holds that the larger you build the submarine, the easier it is to make it quiet.

"Why do we need submarines as opposed to the surface navy? Well, sometimes you want to show the flag,
to let the other guy see you and think about how much
firepower you have off his coast . . . and when that
happens you send in a carrier battle group. But sometimes you don't want him to see you. You want to lurk
off his coast or even slip inside his harbors to see what
he's up to or tap into his submarine communications
cables or drop off a team of SEALs, and for that you
need a submersible, a very *quiet* submersible.

"As for who our enemies are going to be twenty
years from now . . . or even next month, how the hell
do we know? Iran was our bosom buddy in the seventies until their revolution turned them from ally to enemy. Five years later we were covertly helping out
Saddam Hussein because Iraq was fighting Iran, and
eight years after *that* we were at war with Iraq. The
political situation throughout the world is always
changing, and between global terrorism, high-seas
piracy, and the proliferation of weapons of mass destruction, the Navy might find itself going into harm's
way anywhere, at any time. A nuke or a bioterror war-

head in the hands of a nation like . . . what country did you say a while ago? Lithuania. A nuke in Lithuania is just as dangerous, just as destabilizing, just as threatening as the same warhead in China.

"And, damn it, sir, to expect our fleet of L.A. boats to continue operations into the 2020s is like expecting today's Navy to continue employing World War II diesel boats. It's dangerous, it's ineffective, it's short-sighted, and it's stupid. We *need* the *Virginia,* and we need the boats that will follow her."

"But the Los Angeles–class subs *will* function quite well for the next ten years or so, Commander. And by then, we'll have even better technology. The *Virginia* and her sister units will be as obsolete as the *Los Angeles,* and the Navy will be looking to build still *another* high-tech and high-cost submarine! Am I right? Why not wait until then?"

Garrett waved an arm at a group of workers on the scaffolding overhead. "*They're* the reason why, at least in part.

"You know, Congressman, they say we're farther away, right now, today, from putting another man on the moon, than we were back in 1960 when Kennedy challenged us to a manned landing within the decade. The reason is that after the Apollo program was cancelled in the seventies, the team of engineers and technicians and trained construction workers who worked on Apollo had been scattered to the four winds.

"Well, sir, just like with Apollo, it takes years of work to design a new submarine, and years more of construction before the lead boat of a class is launched. That construction requires a small army of highly skilled and experienced workers. Without an ongoing series coming off the ways, that work force will be broken up and lost, wasted. We can't build a new submarine class from a standing start overnight. As it is, the *Virginia* here is doing pretty well. The original NSSN-Centurion studies were done in 1990. Fifteen years from initial cost and feasibility studies to commissioning is pretty damned good in anybody's book."

They continued to walk through the cavernous expanse of the assembly building. Blakeslee was quiet for a long time.

"Excellent speech, Commander," he said. "I wonder if I could lure you into a new career as my speechwriter."

"I'm happy as a sub driver, sir."

"Just kidding. I do appreciate your candor. You, my friend, face danger every time you set sail in one of those sealed coffins. I face danger of a different sort. One of the worst is that everyone tells me what they think I'd like to hear . . . not what I *need* to hear. Right now, the U.S. submarine program is in such an unholy tangle of turf wars and budget battles . . . I don't think anyone in Washington is seeing more than his or her tiny patch of ground. And you know as well as I do . . . the Navy's procurement office is as politically oriented as we are up on the Hill."

"Yes, sir. It leaves us working stiffs kind of caught in the middle sometimes."

"I can well imagine. What I'm interested in here today, Commander, is how you 'working stiffs,' as you put it, feel about the *Virginia*. Do *you* see her as a boondoggle? Politics as usual? Or is she a useful addition to the fleet?" He held up a cautioning hand. "I don't want the Navy's party line, Commander. What do *you* think?"

Garrett thought about that one for a moment. "Sir, I see her as a necessary, as a damned *vital* addition to the fleet. I do believe she's already the product of too many compromises, and I think those compromises will come back to haunt us. But the Los Angeles boats are aging, and we'll be striking a few of them every year from now on. We have three Seawolf SSNs . . . and the *Carter* was being modified as a deep-ocean research, search, and recovery special-mission submarine to replace the *Parche* before she was even launched. That leaves us with just two full-time Seawolf boats. Right now, the *Virginia* is all we have." He thought for a moment. "Congressman, we might not know who our future enemies are going to be, but we do know that the Navy's future battleground is going to be the third world littorals, shallow and hemmed-in waters in places like the Yellow Sea, the Arabian Gulf, and the Eastern Med. Places that sane submarine skippers dread like rush hour on the Washington Beltway. Yes, sir, we need the *Virginia,* and at least thirty more like her."

Blakeslee chuckled. "Well, I can't promise the thirty more, Commander. In fact, I can just about guarantee that you're not going to get them. The question before my panel now is whether to fund more than the first four and, if so, how many." The tune of "The Stars and Stripes Forever" keened from the congressman's jacket pocket. He reached in and pulled out his cell phone. "Excuse me, Commander. Duty calls."

Garrett stepped away to give the congressman privacy. Jesus . . . was all that storm and bluster just his way to probe Garrett's heart and mind, to find out what he really thought? Scary notion, that such a powerful congressman could be that cynical, that untrusting of what others told him.

Blakeslee rejoined him a moment later, pocketing the phone. "I'm afraid the tour has to be curtailed for the moment, Commander. That was my aide, back at the visitors' center. Something's come up."

"I'll walk you back over there, sir."

"Thank you. And . . . thank you for your insight, Commander. It's given me something to think about."

"You're aware, aren't you, sir, that we call the Appropriations Committee 'Santa Claus'?"

"I wasn't aware, but it seems appropriate, somehow."

Garrett's mouth quirked. "Well, yes, Santa Claus, there *is* a *Virginia*. And we need those other boats. Desperately."

Blakeslee laughed. "I'll see what I can do, Commander. You'll need a damned big stocking for that many submarines, though. Tell me . . . are you looking forward to your new command?"

Garrett looked up at the sleek, unfinished hull suspended overhead. "Yes, sir. More than I've looked forward to anything in my life."

"Even if she's a compromise?"

"Even if she's a compromise. Because in the long run, it's not the weapons load or the sonar suite or the technology that makes a sub work. It's the caliber of the men who sail on her, her crew. And we have the best in the world."

"I'm with you there, Commander. And I wish you the very best of luck with your new command."

Funny. The way Blakeslee said the words, it was as though he'd added "because you'll need it" at the end.

Thursday, 11 May 2006

Submarine Pen
Small Dragon Island
Spratly Islands, South China Sea
1345 hours, Zulu −8

Captain Jian stood on the catwalk extending along the length of the cavernous submarine pen, leaning on the railing as he watched the arrival of the *Shuhadaa Muqaddaseen,* an Arabic name meaning "Holy Martyrs." Other People's Republic naval officers and men stood to either side, watching in silence. *How many of them,* he wondered, *know just what is at stake here?*

His own vessel, the *Yinbi de Gongji,* was already moored inside the base, starboard-side to in Mooring Slip One. Working parties labored on her deck, carrying cases of provisions aboard from the dock and handing them down through deck hatches. The *Yinbi* would be ready for sea soon. Jian would be glad to be free of

21

the dank-walled, confining closet of the Small Dragon sub pen and out beneath the waves of the open sea once more.

The shelter was necessary for the moment, a haven safe from the prying scrutiny of American spy satellites. It was important that the Yankees not be aware that the *Yinbi de Gongji* was operational and in these waters . . . at least, not yet. With luck, the Yankees still thought she was at Darien, unaware that the sleek and deadly shape now moored at the shipyard construction dock was a shell of plastic and plywood.

An elaborate deception, carried out under the thick cloud cover of an approaching typhoon, had enabled the *Yinbi de Gongji* to slip out to sea unobserved. The passage south to Small Dragon had been uneventful. Now, all he wanted to do was to complete the resupply and get back to sea.

But first, there was this small and unpleasant formality.

He could see two men squeezed together in the weather bridge of the submarine as it entered the shelter. One was almost certainly the *Shuhadaa Muqaddaseen*'s captain. The man reached up and removed his cap in salute; Jian ignored the gesture, pretending not to see. Line handling parties on the dock stood ready as the incoming vessel approached Slip Two, sidling up toward the dock port-side to. The submarine's black hull, the rectangular tower of her sail, passed slowly through the glare of spotlights suspended from the latticework of struts supporting the shelter's high ceiling.

The flag hanging limply from the foreign submarine's mast was that of Pakistan, but that was a lie, of course. Or, rather, it was a political misstatement. The submarine, a Kilo-class diesel electric boat, had recently been purchased by Pakistan from the Krasnaya Sormova shipyards in Russia, but the Pakistani admiralty, Jian thought, had no idea who was actually crewing that vessel . . . or why. *Shuhadaa* might be operating under the flag of Pakistan for the moment, and her captain and most of her officers and crew were Pakistani nationals, but her first officer was Saudi, and an Afghani reportedly was aboard as well.

And the doctrine under which she sailed was that of al Qaeda.

How deeply, Jian wondered, did the political cabal within the Islamabad government extend? They were playing a deadly game over there, one with terrifying consequences should they be found out by the United States.

Officially, of course, Pakistan was an ally of the United States in the so-called War on Terror. The CIA had established a covert presence in that country during the Soviet occupation of Afghanistan. Almost two decades later, the U.S. had coordinated much of its military campaign against the Taliban and al Qaeda from Pakistan. But the government in Islamabad was less than perfectly stable, and religious fervor and factionalism ran deep. There were plenty of people within both Pakistan's government and the military who admired Osama bin Laden and the small army of Islamic imams, mullahs, and clerics who continued to repeat and elaborate on his inflammatory, anti-American rhetoric.

The truth of the matter was that Pakistan desperately needed American foreign aid and would do almost anything to keep that pipeline open and flowing. But some individuals and certain cliques within Islamabad's centers of power continued to work behind the scenes, not against American interests directly, but in support of the numerous factions, cells, and networks throughout the Islamic world that continued to wage a shadow war of unrest, revolution, and terror against the Western behemoth.

So far, the People's Republic had managed to stay out of that particular tiger's lair, despite the fact that a significant percentage of Chinese—especially in the western provinces—was Muslim. The PRC officially was an atheist state, at times militantly opposed to religious activity that might threaten Beijing's authority; the state's ongoing policy of suppression and subversion in Tibet was a case in point. Now, however, the state apparently had reasons for covertly supporting al Qaeda.

That reasoning was utterly beyond Jian's understanding.

Eighteen years in his nation's naval service had left him with the ability to turn the occasional blind eye to bureaucratic idiocy or incompetence. One needed such convenient blindness at times simply to survive. This, however, was infinitely worse than the typical clumsiness of Beijing's bloated party system. The possibility of a full-fledged war with America was all too real, and Jian knew exactly what the consequences of such a conflict might be. The knowledge left him feeling bitter, angry, and trapped. His two options—and at the moment he could see only two—were to carry out his orders without question, without thinking, and in so doing involve his country in a war that no one could possibly win; or to refuse those orders, a decision that would mean the end of his naval career, possible imprisonment, and disgrace for his wife, both of his children, his father, and his father's politically powerful brother.

His face impassive, he stared down at the long, rectangular upright of the Kilo's sail, passing slowly now almost directly beneath his position on the catwalk.

Where, he wondered, was his path of duty, and was it also a path of honor?

Attack Submarine *Shuhadaa Muqaddaseen*
Small Dragon Island
Spratly Islands, South China Sea
1345 hours, Zulu −8

Captain Abdullah ul Haq replaced his cap on his head as the *Shuhadaa Muqaddaseen* slid serenely beneath the catwalk perch of the Chinese officers. He was pretty sure he recognized his opposite number—Captain Jian—among them, and felt a small stir of resentment at the man's deliberate slight, his refusal to acknowledge ul Haq's cordial salute. The alliance was off to an uncertain start.

Not alliance, ul Haq reminded himself. *A relationship of the moment only.* The marriage between the Maktum and the People's Republic of China was one strictly of convenience and expediency. Not all within the Maktum thought it was a good idea to ally with infidels.

Maktum—the word meant, roughly, "closed mouth" or "sworn to silence"—had arisen in Pakistan during the evil days of America's invasion of Afghanistan and the destruction of the Taliban. Beginning back in the early nineties as a clique of officers within Pakistan's military, dedicated to fundamentalist Islam and the creation of an army-backed theocracy in Islamabad, the Maktum had been instrumental as a pipeline for key Taliban and al Qaeda leaders fleeing the far-flung nets of the American forces attempting to capture them in Afghanistan. They'd helped bin Laden himself escape the trap at Tora Bora, smuggling him first across the border into northern Pakistan, and then eventually to a safe haven in Indonesia.

The man squeezed into the cockpit at ul Haq's side now atop the sail of the *Shuhadaa* had also fled the Afghan holocaust with the Maktum's help. His name was Noor Khalili, and he'd been one of the immortal bin Laden's most trusted lieutenants. He still was one of the most powerful men within the secretive al Qaeda.

"All back," ul Haq said into the microphone for the sub's intercom system. Instantly, the single screw astern reversed direction, churning a swirl of white water as the slow-drifting vessel began slowing more, edging gently toward the pier. The line-handling crews fore and aft tossed lines across to the men on the dock, who grabbed them and began making them fast to the pier-side bollards. *Shuhadaa Muqaddaseen* shuddered as she came to rest.

"All stop," ul Haq commanded, and the engine fell silent. The first leg of the vessel's long voyage, from Karachi to the Spratly Islands, was complete.

"Well done, my friend," Khalili said. The Afghan grinned broadly, exposing a ragged array of yellow teeth. "Truly, *Holy Martyrs* is a magnificent vessel! A magnificent weapon for striking at the Americans!"

"Perhaps," ul Haq replied. "But at the moment, I'm more concerned about our hosts and the promises they've made. I need to go ashore and arrange for our refueling."

"You don't need to worry about the Chinese, Captain. Every detail has been carefully arranged."

"It's my job to worry. That is what ship captains do. If you'll excuse me?"

He squeezed past Khalili and descended into the dark tunnel leading down into the submarine's belly. *Shuhadaa Muqaddaseen* was a submarine of cramped and antique design, one of dozens of Kilo-class vessels a cash-hungry Russian Federation had been peddling lately to every would-be sea power from the People's Republic of China to Iran. The despised Indians possessed no fewer than five Kilos in their navy, one important reason that Islamabad had decided to purchase one as well. Commissioned as S-137, *Al Saif* ("the sword") at Khalili's suggestion, the Kilo had been renamed shortly after leaving port. Though neither the government in Islamabad nor the Admiralty in Karachi knew it, *Shuhadaa* was now the first warship in al Qaeda's navy, a terror weapon that could strike unseen at the West's mercantile infrastructure from the Arabian Gulf to the northern coast of Australia.

Until recently, Pakistan had purchased all of its submarines from the French. Islamabad's small navy boasted six other diesel attack boats—four of the aging Daphne class, plus two of the more modern Agosta class. The two Agostas, *Hasmat* and *Hurmat*, were excellent vessels; ul Haq had commanded the *Hasmat* for two years in the late 1990s. Displacing 1,200 tons and capable of about twelve knots submerged or twenty on the surface, they were capable and deadly.

But the Kilo . . .

She was twice the *Hasmat*'s tonnage, with a larger pressure hull. Constructed with full and certain knowledge of the U.S. Navy's sonar capabilities, she was quiet, quieter even than the American Los Angeles submarines, quieter even, it was whispered, than their

Seawolfs. She carried fewer torpedoes, true, and she was no faster than the French Agostas, but she had a considerably greater cruising range and greater endurance submerged. She also had a bonus, so far as al Qaeda was concerned. Mounted in her sail was a surface-to-air missile launcher, a feature unique to the Kilo among all of the world's submarines. The Russians didn't usually include that particular accessory on board their export submarines. Evidently, some palms had been liberally greased. Despite American efforts, al Qaeda still had considerable financial resources. How else could they have manipulated the Pakistani government to get access to this vessel?

Stepping off the ladder from the weather bridge, ul Haq entered the submarine's control room. Half a dozen men in Pakistani naval uniforms manned the various control stations there. His first officer, a dark and leather-skinned Saudi named Muhammad Hassan Fitaihi, stood at the periscope well. "Ship-to-shore communications have been established, Captain. The Chinese have just requested inspection rights."

"Tell them that I will come ashore to meet with them," ul Haq said. He didn't want the infidels mingling with the crew freely just yet.

Ul Haq was fiercely proud of *Shuhadaa Muqaddaseen*. Her single limitation as a weapon for al Qaeda was her basing and logistical needs. Once the Pakistani government knew that the *Shuhadaa* had gone rogue, she would never again be able to return to Karachi, nor could she pull into any friendly port to refuel. For al Qaeda there *were* no friendly ports.

That was where the Chinese came in.

For reasons of their own—ul Haq still didn't understand what they were—Beijing had agreed to allow the *Shuhadaa* access to their new and highly classified submarine base in the Spratly Islands. More, they'd promised the assistance of a PLAN attack submarine, that one tied at the other slip ahead, in training the Pakistani crew on the new vessel. The PLAN knew the Kilo; they'd purchased a number of them from the Russians and were rumored to be building their own. They knew submarine tactics, knew how to employ attack submarines against a larger and more powerful adversary.

The advisor the Chinese had promised to send on *Shuhadaa Muqaddaseen*'s first voyage would be invaluable—*if* this marriage of convenience could be made to work.

Ul Haq did not trust the Chinese. They were not altruists, and they were not motivated by religious faith. Clearly, they had an agenda of their own, one that would not necessarily further al Qaeda's interests. It was self-evident that they hoped to use the al Qaeda submarine and crew for their own benefit. Ul Haq wished he knew what that benefit might be. The orders transmitted by his Maktum contact in the Admiralty had given no hints as to what Beijing hoped to gain from this . . . association.

Clearly, too, not all of the Chinese officers involved in this plan were eager to implement it. Ul Haq would have to see what he could do to generate some enthusiasm in that quarter.

And he would have to watch his back. The Chinese were perfectly capable of tossing him, his crew, and the *Shuhadaa* to the Americans like a scrap to a dog if the submarine became an embarrassment to them.

Fortunately, he would not have to rely too heavily on the infidels. He needed Small Dragon Island's submarine pen for refueling and provisioning, and he needed those promised advisors. Once *Shuhadaa* had set sail once more, Beijing's games within games would no longer matter.

In the meantime, he wanted to limit contact with the Chinese as much as possible. He didn't want them on his vessel, didn't want them contaminating the crew with strange ideas.

Most of all, he did not want any of his men to start speculating about their chances for surviving this mission.

Ul Haq did not expect the submarine to survive her first cruise. The idea was to do as much damage to American interests as possible before they finally hunted *Shuhadaa* down and sank her.

Thoughtful, he watched the men in the control room securing their stations. Through Maktum's manipulations, most of the men on board were fervent Muslims, eager for jihad. The story had already been passed among them that Pakistan might soon be at war with the American giant . . . a lie, of course, but a very useful one. The nation of Pakistan continued to play the lapdog to American foreign interests. It was al Qaeda that was waging holy war.

But only a few of the officers were al Qaeda or committed to the path of martyrdom. He needed the full cooperation of *all* his men in this difficult mission to come.

It was too bad, he thought, that all of these brave men would perish with the *Shuhadaa* when the Americans caught her at last.

Friday, 12 May 2006
Bachelor Officer's Quarters
Submarine Base
New London, Connecticut
1525 hours, local time

"Tom, I just don't think we can continue like this."

Garrett heard the words but was having trouble grasping their reality. They were faint with distance, but clear enough. Damn it, not again. . . .

"Don't do this to me, Kazuko." He heard the echo of his voice on the line, marking the half-second's delay as his voice was relayed by satellite from New England to California. "*Please* don't do this to me." *Not like this. . . .*

"How long has it been since we were together, Tom? Four months? Five?"

"The last time I was on leave. In November. I flew out to LAX just to be with you on your birthday." That had been a hell of an expensive vacation, but worth every dollar, worth every moment. "Kazuko, I *love* you."

"I love you, Tom. But we can't continue a relationship where we see each other twice a year, *maybe,* when both of us happen to be in the same town."

Garrett leaned back in the chair—one of the one-size-fits-all wonders of modern furnishing provided in naval BOQs the world over. The room was a pleasant one and tastefully decorated; he was a commander, after all, and the captain of an attack submarine. But it was also sterile, a hotel room, not a home.

He'd almost forgotten how much he missed home . . . or missed, at least, the idea of one.

"I told you last week, baby," he said. Damn, that echo was distracting. Hearing his own words bouncing back at him made him all too aware of how pathetic he sounded. "I've got some more leave coming. I was saving it for our anniversary. I could probably get approval for a long weekend, though. I could come out there. We could talk."

They had to talk. *Had* to. He'd been seeing Kazuko for four years, now, since shortly after his divorce, in fact. She'd been a junior flight attendant working for Singapore Airlines then; she was a senior attendant now, which meant she had a good deal more flexibility in arranging her schedule.

He heard her sigh. "I'll be home in Bangkok next weekend," she told him. "After that, I'll be on the Tokyo-Singapore run again. That'll be at least six weeks."

Garrett closed his eyes, mind racing. It *might* work. "Maybe I could swing seeing you out there, hon. In about a month." He couldn't say more. His new command, the *Virginia,* was at sea now undergoing her trials. He would formally take command when she returned to New London, sometime next week. The scuttlebutt was that she would then be deployed to the Far East—possibly Japan, possibly Hong Kong. The latest intelligence reports suggested that the Chinese navy was up to something, possibly something big, and the rumors suggested that *Virginia*'s mettle might be tested in the same waters where Garrett had taken the *Seawolf* three years before.

It was only scuttlebutt, of course, and not something he would ordinarily count on. *Virginia* might easily be sent anywhere in the world, and her orders hadn't been cut yet. But if there was even a chance of seeing Kazuko face to face, to make her reconsider . . .

Even if the *Virginia* called at Hong Kong rather than at Yokosuka, he might be able to wangle a forty-eight for a quick flight to Tokyo and see her there.

"Tom . . . I don't think you're hearing me. I can't live like this. I can't live on promises and stolen weekends. I can't live with the secrecy and the maybes and the 'I'll try to see you if I'm in port.' I can't go on month after month not knowing when I'll see you again. This is good-bye."

"Not long distance, damn it," he said. "I want to *see* you. I want you to look me in the eyes when you tell me that!"

"It won't change anything, Tom. Give me a call when you're in Japan again. I'll see you if I can. But I *won't* change my mind."

"Kazuko, please . . ."

"I've . . . I've got to go now, Tom. I'm sorry. I know this is hard on you. It's hard on me, too. But, like I said, I can't keep living this way. I want my life back!"

"Kazuko, don't—"

But the line was dead.

Garrett sat there for a long time, the phone still to his ear, listening to the buzz of the dial tone. Kazuko . . . She'd just walked out of his life. Not again. Damn it, not again. His marriage had ended five years ago when his wife couldn't stand the long stretches of sea duty or the uncertainty. A casual romp with a Japanese flight attendant had swiftly grown into something very serious indeed. They'd talked about marriage.

Carefully, he replaced the phone in the cradle on his desk. *If the Navy wanted you to have a wife, they would have issued you one with your sea bag.* The old saw, long popular among enlisted men in boot camp, clawed its way out of long-buried memory, taunting him.

Suddenly, Garrett was terribly, achingly lonely.

No . . . he corrected himself. He'd been lonely all along. Kazuko's call had merely dredged that carefully buried fact out of the muck of his unconscious and smacked him in the face with it. It hadn't been this bad since . . . well, not since Claire had left him.

Part of the price of command, he knew, was the loneliness that came with it. The captain of a submarine, of *any* vessel, needed distance between himself and the men under his command, an aloofness that meant that, while they might come to him with their problems, he could not share his problems with them. The captain simply could not afford to be human.

Nor could he share the burden of command with friends, family, or wife. They couldn't know what it was like to be responsible for 153 men packed into a watertight sewer pipe with delusions of grandeur. The only other people who could possibly understand were other submarine drivers.

And they usually had problems enough of their own.

Eventually, Garrett dealt with the pain the way he'd always dealt with it—burying himself in work. The *Virginia* was not his just yet. She would be, though, next week, after she returned from her trials. A change-of-command ceremony was scheduled for the following Thursday morning, with all of the usual pomp and circumstance demanded by such occasions. They were preparing the dock for the ceremony now, carpenters banging away at the VIP stand and dignitary bleachers. The usual round of invitations had already gone out to most of the politicians, admirals, and civic leaders in New London and Washington and most points in between. It promised to be quite a show.

In the meantime, though, he had plenty to keep him busy—wading through status reports and stores inventories, personnel records and weapons manifests. *Virginia* had been heralded as a truly "paperless" submarine, with all reports and recordkeeping handled by computer. The interface of *Virginia*'s computer records with the paper-logged files and folders ashore, however, formed a major bottleneck. A small army of personnelmen, yeomen, and civilian secretaries were busily inputting data into the electronic files that would shortly be transferred to the *Virginia*, and Garrett needed to check and sign off on much of it—a tedious and thankless job.

But one that kept his mind from dwelling on more painful thoughts.

Office of Global Issues
CIA Headquarters
Langley, Virginia
1610 hours, local time

"This just in, hot from NPIC."

The case officer pronounced the acronym "en-pick," and it stood for the National Photographic Interpretation Center in Washington, D.C.

"Thanks, Chris." John Stevens broke the seal reading TOP SECRET and opened the folder. Inside was a single black-and-white photograph identified only by the cryptic lines of transmission data and time/date stamp in the corner. The shot had been taken less than six hours ago. "Any change in course?"

"They've been zig-zagging all over the ocean,"

Chris Minkowski replied. "But they're not very good at it. They always keep coming back to the same heading."

Stevens studied the photograph. It had been enlarged quite a bit and showed some graininess, but the overall quality was exceptional—considering that it had been taken by a KH-12 satellite some 150 kilometers above the South China Sea. It showed a sharply angled view of the surface of the water, and a single vessel . . . the sleek and graceful lines of a large, oceangoing yacht. The view was from the stern starboard quarter, and the vessel's name, in English and Arabic, was easily read. AL QAHIR.

"They see this yet over in OIA?" The Office of Imagery Analysis was responsible for creating assessments of photographic data provided by NPIC and other sources.

"Yup. They're still working on it." Minkowski tapped the white "V" of the vessel's wake. "They did say the wake shows they're humping it at a good twelve knots. That's pretty good for an eighty-foot yacht."

"Must be a souped-up job. If they're headed for Small Dragon Island, how long till they get there?"

Minkowski shrugged. "Depends how much more zig-zagging they do. At their present rate, three more days, maybe four."

Stevens leaned back in his chair, still studying the photograph as if to leach yet more information from its somber black, white, and gray tones. *Al Qahir*—the name meant "the conqueror"—was officially registered as the property of a wealthy oil sheik named Feisel living in Dhahran, but the agency had managed to peel back several layers of blind trusts and corporate shelters to identify the man who really owned her.

That man, a Saudi national named Sabawy, was a former associate of the bin Laden Corporation . . . and a close personal friend of Zaki Abar.

And Zaki Abar was high on the Agency's ten-most-wanted list of al Qaeda all-stars.

"So the question is . . . what the fuck is Sabawy doing in the Spratlys?"

"He's not. Intelligence puts Sabawy in Paris right now."

"Jesus! Then . . ."

Minkowski nodded. "They think Sabawy's good buddy Zaki is using the yacht for the summer. Kind of like your time-shared vacation getaway, y'know?"

"Huh. Are we talking about a snatch, here?" If Zaki was on board that yacht, it would be the perfect opportunity to send in a team and get him.

"Not until we know what he's doing in the Spratlys. Or how the Chinese might be involved."

"Do the Chinese even know he's there?"

"Hell, yes. What do you think? They've been following him on radar ever since last Tuesday."

"Doesn't mean they know who's on board."

"C'mon. A playboy toy would've been warned off long before this. They haven't even sent out one of their trawlers for a look-see. It's like they don't want to attract attention, y'know?"

"Yeah. That's what it looks like to me, too." Stevens thought hard.

The CIA's Office of Global Issues was responsible for analyzing international issues of all kinds—economic trends, geographic factors, commodities and trade, and technological developments. It was also the bureau responsible for such juicy and often interrelated issues as narcotics production and shipment, sales and shipments of restricted weapons and technology, political instability anywhere in the world . . . and international terrorism. Department emphasis on that last had skyrocketed since 9-11, and Stevens ran the unit that specialized in tracking key assets of al Qaeda—its money, its weapons, and its personnel.

OGI also had a special interest in the Spratly Islands. Located in the South China Sea, the Spratlys comprised some one hundred islands and atolls with a total land area of perhaps 5 square kilometers, scattered across 410,000 square kilometers of ocean. The highest point in the whole island chain was an unnamed point on Southwest Cay, some four meters above sea level at high tide.

The Spratlys might be insignificant geographically, but the mere possibility of natural reserves of gas and oil had transformed them into one of the world's hottest potential flash points. All of the islands were claimed by the People's Republic of China, by Vietnam, and by Taiwan—three mutual and deadly enemies. Some atolls and islets were also claimed by Malaysia and the Philippines. Tiny Brunei claimed an exclusive fishing zone encompassing Louisa Reef in the southern Spratlys, but so far had not publicly claimed the island. There was no native population, but China and the Philippines each had occupied a few of the larger islands with military garrisons.

For many years, the dispute had festered in various nations' capitals, but little had been done beyond the obligatory rattling of sabers. Most of the area remained unexplored, and the oil reserves, if they existed, remained undiscovered.

Recently, though, the People's Republic had upped the ante. Elements of their fleet had crisscrossed the Spratly zone, investigating dozens of the larger islets.

One—Small Dragon Island—had become the center of almost frantic activity.

American spy satellites had followed events from orbit. There'd been no natural harbors in any of the Spratlys, but the Chinese had constructed one, blasting it out of submerged coral rock. Part of the blasting had cut deep into the island itself, creating an anchorage which was then roofed over. A structure something like an offshore oil platform had gone up alongside, a three-story tower with windows and decks, and a helicopter pad connected to the main building by a causeway or ramp. The OIA thought it might be a base for prospecting for oil and gas. The OGI believed it was a sheltered anchorage for military ships, complete with a sheltered dock where weapons or other supplies might be offloaded in privacy, unseen by U.S. satellites.

Whatever the truth, Beijing had invested a lot of time, effort, and money in building the base at Small Dragon, enough to give them a very large stake indeed in the area. The base was particularly worrisome because of its location. Small Dragon was one of the easternmost of the Spratlys, positioned astride important international shipping lanes running southwest from the Philippines toward Singapore, a shipping chokepoint called the Palawan Passage. Much of the Spratlys' area was a treacherous maze of coral atolls and shoal water, deadly for all but the most shallow-draft vessels. Deeper-hulled craft—such as the oil tankers that kept Japan's faltering economy afloat—skirted the main body of the Spratlys and their dangerous reefs by running up the Palawan Passage, a deep-water channel that measured just a hundred kilometers from the shores of Palawan to tiny, strategic Small Dragon Island.

That much of the situation was worrisome enough to the analysts at OGI. But now there was evidence that one of the highest-ranking surviving officers of al Qaeda was heading for Small Dragon, and apparently taking steps to keep that visit secret.

"I think it's time," Stevens said at last, "to have a closer look at Small Dragon Island."

"I thought you'd feel that way," Minkowski replied.

Stevens reached for the phone on his desk.

Thursday, 18 May 2006

Submarine Dock One
Submarine Base New London
Groton, Connecticut
0910 hours, EST

"*Comp'ny*, atten . . . *hut!*"

Seaman Calvin R. Wallace came to attention, one of 140 sailors standing in tightly formed ranks. His crisply starched whites scratched at his shoulders and hips; submariners were sometimes referred to as the "dungaree navy," since they rarely appeared in any other uniform. Even though it was late spring, the stiff breeze hissing in off Long Island Sound chilled. How long, he wondered, was this shindig going to last?

He was in the second rank. Looking past the broad shoulders of the man in front of him, Wallace could see his new home for the next few months, the brand-new attack submarine *Virginia*, moored to the dock, huge, death-black, the numbers 774 high on her sail the only identifying features visible at all.

Even those numbers, he knew, were held in place by magnets, and would be removed once the vessel left port. *Virginia* held for him an aura of barely restrained power, of menace somehow given form by her very anonymity.

Her commissioning crew stood in ranks on her aft deck, behind the sail and the gangway, their white uniforms in stark contrast to the black hull beneath their feet. The two masses of white-clad sailors faced each other impassively across the narrow gap between submarine and dock, with the dark water lapping at the curve of the hull below. To Wallace's right, the gangway stretched across that gap, a slightly rising bridge festooned with flag bunting and a large logo shield representing the *Virginia*, SSN 774.

Farther to the right, near the rounded bow of the submarine, was ground zero for the main party. There, an enormous video screen rose three stories above the dockside, displaying, at the moment, the same *Virginia* logo that decorated either side of the gangway. Temporary bleachers and a forest of folding chairs had been arranged on the shore, facing *Virginia*'s prow. A covered dignitaries' stand held seats for the dozen or so scheduled speakers; nearby, a smaller, open stand was reserved for members of the press, a small army of men and women crowded together in the breeze, armed with everything from digital cameras to shoulder-held and tripod-mounted TV cameras.

I guess we're news, Wallace thought, bemused . . . and a little awed. He still felt as though he didn't quite belong at the eye of this incredible hurricane of media attention and full-dress pomp and circumstance.

Damn. His black Corfam dress shoes were just a

shade too tight, and he wasn't used to the pinch of the things. His feet were threatening to go to sleep.

"Stop fidgeting, Wall-eye," the man to his left said, his voice a fierce whisper too low for any but Wallace to hear. EM1 Jack Kirkpatrick had for some reason elected himself Wallace's keeper . . . and nemesis. "Make this division look bad and you'll find yourself guest of honor at a blanket party tonight."

He tried to grow roots, unmoving, in the hard pavement of the pier and ignore the pins and needles pricking at his feet.

Wallace—the nickname "Wall-eye," for the black-framed glasses that looked so huge on his thin face, was a hated handle he'd acquired in submarine school—had been in the Navy for just eight months, with twelve weeks of boot camp at Great Lakes, north of Chicago, five weeks of basic submarine school here at New London, and sixteen weeks more in submarine ET school—classes to train him to be an electronics technician. He'd already changed—grown—more than he'd ever believed possible when he'd left home for the first time, right out of high school. But he was painfully aware of just how much more he needed to learn. All the books, all the lectures, all those hours in submarine simulators of various types . . . none of that had even come close, he thought, to preparing him for the adventure on which he was about to embark.

Adventure . . . yeah. That was the word for it. *Adventure.*

Why did it feel like a death sentence? Damn it, did the fear ever stop?

Wallace was nineteen. A thin, gangly kid born and raised in Monroeville, Pennsylvania—a near suburb of Pittsburgh—he'd seemed an unlikely candidate for the Navy's submariner program, an unlikely candidate, in fact, for the U.S. Navy. His father had been an Army draftee, serving in Vietnam; his mother's dad had been an Army private killed in the hellfire of Omaha Beach. An uncle was a career Army sergeant major who'd just returned from a tour in Iraq. Any tradition of military service in his family seemed to point him toward the infantry. Wallace still wasn't entirely sure why he'd joined the Navy, much less why he'd volunteered for the submarine service.

In part, of course, there was his love of computers to blame. He'd wanted to go to a computer training school after high school, but his family hadn't had the money. Both the Army and the Navy had computer training programs for promising recruits. He'd told a buddy once that he'd chosen the Navy because it was *cleaner* than the Army—no muddy foxholes, no crawling through swamps.

In fact, the Navy had promised him a chance to get out of Monroeville and see something of the world. Not that the Army couldn't do the same for a penniless young man fresh out of high school . . . but Wallace wanted as complete a break with the past as he could manage. Army recruiting slogans like "Be all that you can be" and "An army of one" left him cold; the old "Join the Navy and see the world" still had a powerful hold on his mind.

So here he was, six hundred and some miles from Monroeville—which was, he thought, a *good* thing—but about to allow himself to be sealed inside a steel cylinder where he would live and sleep and work for months at a time, possibly, and never see anything of the world of light and sun and fresh air. All of the training, all of the psychological screening he'd endured over the past year . . .

Was it possible he was a secret claustrophobe? Damn it, he was scared.

And he didn't dare admit that fact to any of the other men standing in the white-clad ranks around him.

Someone was talking over the sound system. A guy who'd introduced himself a few moments ago as the president of Electric Boat was now, in turn, introducing one of the senators from the state of Virginia.

Politics. . . .

VIP Stand
Submarine Dock One
Submarine Base New London
Groton, Connecticut
0925 hours, EST

Politics. . . .
Commander Thomas Frederick Garrett sat uncomfortably ensconced on a folding chair in the VIP stand set up at the head of Pier One, facing the colorful crowd of mostly civilian spectators in the bleachers and seats below. The wind off the sea to the south was freshening, carrying a sharp chill and the promise of rain.

Maybe it would cool some of the hot air being released by the politicking.

The senator from Virginia leaned against the podium a few feet in front of Garrett and to his right, as though trying to weave a magic spell of words over the audience. "We set sail today," he said, "to the future! This proud submarine vessel, SSN 774, is about to take her crew . . . and the armed services of her proud nation . . . into the wonderland of tomorrow, a future where technology rules the ocean depths, where technology seems like nothing so much as sheer, wondrous magic!"

The senator's craggy features and his lovingly coiffed, silver mane were displayed in close-up on the giant video screen towering to one side of the VIP box, his image weirdly distorted by the screen's angle, easily visible to the audience, but not to the occupants of the stand. The man had a lot to say, it seemed, about the future and about the glories of technology, about "young, intelligent, and dedicated young men standing in harm's way," and about "young people who stand ready to answer the Minuteman's call."

Well, the guy was right about the young men. Garrett let his gaze pass the ranks of family members, dignitaries, shipyard workers, and executives to rest on the neatly ordered block of white uniforms standing farther out on the dock. *My new crew.*

There was a very great deal in the speech about America setting sail into the future. In fact, *Virginia* had already been to sea. Today was her *commissioning* date, as opposed to the actual date of her launching, which had taken place more than five months ago. Submarines, especially, generally were launched and crewed for a precommissioning shakedown cruise, a short voyage during which bugs in the vessel's design or systems, if any, were found and corrected. In a short while, those ranks of white-clad sailors across the water on *Virginia*'s aft deck would come ashore, replaced by the sailors standing now on the dock. Part of the ceremony today would include the formal change of command, as *Virginia*'s new captain took over from the old.

So far in his career, Garrett had commanded two attack submarines—the USS *Pittsburgh,* a Los Angeles boat, and the USS *Seawolf,* though that last assignment had been a temporary command only, with Garrett stepping into the shoes of the sub's original skipper when that man had been killed. Both counted in his personnel record, though, and both had contributed to his knowledge and his appreciation of the men under his command. The crews of both boats had been exceptional—good men, well trained, sharp, professional. Navy training standards being what they were, he had no doubt whatsoever that this crew would be just as good.

Still, there was always a bit of anticipation, even a bit of worry in the promise of a new crew. Those 140 sailors and 13 officers standing out there might be exceptional in training and character, every one of them, *as individuals,* but how would they shake out as a crew? A submarine crew was as much an individual in its own right as any one of those young men standing in ranks, and, like any organism made up of many smaller cells or living parts, was only as strong as the weakest one within it. How those young men worked together as a team under next-to-impossible conditions would spell the difference between a successful deployment and a failure—and failure in this business could all too easily mean death.

Garrett let his gaze drift from *Virginia*'s new crew to her old. Most of the members of her shakedown crew would be going on to other duty, but a select few would be staying on. Senior Chief Bollinger was slated to be *Virginia*'s COB, her Chief of the Boat, the most important enlisted man on board. He would be the all-important link between captain and crew, more so even than Lieutenant Commander Peter Jorgensen,

Virginia's exec. Garrett had already worked long hours with both men, getting to know them and how they thought, getting to know them, in fact, as well as he already knew the *Virginia* herself. Good men, both of them. Bollinger had been in the Navy for twenty-three years and could be depended on as a sturdy, steadying influence on the younger men. Jorgensen had served as navigation officer on board an L.A. boat before this—the *Miami*—and had racked up ten years of experience so far in the submariner service.

Another asset Garrett was happy to have on board was Sonar Technician First Class Ken Queensly, "Queenie" to his shipmates. Queensly had been a third class and the junior sonar tech on board *Seawolf* but had proven himself to be a superb set of ears, one of those proverbial wunderkinder of sonar who, purportedly, could hear someone drop a pocketful of change on another submarine somewhere out in the cold, dark depths, and report the total at sixty cents—a quarter, three dimes, and a nickel, and the nickel had come up "heads."

Exaggeration, of course. Still, a good sonar man could perform acts of apparent wizardry, pulling vital information out of the hiss and roar and throb of the deep. Queenie was one of the best. Garrett was glad to get him.

The senator from Virginia, at long last, droned on to the end of his speech. The president of Electric Boat took his place at the podium once more, this time introducing a senator from Connecticut.

More droning, this time about the jobs that Electric Boat continued to bring to the sovereign state of Connecticut. There was some playful sparring with the Virginian senator over how much better the New London–built boats were than those built in Norfolk. My

God, Garrett thought wearily. How can you joke about that sort of thing?

American submarines—*all* American submarines, no matter where they were built—were technological marvels, superior in every way to the submarines of other navies in the world.

There was a joking intimation in the Connecticut senator's speech that New London–built boats were just a bit more likely to resurface after a dive than those built at the Norfolk Navy Yard. The laughter from the audience was polite, and just a bit strained. Many of those visitors were family to those who would serve aboard the *Virginia*, and, Garrett guessed, they didn't like to be reminded of the chance, however remote, of a *casualty* . . . the lovely bit of naval doublespeak referring to an emergency on board a submarine.

Garrett wondered if, come next year when the second Virginia-class boat was launched, the Virginian senator would joke about the inferiority of New London boats?

Funny, that that boat would be the *Connecticut,* launched in Virginia, while this one was the *Virginia,* launched in Connecticut. That seemed a doggedly bass-ackward way to go about things. Why not build the *Virginia* in Virginia? It sounded like bad planning all the way around; he hoped the actual design work on this so-called miracle of modern technology was a bit more straightforward, and less tainted by politics.

He remembered again the time a year ago when he'd taken that congressman what was his name? Blakeslee, that was it—when he'd taken Congressman Blakeslee on a tour of the assembly building where they'd still been putting the *Virginia* together. He wondered if that afternoon of shared viewpoints had done any good. At least the Virginia program hadn't been canceled altogether. But just because they hadn't chopped off support yet didn't mean it wouldn't happen.

Garrett was little less than fanatical in his support for a military that by law could not take sides politically. It was a real blessing that the military couldn't set national policy. But sometimes it seemed just as bad that civilians were tasked with setting military policy, especially in areas like appropriations and budgets. They didn't have to trust their lives and their sanity to the structural integrity of a narrow steel cigar manufactured by a shipyard chosen by pork-barrel politics, using machine parts supplied by the lowest bidder.

Virginia was a good boat. He'd watched them assemble her, almost plate by plate, and he knew what sheer, sweating labor had gone into her construction. But the pressure to produce a *cheaper* submarine, using as much off-the-shelf engineering as possible, had been as crushing at times as the pressure at the bottom of the Marianas Trench, 35,000 feet down.

He hoped they wouldn't pay for it later, especially when the payees would be the officers and men who crewed her.

The senator from Connecticut was still talking about the New London shipyard and jobs. God, wasn't this guy *ever* going to shut up? . . .

Submarine Dock One
Submarine Base New London
Groton, Connecticut
0948 hours, EST

Wallace had tried to listen at first, but it was all too easy to simply stand there, zoning out as the senator's words washed over him and around him like the flag-snapping breeze off the sound. Keeping his head facing rigidly forward, Wallace tried to eyeball the VIP stand. There were several officers sitting there in the chairs behind the senator at the speaker's podium, along with several civilians. Which one, he wondered, was his skipper? What would he be like? Sub school had stressed the god-like authority and power of a submarine's commanding officer, and Wallace couldn't think about the man, whoever he was, without just a touch of trepidation.

His musings made him miss the rest of the Connecticut senator's speech and part of the next one as well. He wished he could glance at his wristwatch to see how long they'd been standing here, but he didn't dare. His division officer would be certain to note any infraction while in ranks, and take it out of his hide in extra duty later—if he didn't slap the offending sailor on report.

Another representative from EB—Electric Boat—made a speech, as did a congressman from Connecticut on the Armed Services Committee. They were followed by a few comments by a sleek and silver-haired woman introduced as the wife of a congressman from Virginia who couldn't make it that day. By this time, Wallace's feet had gone, in turn, soundly asleep, awake in an agony of pins and needles, and finally into a semisomnambulant state somewhere between numb and aching. Was it his imagination, or was the temperature steadily getting colder? The bright, partly cloudy sky they'd begun with was gradually giving way to gray overcast, and with the masking of the sun the wind felt colder. He tried not to shiver openly.

Submariners were volunteers, every one of them. *He* was a volunteer. The training program he'd signed on for had been a good one, but he could have ended up safely working the system at some shoreside billet . . . or served, perhaps, on board an Aegis cruiser—a computerized miracle of electronics that would have at least given him access to daylight on off-duty hours. Why had he picked submarines, for God's sake?

Jack Heil had a lot to do with it, damn him. Jack had been the closest friend he had in the Navy. They'd met in boot camp at Great Lakes, then gone across the road to Mainside and A-school together. Jack had volunteered for submarine duty, and Wallace had volunteered, too, so they could stay together. Jack had been full of stories about how luxurious life could be serving aboard one of the big boomers, a member of a gold or blue crew alternating with each other in six-month tours ashore and at sea, America's first line of nuclear defense and deterrent. The best food in the Navy, and some of the best perks. Jack made it sound like a freaking country club.

And then they'd shipped out to sub school at New London, and three weeks later Jack had washed out, almost literally. He'd lost it in their first flooding casualty in the simulator tank, punching out a fellow trainee in a shrieking attempt to reach the hatch as ice-cold water came flooding in.

And so Jack was gone, shipped back to the "target fleet," while Wallace continued with the program.

For a time, he'd thought about backing out of the

program, but his dad's admonitions to "stick with whatever you start" stayed with him, and quitting at that point would have been an admission that he couldn't cut it, couldn't make the team. He'd done well, graduating fifth in his class. His scores in the various computer classes had been high enough that he'd been offered a very select billet indeed—as a computer technician on board the Navy's newest and most advanced submarine . . . the USS *Virginia*.

But now he was out of school, about to set foot on the vessel that would be his home for the next couple of years or so, and all the doubts he'd ever had were crowding back. He'd been through the schools and classes, yeah, but did he have what it took to be a real submariner?

They'd been constantly in-your-face about that during sub school. He might have graduated from the course, but he still had a full year of what amounted to probationary service ahead of him. The schooling would continue as he worked his way through every one of the departments aboard the *Virginia*, studying and taking tests, "making his quals" in order to prove that he could stand watch anywhere from main engineering to the torpedo room. Only then—and only with an OK from each of the department chiefs and officers—would he win the right to pin on a set of the coveted gold dolphins that were the badge of honor for a *real* submariner.

Something in the senator's speechmaking just then caught Wallace's attention. "The young men who serve aboard these vessels are the sharpest, the smartest, the very best trained sailors of any navy in the world," the senator was saying. "They are patriots, every one of them, and they deserve our undying thanks. . . ."

Fuck. . . .

Sharpest? Smartest? Best-trained? In theory, yeah, maybe, but right now he felt as though he didn't know a damned thing, that all of that training had been for nothing.

How long, he wondered, before his shipmates found him out?

VIP Stand
Submarine Dock One
Submarine Base New London
Groton, Connecticut
0957 hours, EST

"They are patriots, every one of them, and they deserve our undying thanks. . . ."

Well, the congressman had gotten that part right, at least. Garrett glanced at his watch. Couldn't a grateful nation thank its smart young patriots by letting them get on with their work?

The guy was wrapping up, now, and turning the podium back over to the VIP from General Dynamics. He, in turn, introduced Commander Daryl Fitch, *Virginia*'s skipper for her sea trials.

Fitch bounded up to the podium, grabbed the microphone off the stand, and bellowed, "*What a beautiful, incredible, and* amazing *submarine!*"

The crowd erupted in wild cheers and applause, and even Garrett and the others on the stand clapped long and hard. After so much pomposity, Fitch's exuberance was fresher than the breeze coming in off the sea, and considerably more welcome. He was a young man, short, with a thick but neatly trimmed black mustache. He and Garrett were friends; Garrett had been aboard during one of the early sea trials—strictly as a passenger—and the two had worked together for long hours just last week, running through the lists and manifests required for the changeover in command.

Fitch's speech was mercifully short and to the point, a litany of praise for the *Virginia* and her builders. No politics there. The New London shipyard workers *were* good—the very best—and it was only right to acknowledge their skill.

"In the *Virginia*," Fitch said, in conclusion, "we have a submarine that can go anywhere in the oceans of the world, go there undetected, go there and carry out her mission, whatever that may be and return safely home. And that is all anyone could ask of such a vessel, and more. I salute her builders. Well done!" Again, the audience exploded into cheers. The majority were probably shipbuilders or Electric Boat execs. "And to her new skipper, I say—with heartfelt jealousy—you are one *hell* of a lucky SOB!"

Lucky? Yeah, Garrett had to admit that he was that. For a while there, it had looked as though his career was going to be thoroughly stalled, thanks to a letter of reprimand when he was skipper of the *Pittsburgh*, six years ago. And, since his command of the *Seawolf* was strictly temporary, a stand-in for Captain Justin, he might well have found himself spending the rest of his Navy career on the beach.

Virginia had been a reward for his handling of the *Seawolf* during the Taiwan crisis in '03. He was lucky, all right, but determination had a lot to do with it, too. He'd passed on a chance to go before the promotion board—a shot at his fourth stripe—so that he could have her.

And now it was Garrett's turn. The president of Electric Boat was introducing "the exceptional young officer" who'd been selected to take the *Virginia* out on her first operational deployment, her "voyage into the crystalline waters of the twenty-first century, and beyond. Ladies and gentlemen, I give you Commander Thomas Frederick Garrett, the new captain of the USS *Virginia*!"

Bemused, he stood and walked to the podium. Exceptional young officer? He was old for a commander—thanks to his passing up the rank of captain. And right now he was feeling pretty old. His first wife had divorced him when he couldn't give her a normal kind of life, with a husband who came home from work at night and wasn't gone six or eight months at a time. And then there's been Kazuko. . . .

Being a submarine skipper, it seemed, precluded anything like actually having a life.

"Like Commander Fitch," he said, placing the single sheet of paper with his speaker's notes before him on the podium, "I won't speak for long. I'm a sub driver, not a speech-maker. This is, after all, the *silent* service. Submariners put a high premium on being quiet."

The audience laughed, and a few people applauded. They were as tired of this ritual as he was, he decided. He glanced again at his notes and decided to ignore them. Garrett was better at speechmaking when the words came from the heart rather than from notes, and he knew it.

"We've already heard all about what a fine boat the *Virginia* is, about the tradition of superb shipbuilding at this yard, about what marvelous technology we put into our submarines, about what fine young men *Virginia* has as her crew. All true.

"But one thing more we haven't mentioned yet . . . and that is the *dedication* of the men who serve aboard this nation's submarines.

"You know, there are certain perks about submarine service. The food is the best in the Navy. The pay scales are good—at least so far as the Navy is concerned. And submariners know that they're the best. We are an elite, and we know it. That translates as self-confidence, as competence, and as an esprit de corps that just won't quit. We have a saying in the submariner service, you know. There are only two kinds of ships in the Navy: submarines . . . and *targets*. We are the hunters, the stalkers, the killers.

"But all of that comes with a price, and all of us wonder, sometimes, if the cost is worth it. Service on board a submarine is *tough*, and it is demanding. We stand watch and watch, usually, which means our internal clocks are *always* out of sync with the rest of the world, and that half the time we're trying to sleep when everybody else is awake and making more noise than you'd think was possible on board a submarine.

"Unlike the rest of the Navy, we don't have women aboard as part of the crew, and, submarines being what they are, we're not going to. We go for so long without even *seeing* the fair sex that we forget what they look like." He paused as the audience laughed.

"And it's crowded. Things are a little better, I hear, on the boomers—the big ballistic missile subs—and the *Seawolf* had a bit of room to spare, at least when we didn't have a team of Navy SEALs on board—but the Los Angeles–class attack boats, and now, the *Virginia*, just have too many men living in too small a space. You have to 'hot bunk'—racking out on a mattress just vacated by someone else going on watch. There is no such thing as privacy. I've seen closets bigger than the quarters used by a boat's officers, and if you're an enlisted man, the only nod toward privacy is your rack—a space seventy inches long and just eighteen inches high, walled off from the corridor by a curtain.

"And yet, every man on board an American submarine is a volunteer. He *asked* to be there, and had to jump through some pretty demanding hoops to be accepted. Submariners are among the smartest kids in the Navy. I think they're also the *craziest*, giving up a sane, normal, spacious life ashore or on board one of those floating cities we call targets in order to live like a sardine, wedged into a claustrophobe's nightmare with over a hundred other sardines, sometimes not even able to see the sun or taste fresh air for months at a time.

"They are volunteers. And by volunteering—and by sticking it out—they show a level of sheer, raw dedication, to their country, to the service, to their shipmates, to themselves, that is, to my mind, astonishing.

"And that, people, is what makes the *Virginia* an amazing submarine. Not her technology . . . but the dedication of her crew.

"I only hope I can live up to the standards *they* will set."

Submarine Dock One
Submarine Base New London
Groton, Connecticut
1015 hours, EST

The speechmaking was over at last. Wallace had been transfixed by the last speaker—Commander Garrett, his new CO. He sounded like an okay kind of guy, an *understanding* guy, not at all like the tyrants he'd heard so many stories about in boot camp and school.

He was also older than Wallace had expected. During the inspection following the speeches—when Commander Fitch and Commander Garrett walked up and down the ranks of sailors on the dock—Garrett passed right in front of him, two feet away. Garrett seemed to possess an energy that felt . . . restless, barely contained, but it was an energy reined in by a formidable self-control. Wallace's own father had never possessed that aura of maturity.

Wallace found he was less worried now about being "found out" by his shipmates than he was about living up to this new commanding officer's expectations.

Friday, 19 May 2006

Headquarters, SUBGRU-2
Submarine Base New London
Groton, Connecticut
0910 hours, EST

Garrett trotted up the steps of the graceful, turn-of-the-century mansion housing the headquarters of Naval Submarine Group Two, returning the salute of the two Marine sentries outside the door. It was a beautiful New England spring day, with gulls wheeling and keeking overhead. He'd been at the dock supervising the provisioning of the *Virginia* but Admiral Fore's summons had been brutally direct, with an air of urgency. What could be the problem?

Vice Admiral Richard Fore's office was a bastion reached through layers of outer offices and official buffers of progressively higher and higher rank. Garrett was passed through with little delay until he was ushered through into the carpeted office of the commanding officer of Submarine Group Two. SUBGRU Two was the command organization for all SSNs—attack submarines—in the Atlantic. The strongest such fleet in the world, it included SUBRON 2 and SUBRON 10, as well as SUBDEVRON 2 which evaluated new undersea technologies, all based out of New London. It was also the headquarters for SUBRON 4, down in Charleston, South Carolina, and for SUBRONs 6 and 8 operating out of Norfolk. At any given time, SUBGRU Two might command as many as forty-five attack submarines, various tenders and support vessels, and the special Navy Research submarine NR-1.

He came to attention in front of the admiral's massive oak desk. "Commander Garrett, reporting as ordered, sir."

Fore glared up at him from beneath a formidable pair of shaggy white eyebrows. "What the *hell* were you playing at, Commander?"

"Sir?" Garrett scrambled through his memory, searching for whatever it was that might have made his boss this angry. He couldn't remember. . . .

"That speech you gave yesterday, at the change of command ceremony. Do you have any idea what a hornets' nest you've managed to kick over?" Fore shoved the newspaper across the desk. It was a copy of the *Connecticut Reporter* and the headline read, "FAIR SEX" NOT WANTED ON BOARD. The subhead added, cryptically, SUB SKIPPER SAYS "NO" TO WOMEN IN SUBMARINES. A grainy photograph showed him at the podium during the ceremony the day before.

"What the hell is this?" Garrett asked, before remembering where he was, and adding, "sir."

"It's a liberal rag pushing women's rights, is what it

is," Fore said. "Normally it doesn't get very much attention. But your little speech yesterday was seen as proof that the Navy is not interested in equal rights for women in the service. Apparently the wire services have picked it up and are even now echoing your words across the country. Damn it, Garrett, we had the whole issue pretty well back in the box, and your speech just let it all out in the open again. Would you mind telling me just what you had in mind with that talk you gave?"

Garrett tried to remember just what it was he'd said. "I think I was taken out of context, sir. I wasn't talking about whether or not women should be allowed on subs. I was talking about the hardships our sub crews have to endure . . . months at sea without seeing a woman."

"Oh, they got that part, too." Fore's finger stabbed at a paragraph farther down the column. "There's considerable talk here about your 'sexist remarks,' and there's an editorial in here that explains that you—and by extension, *we*—think of women as ornaments and kitchen drudges. You called them 'the fair sex,' for God's sake. How condescending can you get?"

"Damn it, sir, it was a *joke*."

"Your joke may have set the Navy's public relations program with regard to women in the service back twenty years. You are aware, are you not, that both NOW and the Patriotic Women's Front have been angling for years to get the Navy to admit women to male-only billets?"

"Yes, sir."

In fact, female naval personnel had already been brought aboard most ships in the Navy. After some tentative experiments back in the '70s and '80s, women now served aboard a number of U.S. ships, including her aircraft carriers, and a number of women were combat pilots.

But it took considerable effort—and therefore *money*—to redesign a ship to permit women the privacy of their own quarters and heads. That had been done, one way or another, on board surface ships, but a sub was something else. There was almost *zero* privacy on board a submarine, as Garrett had been trying to say in his speech, and the habitable spaces were so tightly packed with equipment, electronics, and life-support gear there was no room to expand. You couldn't simply add, say, a separate shower head and berthing compartment for women's use only without throwing out something else—weapons systems or reactor shielding or sonar gear or air scrubbers . . . and every single system on board a submarine was absolutely essential either to her mission or to the survival and well-being of her crew.

Women would not serve on board American submarines until those submarines were designed, from the keel up, to include them.

"When we start working on the next new sub design, sir, maybe we should talk to EB about installing quarters for women."

"That's just it, Garrett. The *Virginia is* a new design, the 'submarine for the twenty-first century,' remember? Your speech has stirred up all kinds of controversy out there about why the Virginia class is still . . . let's see. What did they say?" He turned the paper so he could read from it. "Yes, here it is. ' . . . a no-girls-allowed clubhouse for the Navy's old-boy network.' They go on to say, 'Obviously, Commander Garrett does not believe women capable of the same degree of dedication and patriotism as men.' "

"I'd be happy to have female sailors in my crew, Admiral. Somehow, I don't think they'd care for the accommodations."

"And that is not the point. You departed from the text of your approved speech. Why?"

Garrett blinked. He'd submitted the text he'd written out ahead of time, yes, but somehow he'd thought that a formality. "I didn't realize my speech had to be approved in advance, sir."

"If it touches on political, controversial, or sensitive issues, of course it does. Damn it, you know the regs."

"Yes, sir." He just hadn't realized he was dealing with a controversial topic in the first place.

"There wasn't anything that would set off the NOW people in what you submitted. Why did you start shooting from the hip?"

"I don't know, sir. It seemed right at the time. The speeches were long and boring. I thought some light comments and some appreciation of the enlisted men's dedication would go down more easily."

"And the Patriotic Front is using that to claim you don't think women are dedicated enough to serve their country."

"That is not true at all, sir."

"True or not, the Navy Department is now engaged in some pretty extensive damage control. We've taken a pretty bad hit, here. I needn't remind you, Commander, that carelessness like this has ruined more than one promising young officer's career."

Garrett started to reply, then thought better of it. He'd not seen things in quite that light before. Damn it, the powers-that-were could scuttle him for a few chance comments.

"What can I do, sir?"

"To start with, no more comments to the press. If they phone you, and they will, I have no doubt, refer them back to my office. Second, all, repeat, all speeches you make will be submitted to my office for prior approval . . . and no departing from the prepared text. I don't care if you put them all to sleep in their chairs, you stick to the approved speech, with no ad-libbing. Do I make myself clear?"

"Yes, sir."

"Finally, you will prepare a public apology. Doesn't need to be long . . . a few paragraphs. Say that you had no intention of slighting the dedication and willingness to serve of our nation's female sailors and officers, that you would be proud to serve with them at any time, that the Navy has taken heroic strides to include women in all areas of endeavor . . . you know the drill. Submit it to my office for approval and distribution before 1600 hours today."

Garrett winced inwardly. His schedule today with the loading and provisioning of the *Virginia* was packed solid already. When would he have time? . . .

"Clear, Garrett?"

"Clear, sir." He would just have to *make* the time.

"Very well. How goes the provisioning?"

It took Garrett a moment to shift mental gears from the chewing out to ship's business. "Uh . . . fine, sir. We're on the sched for loading torps and TLAMs this afternoon. Final provisioning after that. We'll be ready for our planned 0700 departure tomorrow."

"Good. Your orders have already been sent aboard by messenger. You'll open them, as usual, when you're under way."

"Yes, sir."

"I will tell you this. You're going to have some new bluenoses in your crew."

Garrett's eyebrows reached toward his hairline. Bluenose was the name for personnel who'd crossed the Arctic Circle, much as the Royal Order of Neptune was awarded to men who'd crossed the equator, or the Golden Dragon was won by those who'd crossed the international date line. They were going north, then.

"Under the ice, Admiral?"

Fore nodded. "You'll be shaking out *Virginia*'s new under-ice sonar. And you'll be transiting to the Pacific. Because of the radical new technology involved, and because your mission will involve developing and evaluating strategy and tactics for a new weapons platform, *Virginia* will remain under the operational umbrella of SUBDEVRON 2. However, we want you back in your old stomping grounds for the next couple of months. Things might be heating up again in the South China Sea, and the planning staff thinks this will be a good test of *Virginia*'s operational capabilities. They seem to think it won't hurt to have a man at the conn who's faced the Chinese before. Full details will be in your sealed orders, of course."

"Yes, sir."

"Questions?"

"No, sir."

"Okay. And have that formal written apology on my desk before 1600 hours, or I'll have Commander Fitch extend his tour of duty as *Virginia*'s skipper. Understand me?"

"Aye aye, sir."

"Then get out of here. And for God's sake, don't talk to the reporters!"

Garrett turned and hurried from the office, feeling lucky to be alive.

Outside, he stopped and took a deep breath before walking around to the HQ parking lot and getting into the car requisitioned for his use. Fifteen minutes later he was walking up the dock, a critical eye scanning the activity on *Virginia*'s forward deck, where a working party was gently, *gently* lowering a Mark 48 ADCAP torpedo at an angle down through the weapons-loading hatch forward of the sail. A number of enlisted men in dungarees and poopie suits—the navy blue coveralls used by submarine crews—were gathered around the descending torp as it rested on the cradle-like loading tray, guiding its nineteen-foot length down the narrow hatch. A loading crane on the dock was preparing to sling the next ADCAP into position. He watched as the first bright blue Mark 48 vanished tailfirst down the hatch, where a second working party hidden below deck was manhandling the pencil-thin giant into a storage rack in the torpedo room. The empty loading tray, meanwhile, was lowered back to its horizontal position on the forward deck, ready to receive the next torpedo.

Virginia could carry only thirty-eight weapons—a variable mix of Mark 48 ADCAPs, tube-launched mines, Harpoon antiship missiles, and Tomahawk TLAM missiles—as opposed to the weapons load of fifty carried by the *Seawolf*. It was part of the trade-off *Virginia*'s designers had been forced to accept to create the smaller and less-expensive attack boat. *Smaller, cheaper, better.* The *Virginia* was certainly smaller and cheaper than the mammoth *Seawolf*. Would she be better as well? That remained to be seen.

Lieutenant Bill Carpenter, "Weps," *Virginia*'s weapons officer, was supervising the loading of the torpedoes. He saw Garrett standing on the dock alongside and saluted; Navy tradition held members of a working party exempt from saluting while carrying out their duties, but the senior man could salute if he himself was not otherwise engaged. Garrett returned the salute, then walked the rest of the way aft to *Vir-*

ginia's gangway, empty now of the banners that had festooned it during the ceremony yesterday. A first-class machinist's mate in whites, standing the officer-of-the-deck watch in a temporary shelter erected on board close by the gangway, made the announcement of Garrett's coming on board into his communications headset—"*Virginia*, arriving"—then came to attention and saluted. Garrett, by tradition, saluted the boat's ensign, fluttering on her aft deck, then saluted the OOD. "Permission to come aboard."

"Permission granted, sir. Welcome aboard."

"Thank you . . . Pettigrew," Garrett said, glancing at the name tag on the sailor's whites. He tried to memorize the man's face. It would take him a while to get to know all 140 men and 13 officers of the crew by face alone . . . but in the inevitable crowding on board, that *would* happen, and sooner rather than later. For Garrett, it was vitally important that he know his men as individuals.

Walking toward *Virginia*'s forward personnel hatch, located just abaft her far-forward sail, he felt the slight give in the deck beneath his feet, a sensation almost like walking on rubber or thick carpet padding. Like the *Seawolf* and both the improved and retrofitted L.A.-class boats, *Virginia* came with brick-sized anechoic/decoupling tiles covering every square inch of her hull except for hatchways, control surfaces, and sonar dome and windows. The tiles helped defeat enemy active sonar and served to further insulate onboard noise, part of the engineering that made her as silent as the *Seawolf*.

He descended the ladder inside the hatch, then turned and walked forward to the command center. Lieutenant Commander Peter Jorgensen, *Virginia*'s exec, stood in the control room, already holding out a coffee mug—complete with *Virginia*'s logo—for Garrett to take. "Welcome aboard, sir."

"Thank you, Number One," Garrett said, accepting the coffee. "How are things going?"

"We're an hour and a half behind sched, Captain," Jorgensen replied. "We had a man injured during the torpedo load."

"Bad?"

"A broken wrist. The guy got his hand in the way of an ADCAP coming down onto the cradle. He's been taken Mainside to the hospital."

"Shit. Who was it?"

"TM3 Connors, sir. The incident has been logged and reported."

"What went wrong?"

Jorgensen stiffened. He was directly responsible for everything that happened on board the *Virginia*, both as the boat's executive officer and as the captain's representative when the captain was ashore. He hadn't worked with Garrett long enough yet to know how he would respond to news of the accident. "It's all in the accident report, sir."

"I want to hear it from you, Number One. Was Connors an experienced hand?"

"Yes, sir. Well, pretty much. *Virginia* uses a different style loading tray. The new sail placement, you know."

Garrett nodded. *Virginia*'s sail, the above-deck structure once known as a conning tower that housed the boat's sensor array masts, was located much farther forward than on other submarines. It gave her an odd, snub-nosed appearance, with just barely enough deck space forward of the sail for twelve vertical-launch TLAM tubes, the rounded half-globe of her nose, and the weapons-loading hatch itself. The change in architecture had necessitated a number of changes in the equipment used to service the boat.

"Well, Connors hadn't worked with the new rig, sir. Nobody had. Fact is, he had his hand resting where he shouldn't have. He got it caught between the fish and a support bar."

"Damn. He could have lost his hand."

"He almost pulled it out in time, sir. He just wasn't quite quick enough."

"It shouldn't be a matter of being quick enough. The men have to know their equipment."

"Yes, sir."

"Very well." He frowned. That was not an auspicious beginning to things. He made a mental note to stop by the hospital on his way to the BOQ—his quarters on shore—tonight. "Any other problems?"

"Not so far, sir." Jorgensen sounded wary, as though he was waiting for the drop of another shoe. "Lieutenant Carpenter says they can make up the lost time tonight and still have time to complete provisioning."

"Sounds good, Number One." He checked his watch. "I'm going to my office. You have the watch."

"Aye aye, sir."

Garrett's stateroom and office was located on the first deck forward of the control room. He stopped at the door to watch another Mark 48 ADCAP slide down from the loading hatch. Forward of his stateroom, the deck itself had been pulled up and the grating converted to rails that received the incoming torpedo from the loading tray topside, guiding it down past this deck, through the second deck, and into the torpedo room, which was located amidships on the third deck. Senior Chief Bollinger was standing in the passageway just short of the drop-off, hands on hips, staring down into the chasm created by pulling up sections of *Virginia*'s first and second decks. A working party was noisily engaged in the opening, maneuvering their ton-and-a-half charges down to their on-board storage racks.

"What's the matter, COB," Garrett asked. "Can't reach the goat locker?"

"Goat locker" was shipboard slang for the quarters shared by a submarine's chiefs, located on the second deck and forward.

"As a matter of fact, Captain, I can't. Seems there's a fish in my way."

"Doing anything urgent? Besides sitting on your thumb, I mean."

"Just watching the *Ginny* swallowing goldfish, sir." Goldfish indeed. A single Mark 48 ADCAP cost something like two million dollars. A TLAM Tomahawk ran more in the neighborhood of ten million. But to Garrett's mind the cost was less important than the fact that they could be relied upon when it counted.

Garrett smiled. It was a good sign that the *Virginia* had acquired a nickname already. "Come on into my office. I need to talk to you."

"Sure thing, Skipper."

The captain's office was smaller than some closets Garrett had seen, with just barely enough room for two chairs and a tiny desk. His stateroom was just forward of the office, with a bunk and the only private head—a bathroom and shower—on the boat. Much of the bulkhead space was taken up by communications equipment, a computer monitor and keyboard, and a small printer. Space was cramped, but the *Virginia* did offer the very latest in computer and communications technology.

"What can I do for you, sir?" Bollinger asked, wedging himself into the visitor's chair.

"Jorgensen told me about the accident."

"Yes, sir. Leaves us a hand short."

Garrett glanced hard at Bollinger, looking for an indication that that had been a deliberate pun. The Chief of the Boat maintained a bland and noncommittal expression.

"How long to get a replacement?"

"Should be able to have someone out from the holding company by tomorrow. I've already put a request through channels."

"Excellent."

"It'll mean delaying our departure, though." *Virginia* was scheduled to depart New London at 0700 hours the next day.

"Can't be helped."

"If it turns out there's going to be too much of a delay, we could always have them meet us by Sea King, an at-sea transfer."

"I'd rather avoid that if possible." Dangling a man from a harness attached to a cable lowered from a Navy helicopter was acceptable practice in an emergency—when a crewman had to be taken off for surgery, for instance—but could rarely be justified otherwise. The chance of mishap was too high, the advantages too slight, the sea far too cold and unforgiving to try an at-sea transfer in any but the most urgent circumstances.

"Of course," Bollinger replied.

"We can go a man short if necessary. I'm more concerned about the training standards. Number One said the injured man wasn't experienced with the new loading tray. I don't want this accident repeated, not with Mark 48 ADCAPs weighing over a ton and a half apiece, and not while we're at sea."

The loading tray the working party was using on the

forward deck was essentially identical to the loading trays used in the torpedo room. Torps were manhandled off their storage racks and into the tray, which allowed them to be slid forward into the torpedo tubes during loading. A certain amount of muscle power was necessary, especially during the urgent heat of combat, and conditions could be less than ideal, in rough water or while the submarine was performing violent evasive maneuvers, for example. The torpedo room crew had better know exactly what they were doing under such conditions, and they'd better know the equipment they were working with, know it better than they knew themselves.

"Sounds to me like we have some drill in our future," Bollinger said, grinning.

"COB, you've just read my mind. This deployment is supposed to evaluate the *Virginia* and her capabilities for SUBDEVRON 2. But to do that, I first need to evaluate *Virginia*'s crew. Do you copy?"

"Loud and clear, Captain."

"Good. It is my intention to call a meeting of all officers and senior enlisted personnel to work out a training schedule as soon as we're under way."

He was interrupted by a loud clangor from forward—another weapon coming down the weapons-loading hatch, bound for the torpedo room two decks down.

He stood up. "I don't think we'll get anything else done while that's going on," he said. "We'll discuss the details later."

"Aye, aye, sir. I'll look forward to it." Another loud clang sounded, accompanied by the echoing yells of sailors and a burst of paint-scorching profanity. Bollinger chuckled.

"What?"

"It just occurred to me, sir. Whoever first called us the silent service was never on board one of these things in port!"

"Makes you wonder about L.A. boats in port, doesn't it?"

Bollinger laughed, nodding. One of the chief claims to silent fame for the *Seawolf*—and, by extension, for the just-as-silent *Virginia*—was that they were actually quieter, while under way, than an improved Los Angeles–class submarine tied up at the dock. If the *Virginia* was *this* noisy, what did it say about the L.A.?

"Be fair, Captain," Bollinger replied. "Maybe the L.A. boats are quieter when they're under way. I damn well hope that's the case for us!"

"Me too, COB. Right now, they can probably hear us in Beijing."

Bollinger pricked metaphorical ears at that. "Beijing, Captain? Are we headed for the Pacific?"

"Looks that way, COB, though we'll wait and see what the orders say. Until then, keep it to yourself."

"Of course, sir. But it'll help in some of the stores requisitioning, know what I mean? I might have a private word with Lieutenant Kendall." Kendall was the boat's supply officer.

"By all means."

"Thank you, sir."

Garrett tried to catch up on some of the backlogged office work waiting for him on his computer. Like *Seawolf*, the *Virginia* was a "paperless" submarine, with all reports, memos, and requisitions handled electronically. That didn't mean there was any less work to do, however, and it seemed to Garrett—a command veteran on both the *Seawolf* and on Los Angeles boats—that the office workload was getting worse and worse . . . and backbreaking, nosegrinding *worse*. At this rate, he would be lucky if he emerged from his coffin-like office once in the course of an entire three-month deployment.

But first, he had an apology to write. Trying to ignore the crash and clang, the shouting and swearing just beyond the thin bulkheads of his office, he began pecking out words on his keyboard.

Surely, he thought, a naval officer had more vital things to do than wading into the cold and murky pool of public relations.

Or of political damage control.

"Both as an officer of the United States Navy and as commanding officer of one of that Navy's submarines, I deeply regret my choice of words during a speech delivered on Thursday, 27 May, at the commissioning ceremony for the USS Virginia. . . ."

Saturday, 20 May 2006

Sail, USS *Virginia*
Submarine Base New London
Groton, Connecticut
0700 hours, EST

"Captain, we are ready in all respects for sea."

"Very well," Garrett said, speaking into the headset mike he was wearing. "Transfer the ensign."

A deck party swiftly detached the American ensign from the jackstaff aft, then began securing the jackstaff itself. *Virginia*, like all recent American subs, had been designed with absolute silence in mind, which meant that permanent deck fittings—the capstans to which mooring lines were secured—all were located along the centerline where the water flow was already disturbed, while temporary fittings, like the flagpole or the secure points where deck handlers could clip their safety lines, could either be removed or hidden away in sealed recesses in the hull.

A moment later, a second American flag broke out from the masthead at Garrett's back, snapping in the freshening breeze off the Thames.

Garrett took another look around, checking the water alongside and aft of the *Virginia*. There wasn't much room to move in the tiny space. The bridge area of the sail was barely large enough for Garrett and the quartermaster chief—Harry Vance—wedged in side by side with the bare minimum of navigational and communications equipment. Two enlisted men stood in the lookout bins just behind them, to either side of the optical mast array, high-tech replacements for the venerable periscope that, with *Virginia*, had gone the way of the dinosaur.

A huge crowd had turned up on Pier One this morning to see *Virginia* off—mostly family and friends of her crew, with a fair number of dignitaries and politicians as well. A small Navy band had struck up "Anchors Aweigh" with an enthusiastic thump of brass and drums.

"Deck, single up lines, fore and aft," he said. The brow had already been swung ashore, and the brow lines and springs released and stowed. In a moment, the only ties still binding the *Virginia* to land were one mooring line forward and one aft, both attended by small line handling parties. They were highly visible on the black deck, in dungarees and bright orange life vests. One extra hand, a diver, stood ready in full scuba gear as well, fast-rescue insurance in case someone fell overboard. *Virginia*'s narrow deck afforded very little room for maneuvering, and none whatsoever for missteps or accidents.

With that crowd ashore, it would *not* do to have someone trip over a line and end up in the drink.

"Deck lines singled up, fore and aft, aye," Chief Vance announced.

Garrett took a last look aft and to starboard, checking to see that the water was clear. A pair of harbor tugs stood ready in midriver, waiting. "Sound horn, backing down."

"Sound horn, backing down, aye, sir." Three sharp blasts sounded from the ship's horn mounted in the sail, a deafening triple honk.

"Cast off aft line," Garrett said. "Helm, come ten degrees left rudder."

"Aft line cast off, Captain," Vance told him.

"Helm, ten degrees left rudder, aye, sir" sounded in his headset.

"Maneuvering, slow astern."

"Maneuvering, slow astern, aye aye!"

With *Virginia*'s pumpjet propulsor just barely turning over, and with the rudder swung left—the opposite direction for a right turn since the vessel was backing down—the submarine began slowly to move, her tail swinging out into the river away from the dock.

Garrett watched critically for a handful of heartbeats, then snapped the order, "Cast off forward line!"

"Cast off forward line, aye aye, sir!"

Bound to the land no more, *Virginia* moved slowly astern into the river, gently sliding past the *San Juan* moored opposite. The sailors on *San Juan*'s deck came smartly to attention, rendering honors; Garrett faced them and responded with a hand salute.

By the time *Virginia* had cleared the dock, still moving astern, the tugs had moved in, passing lines over to the sub's deck parties. Garrett felt a soft, almost caressing bump as one of the tugs slipped in on *Vir-*

ginia's port side and began nudging the submarine into the main channel heading south. A small Coast Guard security boat fell into line ahead forward, with a second one bringing up the rear. Security was pretty tight today. There'd not yet been a successful terrorist attack on a U.S. ship getting under way from American waters. Emphasis on *yet*. The attack on the USS *Cole* while she was refueling at the port in Yemen had been a major victory for the terrorists who'd launched it— men now known to have been members of al Qaeda. That kind of publicity was bound to make the bastards want to try again . . . in a way intended to get even more attention.

Garrett leaned against the spartan instrument console beneath the Plexiglas spray canopy and let the tug drivers do their job, guiding the *Virginia* south past the point at Fort Trumbull and tiny Powder Island. Quarters were tight here within the lower reaches of the Thames, and no criticism of a sub skipper's skill was intended when the rules mandated the tugs' assistance in putting out to sea.

Twenty minutes later, the wind began picking up as the headlands to either side at the river's mouth fell away, and the *Virginia* entered Fishers Island Sound. East were Avery Point and the low and swampy bulge of Pine Island. West was the New London Lighthouse, marking the treacherous shoals of the Quinnipeag Rocks. As soon as they were clear of the Thames Channel, the tugs cast off and, with a mournful hoot of farewell, fell off to starboard.

"Maneuvering, bridge," Garrett said into the intercom mike. "Make revolutions for twelve knots. Change course to one-seven-zero."

"Bridge, maneuvering" was the reply. "Make revolutions for twelve knots, aye. Change course to one-seven-zero, aye." He felt the surge of power as *Virginia*'s screw bit harder at the ocean, thrusting her forward. The two security boats fell into step to port and starboard, trailing slightly astern.

Two lookouts stood in raised niches above and behind Garrett's place on the weather bridge, scanning the opposite horizons with binoculars. The man to starboard suddenly called out, "Surface target! Starboard quarter, possible collision course, range six hundred yards!"

Garrett turned, raising his binoculars and scanning the water in the indicated direction. *Virginia* was still just barely clear of the mouth of the Thames. The shore to the west was close, less than nine hundred yards distant, a low and rolling panorama of hills covered by the neatly clustered buildings of southwestern New London. A number of boats—mostly small recreational craft—motorboats and sailboats—were visible. The lookout's use of the word *target* wasn't meant literally, of course, but he'd spotted something that could be trouble.

And it was. Through his binoculars, Garrett could see the long, low lines of a bright red Cigarette boat, moving fast off *Virginia*'s forward quarter, bow planing above the white slash of its wake. Its driver was in a hell of a hurry, and from the angle on the bow, it looked as if he was trying to cut across the *Virginia*'s path.

"Radar, this is the Captain," he barked. "We've got a visual on a high-speed contact six hundred yards to starboard! Wake up down there and give me a bearing and speed!"

"Sir . . . aye aye, sir!" The voice sounded shaken.

"Comm, Captain. Raise our security escort. Point them at the Cigarette boat cutting across our bow!

And put a flash out to New London. Tell them we have a civilian craft trying an intercept." He watched the other craft a moment longer. "Maneuvering, bridge. Come left ten degrees. Make revolutions for twenty-five knots!"

"Bridge, maneuvering. Come left ten degrees, aye. Make revolutions for two-five knots, aye!"

A 7,500-ton submarine does not stop on the proverbial dime. That racing boat driver was a civilian and probably wasn't used to handling craft heavier than the one he was in now. Garrett wasn't sure what the guy's game was, but it could easily end in disaster.

A high-speed racing boat probably wouldn't more than dent *Virginia*'s hull if they collided, but there would be a bad PR fallout indeed if a civilian boat hit the sub and a civilian was killed. Every attack sub skipper in the Navy had nightmares about that; a few years ago, the *Greeneville*, a Los Angeles–class boat, had pulled an emergency surface drill and come up directly under a Japanese fishing boat loaded with students just off the Hawaiian coast. Nine civilians had died, and the *Greeneville*'s captain had lost his command.

And there was another possibility to consider. Palestinian terrorists had used such boats for years in suicide bombing attempts against Israeli naval vessels, and there was the small boat packed with explosives that had put a hole in the hull of the USS *Cole*.

It didn't seem likely that al Qaeda would have a suicide boat waiting for a U.S. attack sub less than a mile off the coast of Connecticut . . . but then, before it happened, no one would have believed bin Laden's terrorists capable of taking out the World Trade Center and a chunk of the Pentagon with three hijacked airliners. The Navy in general, and ship captains in particular, took such possibilities very seriously indeed.

Garrett wasn't going to let that speedboat anywhere near his vessel if he could help it.

"Bridge, Radar," a voice called over the intercom headset. "Target designated Romeo One, bearing two-zero-five, range five-five-zero. Estimate speed at fifty knots. Probable intercept course. Time to impact . . . approximately two minutes."

"This is the Captain. Sound general quarters."

"Now general quarters, general quarters" blared from every 1MC speaker on the boat. "All hands, man your battle stations." As the vessel's crew came to a state of full alert, Garrett grappled with the variables of speed, range, and direction. He could extend the time to collision by turning away from the oncoming speedboat and increasing speed. Or he could order an emergency dive.

The trouble was, *Virginia* was still moving through dangerously restricted waters. Dead ahead was the shoal water of the New London Ledge, marked by another lighthouse. To the right of that lay the shoals of Black Ledge and Vixen Ledge, marked by warning buoys, while to the right were Long Rock, Shoal and Middle Rocks, and the Sarah Ledge. There was damned little room in here for maneuver.

"Diving Officer!" he snapped. "This is the Captain. Give me DBK!"

"Captain, Dive Officer. Depth beneath keel . . . thirty-eight feet."

Shallow. *Very* shallow. *Virginia* had a draft of thirty-four feet, meaning the actual depth here was seventy-two feet. From keel to the top of her sail she measured just under fifty-five feet, which gave her almost no leeway at all if she submerged totally. The slightest miscalculation in trim or angle of descent could slam the *Virginia* into the bottom. The charts listed the bottom hereabouts as mud; probably nothing would be damaged but pride . . . *probably*. Garrett wasn't willing to risk it, however.

"Helm, Bridge. Come left twenty degrees."

"Bridge, Helm. Come left two-zero degrees, aye aye!"

"Maneuvering! Bridge! Increase revolutions to three-zero knots."

"Bridge, Maneuvering. Increase revs to make three-zero knots, aye aye!"

"Comm, signal our intentions to our escort." It wouldn't do for *Virginia* to avoid the oncoming civilian boat, only to run down a Coast Guard security craft in the process.

Virginia seemed to hunker down as her speed increased. The wash coming up and over her rounded bow and breaking up and across the slanted foot at the forward edge of her sail turned to a white cascade lashing at the cockpit. In seconds, Garrett was soaking wet, and the windshield was practically opaque with driving salt spray. Turning in the cockpit, he tried to spot the Cigarette boat, almost lost against the clutter of small boats and houses along the shore. There it was . . . almost bow-on now to starboard, high on a plane as it raced to catch up with the speeding submarine. The Coast Guard boats were both turning to intercept him.

Garrett continued to study the boat through his binoculars, trying somehow to read the mind of its pilot. An idiot rich kid out for a joyride in Daddy's expensive racing boat? That stretch of the Connecticut coast behind the New London skyline was definitely the high-rent district, home to plenty of rich doctors, lawyers, and New York City stockbrokers.

Or could it be a terrorist, an AQ fanatic trying to go out in a blaze of martyr's glory by taking out America's latest nuclear attack submarine with a speedboat full of explosives?

If it was a terrorist, Garrett thought, the guy wouldn't be alone. He would know his chances of catching the *Virginia* were slender, even within the maze of rocks and shoal waters south of New London. He might well be out there as a highly visible diversion, attracting attention with a bright red speedboat throwing a towering rooster tail of spray, while other suicide bombers moved into position in the south or east. Turning, he carefully swept the horizon ahead and to port. Fishers Island was four miles to the southeast, beyond the New London Ledge Light. That was the only piece of high ground that would afford much in the way of concealment for other attackers.

Garrett needed to make a navigational decision quickly. On his new heading, he would scrape past the New London Ledge and run smack aground on Fishers Island in another eight minutes or so. He could come back to starboard onto his original heading, taking the main channel south into Block Island Sound before turning southeast again and moving into the open vastness of the Atlantic. Or he could swing further to port, with the intention of threading the *Virginia* past the Dumplings and through narrow Lord's Passage between Wicopesset Island and East Point on the far tip of Fishers Island.

He would be in deep and open water faster with the first choice. *Virginia* needed maneuvering room, and fast. He took another look at the Cigarette boat, now almost directly to starboard. Yeah . . . to his eye, *Virginia* was definitely winning the race.

"Helm, Bridge. Come right three-zero degrees."

"Bridge, Helm. Come right three-zero degrees, aye aye!"

Back on a southerly heading, the New London Ledge Light now lay five hundred yards off the port bow. The Cigarette boat, now off *Virginia*'s stern quarter, continued to make a valiant attempt to catch the fast-moving sub, but the two Coast Guard vessels were moving to block it. Swerving wildly, he avoided one of the Coasties, but the second expertly slid into his path.

By this time, the alert Garrett had flashed to the shore authorities had begun to produce results. A pair of Navy Sea Cobra helicopters was approaching low across the water from the airfield to the northeast, like small, deadly gray insects. Along the shoreline to the northeast, a small flotilla of Navy and Coast Guard patrol boats was scrambling. They'd be bearing down on the scene of the unfolding drama in another few minutes.

The Cigarette boat driver evidently saw that he wasn't going to get closer. At a distance range from the *Virginia* of just 150 yards, he turned broadside and cut his power. Through his binoculars, Garrett could see two people on board beside the pilot, a man and a woman, struggling to unfurl a large green and white banner along the craft's side.

The banner read GREENPEACE.

Greenpeace! So they weren't terrorists and they weren't joyriders after all. *Damn* it all!

That organization, he knew, had a number of agendas worldwide, and they'd done a lot of good for conservation and for the raising of an ecological consciousness, both in the U.S. and abroad. Garrett approved, in general, of such goals. But Greenpeace was also dedicated to blocking the deployment of naval vessels with nuclear power plants, or that might be carrying nuclear weapons.

Garrett had encountered them before more than once. They'd tried a similar ploy a few years ago in San Francisco Bay as he'd captained the *Pittsburgh* from Mare's Island to the Golden Gate. They were nuisances, nothing more. He supported their right to protest, even if he thought some of their political goals were misguided.

Such antics were especially risky now, in the ongoing aftermath of the *Cole* and of the paranoia of 9-11. The United States was at war, whether her citizens were always aware of that or not. Garrett would have been justified in opening fire on that speedboat. Those Sea Cobras buzzing overhead most certainly *would* have fired if the Cigarette boat hadn't cut power.

What price freedom?

An old, old question, one American military personnel had pondered since Lexington and Concord. *Virginia*'s primary ongoing mission was to safeguard American lives, property, and rights ashore and at sea. By extension, that included the rights of those Greenpeace advocates to protest the policies of the U.S. government.

But when those protests risked damage to an American naval vessel, worse, when they risked *lives*, civilian or military . . .

He could see the security boat grappling with the speedboat now, and armed Coast Guardsmen in black Kevlar vests clambering into the wallowing craft's well deck. Her crew would be in for some rough handling, he thought—complete with handcuffs and arrest. He hoped they thought it was all worth it, a fair exchange for making their dramatic statement. They were damned lucky not to have been blown out of the water.

"Conn, this is the Captain. Secure from general quarters." He would have to file a report on the incident later, justifying his decisions and orders. In the meantime, he needed to see to a harsher duty. "Who's got the radar watch?"

"Uh . . . Seaman Wallace has the radar watch, sir."

What the hell was a seaman doing on the radar watch at a critical moment like the *Virginia*'s passage out of New London's crowded waters? "Tell Wallace that he is relieved from duty and that he is on report. Who is his department head?"

"Sir, that would be Chief Kurzweil."

"Tell him I want to see him in my office at . . ." He checked his wristwatch. "Ten hundred."

"Aye aye, sir."

Garrett remained on the weather bridge for a time longer, watching the rolling hills of Connecticut fall away astern. An hour later, *Virginia* was cutting through the heavier seas beyond the shelter of Block Island Sound. Fishers Island now lay well astern, sixteen miles, to be exact, and was little more than a shadow against the horizon. Seven miles to the northeast, off the port quarter, lay Block Island, marked by the 200-foot prominence of Beacon Hill. Eight miles to the southwest lay Montauk Point, easternmost tip of Long Island, and the much gentler swell of Prospect Hill beyond.

Ahead lay only open ocean, and the freedom of the depths—*Virginia*'s proper domain.

"Diving Officer, this is the Captain. Depth below keel."

"Captain, DO. Depth below keel is now sixty-eight feet."

Deep enough—barely. "Very well. Prepare to take us down."

"Prepare to submerge, aye aye, sir."

"Lookouts below."

The two lookouts scrambled down out of their perches and vanished through the sail's hatch. Garrett took a last look around, savoring the taste of the cool, salt-laden air, the warmth of the sun still low in the east. Then he followed the lookouts down the ladder, securing the weather bridge deck grating and hatch above him.

He knew it would be a while before any of them felt sun or sea breeze again.

Crew's quarters, USS *Virginia*
32 miles south of Martha's Vineyard
Massachusetts
1010 hours, EST

"Jesus, Wall-eye, you are in a *world* of shit!"

TM2 Ron Titelman's pleasant jibe did nothing to improve Wallace's spirits. Since he'd been relieved from duty a couple of hours ago, he'd holed up in the one place on board where he could be out of the way—in his rack. Unfortunately, Titelman had found him, yanked back the privacy curtain, and was leaning on the side of the bunk now, grinning with evil pleasure.

"Give me a break, Ron," Wallace said. "I don't even know what I did!"

"Well, you'll find out when you pay a little visit to the captain, that's for sure. Man, he's gonna ream you a new one with a live Mark 48. Warshot loaded!"

"Whadja find there, Titsy?" EM1 Jack Kirkpatrick said, coming up the narrow passageway beside Titelman. "Well! If it ain't the perpetrator hisself! Trying to hide from your shipmates, there?"

Wallace groaned and covered his eyes.

"I told you about making the department look bad, twerp!" Kirkpatrick growled. "Right now, your ass is grass!"

"What is this, a goddamn convention?" TM3 Rodriguez joined the conclave in an already crowded passageway. "Hey, Wall-eye! Out that rack! I'm off-duty until the first dogwatch and I want some rack time!"

Rodriguez was the man with whom Wallace had to hot-bunk, sharing the same rack space in staggered shifts of duty.

Clumsily, Wallace rolled out of the narrow confines of the bunk, landing on the deck and bumping against both Kirkpatrick and Titelman.

"Watch the fuckin' feet, newbie!" Kirkpatrick barked. "Why don't you make yourself useful and go outside and scrape down the hull?"

"Yeah. And requisition a gallon of polka-dot paint from ship's stores while you're at it," Titelman added. Wallace hurriedly pulled on his boondockers and moved off down the passageway forward, as the others exploded into raucous laughter at his back.

That first phrase Titelman had used raised unpleasant memories. Wallace remembered the first march of his newly formed boot company back at Great Lakes, a small age ago. They'd walked across from Mainside, where they'd been in a holding company, through the tunnel to the recruit training center. In time-honored tradition, other, much more experienced recruits—all of six weeks, perhaps?—had leaned out of windows to taunt the scared newbies. "You guys are in a w-o-o-o-o-o-orld of shit!"

As they marched through the tunnel that connected the two halves of the base beneath Sheridan Road, they'd been ordered to sing "Anchors Aweigh" at the top of their lungs.

A bizarre, bizarre experience, and one that for a long time had seemed a world away.

Now, though, he was as scared and as anxious about the future as he'd been then, as though he hadn't changed, hadn't *grown* at all.

He'd known privacy was an issue on board an attack sub, but he'd not expected it to be like this. How was he going to even survive these next months at sea?

If he was lucky, maybe the captain would kill him.

Captain's office, USS *Virginia*
32 miles south of Martha's Vineyard
Massachusetts
1012 hours, EST

"Jesus Christ, Chief! What were you thinking?" Garrett glared across the tiny desk at Chief Kurzweil, a look that others more than once had told him would peel paint from the bulkhead at fifty paces. "Have you forgotten how hard it is to read a radarscope in waters that cluttered?"

"No, sir. I guess . . . I guess I wasn't thinking, sir."

"I think you guess right."

"But Wallace is fresh out of ET school. He's about due for his crow. He's had training reading a scope!"

"Sure, training. But the real thing is never like training. Never. I don't care how good the simulators are."

"Yes, sir. But it's SOP to run all the newbies through every department. It's part of the training regimen."

"Of course it is. But you don't give a problem like that to someone with no experience! Why the hell weren't you backing him up?"

"I was, Captain. I was right behind him."

"Ah. Then why didn't *you* pick up that speedboat?"

"I . . . well, the picture was pretty cluttered, sir."

Yes, it would have been. Even with *Virginia*'s advanced sensor systems and computers, the submarine's radar would have been backscattering like hell—from the sea, from the shore and all of the buildings on shore, from radar reflectors on buoys, from dozens of small craft ranging in size from small sailboats to fifty-foot yachts and houseboats. The radar picture had been a tangle of green splotches and smears. He knew, because he'd already played the recording automatically made of the boat's radar pictures, to see for himself what Wallace had been seeing.

"So cluttered that an ET chief with seventeen years in couldn't read it? If that was the case, what the hell was the point of sticking a seaman with maybe six months of service under his belt in that chair?"

"Romeo One started off just as another pleasure boat, sir. There was nothing to pick him out of the regular traffic. He was just idling along the shore. When he swung bow-on to us, he didn't speed up right away. It could've just been a turn, y'know?"

"I know. But the fact remains that the billion-dollar technology on this boat failed us this morning, and that failure was due to human error. Radar is supposed to be better than Mark One eyeballs, Chief. You guys should have been on the 1MC the instant that bastard put his foot on the gas."

Kurzweil sighed. "I fucked up. Sir."

"Yes, you most certainly did. And unfortunately, Wallace is going to have to pay for it. It's not his fault, you know."

"Yessir. It was my responsibility."

"It's not his fault, but I can't let him off the hook because he *did* screw up. He had the chair. And he didn't spot that Cigarette boat or the fact that it was on a collision course with us for a good thirty seconds. I know. I've seen the tapes."

"Yessir."

"What's more, the automatic alarms were off. Why?" *Virginia*'s computerized sensor suite could be set to sound an alarm if a radar contact was on a collision course with the sub, or if the contact closed to within a certain range.

"That was my fault, sir. With all the traffic inside the Thames, and with the tugboats and security craft and everything, the damned alarm was going off every five seconds."

"Shit, Chief! When's the most likely time for a terrorist to try to hit us? When we're out at sea, a thousand miles from land and five hundred feet down?"

"No, sir. It would be when we were in a crowded harbor or channel. When there was a lot of other surface traffic around. When we couldn't submerge or maneuver."

"Right." Garrett closed his eyes for a moment. "Chief, I'm going to be a goddamn bastard about this. I'm logging it. There will be a disciplinary letter in your personnel record."

"Yes, sir."

He saw the pain in Kurzweil's face, but he had no choice, really. There would almost certainly be an investigation of the incident, and Garrett was determined that the sacrificial lamb, if there was to be one, would not be a seaman just out of boot camp with barely enough experience to tie his shoes. Kurzweil, the experienced man, should have had a more experienced man on the radar this morning—or he should have been there himself.

"Get the hell out of my sight, Chief."

Kurzweil got.

There were times, Garrett thought, when he hated this job.

Saturday, 20 May 2006

Captain's office, USS *Virginia*
18 miles east of Nantucket
Massachusetts
1345 hours, EST

"Seaman Wallace, do you understand that this is captain's nonjudicial punishment?" Garrett said. "A captain's mast, in other words. That means you tell me your side of the story, I tell you my side, and then I tell you what I'm going to do about it."

Wallace stood at awkward attention in front of the desk. He gulped and swallowed, managing an unsteady nod. "I . . . I understand, sir."

Damn. Wallace's voice was shaking. The kid must be scared half to death. But Garrett had to say these things. "You may request a summary or special court-martial instead, if you wish to have legal representation or call witnesses."

"My recommendation is that you take the mast, son," Chief Fred Giangreco said with a wry grin. "A court would hit you with everything a captain's mast would, plus maybe a lot more."

Giangreco, the boat's master-at-arms, sat wedged into the back corner of the office, squeezed in between the desk and the small coffee mess Garrett maintained for informal visits to this cubby. Two made it crowded; three was downright claustrophobic.

But the MAA was *Virginia*'s chief of police, in a sense, the enlisted man responsible for maintaining order and making sure the rules were obeyed. And it was vital to establish the form and working of shipboard discipline from the very start.

"I'll go with whatever you say, sir," Wallace said.

"Good enough." Garrett tried to keep his voice gentle. It would serve absolutely nothing to terrorize the kid. "Do you understand why I put you on report?"

"Uh . . . because I screwed up on watch."

"What did you do? Or *not* do?"

"Well, sir, I didn't see that speedboat on the radar."

"Specifically, you didn't see it, designate it as a target, and report it to me or to the officer of the deck. Do you see why that was a problem?"

"Yes, sir! If that had been a kamikaze boat, he could've sunk us!"

"Maybe. But it's not just the problem posed by that one speedboat. The *Virginia* is a United States warship. And we are, whatever the civilians might think, at war with a vicious, determined, and cunning enemy. It is our absolute duty to our country, to this submarine, and to our shipmates to be alert, to be vigilant, to be situationally aware of what is going on near this vessel at every moment." He paused. "Tell me what you were doing when you had the board."

"Well, it was pretty confusing. Chief Kurzweil was showing me how to try and separate genuine targets from waves and buildings and stuff like that."

"You had a pretty complicated picture to sort out."

"Uh, I guess so, sir."

"Did you ever have to deal with a radarscope picture like that in training?"

"Oh, sure. I mean, yessir. But, well, I guess it wasn't quite the same as the real thing."

"I guess not. Were you confused?"

"I don't know, sir. Maybe, a little. I didn't notice the speedboat. The return was, well, Chief Kurzweil said it was 'intermittent.' "

"The target was low in the water, and the swell would mask it occasionally, sure."

"It was mixed in with the reflections from buoys and sailboats and stuff. I guess I just didn't notice it moving. If it had been on the screen all the time, maybe I would have."

"Did you know there was a control setting that would let the computer sound an alarm if an object was on a collision course with this boat?"

"Yes, sir. We learned about that in school. Chief K switched it off because it kept going off when we were in the channel. False alarms."

"Uh-huh. Chief Kurzweil and I have already had words about that."

He swiveled his chair to check the flat-panel computer screen mounted in the bulkhead. Currently, it was repeating the control room navigation screen, with the image of a nautical chart superimposed with colored lines showing the *Virginia*'s past course and projected future course, along with blocks of navigational data—bearing, speed, depth, positional data taken from a GPS satellite. At that time, they were passing the island of Nantucket, moving northeast. Depth, one hundred feet. Speed, twenty-five knots. It was good to be in *Virginia*'s natural element—running submerged. Even in home waters, a submariner never felt entirely safe on the surface.

What was the best way to proceed with Wallace?

"Tell me this, son. While you were in that chair, watching the scope . . . did you feel on top of things?"

"Beg pardon, sir?"

"Did you feel in control? Did you feel as though you knew what you were doing and that you were able to handle any situation that might come up?"

"Uh . . . no, sir. I didn't."

"Explain."

"Well . . . there was just so much going on, you know? And Chief Kurzweil was talking and pointing out things on the screen, and I was having trouble figuring out what *anything* was. I mean, the buoys with radar reflectors are pretty obvious, and so are the larger ships. But the little ones look just like waves sometimes. And sometimes, all I was getting was this kind of smeared green mess. I didn't know what to look at!"

"So . . . what did you do wrong?"

"Uh . . . I didn't identify the speedboat, sir?"

"No. Chief Kurzweil didn't spot it right away, either. He was right there, and he has a lot more experience than you do. If it had been that obvious, he would have spotted it." *He* should *have spotted it*, Garrett thought, but he didn't tell Wallace that. "Nope, what you did was fail to tell Chief Kurzweil that you were in over your head. He put you in that chair, gave you the watch. You should have told him that you were having trouble separating out the potential targets or correctly identifying them."

"Oh . . ."

"Always ask for help if you don't understand something. Am I clear?"

"Yes, sir!"

"Don't worry about feeling stupid or foolish or anything else. Your shipmates' lives depend on you knowing what you're doing. If you don't, sound off!"

"Yes, sir."

"To drive that home, I'm giving you twelve hours extra duty. One hour a day. You'll log 'em with the MAA here."

"Yes, sir." Wallace looked crestfallen.

"I'm letting you off easy, son, because I don't think what happened is entirely your fault. I want you to think, next time. Let someone know if you're in over your head. Do you hear me?"

"Yes, sir!"

"Dismissed."

"Aye aye, sir!" Wallace turned and fled through the door.

"You *were* light on him," Giangreco said. "Twelve hours is a slap on the wrist."

That, Garrett knew, was very true. A captain was authorized to hand out stiff punishments indeed at mast—up to and including two hours a day extra duty for forty-five days, thirty days correctional custody, or a fine amounting to half of two months' pay.

"You know and I know, Chief, that he wasn't the problem. He shouldn't have been there in the first place."

"Poor judgment on Kurzweil's part, I agree, sir. What are you going to do about it?"

Garrett sighed. "There's not much I can do. I cannot and will not undercut the authority of my CPOs. Letting Wallace know I've talked to Kurzweil about it is as much as I could get away with. And I can't let Wallace learn the lesson that it's okay to goof off on watch . . . or to just let things slide when he's not sure. Otherwise I would have dropped it."

"I think Wallace is a good kid, sir."

"I think so, too. He's eager to please. I think he'll do okay. I'm more worried about Chief Kurzweil. He's going to have to prove to me that he understands the men in his charge. What they can do. And what they *can't* do."

"You want me to say something to him, sir?"

Garrett shook his head. "No. He knows he's on notice. We'll see what happens."

"I expect so, sir. You know, being locked up in one of these things for months on end is just about guaranteed to bring out the worst in men."

"True. It also brings out the best."

In Garrett's experience, it was tough predicting which would have the upper hand.

A knock sounded at the open door. Commander Jorgensen stood in the opening. "Captain Garrett? Fourteen hundred hours, sir. Time to break out the orders."

"Thank you, Pete. Call in Lieutenant DeKalb and the COB, will you?"

"They're both here, sir." He moved aside so that Garrett could see both Lieutenant DeKalb, *Virginia*'s navigational officer, and Senior Chief Bollinger standing in the passageway.

"Ah. Well, come in as much as you can."

"Everyone inhale," Giangreco joked.

"Master-at-arms, I think our business is concluded."

"Yes, sir. Time for me to make my rounds, anyway."

Giangreco squeezed past the others. The exec took

his seat, while the navigational officer and the chief of the boat both stood just inside the doorway. Garrett keyed in the combination of the safe, opened the door, and pulled out *Virginia*'s sailing orders. After the exec verified that the seal was unbroken, Garrett used a penknife from his desk to cut the string and pull out the sheaf of papers inside.

The others waited while he read.

TO: COMMANDING OFFICER, USS VIRGINIA, SSN-774
FROM: COMSUBLANT
RE: OPERATIONAL ORDERS
HAVING DEPARTED NEW LONDON NOT LATER THAN 1200 HOURS 27 MAY 06, USS VIRGINIA WILL PROCEED SUBMERGED VIA THE LABRADOR SEA TO BAFFIN BAY BY WAY OF THE DAVIS STRAIT. . . .

"Well, my informants were right," he said at last.

"What course, Captain?" DeKalb asked.

"North. We're going under the Pole." He heard the intake of breath from the others. "Our orders are to evaluate *Virginia*'s under-ice capabilities and technologies. And after that, we take the Bering Strait south, putting in at Yokosuka for supplies."

"Japan!" Bollinger said. "It's been a while."

"Should be interesting," Garrett said. "If you think Greenpeace is a pain in the ass over nukes, you should see the Japanese."

"They have reason," Jorgensen said.

"It's not like we have nuclear weapons on board," DeKalb pointed out. "Just a nuclear reactor."

"Some folks over there are still touchy about that," the COB pointed out. "They assume any U.S. warship is carrying nuke warheads, and, of course, official U.S. naval policy is to neither confirm nor deny. . . ."

Garrett was paying little attention to the animated conversation as he dropped the orders on his desk. Japan! Already he was wondering if he would be able to wangle the time and the opportunity to see Kazuko while he was there.

If he could just talk to her, convince her that they could make their relationship work. . . .

Sunday, 21 May 2006
PLA Base, Small Dragon Island
Spratly Islands
South China Sea
1610 hours, Zulu −8

General Han Do Liu grinned broadly, spreading his arms. "Welcome, brothers, to Small Dragon Island!" He spoke in broken Arabic, for the benefit of the visitors. Captain Jian masked the scowl he felt behind a bland and indifferent face. Han was going out of his way to impress these . . . foreigners.

The irony of that thought surprised him. The word he'd used was *gwailo*, used much in the same manner as the Japanese *gaijin* . . . and meaning, roughly, "foreign devils." That was what the citizens of the Middle Kingdom had called the foreign barbarians for centuries, but by the nineteenth century it was synonymous with the white foreigners of Europe and America. These foreigners were sworn enemies of the Americans, and somehow the name didn't seem to quite fit.

On the other hand, foreign barbarians were pretty

much the same, whether they came from New York City or Karachi.

Or Kabul.

They sat around the long, broad table in the base conference room, Jian and Han and members of their staffs, and the motley collection of al Qaeda fanatics. Men so dedicated to their religion that they were willing to die for it were an enigma to Jian. A lifelong atheist, he did not trust such people, or their motives. Men dedicated to a *cause*, however, he understood well indeed, and he tried to focus on that aspect of the visitors.

"We appreciate your hospitality, General Han," the tall newcomer said. The intelligence dossier Jian had seen called him Mahmud Salah Zahid, a wealthy Saudi expatriate who now used the nom de guerre of Zaki Abar. He and his associates had arrived at Small Dragon Island only a few hours ago on board a palatial motor yacht, the *Al Qahir*. The yacht was tied up now alongside the Pakistani submarine in the big sea shelter; the eighteen-man crew had been quartered with the Pakistani sailors from the *Shuhadaa Muqaddaseen*.

And now Zahid, two disreputable-looking Afghanis, and ul Haq, the Pakistani captain of the *Shuhadaa*, were gathered in the briefing room as if they were honored foreign dignitaries.

"Not at all, not at all," Han said affably. "How was your voyage?"

"Smooth enough, though the Vietnamese gave us some trouble when we first entered these waters. We were stopped by one of their patrol boats south of Spratly Island. We had to bribe them to be allowed to proceed."

"Ah, yes. The Vietnamese have been a problem for

us in this region for some time now. They claim these islands, as do we. Ours is by far the older, and superior, claim."

"Of course, of course. But something needs to be done about these . . . pirates."

"It will be," Han promised. "Actually, Captain ul Haq, here, will be assisting us in that regard. Part of our mutual assistance pact, you know."

"*If* that can be done without jeopardizing our primary mission," ul Haq put in, speaking fluent Mandarin.

"Of course."

Jian listened to the verbal sparring with barely concealed impatience. How were these foreign devils going to be of any possible use to the People's Republic? "General Han," he said in Arabic. "Perhaps we should address the issue of inspection? Our people still have not been allowed aboard the Pakistani submarine . . . as was agreed upon."

Ul Haq locked eyes with Jian. "The agreement was for one of your officers to come on board as an advisor. We wish to limit contact between your people and my crew, however. It is important that they not discuss our mission."

"Our people know the meaning of security, Captain," Jian replied. *His crew hasn't been told the nature of their mission,* Jian thought. It confirmed the impression he'd already formed in earlier briefings with the Pakistani submarine captain. "Commander Hsing is ready to join the *Shuhadaa Muqaddaseen*'s crew at any time."

Commander Hsing Yng Tak, sitting at Jian's left, inclined his head. *That* was a man dedicated to a cause, one that Jian understood perfectly. Serving as Jian's weapons officer on board the *Yinbi,* Hsing lived and worked beneath a shadow of grief-driven need for vengeance. His older brother, another PLAN submarine officer, had been captain of a Kilo-class attack submarine sunk by the Americans three years ago. Hsing had eagerly volunteered to serve as advisor on board ul Haq's vessel, merely on the promise that he would be able to strike back at the hated Yankees.

"Commander Hsing understands that he is to communicate solely with me and my officers?" ul Haq said.

"Perfectly, sir," Hsing said, responding in Arabic. "I will not interfere with your crew."

"Then he may come on board the *Shuhadaa Muqaddaseen*," ul Haq said. "And he is free to inspect her weapons and facilities, as you wish. We have nothing to conceal from you, our allies. But we must be careful about what the enlisted personnel hear from . . . outside."

"Perfectly understandable," Han said.

Jian maintained a bland expression. *Fighting men should know the truth when they are sent on a suicide mission,* he thought. *Sending them to their deaths blindly is murder.*

He wondered if Hsing fully understood. The *Shuhadaa* would not be returning from her deployment. Not if she was going to take on the United States Navy.

Jian decided that it was enough that he concern himself with his own submarine, his own crew. They knew why they were here, and they knew what was at stake. That knowledge, he was convinced, made them better sailors. Better warriors.

"It is settled, then," General Han said. "To review, then . . . *Shuhadaa Muqaddaseen* will commence operations in the western Spratlys as soon as provisioning is complete. Commander Hsing will serve as naval liaison, and as advisor to her officers. Captain Jian will station *Yinbi de Gongji* in a position from which he can protect the *Shuhadaa Muqaddaseen* in the event of foreign naval intervention."

A neat plan . . . almost too neat, too perfect, and one with layers upon layers. The al Qaeda officers would be using the Pakistani submarine to carry out terrorist operations against western targets in the South China Sea . . . and, if possible, would include among their targets elements of the Vietnamese forces stationed among the western Spratlys. Inevitably, U.S. naval forces—in all likelihood, one of their supercarrier battle groups—would deploy to the region, hunting for the *Shuhadaa*.

That was where the *Yinbi* came into the picture.

In a sense, the *Shuhadaa* was the bait. While the Americans were hunting the Pakistani sub, the Chinese submarine, silent, unsuspected by the enemy, would stalk and kill the U.S. aircraft carrier. The destruction of one of their billion-dollar supercarriers might well make the cost-conscious Yankees think twice about their policy of maintaining a naval presence within Chinese waters—or of protecting the rebel province of Taiwan.

It would be revenge, too, for the losses inflicted on the PLA Navy three years before . . . and the best part of all was that, if all went well, the Americans would not even see the Chinese hand behind the attack. They might suspect that Beijing had provided covert assistance—bases and logistical support—but they would be unable to prove it in the court of world opinion. They would have to assume it was al Qaeda that had sunk their precious supercarrier.

The one American threat that most concerned Jian

was the American attack submarine force—especially their new Seawolf class. An axiom of naval strategy was that the best way to kill a submarine was *with* a submarine, and the American attack subs—Los Angeles class, Seawolf class, and a new class that according to Chinese military intelligence had just become operational—were the best sub hunters in the world.

The operational plan had taken that into consideration, he knew. While he was stalking the carrier battle group that would be stalking ul Haq's *Shuhadaa,* other Chinese submarines would be moving into position to protect Jian's *Yinbi,* stalking the Yankee submarines that were certain to be operating with their CBG.

Circles within circles, plans within plans. Operation Yangshandian had taken on a vast and complex life of its own.

That last bit of information had come to him by way of his Uncle Jiasuo, an e-mail message relayed by satellite to Jian's office computer. Jiasuo had been careful with his words; government censors were certain to be screening all mail, both paper and electronic, and both men would have been in trouble if they'd typed their messages in plain romanized Common Speech. Jian had asked if there was anything his uncle could tell him about the "hopelessness of the march," an indirect reference to *Yinbi*'s deployment. Jiasuo, guessing what was on Jian's mind, had replied with a rambling story about a man hunting a tiger by using a tethered goat. His offhand reference to other hunters protecting the first from other tigers told Jian that *Yinbi* would not be alone.

How many other PLAN submarines would be in the area? That he had no way of knowing. Clearly, Beijing considered it unimportant to tell him; their ideas of duty frequently held that a commander need only follow orders, not understand the plan as a whole.

Sometimes that approach was necessary, Jian knew, but he disliked being treated like a child. He would do his part, without question, but it helped to know that *Yinbi* would not be facing Yankee submarines alone.

Perhaps, he thought, the larger plan embraced the hope that one or more of the American attack subs would be caught and sunk as well. The *Seawolf*, reportedly, was fabulously expensive—more expensive even than the notorious Soviet "Golden Fish." If an American aircraft carrier *and* one of their Seawolfs or the new attack sub could be brought down . . .

Yes, it made sense. Faced with such a loss from "terrorists," America, known throughout the world for its cost-consciousness, would almost surely pull back from the western Pacific.

And that would give Beijing a free hand at last with the rebellious population of Taiwan.

He just wished that China's allies were a bit more reliable. He had no respect for these Muslim fanatics, and less trust.

Zaki, the tall Saudi, was sliding an envelope across the table to Han. "Here is the record of payment, as promised."

Jian watched as Han opened the envelope and read the slip of paper inside. It was a record of money—a very large sum of money—transferred from Riyadh to the Bank of Hong Kong. Evidently, American attempts to shut down al Qaeda's global financial network had been less than successful.

Perhaps that was the real reason Jian did not trust these foreigners. It wasn't just the fanaticism of their beliefs; it was the fact that they spent money like water. They'd bought a fair number of Pakistani military and government officials to get control of the *Shuhadaa*. Now they were paying Beijing for the right to use the Small Dragon base and for the assistance of the *Yinbi*. Such people, in Jian's experience, came to believe that they owned the people they'd paid.

And Jian belonged to no one and no thing but himself and the naval service.

"My orders," Han said, "are to await confirmation from the mainland."

"Of course."

"However, this all appears to be in order. I expect to receive the final orders to proceed no later than this evening."

"I would suggest the *Shuhadaa Muqaddaseen* be under way tonight, then," ul Haq said. "The sooner we are at sea, the better."

"I agree," Zaki said. "With your permission, General, my associates and I will also leave tonight. We took precautions to distract the Americans and their satellites, but if they tracked us anyway, it will be safer for you if we are gone."

"So long as I have confirmation of the payment, you may leave when you wish," Han said with a shrug. "If the Americans did see you arrive, we can always tell them we ordered you in for violating our sovereign waters!"

Zaki chuckled. "That would be a difficult claim to maintain. As far as the rest of the world is concerned, nobody owns these islands."

"Nobody and everybody. We *are* asserting our historic claims to the Spratly Islands, however. Which is why Captain ul Haq here is going to help us with the Vietnamese problem."

"The Vietnamese will be the least of your problems, General," ul Haq said. He locked eyes with Jian.

"Your naval officers will have their hands full when the Americans respond with a carrier battle group."

"That, Captain, will be my worry," Jian said smoothly. "Not yours. If you carry out your part of this operation, we will take care of ours."

"I am gratified," ul Haq said, addressing Han, "that your people are so confident. I trust they will not be hampered by overconfidence."

"Captain Jian is one of the best submarine officers in the PLAN," Han said, surprising Jian with the overt compliment. Han was not known for being gracious or for bestowing praise. "This plan has been carefully and methodically developed, both by your people and by ours. There is little that can go wrong."

"One thing can go wrong, General," Jian said.

"Eh? What is that?"

He held ul Haq's eyes with his own, trying to judge the man's strength. "A failure of nerve, sir. By either party. But I trust that is not a serious possibility."

"It is not," ul Haq said, his voice steady. "Not for our part, at any rate."

"Nor is it for ours."

"Then," Han said, smiling, "perhaps we should toast our victory!"

Zaki scowled. "We cannot—"

"We know the restrictions of your religion." Han snapped his fingers, and an aide standing silently near the door vanished through it, to return an instant later with a silver platter bearing cups and tea. "You can join us in tea?"

The Muslims relaxed, and Zaki nodded. "Of course."

Jian, however, did not relax. It was entirely too soon, he thought, to be celebrating victory with *any* toast, no matter what the beverage.

He would be glad when they no longer needed to rely on foreigners.

The People's Republic of China could fight its own battles.

Friday, 26 May 2006

Control Room, USS *Virginia*
Entering the Beaufort Sea
22 miles north of Banks Island
Canada
1512 hours, EST

"Ocean floor is dropping fast, Captain," Jorgensen reported. "Somebody just yanked the deck out from under us."

"Very well," Garrett said. "Helm, steady as she goes."

"Steady as she goes, aye, Captain," the man at the helm station replied.

Garrett sat in the center seat, surveying his domain. *Virginia*'s control center was unlike that of any submarine he'd ever served aboard.

The periscope was gone, first of all. Input from *Virginia*'s Photonics mast was displayed on the big for-

ward screen for all in the control room to see. Without
the massive, gleaming column of a periscope mount in
the middle of the control room, there was room for a
seat for the captain, set on a swivel so he could see
every console and station without moving from the
spot.

In front of him and to his left was the seat for the diving officer, and ahead of *that* were the side-by-side
seats for the enlisted men at the dive plane and helm
stations, their consoles set against the left-forward half
of the control room bulkhead, just beneath the forward
screen. On previous U.S. attack subs, those two stations had been controlled by aircraft-style steering
yokes. On the *Virginia*, the yokes had been replaced by
touchscreens and grip-contoured joysticks, giving them
the feel of a simulator game in some fantastic, ultra-
modern video arcade.

As on earlier U.S. submarines, along the left side of
the control room were the navigational consoles and
the NAVSTAR GPS board. Down the right side were
weapons and fire-control panels—including the Command and Control System, or CCS-2, from which
Tomahawk missiles could be programmed and fired—
and the BSY-2—"Busy-Two"—board, which could
track dozens of sonar targets simultaneously. The
sonar shack itself was in a long, narrow room through
a door in the aft bulkhead. Forward, well marked by
glaring security signs, was the communications center,
or radio shack.

Behind Garrett's seat, also on the control room's aft
bulkhead, was the big automated plot board, where
Lieutenant DeKalb and the yeoman of the watch kept
careful track of *Virginia*'s position, course, and speed.
Garrett swiveled his chair to check the screen. *Virginia*'s current location was marked by a moving circle

at the end of a long and slowly growing green line.

As the boat's exec had just reported, the bottom was dropping away as *Virginia*'s northwesterly course carried her through the McClure Strait, past the shallows of Banks Island and out over the black depths of the Canada Basin. A moment before, the water depth had been 100 meters. Now, as the sub flew out over the edge of a submarine cliff, the bottom was at 280 meters—almost 900 feet—and still falling. The deepest point of the ice-locked Canada Basin still lay 600 miles due west—and 15,000 feet down.

A screen showing the sub's key positional data continued to change as *Virginia*'s navigational computer updated the information moment by moment. Garrett could read it from his chair, though a small screen by his left hand repeated it:

N74°27.91'
W132°5.02'
DEPTH: 35 METERS
DBK: 352 METERS
BEARING: 260°
SPEED: 22 KNOTS

As he watched, the latitude changed to N74°27.55', the longitude to W132°5.12', and the depth below keel to 380 meters. In the old days, those cryptic navigational markings would have been made with grease pencil on a navigational chart every twenty minutes or so. In *Virginia*'s paperless world, the chart had been replaced by detailed computer mapping. A keyboard command could call up an electronic chart for any portion of the sea bottom in the world—or of the land, for that matter, since *Virginia* might be called upon to launch a Tomahawk TLAM at a target a thousand

miles inland. The boat's undersea passage so far was
stored as a snaking green line from Baffin Bay to the
Beaufort Sea, threading the twists and turns of the
Barrow and McClure Straits. He could instantly review any portion of the cruise all the way back to New
London. Far more—and far more accurate—navigational data was literally at his fingertips than he'd ever
enjoyed on board the *Seawolf*.

"Incredible," Garrett said, whispering to himself.

"Just like the fucking *Enterprise*," Jorgensen said
softly at Garrett's elbow.

"I assume you don't mean the carrier, Number
One." Aircraft carrier bridges were known for their
sheer spaciousness.

"I meant the starship," Jorgensen replied with a
chuckle. "You look like Captain Kirk there, center seat
and all."

"I wonder if Roddenberry's estate is getting royal-
ties for this thing."

"Beg pardon, sir?"

"Back in the sixties, when *Star Trek* was first on TV,
the U.S. Navy actually contacted Gene Roddenberry—
the show's creator—and told him they were looking at
his design for the bridge on his fictional starship as a
model for the bridge on real-life Navy ships. Someone
in the Navy's design bureau thought it made a lot of
sense, putting the captain or the OOD in a chair smack
in the middle of things where he could turn back and
forth and see all of the consoles and screens around
him without having to move. At least, that's the story.
So . . . it took us, what? Forty-some years, but we've finally caught up with the USS *Enterprise*."

"Yup," Jorgensen agreed. "Though I'm not sure
what the stores people ashore would make of a request
for *photon* torpedoes."

Garrett turned to face forward once more, glancing up at the main screen—another adaptation from Roddenberry's science fictional world. The Photonics mast view wasn't particularly informative at the moment. The scene showed an almost impenetrable murk, a deep, dark pea green shading to midnight black at the bottom. Myriad flecks of debris caught in the sail lights streamed past the camera like clouds of stars. Garrett could make out just a hint of the "ceiling," the underside of the polar ice cap stretched overhead like a dark gray, inverted landscape thirty feet overhead.

Submarines had always relied very little on the sense of sight. Except for those rare occasions when they might be tracking targets through their periscopes, submerged boats ran blind, relying instead on their sonar ears to tell them about what might be in the sea around them. *Virginia*'s forward view screen threatened to change that . . . and not for the better, so far as Garrett was concerned. Even with the high-tech sensors of the Photonics mast, visual input carried very little useful information. Even with the lights on, visibility was at best a hundred yards. *Virginia*'s sonar ears—honed by decades of the U.S. Navy's high-tech prowess in the field—were infinitely more sensitive and informative.

Here, too, the technology had transformed the nature of the submarine beast. *Virginia*'s main sonar was the BQQ-10 Acoustic Rapid COTS Insertion system, or ARCI, an upgrade to the spherical bow-mounted BQQ-6 active/passive array, which was already acknowledged as the best sonar system in the world. The COTS acronym stood for Commercial Off-The-Shelf, a measure designed to keep the *Virginia* class's per-unit cost down, but also to allow for easy upgrades as technology progressed. Besides her TB-16 towed and

TB-29 thin-line towed sonars, she also mounted the new BQG-5A Wide-Aperture Array. The WAA had been designed as *the* premier sensor for tracking what the Navy anticipated *Virginia*'s number-one prey would be: diesel-electric submarines operating in shallow littoral waters.

At the touch of a screen, data from any of those sonar systems could be displayed on the main screen, or on the small console screen mounted on Garrett's armrest.

Some things did not change with the technology, however. The sonar was still operated by enlisted men trained to use their ears as well as the computers, visual sonar displays, and computerized sound libraries. The men at the various control-room stations remained calm and alert, focused on their jobs. Commands were, as ever, repeated back word for word in formal litanies designed to make certain that the order was heard, that it was fully understood, and that it was being properly carried out. Stress or overeagerness could make a man anticipate an order and get it wrong. Repeating a command back assured understanding and helped disarm what could become crippling stress.

The key word was *professional*; the boat's crew were consummate professionals, very, very good at what they'd volunteered to do.

Which, at the moment, was probing the underbelly of the Arctic ice cap. *Virginia*'s operational orders included an under-the-ice passage from Baffin Bay, west of Greenland, to the Bering Strait between Alaska and Siberia. While under the ice cap, they would thoroughly test *Virginia*'s under-ice sonar and navigational capabilities. An add-on to those orders required them to take periodic soundings of the ice along the way for NOAA, the quasi-naval National Oceanographic and Atmospheric Administration. Information gleaned from this run would be added to the database now being compiled on the worldwide effects of global warming.

"Conn, Sonar," a voice said in Garrett's headset.

"Sonar, this is the Conn. Go ahead."

"Sir, the ice is thinning. Looks like we have an open lead coming up."

"Very well."

On the view screen, the water appeared to be lightening substantially. A touch of his armrest controls angled the Photonics mast camera upward. Murk-gray-green gave way suddenly to an explosion of white radiance. Shafts of sunlight sliced through the water overhead, dwindling rapidly as they descended.

The ice was a lot thinner than normal for this latitude at this time of the year. The first time Garrett had crossed under the ice, as a junior officer on board a Los Angeles boat almost two decades ago, the ice here a thousand miles from the North Pole had measured around two or three meters thick. Now, the ice was only rarely thicker than half a meter, and there were frequent leads of open water.

Would it reach the point that the North Polar ice cap melted away completely, he wondered? And what would happen in warmer climes if it did? The Arctic ice held something like 8 percent of the world's supply of fresh water. The sea levels worldwide were bound to rise, at least a little.

He considered ordering *Virginia* to stop and surface—part of the test of her under-ice capabilities—but decided to put that off for a while. A moment later, the sunlight overhead was eclipsed by gray shadow once more. He returned the camera to its forward-looking position.

Time passed in dark seclusion, the silence broken only by the gentle hum of electronics. "Captain? Request permission to enter the Conn."

He turned his chair aft. "Sure, COB. Come on in."

Senior Chief Bollinger came closer. "A word, Captain?"

"Of course. What's up?"

The COB leaned close, speaking quietly. "Nothing major, Captain. But some of the men are wondering about the Blue Nose ritual. Are we still going to have one? Or are we canning it for this voyage?"

Garrett smiled. Over the centuries, a number of navigational crossings had become time-honored rites of passage, markers for the men who sailed the seas . . . and beneath them. Crossing the equator was one, a ceremony bestowing the Order of the Shellback on any officer or man who'd not made the passage before. Crossing the international date line was another, bestowing the Order of the Golden Dragon.

A third was reserved for sailors who first crossed the Arctic Circle, granting the Order of the Blue Nose in a hazing ceremony similar to the others. *Virginia* had crossed the Arctic Circle while traveling north through the Davis Strait five days ago, just before they'd reached the pack ice limit. At that time, Garrett had ordered Bollinger to hold off on the festivities. *Virginia* was coming up on a tricky bit of pathfinding, moving under the ice and through the narrows of Lancaster Sound and the Barrow Strait. Ceremony could be deferred, he'd decided, until they were in the unrestricted depths of the Beaufort and Chukchi Seas.

"Is old Neptune getting antsy?" he asked.

"Oh, I don't know about antsy, Captain," Bollinger replied with a grin. "Pissed, maybe. We *are* trespassing in his domain, you know."

"Just a second. Mr. DeKalb?"

"Yes, Captain!"

"Estimated time to arrival at the IDL?"

A blue line projected itself ahead of the green circle marking *Virginia*'s position, extending southwest. The scale changed, pulling back to reveal the north coast of Alaska.

"Sir, that would be when we approach the Bering Strait. At our current speed, that's forty hours."

"Very well." He looked at Bollinger and cocked an eyebrow. "COB, I suggest that we do two ceremonies in one. Give 'em the Golden Dragon and the Blue Nose, all in one big party."

Bollinger's grin grew wider. "That'll be a hell of a party, Captain."

"It should be. The men have done a good job, so far. A *very* good job. They deserve it."

"Right you are, Captain. Would . . . lessee. Sunday night be okay?"

"Absolutely, COB."

"Thank you, sir. I'll make the necessary arrangements with his Oceanic Majesty."

"You do that."

"And of course Davy Jones'll have to put in an appearance Saturday night."

"Arrange it with the chiefs on the boat. Keep me informed."

"Conn, Sonar."

Bollinger patted the arm of Garrett's chair. "Talk to you later, sir. Thanks."

"Right, COB. Sonar, Conn. Go ahead."

"Conn, we have a pressure ridge coming up, bearing approximately two-three-zero through two-eight-zero, range five thousand."

Occasionally, drifting masses of pack ice collided, creating walls of ice extending deep below the usual ceiling depth, a kind of upside-down mountain range that posed a real hazard for submarines that weren't watching where they were going.

"Sonar, Conn, roger that," Garrett replied. "Where's the ceiling?"

"Conn, Sonar. Ceiling now fourteen meters above the mast . . . and dropping."

Garrett called up the new data to see for himself. *Virginia*'s under-ice sonar was constantly pinging the underside of the ice cap, letting them know how much overhead clearance they had. Fourteen meters dropped to twelve as he watched.

There was plenty of room beneath *Virginia*'s keel.

"Sonar, Conn. Estimate depth of the pressure ridge."

"Conn, Sonar. It's hard to say, sir . . . but I'd guess ten meters, maybe fifteen." Sonar was less than precise when it came to variables such as depth. A narrow angle between separate sonar returns was notoriously difficult to read. Besides, echolocation could be confused by thermal layers in the sea or by backscattering echoes off the ice or the bottom.

"Stay on it, Sonar. I need facts, not guesses."

"Sonar, aye."

"Diving Officer, make depth six hundred feet."

"Make depth six-zero-zero feet, aye, sir," the diving officer, Lieutenant Falk, said. "Planesman, set bow planes for fifteen degrees down bubble. Make depth six-zero-zero feet."

"Fifteen degrees down bubble, aye, sir. Make depth six-zero-zero feet, aye aye."

As the first class on the diving plane station pushed his joystick forward, the deck tilted gently forward. The murk on the main screen darkened until it showed a background of pitch blackness, relieved only by the illuminated specks of drifting crud which now, more than ever, took on the appearance of tiny stars streaming past the camera.

"Come up fifteen degrees," Falk ordered. "Zero degrees on the bubble."

"Coming up fifteen degrees," the planesman reported. The deck leveled off. "Zero degrees on the bubble. Depth six-zero-zero feet."

"Depth six hundred feet, Captain," Falk repeated.

"Very well." The down-thrust grasp of the pressure ridge slid harmlessly past, far overhead. The main screen still showed nothing but shadows and whirling specks of organic debris illuminated by *Virginia*'s exterior lights.

A quiet trip, Garrett thought. *Let's hope it stays that way.*

Sunday, 28 May 2006
Attack Submarine *Shuhadaa Muqaddaseen*
North of Nanshan Island
South China Sea
1145 hours, Zulu –8

"Our bearing is now two-nine-zero degrees," the helmsman reported. "As ordered, sir."

"Sonar reports depth below keel at twenty-five meters," the diving officer added.

"Very well. Gently, now, Lieutenant Daulat," ul Haq told him. "Put us on the bottom."

"Yes, sir." Daulat studied the gauges and readouts on his board. "Planesman! Five degrees down bubble . . . Depth below keel now . . . eighteen meters . . ."

"Captain!" Noor Khalili was furious. "Why are we stopping *now*?"

No, ul Haq decided, turning to study the man, it wasn't anger that drove him. It was a restless, roiling impatience, a mental pacing that reminded ul Haq of a caged jungle cat.

"You should know, my Taliban friend. It is time for prayer."

"Allah the Merciful, the Compassionate, makes allowances for the faithful when they are engaged in holy jihad," the Afghan replied. "If we had stopped for prayer five times a day when the American devils came for us in Tora Bora—"

"But this is not Tora Bora," ul Haq said. "And the Americans are not coming for us." *Not yet, at any rate,* he reminded himself.

With a soft, grating crunch of steel on coral sand, the *Shuhadaa Muqaddaseen* settled gently onto the bottom, coming to rest with a slight heel to starboard.

Ul Haq picked up the microphone hanging on the periscope mount. "Attention, attention, this is the Captain. *Shuhadaa Muqaddaseen* is now at rest on the bottom. Face the bow, and you face holy Mecca."

A moment later, the voice of *Shuhadaa*'s imam sounded over the intercom, intoning the ancient, wavering call summoning the faithful to prayer.

"This is insanity," Khalili said. "We are within a kilometer of our first target!"

"A good time to ask Allah's help, then." His prayer rug was already on the deck at his feet. Facing the bow, ul Haq knelt, composing himself. "I suggest that you join us. For the sake of the crew, if not for your-self."

Khalili really was furious now, his face red, his eyes dark. But he kneeled nonetheless.

Good, ul Haq thought to himself. *This one will be a problem if we do not bring him to heel immediately.* He saw with approval that the Chinese liaison officer was also kneeling, performing the ritual series of bows toward Mecca. Hsing was supposedly of Chinese Muslim extraction, but ul Haq hadn't fully believed that. How could someone of an alien race, of such an alien culture, understand?

Perhaps, ul Haq thought with a sudden flash of in-sight, it was not the culture of Islam that bound Hsing so much as the culture of naval service within sub-marines. Whatever the man might believe privately, deep within the secret reaches of his own soul, he was an experienced submariner and knew the men who sailed such craft, knew how vitally important unity of spirit and purpose was to such men. Noor Khalili pos-sessed an admirable warrior spirit, but he bordered too much on the fanatic for ul Haq's taste. Service on board an attack submarine did not require fanaticism. It required dedication, purpose, self-sacrifice for a common goal, and, above all, *patience.*

By observing the Prophet's commandment of five-times-daily prayer, ul Haq intended to deepen the bond of trust, dedication, and spirit between the men and officers under his command. They'd taken time for the ritual each day since they'd left Karachi, and it was his intent to continue for as long as possible.

Soon enough, when *Shuhadaa Muqaddaseen* be-came the hunted instead of the hunter, such formali-ties would be set aside. It would be insanity indeed to issue a call to prayer while American submarines were in the area with the keen ears of their sonars tuned for any noise within the ocean depths. And it would be insane to expect the Americans to allow the crew of the *Shuhadaa* time for their devotions once the hunt had begun.

But for now . . . *Shuhadaa Muqaddaseen* was the hunter and had the luxury of choosing its own time for attack. The target, a Filipino fishing boat, was utterly unaware of the submarine's presence in these waters, and, in any case, neither the Filipino nor the Vietnamese navy possessed advanced ASW techniques or weapons. There was some risk, he knew, but that risk was far offset by the benefit this simple ritual would bestow upon the crew.

And the fishing boat would not get far.

The imam's voice continued to waver from the intercom. "In the name of Allah, the Merciful, the Munificent . . ."

Saturday, 27 May 2006
Control Room, USS *Virginia*
Chukchi Sea
180 miles northwest of Point Barrow
Alaska
0919 hours GMT/shipboard
2119 hours, Zulu +12

"Open the escape trunk, Mr. Kirkpatrick," Garrett told the first class electrician's mate standing next to the securely dogged watertight door. "Let's let our guest come on board."

"Aye aye, sir," Kirkpatrick replied, turning to the door. He didn't sound too certain about this.

Kirkpatrick spun the locking wheel and pulled the door open. Seawater cascaded into the passageway and the control room beyond, a spectacular splash washing across the deck. Most of the hands in the control room were crowded around the passageway entry to see the spectacle.

And spectacle it was. Davy Jones, Royal Secretary to His Majesty, King Neptunus Rex, stepped out of the dripping escape trunk, painted green from head to bare foot, wearing swim trunks and yard upon yard of fishnet and seaweed, with a curly white beard reaching almost to his navel.

"What vessel?" Davy Jones demanded, in a rumbling voice guaranteed to twig sea-bottom sonars as far south as Kamchatka.

"USS *Virginia*," Garrett replied. "SSN 774!"

"On what course?"

"Heading one-eight-zero . . . due south!"

"Very well! I have been awaiting your arrival."

"And we have awaited yours, Davy Jones. Welcome aboard!"

"Thank you. Are you the captain?"

"I am, sir."

"My congratulations, Captain, on your fine command." He looked about him. "And my condolences, sir, that you command such a scurvy lot as your crew!"

Garrett grinned. "They're not such a bad lot, Mr. Jones."

"That's as may be, Captain. I have orders for you and summonses for your pollywogs from Neptunus Rex."

"I'll be happy to receive them, sir."

Davy Jones—actually Chief Kurzweil, though it was tough to tell through the beard and seaweed—produced an impressive-looking scroll bound in green ribbon. Opening it, he proceeded to read aloud.

"I, Davy Jones, come from the depths of the sea this night to bring from His Oceanic Majesty, King Neptune, Ruler of the Seven Seas, all the summonses for the landlubbers, the pollywogs, the sea vermin, the crabs and eels and slimy bottom dwellers that have not yet been initiated into the Supreme Order of the Deep. We of the great Neptune's Court bring serious indictments against those who still have traces of farm soil and city dust on their feet. No matter. All will be blue-nosed golden dragons after the rough treatment of the morrow, at which time those summoned will appear before the Royal Judge of His August and Imperial Majesty, Neptunus Rex, and there answer for offenses committed both aboard and ashore!"

"Sir," Garrett said, grinning, "I must respectfully ask for leniency of the Great Neptune. These are good men, and true. . . ."

"No, Captain! King Neptune plays no favorites! All landlubbers since men first followed the sea have endured the strict initiation required by the King of the Sea! There will be no leniency! *All* pollywogs will receive appropriate punishment on the morrow!

"And remember! Sorrow and woe to those who resist or talk in a light and jesting manner of the ceremony or of His Majesty, the Ruler of the Seven Seas, or of Queen Amphitrite or of His Majesty, the Ruler of the Arctic Wastes, Borealis Rex! And woe on any who belittles Royal Members of His Supreme Court! Beware! Beware!"

"We will await the arrival of the Royal Party with keen anticipation, Davy Jones."

"Very well! Goodbye, Captain. I will see you with the Great Neptune on the morrow!"

With haughty dignity, Davy Jones turned and slogged through patches of seaweed and ankle-deep water back to the escape trunk. "Gangway for Davy Jones!" he bellowed, and Kirkpatrick jumped aside out of his way. He stepped across the knee-knocker into the trunk's dark recesses, and waited as Kirkpatrick dogged shut the watertight door.

For a moment, those crewmen present stood in what could only be described as stunned paralysis. "Let's get back to work," Garrett said, breaking the silence.

"All right!" Senior Chief Bollinger bellowed in a voice to rival that of Davy Jones. "You heard the man! What's this lollygagging in the passageways! Back to your stations!"

Garrett was thoughtful as he returned to the center seat. The ritual of crossing the line was ancient, its roots going back to Greek seamen passing the Pillars of Hercules, to Phoenician seafarers crossing the 30th parallel as they rounded Africa. There were a number of different modern incarnations of the rite. If the Golden Shellback and Order of the Dragon awards were the best-known line-crossing ceremonies, the Order of the Blue Nose had a special significance for submariners. That ordeal, supervised by Jack Frost, had attended submarine passages under the ice ever since the *Nautilus* and the *Skate* became the first submarines to reach the North Pole.

The ritual just announced by Davy Jones combined the Order of the Dragon with the Blue Nose ceremony. The old hands who'd been across the lines in question looked forward to hazing those who hadn't; those poor newbies who would face Neptune's court tomorrow would soon look forward to the time when they got to have *their* chance at the tenderfeet.

More important, though, the ritual would help the men bond. Once all were on the same side of the ceremony, they would be more of a team, even if they didn't think about that consciously. Because officers—especially junior officers—weren't spared, the ceremony would bridge the gulf between them and enlisted men.

Perhaps more important for a submarine crew, it would even help close the gap between those who'd won their dolphins already and those new to the service who were still in their year-long probationary period. Submariners were a clannish bunch and didn't easily accept outsiders, "surface swimmers," until they'd proven themselves.

That unity of spirit was a necessary prerequisite to a mob becoming a *crew*.

As captain of the *Virginia,* Garrett was prepared to sacrifice just a bit of his personal dignity and the orderliness of the vessel's daily routine to make that happen.

It was a sacrifice ship captains had been making now for several thousand years at least, a time-hallowed offering to the traditions of the sea.

Monday, 29 May 2006

Attack Submarine *Shuhadaa Muqaddaseen*
Southeast of Amboyna Cay
South China Sea
1430 hours, Zulu −8

Black-hulled and silent, *Shuhadaa* again slipped like a
great, hunting cat through the shadowed forests of the
sea. The water here was shallow—less than thirty meters, just barely deep enough to allow the vessel to remain submerged.

If the Vietnamese possessed a decent antisubmarine
search force, ul Haq thought, with ASW helicopters, it
would have been a hopeless mission. They would have
been spotted long ago, as visible in these brightly sunlit and shallow waters as a beached whale. But the target appeared oblivious to the threat closing in now
from the southeast.

"Target in sight," ul Haq called from his place at

the periscope column, peering into the eyepiece. "Bearing three-zero-eight, range . . . seven hundred meters."

"Target bearing three-zero-eight," Lieutenant Mahmud Jamal replied from the weapons board. "Range seven hundred meters."

Ul Haq took a last, long look through the periscope optics. This was no wood-hulled Vietnamese or Filipino fishing boat.

The Spratly Island facility was similar in many respects to the Chinese base at Small Dragon Island—a large marine platform built on pedestals like an oil rig, rising from a patch of coral barely above the surface of the water even at low tide. To the left, a heliport was connected to the main structure by a causeway. The base itself resembled a four-story apartment building, with clusters of microwave relays, radar masts, and satellite dishes on the roof.

Amboyna Cay—the Chinese called that speck of coral Anbo Shazhou—was a powerful symbol. It lay just 150 kilometers southeast of Spratly Island itself, the rock that gave its popular name to the entire archipelago stretched across 410,000 square kilometers of the South China Sea, and could, therefore, be considered to be the capital of this entire region. It also lay close to the border of a large patch of mostly empty ocean west of the Amboyna Cay that now, according to Chinese intelligence, was being actively prospected for gas and oil.

The Vietnamese base facilities on Spratly Island itself were out of the submarine's reach. Spratly was one of the few islands in the group with any land area at all, and *Shuhadaa Muqaddaseen* did not carry cruise missiles that could strike inland targets. But Amboyna

Cay was another matter. The Vietnamese base was built, in part, over the water.

Reportedly, it was serving as a supply center for the oil prospecting vessels operating to the west. Striking this base would send a decisive message to Hanoi: *Your assets in these waters are vulnerable.*

By using the rogue Pakistani submarine to make the attack, China distanced herself, could, as the American intelligence phrase so elegantly put it, "plausibly deny" any involvement in the incident. Hanoi might suspect Beijing's complicity, but once the attacks on western shipping began a few days later, they would have to publicly accept this as simply another terrorist outrage. With luck, they might decide that defending these islands was futile and withdraw. Or, again with luck, they might take overt action against Chinese interests in these waters, providing Beijing with the excuse necessary to move in with its own overt military muscle.

At worst, Vietnam would lose an important petroleum prospecting base, and their development of commercial assets in these waters would be delayed, possibly for years.

"May I see, please? Captain."

Ul Haq nodded and stepped back from the eyepiece, so that Commander Hsing could take his place. "Would you like the honor of ordering the attack, Commander?"

Hsing studied the target for a moment, then turned, shaking his head. "No, sir. I wished merely to verify your target."

Still letting us do your dirty work, ul Haq thought. The man was less advisor than spy.

No matter. During the past forty-eight hours,

Shuhadaa had tracked and destroyed three fishing boats—two flying the flag of the Philippines, and one the flag of Vietnam. In each case, a boarding party had gone across in a rubber boat ostensibly to check their papers, assembled the crew on the afterdeck, machine-gunned them, then planted explosive charges in the vessel's bilge. There was no sense in wasting an expensive torpedo on a fifteen-meter wooden hull.

The Spratlys were an important fishing ground for both the Philippines and the Vietnamese, with several million tons of fish being taken from these waters each year. Sinking those fishing boats was, at best, an economic pinprick, more symbolic than anything else. Destroying the base now centered in the periscope's crosshairs, however, would be a far more savage blow, to both Vietnamese pride and economic interests.

Best of all, destroying that base would also strike directly at the soft, economic underbelly of the hated West—a strike at the Western oil interests, and at one of the governments supporting them.

"Very well." Ul Haq took his place at the periscope once more. It looked as if a helicopter, an ancient, Soviet-era MI-8 cargo transport, was being readied on the heliport. He could just make out the black specks of men moving about the aircraft. "Ready tubes one and three," he said.

"Tubes one and three, ready to fire," Lieutenant Jamal reported.

"Set running depth at one meter." That was, in effect, right on the surface. Any alert lookout on the Vietnamese base would almost certainly see the torpedoes as they approached.

But a fixed base would have some problem maneuvering clear of the threat. And the water was so shallow here; ul Haq wanted to make certain his torpedoes didn't slam themselves harmlessly into sand.

"Running depth set at one meter, Captain."

"Open outer doors, tubes one and three."

"Tube doors one and three are open, Captain."

"Fire one!"

The hiss of compressed air flinging the torpedo from its bow tube was audible throughout the boat. Ul Haq felt the deck shift with the change in trim, until the enlisted man on the trim tanks could compensate.

"One fired, Captain!" Jamal said. "Torpedo one is running straight and normal!"

"Fire three."

Again, the hiss of compressed air shrilled through the submarine.

"Three fired! Torpedo three running straight and normal!"

"Estimate time to target."

"Time on target for first torpedo . . . forty-five seconds."

Ul Haq glanced at the sweep hand on the control room clock, then returned his full attention to the periscope eyepiece. *Patience . . . patience . . .* A quick check to make certain the periscope camera was running. Beijing would want to see the films, if it was possible to return them to the Chinese.

There was no indication that the Vietnamese base was aware of the approaching torpedoes. The helicopter appeared to be about to take off. Its rotors were running. He could see no other activity at all.

After a time—he would not let himself look at the clock again—he became aware of a soft, rhythmic chanting in the control room. *"Sab'a . . . Sitta . . ."*

Counting. The officers and men in the control room

were counting down the seconds. He locked glances with Commander Hsing, who shrugged and looked away.

"*Khamsa . . .*"

"*Arba'a . . .*"

Their voices were becoming louder now, the chant more insistent. Khalili appeared to be leading it, standing near the weapons board next to Jamal, beating off the time with one clenched fist.

"*Talaata . . .*"

"*Itneen . . .*"

"*Waahid . . .*"

The countdown reached one . . . and nothing happened. The faces of a dozen men were turned toward his, questioning. Had something gone wrong? Had they missed? . . .

Seven hundred meters away, the first of the two torpedoes, running slightly slower than expected, reached the target. The weapon was a 533-mm naval torpedo based on the old Soviet 53-VA design, built in China, purchased by Pakistan. It was twenty-one feet long, twenty-one inches thick, and carried a warhead weighing 1,250 pounds.

Skimming at thirty knots just above the shallow, sandy bottom, it passed within ten feet of one of the massive steel and concrete pylons supporting the Vietnamese naval base overhead. The electromagnetic exploder detected the steel supports above and to the sides, and detonated.

On board the *Shuhadaa*, half a mile away, ul Haq was watching the MI-8 helo lifting off from the heliport. Then with startling suddenness, a towering, mountain-sized geyser of water, white foam and black mud spewed skyward high above the very top of the main building. Over half a ton of high explosives erupted in a savage blast that all but engulfed the base in spray. The shock wave, magnified by the shallow sea bottom, rolled across the *Shuhadaa* with a thunderous roar a second later.

The second torpedo detonated to the left of the first, beneath the base side of the heliport, close by the causeway. The hovering MI-8, caught by the blast, lurched sideways, its main rotors slamming into the crumpling steel of the deck. Stores of aviation gasoline on the platform itself erupted in a secondary explosion, sending an immense black and orange fireball roiling into the sky. The helicopter, fragmenting in midair, struck the heliport pad and then tumbled into the water.

Around him, the submarine's crew screamed and shouted at the sound of the double explosion, some dancing up and down, some hugging one another, some chanting, *"Allah akbar! Allah akbar! Allah akbar! . . ."*

God is great. . . .

Through the periscope, ul Haq watched the fire spread as burning gasoline spilled into the ocean, fed, he guessed, by ruptured pipes. The helipad was engulfed in flames. The main building still stood, but at least two of its support pylons had buckled, and the entire structure was now tilted sharply to the left, perilously balanced above waves and flame. Ul Haq considered sending a third torpedo . . . but a moment later, gravity completed the work of the first two. One by one, struts and supports, strained beyond engineering limits, gave way, and with a ponderous shudder, the base facility collapsed, the sound of the destruction rumbling and creaking and booming through the submarine's bulkheads. In seconds, all that ul Haq could see was the right side of the building, canted sharply at a forty-five degree angle above the sea and all but lost in the smoke.

How many were on that thing? he wondered. Chinese intelligence reported as many as a hundred or a hundred fifty at any given time. Most would still be alive . . . and facing now the unenviable choice between burning alive in the wreckage or jumping into the shark-infested water fifty miles from the nearest other speck of land. A few might manage to launch rafts or lifeboats, but the toll in human life would be high.

"Stations!" he barked into the microphone, trying to be heard above the raucous cheering. "All hands to stations!"

Slowly, the cheering subsided. Commander Hsing took a turn at the periscope, stepping back a moment later with a satisfied nod.

Noor Khalili asked for a look as well. The former Taliban warrior looked at ul Haq with a gap-toothed grin. "Victory, Captain! It reminds me of the World Trade Center!"

Hardly that, ul Haq thought, but the comparison was disquieting. Jihad warriors around the globe still thought of the suicide attacks on the twin towers of the World Trade Center in New York City as a splendid, spectacular, and God-given victory in the holy war against the hated American infidels and the West. Somehow, none seemed to make the connection that if there'd been no 9-11, as the Americans called the attack, there would have been no invasion of Afghanistan, no eradication of the Taliban regime, no second war in Iraq, no wholesale, worldwide hunt for members of al Qaeda and other jihadist groups. War against the West this might be, but, so far, the armies of Allah had been getting the worst of it by far.

Violence always begat violence. Attack invited retribution. These waters would soon be swarming with the agents of retribution—Vietnamese and, in all likelihood, Americans as well.

Those sentiments, he knew, might be less than ardently martial for a leader of the Maktum, but they reflected something of his own ambivalence. He believed passionately in striking at the hated West by any means possible, yes . . . but did not believe the Maktum could hope to match the U.S. Navy, blow for blow. Speedboats were cheaper than submarines, and required the sacrifice of fewer men willing to die for the cause.

Ignoring Khalili's joy, he picked up the microphone. "Our target has been destroyed."

The cheering began again. "Silence! Silence on all decks!" He waited until the shouts of "God is great" died away once more. "Helm, bring us left to three-five-zero degrees. Maneuvering, ahead one quarter." Replacing the microphone, he looked at Commander Hsing. "I trust this satisfies the letter of our contract?"

"It does, Captain. Most satisfactory."

"Then it is time for us to seek other prey."

Sailing Yacht *Sea Breeze*
Southwest of Spratly Island
South China Sea
1610 hours, Zulu −8

"Damn it, Ginger, Katie," an angry George Schiffer said. "I wish you girls wouldn't do that. I've told you about it before!"

He stood on the yacht's forward deck, braced

against the sailboat's gentle list as it cut through glass-calm water, hands firmly planted on hips as he stood above the two basking women. Ginger Tompkins and Kate Milford rolled over on their beach towels, both gloriously, exuberantly naked.

"Why, Mr. Schiffer," Ginger said in a mock-innocent voice. "Whatever do you *mean*?"

"You . . . you know damned well what I mean," Schiffer said. He tried to speak firmly, but the sudden double display of full-frontal nudity, one blond, the other redhead, made him falter and take a step back. "I mean you girls running around the boat like . . . like *that!*"

"But Mr. Schiffer," Kate said, running her hand down the taut front of her body from breasts to thigh in a lascivious stretch, "we're not running around. We're just laying here sunning ourselves! You wouldn't want us to show the clients *tan lines* now, would you?"

"Besides," Ginger added, "Mr. DuPont told us to be *extra* nice to the clients." Smiling, she waved at the two Vietnamese officials, watching the scene from the well deck aft. "And . . . that's what we're doing."

"Sure! I think they're enjoying the view."

"I don't hear Mr. Nguyen or Mr. Phuong complaining, do you?"

He glanced back at the two Vietnamese nervously. It was tough to read their impassive faces.

"Do you remember what happened on Tuvalu last month?" he asked. "The police were very upset . . . and you two were just topless then. The People's Democratic Republic of Vietnam is still Communist, I don't care how free market they've become, and some of them are pretty conservative. I don't want you to offend them."

"Sounds to me like you're the conservative, Mr. Schiffer," Ginger said. "Why are you so uptight?"

"I am *not* uptight! It's a matter of morality. Of common decency!"

"George, what's your problem?"

He spun, startled. His boss had padded forward on bare feet, and he'd not heard his approach.

"Uh . . . Mr. DuPont, sir. I was just suggesting that the girls might want to put on swimsuits. You know, so they don't give offense to the natives."

Matthew DuPont's expression was also unreadable, masked behind his expensive aviator's-style sunglasses. "The girls' bikinis make them look more naked than plain, bare skin. As for Mr. Nguyen and Mr. Phuong, they are not *natives,* so you can drop the patronizing bullshit. Ginger and Katie are doing what we pay them to do. I suggest you do the same and not interfere with their job."

"Sir, the police chief on Tuvalu was *most* upset. . . ."

DuPont sighed. "George, two hundred years ago, the natives on those islands were happy and uninhibited. A woman's bare breasts were milk glands for feeding children, nothing more, and they certainly weren't objects of shame. Then *your* missionaries showed up and taught them how to be ashamed of their bodies. Yes, they get a bit upset nowadays at tourists to the islands who shuck their clothes and go natural. I don't blame them a bit.

"But out here we're fifty miles from the nearest land, and the only prude with a stick up his ass on this boat is *you.*"

"Sir! I don't have—I'm not uptight!"

"Then stop acting like it. Your religious right is showing."

"That's not fair!"

"No? You're Baptist, aren't you?"

"No, sir." He'd been raised in an independent Bible church, though, in fact, he hadn't been to church in years. His ideas of right and wrong, however, were firmly entrenched in fundamentalist Christian doctrine. "This isn't a religious issue," he insisted. "It's just common decency!"

"George, there is no such thing as absolute morality. Those native people, two hundred years ago, thought nothing about women going around with their bare boobs showing. No big deal. *Kissing,* though, that was another story. They thought rubbing mouths together was about the dirtiest, most disgusting thing a couple could do. That was *their* morality . . . at least until the missionaries got through with them."

DuPont was wearing rather tight swim trunks. The bulge at his crotch proved that he was more than casually interested in the women's current state of attire. Schiffer suspected that his boss had been having relations with both women the whole way across from Hawaii, but he had been doing his best not to think about it. DuPont, after all, was married, and a senior vice president of Global Oil to boot. Even in this libidinous day and age, scandal could play havoc with stock market numbers.

The state of DuPont's swimwear was making Schiffer increasingly conscious of the swelling discomfort in his own suit. Ginger stretched out on the deck, arms high above her head, her movements luxuriously catlike . . . then absently reached down and rubbed the gold-furred delta between her legs.

Jesus! He tried thinking about icebergs. "That doesn't prove there isn't such a thing as right and wrong, sir. . . ."

"George, you're giving me a pain. Get out of here. Go below and help them fix lunch, will you?"

He glanced at the two women again. Maybe going below was a good idea. Their nakedness was . . . distracting, and the iceberg ploy wasn't working.

"Hey, Mr. Schiffer," Katie said. She rolled over and deliberately took Ginger in her arms. "Maybe we should kiss instead, huh?" They started kissing full on the mouth, hands restlessly sliding everywhere, and Schiffer turned and fled.

He heard their laughter at his back, raw and taunting.

**Attack Submarine *Shuhadaa Muqaddaseen*
Southwest of Spratly Island
South China Sea
1615 hours, Zulu −8**

Ul Haq pressed his face against the periscope's eyepiece, studying the target.

"What is it?" Khalili demanded. "What do you see?"

Ul Haq ignored him for a long moment. The ex-Taliban officer would not have approved of what he was watching.

Though the range was just over one hundred yards, the periscope optics magnified the image enough that ul Haq could see the deck of the two-masted sailing yacht clearly. Several men stood aft, in the well deck, while two more stood forward, just in front of the mainmast. On the deck were two women, either naked or wearing extremely skimpy bathing attire.

As a good Pakistani Muslim, ul Haq believed that women should cover up in order to avoid tempting males. The Taliban, though, was notorious for its mistreatment of women. When they'd ruled Afghanistan a few years before, gangs of Taliban thugs had stoned, raped, or mutilated women, sometimes for crimes as slight as exposing their faces, or for failing to brick over the bedroom windows in their homes. Ul Haq had never approved of such an extreme interpretation of religious law. Pakistan—especially in the cities, tended to be more tolerant of uncovered women, especially with the influx of foreign films and foreign tourists.

Besides, he'd seen something of the world. Twice he'd visited England, and he'd even been to the United States, attending a year-long exchange student program in college. He knew that other peoples' ways were not necessarily his ways. That didn't lessen the extent of their sin against God, of course, but he did understand that other cultures viewed skin—specifically female skin—differently than did the clerics of fundamentalist Islam. Those women displaying themselves in front of those men simply didn't know what they were doing.

He was glad that only he could see what the periscope saw, however. The scene would surely have enflamed the crew, and Noor Khalili would have become insufferable.

"*In Allah's name, have we found the target?*" Khalili demanded.

"Yes," ul Haq said, continuing to peer through the scope. "At least . . . we have a large sailboat . . . twenty meters, at least. I cannot see the name or registry, but it appears to match the information your colleagues provided. It flies an American flag."

"The American yacht!" Khalili's fist cracked against his open palm. "Then we should take them! Now!"

Ul Haq turned from the periscope eyepiece. "My friend, you should learn the first order of the submarine sailor. It is *patience*. We have the target in sight. We stalk him. We make certain of our prey's identity. And, when the time is right, we attack . . . not before."

"And I remind *you* of *our* mission." Khalili glanced aft, at the taciturn Chinese officer standing by the chart table. "We were forced to strike at the Vietnamese base to satisfy the Chinese, but now we are free to hit the Americans. If the sonar contact is, indeed, the sailing yacht *Sea Breeze,* we have both targets in our sights at once—Vietnamese and Americans! We should surface and take her passengers on board!"

Ul Haq sighed, returning his attention to the periscope. Khalili's joy at the destruction of the Vietnamese base had swiftly taken on a dark and fanatic aspect. He was grating on ul Haq's nerves.

An hour ago, *Shuhadaa* had come to snorkeling depth to recharge her batteries, and to radio a detailed report of the attack against the Vietnamese base. The al Qaeda courier and liaison, Zaki, was cruising somewhere in the general Spratly area on board the motor yacht *Al Qahir,* serving as a communications relay for the *Shuhadaa* . . . or was Zaki himself giving the orders for this mission? Ul Haq had not been told who was ultimately in command, nor was it important that he know. Over the radio, Zaki had congratulated him on the successful attack, and had then passed on some interesting news.

According to Chinese intelligence, two months ago, the sailing yacht *Sea Breeze* had set sail from Hawaii for Danang in Vietnam. The sailboat was registered as the property of the Global Oil Corporation, and on board, supposedly, was a senior official of that company. In Danang, *Sea Breeze* had picked up two representatives of the Vietnamese government, then set sail again, this time for either Spratly Island, or for the base at Amboyna Cay.

The intelligence report suggested that Global Oil was trying to impress the Vietnamese officials—the incongruous American phrase ul Haq remembered from his stay in the United States was "butter up"—to secure lucrative petroleum concessions and exploitation rights in the Spratly Island area. According to Zaki, the *Sea Breeze* was now somewhere between Spratly and Amboyna Cay.

By taking the passengers hostage, *Shuhadaa Muqaddaseen* would both embarrass the Vietnamese attempting to stake commercial claims in the region, and hurt American interests. Besides, having hostages on board would help safeguard the *Shuhadaa* as she continued her mission. Guided by Zaki's information, ul Haq had located the American yacht almost at once.

The two women on the deck appeared to be . . . *what* were they doing?

Perhaps it was time to interrupt the party after all.

"Prepare to surface!" he barked, snapping the handles of the periscope home. "Down scope! Boarding party, report to the forward escape hatch, with arms and life jackets!"

Khalili was right. There was no point in delaying further. The horizon was empty, save for that single tiny, vulnerable, unarmed yacht. There would be no better time.

"Take us up!"

Monday, 29 May 2006

Sailing Yacht *Sea Breeze*
West of Spratly Island
South China Sea
1620 hours, Zulu −8

"You shouldn't tease poor George so much," Matthew
DuPont said, sitting down on the deck next to the two
women. "He's a prig . . . but he's a well-meaning
prig."

"It's a shame, really," Katie said, letting Ginger go
and sitting up. She shaded her eyes as she watched
Schiffer walk aft, turn, and descend below deck into
the yacht's salon. "He's a nice guy . . . good-looking,
smart. Why can't he loosen up?"

"He's a Bible-thumper," Ginger said with a dismis-
sive toss of her blond mane. "Bible-thumpers don't
want *anyone* to have fun."

"I don't think it's that simple," DuPont said.

"He never quotes scripture at us, or anything like that," Katie said. Lying back, she stretched happily on her towel. "Oh, God. This is the best. I wish this job would never end! Why can't George just, you know, go with it? Enjoy life?"

"He's a good man, Katie. Worked his way up to assistant vice president from the very bottom of the corporate ladder." DuPont shrugged. "My impression is he was raised by pretty strict parents. My guess is he's afraid of what might happen if he *did* let go. Had a friend like that in college, a few centuries ago. . . ."

Ginger laughed and reached out, stroking his thigh. "Mr. DuPont! You're not *that* old!"

"Thank you, Ginger. I just sometimes feel—"

"Hey!" Katie called, pointing out to sea. "What's *that?*"

DuPont turned, looking off the starboard beam. Something like a vertical pipe was emerging from the water less than a hundred yards away, dragging a white curl of spray in its wake. The white water exploded then, the wake becoming much higher and longer as the upper reaches of a massive black rectangle shouldered itself above the calm surface of the sea.

It took DuPont a moment to identify the apparition as a submarine.

"You girls better put some clothes on," he said, standing. "We may be about to have some company."

"Yes, Mr. DuPont."

Walking aft, he joined the two Vietnamese, both of whom were standing by the starboard mainstays, staring at the newcomer. "Is it one of yours?" he asked, hopeful.

"Mr. DuPont," Nguyen said. "The Socialist Republic of Vietnam *has* no submarines."

"I have some naval experience," Phuong added.

"That is what your navy people would call a 'Kilo-class' submarine. It is almost certainly Chinese. Our intelligence service warned us that they may have one in these waters."

"And that means trouble," DuPont said. "George! *George!*"

Schiffer stuck his head up out of the hatchway below. "Yessir?"

"Quick! Tell Davis to get on the horn to Oahu Corporate. Tell 'em there's a Chinese Kilo submarine surfacing next to us. Give our position exactly. Tell him to keep broadcasting until I tell him to stop."

Schiffer raised high enough out of the hatchway to see the submarine, his eyes wide. "Yes, *sir!*" he snapped, then vanished back down the hatch.

Davis was the yacht's radio operator, and the custodian of her state-of-the-art satellite communications and navigational equipment. If the *Sea Breeze* was about to become the focus of an international incident, Global Oil needed to know the particulars, and fast.

The submarine was on the surface now, running parallel to the *Sea Breeze* and less than the length of a football field away. The solid-black rectangle, clearly, was the conning tower, a windowless two-story building considerably longer than it was tall. The deck was only just visible above the water; he guessed the submarine was three times the length of the *Sea Breeze,* which made it something like two hundred to two hundred fifty feet long.

Men were spilling onto the deck now from a hatch in front of the conning tower, and he could see men in the tiny bridge atop the front of the conning tower itself. DuPont walked aft to the tiller, where Kingsfield was standing at the *Sea Breeze*'s wheel, and picked up a pair of binoculars hanging from the binnacle.

"Whaddaya think, Mr. DuPont?" Kingsfield said. "Should I have the boys break out small arms, just in case?"

DuPont raised the binoculars and scanned the submarine's deck and sail. The men on the forward deck, he saw, wore bright orange life jackets . . . and several were carrying weapons. He recognized the wickedly curving magazines of AK-type assault rifles.

He considered the question. Michael Kingsfield and two of the other crew members had been drawn from Global's security division. Kingsfield himself was a former Army Green Beret. Davis was a former Marine, and Carle had been a Navy SEAL. A fourth hand, Greg Marshall was a former New York City cop, serving now as one of *Sea Breeze*'s general hands. On a quasi-diplomatic business cruise like this one, it was good to have some competent security people along, just in case. The South China Sea was infamous for its modern-day gangs of pirates.

But pirates don't use submarines, and they were rarely this well armed. "I don't think so, Michael," he said. "But it won't hurt to be on your toes."

"Right, sir." He began speaking quickly into the needle mike of the headset he wore.

"Ahoy the sailboat!" The voice boomed across the water from a handheld loudhailer. DuPont was surprised it was English . . . until he remembered the American ensign flying from the taffrail. "Lower your sails and prepare to be boarded!"

A loudhailer was stored in a locker aft. He pulled it out, turned it on, and raised it to his mouth. "We are . . ." A squeal of feedback howled across the water. He adjusted the volume, and tried again. "We are a United States vessel in international waters!" he called back. "You have no right to detain us!"

For answer, a chain of waterspouts geysered across the surface of the sea directly beneath *Sea Breeze*'s bowsprit, followed a second later by the crack-crack-crack of full-auto gunfire. Ginger, balancing one-handed against the mainmast as she stepped into her bikini bottom, squealed and fell to the deck. At first DuPont thought she'd been shot . . . but then he saw her scrambling for cover behind the forward deck-house, unhurt but badly frightened.

"Lower your sails and prepare to be boarded!"

"Shit!" Kingsfield said at DuPont's back. "I don't think we have a choice, not against *that* firepower!"

Sea Breeze's fiberglass and aluminum hull would provide about as much protection against machine gun fire as tissue paper. DuPont nodded. "Strike the sails, Michael. I'll try to stall them." He hoped Davis was talking to Oahu by now. It was . . . what? Six hours' difference . . . so 4:30 on a Monday afternoon here would be 10:30 at night in Honolulu, but *yesterday,* Sunday, because of the date line. No matter. The people at Corporate in Oahu were supposed to maintain a 24-7 watch in the comm office. Somebody would be there to hear and pass the news.

Another burst of gunfire cracked across the water, and this time a line of five neat holes punched their way through the mainsail ten feet above the deck.

"Hold your fire, damn it!" DuPont called through the loudhailer. "We're bringing down the sail!"

Sea Breeze's entire crew—all save Davis—was on deck now. Kingsfield put the wheel over, bringing the yacht around to the right, toward the submarine and into the wind. As the jib fluttered and cracked fitfully in the breeze, the mainsail slid down the mast and was swiftly secured to the main boom. Spanker and jib were secured in short order, leaving the *Sea Breeze* rocking uncomfortably on the gentle swell.

A number of the armed men on the submarine were scrambling down into a pair of rubber rafts that had been dropped over the side. Kingsfield secured the wheel, then approached DuPont. "We could take 'em as they come across in the rafts, sir."

"And then what?" DuPont asked. "They machine-gun us from the submarine? I don't think the four of you would do much good treading water."

Kingsfield shrugged, unable to find a better answer.

DuPont turned to Nguyen. "What's likely to happen?" he asked. "Are we going to be interned?"

Nguyen's face was bland. "You Americans always assume people . . . what is it you say? Play by the rules. Out here . . . well, you will find it difficult to place a call to your consulate."

"What's that supposed to mean?"

"It means the Chinese will do with us what they want. They claim these waters, as do we. Unfortunately, they have the upper hand at the moment. They could use you—and us—as examples of what happens to . . . I believe your word is 'trespassers.' "

DuPont took another look at the approaching rafts, getting a good look this time at the men on board. "Shit!"

"What is it, sir?" Kingsfield asked.

"Those don't look like Chinese to me." Most of the men appeared to be in some kind of uniform, though he didn't recognize the nationality. Some, though, wore civilian clothing, with either turbans or scarves pulled tightly over their heads and tied at the back.

Kingsfield took the binoculars. "Huh. You're right. They look Middle Eastern to me. Or maybe . . . hell. Iranian? Afghan?"

"Afghanistan doesn't have a fucking navy."

"I know. But some of them have that look, y'know? I was in Afghanistan, sir, right after nine-eleven. Task Force Dagger."

"I know." If they weren't Chinese . . . what the hell were they? And what did they want with a private American yacht? He thought again about the high incidence of piracy in these waters . . . but that tended to be focused on fishermen and coastal traders.

And again, pirates did not have submarines.

"Mr. DuPont?" Schiffer was at his side. "Davis is sending the message. He'll keep transmitting as long as he can."

"Good."

"There's something else, though."

"What's that?"

"He picked up a message a few minutes ago. In Vietnamese and then in English. It was kind of fragmented, but . . ."

"But what?"

"The Viet base at Amboyna Cay, sir. It's gone."

"Gone? What do you mean, gone?"

"It stopped transmitting a couple of hours ago. Sounds like there was an explosion. A big one."

"Well . . . accidents happen. . . ." But as he stared at the sharklike black silhouette of the foreign submarine off the starboard side, he had a feeling that very little accident was involved.

Crew's Mess, USS *Virginia*
Bering Strait
12 miles west of Cape Prince of Wales
Alaska
0027 hours, GMT/shipboard
1227 hours, Zulu −12

"I asked you a question, pollywog! *What day is it?*"

Wallace tried to clear his mind. He was on his hands and knees, stark naked, and shivering from the ice-water dousing he'd been getting each time he failed to answer a question to the satisfaction of the beings in front of him. Only his nose was painted bright blue, but he suspected the rest of his body was fast approaching the same hue.

"The pollywog defies us!" King Neptune roared. It was, in fact, Senior Chief Bollinger, but the COB was damned near unrecognizable—bare-chested, painted green from head to foot, and sporting a bushy white beard that would have done Saint Nick himself proud. He pointed at Wallace with his trident. "Methinks he needs another whack with the royal paddle!"

The Royal Baby stepped forward, wielding a smoothly sanded and varnished paddle. EM1 Hutchinson was the biggest man on board the *Virginia*, with a massive, jiggling paunch that spilled alarmingly over the waistband of the oversized diaper he wore.

"No! Wait!" Wallace cried. "It's . . . it's Sunday! No, *Monday!*"

"Well?" King Borealis Rex demanded from the throne at Neptune's side. "Which is it, pollywog? Sunday? Or Monday?" Chief Vance, rail-slender with a pinched face, looked terrifying with his skin painted bright blue and plastic icicles dangling from his white wig and beard.

Queen Amphitrite laughed. "I don't think the polly-wog has the faintest idea, your Majesty!" TM1 Burnham looked quite fetching as Neptune's queen, in scarlet briefs and lipstick to match, fishnet stockings, and a bikini bra stuffed with tissue paper; long blond curls, a seashell necklace, strands of seaweed, and a crown made out of tinfoil completed his garb.

"What kind of seaman doesn't know what day it is?" Chief Kurzweil, in his role as Davy Jones, Secretary to His Majesty, hitched up his swim trunks. "*I* say we dunk him!"

Wallace shook his head, trying to clear it. It was confusing enough since he wasn't entirely sure which side of the international date line they were on right now. He knew that if it was Sunday east of the line, it was Monday to the west. Which was it?

To make matters worse, the bulkhead clock in the crew's mess had been covered, and he didn't have his watch. He knew it was pretty close to midnight, but was it before? Or after? Were they using local time, which would be around midnight? Or GMT—Zulu—which would be twelve hours earlier . . . or was it later? God, he had to *think*!

His thinking by this point was thoroughly muddled. Hours ago, he'd been rousted out of a warm bunk less than fifteen minutes after he'd crawled in, summoned by the bears, also known as the "Royal Masters-at-Arms to Their Imperial Majesties," and to appear before them and answer specific charges of crimes against King Neptunus Rex and King Borealis Rex. Those crimes, an official and impressive-looking warrant declared, included but were not limited to slovenliness, still having manure stuck between his toes, having a non-regulation face, excessive liberty, not knowing larboard from starboard, impersonating a seaman, and being a general disgrace and scum-sodden poor excuse for a landlubber trespassing within His Imperial Majesty's domain.

In the following hours, he'd been stripped, painted, repeatedly doused with ice water, forced to crawl on his hands and knees down a gauntlet while shipmates to either side stung his buttocks with paddles, been humiliated with shouted questions impossible to answer . . . and been generally and bewilderingly tormented until he was so dazed he wouldn't have known what day it was if he'd been back in Monroeville with a calendar in his hand and his watch on his wrist.

"I'll give you one last chance, pollywog!" Neptune roared. "What fucking day is it?"

Somehow, through the haze, inspiration struck. "It's . . . it's whatever day you decree it to be, Your Majesty! Since you are all-powerful, you can make it be any day you wish!"

Neptune roared with laughter. "Ha! I like this one! We'll kill him last! Next!"

Helping hands pulled Wallace aside, as the hazing spotlight fell on QM3 Tom Simmons, another of the shivering, huddled mass of pollywogs waiting to complete this bizarre ritual.

The *Virginia*'s mess hall, the largest compartment on board, had been decorated for the occasion, with fishnets and seaweed hanging from the bulkheads and overhead like curtains, with blue-green filters over the lights, and with an impressive triple throne for Neptune, Borealis, and Amphitrite. Various members of the crew—those who'd gone through this ritual earlier in their naval careers—had taken the parts of various characters: Jack Frost, the Royal Barber, the Royal Bears, a Royal Scribe, Neptune's Officer of the Day, the Devil, and assorted court jesters. Wallace hadn't counted, but there were at least twenty men in various degrees of costuming and paint making up the joint Royal Courts of Neptune and Borealis.

Besides this bizarre assembly, the mess deck was packed with both officers and enlisted crew watching the mayhem or actively taking part. Wallace caught sight of the captain, leaning against a bulkhead with folded arms, laughing. The skipper had played a small part in the drama, formally welcoming Neptune and his entourage as they emerged from the eight-man lockout trunk just aft of the control room. He'd told Neptune that there were several men aboard who'd never crossed the line before, nor ventured into the cold wastes of the Arctic, and asked that he be gentle with them. Bollinger had pretended to consider this request, then said, "I am sorry, Captain, but I *must* be severe with them. You have no idea what craven weaklings and scum-sucking landsmen have been invading my domain of late ... used car salesmen, television evangelists, even *lawyers*! I *will* have a tidy ocean!"

Captain Garrett had bowed before the king and formally surrendered command of the *Virginia* to him, then spent the rest of the time by the bulkhead, watching. He wondered if a ship's captain had to go through this if he'd not done so before. It didn't seem right, somehow.

Odd. RM1 Padgett had just stepped into the mess room from forward, spotted Garrett, and made his way through the crowd to Garrett's side. Wallace saw the radioman whisper something in Garrett's ear. Garrett frowned, then nodded. At that point, Wallace was distracted by a sudden raucous burst of laughter. Simmons had gotten an answer wrong to some trick question or other, and been doused with ice water. When he glanced back again at where Garrett had been, he saw that the captain was gone.

The submarine had not been entirely abandoned to the forces of chaos, of course. Watch standers remained at their stations. When he felt the deck tip gently a few minutes later, the fore end of the mess hall rising higher than the aft, he knew that something unusual was going on. What was the message Padgett had delivered?

And what was important enough to interrupt the Imperial Court of Neptunus Rex?

Radio Shack, USS *Virginia*
Bering Strait
12 miles west of Cape Prince of Wales
Alaska
0038 hours GMT/shipboard
1238 hours, Zulu –12

Garrett stepped into the radio shack. "Anything yet?"

"It's just coming through, sir." Padgett said, tapping on a keyboard. "Coming out of the printer now."

The printer in the back corner began buzzing. *Virginia* might be a paperless vessel, but there were still times when hard copy was preferred. Garrett picked up the sheet from the paper feed and read it.

Padgett's whispered message in the crew's mess had been to the effect that the *Virginia* had received an ELF alert—someone had "rung the bell." A submarine cruising at three hundred feet could not receive ordinary radio messages, which were effectively blocked by just a few feet of water. Extremely Low Frequency signals could penetrate deep water, however, and be picked up by a special long wire antenna trailing in the submarine's wake. The radio waves were so long, however—about four thousand *kilometers*—that information transfer was painfully slow, on the order of .03 bit per second. ELF messages were limited, then, to signals known as "bell-ringers," which meant, simply, "come to the surface to receive orders."

And those orders were what Garrett held in his hand, now that the *Virginia* had come to periscope depth and lifted her satellite communications receiver above the waves. In his experience, such breaks in the routine were either training-related, or they were trouble. He read the message quickly.

Yup. Trouble. And lots of it.

TO: CO USS VIRGINIA
FROM: COMSUBLANT
RE: MISSION UPDATE/NEW ORDERS

1. PASSENGERS AND CREW OF A SAILING YACHT OF AMERICAN REGISTRY HAVE REPORTEDLY BEEN KIDNAPPED IN THE SOUTH CHINA SEA. HOSTAGES INCLUDE MATTHEW C. DUPONT, A HIGH-RANKING EXECUTIVE OF GLOBAL OIL, SEVERAL GLOBAL OIL EMPLOYEES, AND TWO VIETNAMESE NATIONALS. THE SITUATION IS UNCLEAR AT THIS TIME. HOSTILES COULD BE PIRATES OR PLAN ELEMENTS OPERATING IN THE AREA.

2. USS VIRGINIA WILL PROCEED AS PER ORDERS TO YOKOSUKA, ARRIVING NO LATER THAN 1200 HRS, 3 JUN, WHERE YOU WILL TAKE ON BOARD ADDITIONAL SUPPLIES.

3. NO LEAVE OR LIBERTY WILL BE GRANTED CREW IN JAPAN. USS VIRGINIA WILL DEPART YOKOSUKA NO LATER THAN 0600 HRS, 4 JUN, TO RENDEZVOUS WITH SEAL TEAM ELEMENT AT N21°42.50', E120°46.75', AT 0900 HRS, 6 JUN. VIRGINIA WILL TAKE ON BOARD EIGHT-MAN SEAL ELEMENT AND ASDS IN AT-SEA PICK-UP.

4. USS VIRGINIA WILL THEN PROCEED WITH ALL POSSIBLE SPEED TO THE GENERAL AREA OF THE WEST SPRATLY ISLANDS, N9°26', E111°39', DESIGNATED AO THUNDERHEAD. FUR-THER ORDERS WILL BE TRANSMITTED AT THAT TIME.

5. CBG EIGHT IS PROCEEDING TO AO THUNDER-HEAD. USS VIRGINIA WILL OPERATE IN SUP-PORT OF CBG EIGHT, UNDER COMMAND OF ADMIRAL GILLESPIE, COCBG EIGHT. OPERA-TIONAL COMMAND HEREBY TRANSFERRED TO VICE ADMIRAL THORNTON, COMSUBPAC.

6. OPERATION TO SECURE RELEASE OF AMERI-CAN HOSTAGES IN AREA HEREBY DESIGNATED OPERATION CLAYMORE. USS VIRGINIA HERE-BY DESIGNATED TASK FORCE STILETTO. SEAL ASSETS HEREBY DESIGNATED TASK FORCE TRIDENT. CBG EIGHT HEREBY DESIGNATED TASK FORCE BROADSWORD.

7. OPERATIONAL MODALITY FOR TF STILETTO REMAINS UNCERTAIN UNTIL IDENTITY OF HOSTILES IS CONFIRMED. STILETTO'S AND TRIDENT'S FIRST PRIORITY WILL BE TO ASSIST IN CLARIFICATION OF SITUATION BY PER-FORMING SURVEILLANCE OF SHIPS AND STA-

TIONS IN AO IN ORDER TO ASCERTAIN LOCA-
TION AND STATUS OF HOSTAGES.

8. ATTEMPTS WILL BE MADE TO SECURE RELEASE
OF HOSTAGES THROUGH DIPLOMATIC CHAN-
NELS, ASSUMING HOSTAGE TAKERS REPRE-
SENT THE PRC OR OTHER FOREIGN GOVERN-
MENT. A POSSIBILITY REMAINS THAT
HOSTAGE TAKERS ARE PIRATES, TERRORISTS,
OR OTHER ROGUE FORCES OPERATING IN
CONJUNCTION WITH TERRORIST ELEMENTS.
CO VIRGINIA SHOULD ANTICIPATE POSSIBILI-
TY OF MILITARY ACTION IN ORDER TO
SECURE HOSTAGE RELEASE. . . .

There was more, most of it dealing with command
authorities and communications protocol. The orders
were signed James J. Taylor, Vice Admiral, JCS, and
the time stamp showed the orders cut and issued less
than two hours ago. Fast work. Who the hell was this
DuPont character, and why was he so important?
From the sound of things, the Pentagon, possibly the
White House itself, had passed this one down the
chain of command by way of the Joint Chiefs of Staff.
DuPont's disappearance had overturned a real hornet's
nest, and now *Virginia* was on her way straight into
the heart of the swarm.

The Spratly Islands? Garrett knew they'd been the
short fuse on a powder keg in Southeast Asia for decades. Claimed by China, Vietnam, and a handful of
other nations, they were a war waiting to happen . . .
especially if someone happened to strike oil in the region. The presence of Global Oil people on a pleasure
boat with representatives of the Hanoi government
suggested that Vietnam was raising the stakes, possi-

bly bringing in Global to actively prospect. Or maybe they'd already made an oil or gas strike, and Global had been invited in to exploit it.

Either way, the People's Republic of China couldn't be happy about oil company representatives wandering around on behalf of the Vietnamese government. If the PLAN—the PRC's navy—was responsible for the man's disappearance, the chances for a diplomatic resolution were good, but Washington was going to want a powerful force in the area—like a carrier battle group and a few attack subs—to keep the Chinese honest. Given the recent history between the two powers, things could get hot.

And if China wasn't the culprit, there were a dozen different popular insurrections, civil conflicts, boundary disputes, religious wars, and out-and-out piracy going on in the region—in Indonesia, in Malaysia, in the Philippines, and elsewhere—to keep things damned interesting. DuPont might be the target of nothing more than a freelance bid for ransom or political leverage.

Or it could be something far more sinister, and deadly.

One thing was certain. Garrett wasn't going to get to see Kazuko. Once again, his personal life would be on hold until a crisis was resolved.

Well, that was the Navy way. He still might be able to call her, once the ship-to-shore phones were on-line.

He walked back to the control room, where a skeleton watch manned the con stations. The exec rose from the center seat. "Captain on deck."

He exchanged places with the XO. "Thanks, Number One."

"What's the word?"

Without comment, Garrett passed Jorgensen the

printout. The XO read it, his eyebrows rising. Finally, he pursed his lips and gave a low whistle. "The Chinese?"

"Possibly. You'll note Washington doesn't know who the enemy is just yet. That's what they want us to find out."

"So I see. Looks like we have our work cut out for us."

"That we do."

"Are you going to cancel the crossing ceremony, sir?"

Garrett considered the question, his eyes on the control room bulkhead clock. "No. Let them go. The ritual is important. And we're going to be asking a lot of those men in the next few weeks."

"Yes, sir."

"Mr. DeKalb, plot the most direct course for Yokosuka, Japan."

"Aye aye, Captain." A pause. "Sir, recommend coming right fifteen degrees to put us on the desired course."

"Very well. Helm! Come right one-five degrees!"

"Come right one-five degrees, aye, sir!"

"Maneuvering, this is the Conn. Make revolutions for thirty knots."

"Conn, Maneuvering. Make revolutions for thirty knots, aye."

Garrett felt the surge of power as *Virginia* sped southwest through the depths.

Monday, 29 May 2006

Attack Submarine *Shuhadaa Muqaddaseen*
Southwest of Spratly Island
South China Sea
1810 hours, Zulu –8

DuPont sat in the corner on a stinking mattress, one of
a half-dozen spread out over the deck. There was no
room to lie down. He was wedged in tightly between
Kingsfield and Zubrin, *Sea Breeze*'s engineer, and
Carle's back was right in front of him. The compartment was *tiny*, a room the size of a large closet, really,
and never meant to hold ten people.

Sea Breeze's entire complement was packed into the
room; only the two Vietnamese were missing.

The boarding party had stormed onto the yacht,
coming over the starboard gunwale, shouting first in a
language DuPont didn't know, and then in English.
"Everybody! Everybody on boat! Line up here!"

There'd been ten of the invaders altogether, and they stormed through the *Sea Breeze*, rounding up crew and passengers alike with rough efficiency, herding everyone into a tight and easily controlled huddle on the aft deck.

"DuPont!" the man who appeared to be in charge shouted, waving a pistol. He wasn't wearing a uniform . . . or, rather, his dress appeared to be ragged castoffs of several uniforms. He wore a turban and sported a greasy, black beard. "Who is DuPont?"

Kingsfield had put a cautioning hand on his arm, but DuPont pushed forward anyway. "I am." The fact that they knew his name was unsettling. This attack was no random pirate outrage. It possessed the surety of an operation with a considerable military intelligence apparatus behind it.

"You come with us!" the ragged leader had shouted, pointing the pistol in his face.

"Will you let the rest of my people go?" he asked. Somehow, somehow, he had to find a way to bargain with these thugs.

"You come with us!"

"Look!" he'd said. "I . . . I work for a very important company. If you keep all of us alive, my company will pay a *very* generous ransom!"

"You Americans," the man said, with a look of pure disgust souring his face. "You think money can buy anything."

In DuPont's experience, there were very few things that money couldn't buy. And these people, whoever they were, surely needed money to operate, and a lot of it.

"You are prisoners, now," the man said, "of al Qaeda and Maktum. If you do exactly what you are told, you *may* be allowed to live. If you are trouble, even *little* trouble, we throw you to the sharks!"

Al Qaeda! DuPont had reeled at that, stunned. The Islamic fundamentalist terror group that had catapulted the twenty-first century into bloody war. Like most Americans, though, he thought of al Qaeda as ragged desert militia types, hiding out in caves and mountain camps, hunted from nation to nation by U.S. special forces.

My God, he thought. *Where did they come up with a fucking* submarine?

The two Vietnamese were knocked to the deck, pinned down with rifle butts, and their hands locked behind them with plastic ties. "Hey!" DuPont shouted. "You don't need to do that!"

In the next instant, a rifle butt slammed into his skull from behind, pitching him to the deck in a black haze of pain. "Be silent," he was told, "or die!"

For the next twenty minutes, the invaders kept them there, kneeling in a close-huddled circle or flat on the deck, while several of their number went through the *Sea Breeze*'s quarters, gathering papers, passports, and documents. The rest of the prisoners had their wrists roughly bound behind their backs with plastic ties, and were kept under close guard. When anyone tried to protest, he got a rifle butt from behind—not hard enough to kill or render unconscious, but enough to knock him to the deck and keep him silent.

DuPont witnessed only one hopeful sign in the takeover. One of the uniformed sailors, grinning, had begun touching Ginger, stroking her hair and arm, then pulling her from the circle, groping at her bikini top while saying something obviously salacious to the sailor next to him. Ginger screamed, trying to pull away, and then the turbaned man was there, screaming at the sailor in a language that sounded Arabic. DuPont didn't know what was being said, but from the tone of voice and the man's expression, he was willing to bet that the sailor was being figuratively burnt to a crisp.

After that, they left both girls alone.

Oddly, the incident left DuPont feeling even more scared and helpless. Their futures, their safety, their lives all now were entirely in the hands of this turbaned maniac. DuPont, used to giving orders and having his orders obeyed instantly, had never even imagined such a terror-drenched helplessness as this.

The submarine, meanwhile, had maneuvered slowly closer to the *Sea Breeze*, until its conning tower loomed high above the yacht's deck. Once *Sea Breeze* was secured to the submarine's port side, sailors began cutting their bonds and manhandling the captives across one at a time, hauling them up the curved hull onto the submarine's aft deck, then forcing them down the hatch just aft of the sail. For DuPont, that descent through a narrow hatch, down a spindly vertical ladder into darkness, had been a kind of descent into the underworld. The submarine's belly was dark and hot and noisy, a tiny, closed-off Hell defined by pipes, wires, gauges, and dark-eyed men who watched him in hostile silence. Harsh, incandescent bulbs in wire cages cast pockets of illumination surrounded by impenetrable shadow. The humidity was so high that the bulkheads and pipes were sweating . . . and so was DuPont after only a few minutes below deck. The temperature, he guessed, was in the eighties, and was only slightly relieved by the breeze fitfully wafting from fist-sized ventilator shafts.

And the air *stank*. Unwashed bodies, sweat, urine, and the unfamiliar bite of the cooking spices used in Southwestern Asia mingled together to assault nose, throat, and eyes all at once.

He was led through what he guessed was the control room, where half a dozen uniformed men stood or sat at their stations. DuPont tried to observe and memorize everything. Was that a Chinese naval officer he'd seen? He thought so, though the light was uncertain and he'd been forced through into the next passageway with a sharp shove from behind.

Four of *Sea Breeze*'s crew were already there, waiting in the tiny compartment when he was prodded in at gunpoint—Davis the radio man, Zubrin the engineer, a Filipino hand named Castro, and the Global ex-SEAL security guard and boatswain, Carle. The compartment, with its two sets of double bunks on the bulkhead opposite the door and a small desk between, was pretty close quarters for the five of them. With growing horror, DuPont watched as, one at a time, Schiffer, Kingsfield, Marshall, Katie, and Ginger were also pushed through the steel door.

The two Vietnamese passengers never appeared. DuPont wondered what had happened to them.

The prisoners sat on the bunks or on the deck; there was no room to move around. After about half an hour, the door opened again, and members of the submarine's crew began handing mattresses in from the passageway outside. They were thin—only a couple of inches thick, more like thick quilts than actual mattresses—and they stank to high heaven, but they offered something softer than the steel deck to sit on. Their appearance told DuPont that this tiny room was going to be their prison, possibly for some time to come.

Never had he felt this helpless, this terrified. Somehow, he'd managed to assume the professional demeanor he presented in board meetings and interviews with subordinates, but inside his stomach was knotting, his heart was pounding, and he felt like he was going to be sick.

After a long time, he became aware of a low-voiced muttering, a murmur, really, inside the compartment. It took him a few minutes of careful listening to decide what it was.

"George," he said, "shut up. Keep it to yourself."

"S-sorry, Mr. DuPont. Didn't know I was . . . uh, speaking out loud."

"I don't mind you praying, but do it to yourself."

"Yes, sir. Sorry, sir."

"All of you, listen to me. Global will know what's happened by now. You got through to them, didn't you, Davis?"

"I sent the message, and kept sending it, sir. Didn't get a response, but I'm sure they taped it."

"Okay. They'll figure it out, and they'll tell who needs to be told. Global is used to dealing with . . . these kinds of people." He'd almost said "terrorists," but he'd stopped himself. There was no need to dwell on the fact that their captors were al Qaeda. "The fact that we're still alive means these people will negotiate. And Global will do everything possible to get us back."

"What . . . what about the U.S. government?" Zubrin asked. "I mean . . . will the SEALs or Delta Force or somebody try a hostage rescue?"

"I don't know. Probably not, actually. Our best hope right now is that Corporate will pay a ransom, and then these people will let us go."

It was true. DuPont had read the studies and the reports. When hostages in this kind of situation were killed, it was almost always during an attempted rescue, often by so-called friendly fire.

But, then again . . . how often had hostages been in

this kind of situation, held on board a submarine somehow co-opted by international terrorists? His guess was that it had never happened. They were flying blind, right now . . . and that included their captors.

But he didn't want to talk about the negative side of things. They needed to keep their spirits up.

"*Will* they let us go?" Ginger asked.

"Like the boss said," Kingsfield told her, "they've kept us alive for a reason. That's a very good sign."

"Right," DuPont added. "So . . . all of you, do what you're told. Don't give them a reason to regret keeping us alive."

Ginger was sitting on one of the bunks, looking terribly small and vulnerable in her bright blue bikini. "Mr. DuPont! I'm scared."

"Trust me, Ginger. It'll be okay. I promise."

He desperately hoped he would be able to make good on that promise.

Sonar Shack, USS *Virginia*
Bering Strait
Between Mys Caplina and St. Lawrence Island
0615 hours, GMT/shipboard
1815 hours, Zulu –12

"So, Seaman Wallace, how's it feel to be an *experienced* sailor, a real bluenose, now?"

Wallace was still so exhausted he could scarcely think straight. It had been a long, a *very* long, night.

He was sitting next to *Virginia*'s senior sonar technician, ST1 Ken Queensly, facing the waterfall—a monitor screen with narrow, glowing green vertical strips representing the sounds of the ocean around the boat.

Today was his first sonar watch, the beginning of his familiarization with the arcane rituals of that shipboard department, another step in his quest to sign off on every department on board.

But after enduring the Neptune party until 0300 hours . . . then hitting the deck at 0630 to shave, shower, and grab some breakfast in order to be on watch by 0800 . . . well, he didn't feel all there yet. He hoped the missing part of himself was still in his rack, getting some much-needed sleep.

"I said," Queensly repeated, "how's it feel to be a bluenose?"

"Uh . . . what? Sorry. Okay, I guess." He shook his head, groggy. "I'm not really awake yet."

Queensly laughed. "That I can believe. Hey, Grisly! Fetch this man some java."

ST2 Griswold rose from his console seat. "Comin' right up, Queenie. Anything for you?"

"I'm fine, Gris. Thanks." He clapped Wallace on the shoulder. "So, they kept you up late, huh?"

Wallace could only nod.

"It was a hell of party," Chief Evans said. Evans was the boat's senior sonar chief, the man in charge of the department and Wallace's new boss. Off watch, he was enjoying a chief's prerogative and lollygagging—hanging around the sonar shack to gossip. ST2 Dyer was the other watch stander, currently huddled over his console with his ears engulfed by a massive set of sonar headphones. "They turned those poor pollywogs every way but loose!" He reached out and dragged a blunt forefinger down the side of Wallace's nose. "You still have some paint there, youngster."

Wallace rubbed at the spot.

"You got it," Queensly said. "So what all did they do to you?" Queensly had not been in attendance last night. He'd been here, running the sonar watch. Wallace wondered how he could look so fresh after . . . what? Twelve straight hours, now.

"I'm pretty hazy on it all, right now," Wallace admitted. "It was kind of confusing."

"Well, I see you got the royal haircut from the royal barber."

Wallace grinned ruefully and ran his hand over his clean-shaven scalp. Part of the pollywogs' sentence had been to have their heads—and select other parts of their anatomy—completely shaved. His skin was still pretty raw in places. "Yeah. The worst part, I think, was when they made us go fishing for ice cubes." They'd made the pollywogs kneel around a large steel tub—just like bobbing for apples—only the apples were ice cubes, and they were hidden inside a foot-deep mess of something indescribable and very unpleasant. "What *was* that stuff, anyway?"

Evans laughed. "Hey, like old King Borealis told you, you've gotta eat shit to be accepted by the rest of us!"

Wallace grimaced at the mental image. The tub, he was pretty sure, had been full of stuff like cooking oil, grease, and maybe a few pounds of chocolate or cocoa powder to give it its lumpy semisolid consistency, and not what Evans was suggesting. Still . . .

At least his head had been shaved by that time, or else he'd still be pulling the stuff out of his hair.

"Joe," Griswold said, reentering the sonar shack. "Get it while it's hot."

Wallace accepted a mug full of steaming black coffee. "Why do you call it joe?" he asked, hoping to change the subject.

"Ah, therein lies a tale," Chief Evans said, leaning far back in his swivel chair. "In this man's Navy, there are five grades of coffee. They are, from best to worst, coffee, joe, java, jamoke, and battery acid. Only officers rate coffee, of course. On a submarine, the enlisted men can usually expect joe . . . unless it's toward the end of a deployment, of course. Then the coffee's almost gone, and the galley hands are cutting it with God knows what."

"Okay . . . but why 'joe'?"

"Because the guy who outlawed rum on U.S. Navy ships was named Josephus Daniels. He was secretary of the navy in 1914 when he signed General Order 99 which prohibits . . . let's see, 'the use or introduction for drinking purposes of alcoholic liquors on board any naval vessel, or within any navy yard or station.' Congress had been pushing for using coffee as a substitute for twenty years before that. So they called coffee 'joe' in his honor."

"You're full of shit, Chief," said Dyer, removing his headset and turning to join the conversation. "It was a fuckin' racist slur from an old song, 'Old Black Joe.' " James Dyer was African American.

"The hell it was. Who's telling this story, you or me?"

"You are, Chief. I'm just telling you—"

"It was from Joe Daniels, man. Everybody knows that." He took a swig from his own mug. "Hey, here's a bit of trivia for you guys. Did you know the U.S. Navy uses more coffee per man than any other naval or military organization in the world? Fifty years ago, the Bureau of Supplies and Accounts figured the Navy used over twenty-five tons of coffee per day."

"Man, you are just chock full of fascinating data," Queensly said. "How much do we use today?"

"How the hell should I know?" Evans said. "I don't work in supply."

"So what's with the names java and jamoke?" Griswold asked.

"Probably just, whatcha call 'em, euphemisms," Evans said. "You know, they sound good together." He snapped his fingers, chanting, 'joe,' 'java,' 'jamoke' . . ."

"I think you mean 'euphonious,' Chief," Queensly said. "And you forgot 'murk' and 'shot-in-the-arm' and 'caffeine fix' and 'battery acid.' "

Wallace dared a sip of his coffee, then grimaced. He usually took it with creamer and sugar, and the black potion was way too bitter by itself.

"How is it?" Griswold asked.

"At least I know how it got the name 'battery acid,' " Wallace replied. "Yagh. Is this still part of the initiation?"

Evans laughed. "No, youngster. You are now a full-fledged and genu-wine blue-nosed gold dragon, with all rights and privileges thereunto, including, I might add, the right to bitch about the coffee. I think that pot's been on the hot plate since the forenoon watch yesterday."

"So . . . yesterday," Wallace said. "Was that Sunday? Or Saturday?"

Griswold chuckled. "Still wondering what day it is?"

"Well, I know we crossed the international date line last night . . ."

"Right," Evans said. "Actually, we're not up to the 180-degree meridian, yet, but the line takes a jog through the Bering Strait to avoid cutting off a piece of Siberia. When we crossed the line, we lost a day. It was Sunday. Now it's Monday."

"What was it last night, when Neptune was asking me questions?"

"Trick question, youngster," Evans said, chuckling.

"It was about 2400 hours, give or take. Midnight. And when it's midnight on the international date line, it's high noon in Greenwich, England."

"So? What's the point?"

"When it's noon in Greenwich is the *only* time when it's the same date everywhere on Earth. It was—and still is—Monday."

"But I thought you said we'd lost a day. I remember Sunday . . . yesterday. And you say today is Monday . . ."

"Don't worry about it, son," Queensly said. "It catches up with you, see? They'll probably adjust the shipboard calendars later in the cruise, when it's convenient."

"Maybe they'll get rid of Thursday," Griswold said, looking up at the fluorescent-lit overhead. "I never did get the hang of Thursdays. . . ."

Wallace shook his head. "I still don't get it."

"Not important that you do, Seaman Wallace. It *is* important, though, that you get checked out on this board."

"Okay." He was feeling a bit more awake, now, but the mysteries of the sonar board were still daunting. "But I still don't know what I'm supposed to be doing."

"Listen and learn, Seaman Wallace. Listen and learn. And . . . have a listen to this."

Reaching out, he tapped a point on a touch-screen display. Instantly, the sonar shack was filled with a roar, a rushing, white-noise rumble that reminded Wallace of an oncoming train.

"What do you hear?"

Wallace wasn't sure how to answer the question. "Uh . . . I don't know. A roaring noise. Is that a surface ship?"

"No. If it were a surface ship—or another submarine—you'd hear a kind of a throb to the sound . . . like this." He touched the controls again. The rushing roar vanished, replaced by a muffled *thud-thud-thud.* "From our sound library," Queensly said. "That was a Japanese *maru*, what they call their freighters. No . . . what do you hear when I do this?" Instantly, the compartment filled once more with a featureless roar . . . kind of like a waterfall, Wallace decided.

He listened a moment longer. "I don't know," he said. "It just sounds like . . . I don't know. Water rushing past."

"Bingo," Queensly said. "Give that blue-nosed dragon a *see*-gar!"

"Huh?"

"*Virginia*'s current speed, Seaman Wallace, is . . ." He tapped at the controls again, then read what appeared in one corner of a console monitor. "Thirty-three point seven knots. And that, my friend, is flying. *Virginia* has sonar sensors all up and down her hull, and in the big dome up on the bow, of course. You are exactly right. You're hearing water rushing past those sensors at a good forty miles per hour. And brother, that makes such an unholy racket you can't hear a damned thing else."

"We're lucky to hear anything at all above eighteen knots," Evans put in. "Twelve is better."

"A *lot* better," Dyer said.

"And if the skipper *really* wants us to do some careful listening, he'll slow the boat to a crawl, or just hover in one place. When we're hunting a bad guy, it's a matter of moving a bit, stopping and listening, moving a bit more. Takes a lot of patience."

"My dad used to take me hunting in the woods,

back in Pennsylvania," Wallace said. "You do a lot of just sitting and listening."

"Good analogy," Griswold said. "You don't want to make any noise and spook the deer. And you have to stop to really study the woods around you."

"We *are* hunters," Dyer pointed out. "Remember, Wallace. There's just two kinds of vessels—SSNs . . ."

"And targets. I know." He'd heard the old sub-mariner's saying endlessly in sub school. "So, if we can't hear anything at this speed, how do I learn?"

"Simulations, Seaman Wallace," Queensly said. "Simulations . . . and the magic of computers." He tapped out a new command, replacing the waterfall noise with . . . a kind of a deep, hollow emptiness. "You did this in sub school, right?"

"Sure. Listening lessons, we called them."

"Right. You took some tests like this all the way back in boot camp, too. They had to find out who had good ears. The really talented ones, they send to sonar school. Like yours truly. Here. Try it with these." He handed Wallace a set of headphones.

With the phones on, Wallace still heard nothing but a kind of watery silence. Or . . . was that a kind of a deep, plaintive groaning in the distance? He tried to hear, tried to separate it from the background emptiness.

"Hear anything?" Queensly's voice sounded muffled and far off.

"I'm . . . not sure." His own voice sounded preternaturally loud, and curiously dead.

"Okay, I want you to do something for me. When I tell you . . . you're going to take in a deep breath for a count of four. Then you're going to hold it for a count of four. Then you'll let it out for a count of four. Then you'll hold it for a count of four. Then you'll repeat. We'll do that five or six times. Okay?"

"Uh . . . okay. Why?"

"It's an exercise I'm going to do with you quite a bit for the next few days. Just humor me, okay? Ready? I want you to take a few deep breaths first. Relax . . . relax. Just let everything go. Now, close your eyes. Stay relaxed. Let yourself just kind of sink down into the sound, okay? Now, breathe in . . . two . . . three . . . four. And hold . . . two . . . three . . . four. Breathe out . . . two . . . three . . . four. Hold . . . two . . . three . . . four. Breathe in . . . two . . . three . . . four . . ."

Wallace breathed as Queensly guided him through the exercise. The sonar tech's voice was monotonous, almost hypnotic, and Wallace felt as though he were sinking into that silent emptiness in the headset. Somehow, the silence was growing larger . . . and . . . louder? No, that wasn't it. But he was beginning to separate something like a sound from the background nothingness. A groan . . . followed by a popping, scratchy squeak, like a rusty hinge, unimaginably faint and far off.

"I hear it!" he said.

"That, Seaman Wallace, is what we call a biological. A *whale*, in fact, about a thousand miles off. Now here's another . . ."

And the listening lessons began in earnest.

Saturday, 3 June 2006

Sail, USS *Virginia*
Entering Yokosuka Harbor
Japan
0215 hours, GMT/shipboard
1115 hours, Zulu −9

"Steady as she goes," Garrett said over his headset.

"Steady as she goes, aye aye" came the response.

Virginia was on the surface once more, cruising slowly through the placid waters of the Uraga Strait. The headland of Sunosaki was well astern now, and the submarine had rounded Cape Kannon, picking her way with careful deliberation through a swarm of shipping and boats of every size, shape, and description. Directly ahead rose the bristling forest of masts, antennae, and U.S. naval buildings that was Fleet Activities, Yokosuka. A pilot boat led the way through the crowded shipping lanes.

Yokosuka lay on the Mura Peninsula, astride the entrance to *Tokyo-wan*—Tokyo Bay itself—and was right on the main drag leading to the ports of Yokohama, Kawasaki, Chiba, and Tokyo itself. Hundreds of ships were visible from *Virginia*'s sail in all directions, from pleasure boats and fishing smacks up to a monstrous supertanker lumbering north a mile to starboard of the American sub.

Jorgensen stood beside him on the sail's bridge. "You know, sir, the crew think it's a bitch that they're not getting liberty."

"They can *think* anything they like, XO. But our orders don't cut us any slack. We're out of here tomorrow, zero-six hundred."

"Aye aye, Captain." He didn't look pleased.

"You know, XO . . . it's your job to be a bastard." Technically, the executive officer of a ship handled the routine responsibilities concerning the crew, all internal matters, leaving the captain free to think strategically and concern himself with more global matters. The way that usually played out, however, had the exec playing the villain, the guy who handed out the unpleasant news and details, the officer the men could freely hate.

"Yeah, I know. But I don't have to like it."

"No, you don't."

With a final blast from its whistle, the pilot boat sheered off. Pier Two was ahead and to port, a hundred yards off.

"Maneuvering, Captain. Come left three-zero degrees. Bring engines to dead slow."

"Maneuvering, aye aye. Come left three-zero degrees. Engines to dead slow."

"Line handling parties, man your stations."

Virginia entered Yokosuka's harbor as men clad in dungarees and the blue coveralls known as poopie suits filed up out of the hatches and formed up at bow and stern. Garrett judged the approach carefully, watching for just the right moment.

"Maneuvering, Sail. Engine astern, one half."

"Sail, Maneuvering. Engine astern, one half." He felt the throb of the engines change pitch and timbre, felt the slight jolt as *Virginia*'s forward speed was negated. The sub still possessed considerable momentum, however, and continued to drift forward, slowing now with each passing second.

"Helm, do you have the dock?"

"Captain, Helm. We have the dock in sight."

"Very well, then. Let's see what video gaming can do."

He heard Lieutenant Lanesky's dry laugh. "Will do, Skipper."

On other submarines, Garrett or another officer would have talked the submarine into dock, calling for left or right rudder. On *Virginia*, however, the helmsman and helm officer could watch the approach on the TV feed from the Photonics mast. The helmsman would be steering the boat in with his joystick—hence Garrett's crack about video games. There were those who argued that a generation of American kids raised on such games would transform the face of war. *Virginia* was one small proof of that argument.

It took considerable self-control for Garrett not to feed the helm instructions. He needed to show the crew his trust in their abilities.

At the same time, it wouldn't do at all for *Virginia* to take out that dock just off the port bow.

In silence he watched his command sidle up to the dock, watched the line handlers toss their lines across to sailors waiting ashore, and wondered if he would ever get used to this new kind of war.

Attack Submarine *Shuhadaa Muqaddaseen*
Southwest of Spratly Island
South China Sea
1210 hours, Zulu −8

Captain ul Haq dropped the arms of the periscope and leaned into them, walking the scope in approved fashion through three complete circles as *Shuhadaa* approached periscope depth. He could see the water growing light, then becoming a froth of white spray. As the periscope cleared the surface, he continued walking the scope, checking the entire horizon. Submarines had been lost when they surfaced inadvertently directly beneath—or in the path of—an oncoming surface ship.

There was only a single ship visible, and she was at least three miles off. "Allah be praised," he said with soft but heartfelt sincerity.

"What is it?" Noor Khalili asked.

"Our prey."

Four times in the past five days, *Shuhadaa* had stalked a target, and four times the target had eluded them. The last time, two days ago, they'd picked up a very large surface contact—almost certainly a supertanker—but the vessel had proven to be too far away to make visual contact. Evidently, sound waves played interesting tricks on the sub's sonar displays in these shallow waters. Convergence zones could make a target seem to be thirty kilometers away, when in fact it was hundreds.

A Kilo-class boat could only manage about twenty knots, running all-out on the surface using her diesels, which was dangerously noisy. Creeping along submerged on batteries alone, she could only manage twelve knots. Almost *anything* could outrun that. As with predators in the wild, the submarine needed to exercise supreme patience . . . and to expect that too often chance would favor the prey.

Now, though, ul Haq watched the target moving slowly along the horizon, an almost perfect setup.

The vessel's lines were unmistakable, impossibly high and sharply square, with a very low, two-story bridge structure forward, a single stack aft. As if to confirm the initial identification, the name NISSAN was spelled out in titanic characters along the vessel's side.

According to intelligence reports passed on from Zaki, she was the *Innoshima Maru*, a bulk car carrier sailing under Panamanian registry—gross weight of 51,858 tons, deadweight tonnage of 28,070 tons, length overall 185 meters, draught 11.7 meters. Her Hitachi/BMW single-shaft diesel propelled her at a steady 19.5 knots. On board, loaded onto fourteen full cargo decks from keel to main deck, were 3,100 automobiles and 500 trucks, en route from Yokohama to Europoort/Rotterdam.

She was, in fact, a submariner's dream target.

She was also a prime terrorist's target—epitome of Western capitalist consumerism. Ul Haq's orders from Maktum in fact were to give special attention to hunting and killing such highly visible symbols of the West—cargo carriers piled high with consumer goods, cruise ships loaded with wealthy tourists . . . and the oil tankers that represented the lifeblood of America, Europe, and the West.

"Target bearing . . . mark!" he snapped.

"Target bearing two-five-seven," Lieutenant Mahmud Jamal replied, reading the figure off the circle marker on the opposite side of the periscope casing.

"Range, 5,500 meters. Sonar, designate contact as Target One-five. Fire control, ready tubes two and three and prepare to fire."

"Captain, tubes two and three are loaded and ready to fire."

"Set running depth at fifteen meters." That was deep, but the Russian-built torpedoes were designed to explode beneath the target ship's keel, breaking her back. And, according to the warbook, that car carrier had a draught of almost twelve meters.

"Running depth set to fifteen meters, Captain!"

"Open outer doors."

"Outer doors open."

"Match sonar bearing on tube two and . . . shoot!"

A loud hiss sounded through the submarine, accompanied by a shudder in the deck. "Tube two fired electrically!"

"Match sonar bearing on tube three and . . . shoot!"

A second hiss. "Tube three fired electrically. Both torpedoes running straight and normal, Allah be praised!"

Ul Haq suppressed a wry grin at that last. As a ship captain, he frowned on invoking Allah aloud during ship operations, *especially* during combat. It could get in the way of orders and understanding. And that fervent Allah-be-praised carried just the faintest hint of surprise . . . as though Lieutenant Jamal hadn't expected the torpedoes to work at all. That could be bad for discipline.

But Jamal's excitement, with the excitement of the moment, was contagious. After five days of stalking, the tiger was pouncing at last!

"Down scope!" He slapped the periscope handles up and stepped back as the gleaming cylinder slid down into its well in the deck at his feet. The ocean had appeared clear and there was no reason for that carrier to be escorted, but a submariner did not casually ignore his training. "Running time to target?"

"Three minutes, forty seconds, Captain." Ul Haq checked the clock on the bulkhead, noting the position of the sweep second hand, and began counting off to himself.

A minute passed . . . then another . . . and another. The tension in the control room grew, a palpable presence as crushing as the weight of the ocean outside. Those torpedoes were acoustically homing, with sound receivers that picked up the target's propeller noise and steered them in unerringly. But even the best technology was known to fail.

And then, transmitted through the water, came the far-off thud of an explosion.

The men in the control room erupted into cheers and shrill-chorused cries of "*Allah akbar!*"

"Silence!" Ul Haq shouted, and the tumult quieted. Martyrs and angels! He'd missed hearing a second explosion, if there'd been one. "Sonar, conn! What do you hear?"

"Conn, sonar! Two definite underwater explosions. And . . . and breaking noises! We got her, Captain!"

And now it was time for ul Haq to mutter a quietly voiced *Allah be praised*. . . .

"Up periscope!" he ordered, stepping up to the scope mount once more. Snapping down the handles, he leaned against the eyepiece, walking the periscope back onto the heading of the target.

Pandemonium. . . .

The *Innoshima Maru*, despite her deep draught, towered high out of the water and, with a full cargo, tended to be uncomfortably top-heavy. One of the tor-

pedoes appeared to have detonated directly beneath
her stern-quarter roll-on/roll-off door, crumpling the
vessel's stern; the other must have exploded almost directly beneath her center keel, for the carrier had buckled partly amidships, as though punched from below
by a titanic, upthrust fist. She was far down by the
stern already as the hungry sea poured in through a
gaping hole torn across her transom. Those car carriers, ul Haq knew, did not have transverse watertight
bulkheads—an omission designed to save weight and
to provide more maneuvering room when loading the
cargo onto fourteen separate decks. The water pouring
in astern and amidships would rapidly flood all the
way forward. Already, the *Innoshima Maru* was taking on a pronounced list to port, its upper deck angling toward the distant submarine.

He thought he could make out members of the carrier's crew, tiny black specks moving along the deck.
They would be terrified, he knew, struggling to lower
boats, or else giving in to panic and flinging themselves
into the sea. There would be no escape, though. The
car carrier possessed a huge volume, and the water
flooding those compartments and deck spaces would
suck down everything in and on the water for hundreds
of meters around.

Worse, thousands of gallons of marine diesel fuel
were spilling from ruptured tanks now, and the fuel
had caught fire. The surface blaze looked tiny alongside the huge vessel, but the clouds of greasy black
smoke roiled into the blue of the tropical noon sky.
The blaze was spreading quickly, providing the men
trapped on board with their choice of deaths—by fire
or by sea.

Ul Haq could now hear a strange, ongoing noise
echoing through *Shuhadaa Muqaddaseen*'s steel hull,

a kind of clanging, clashing sound, part drumbeat, part crash. It took him a moment to figure out what that noise was . . . hundreds and hundreds of cars and trucks, torn from their fastenings as the deck tilted sharply beneath them, slamming ten, twenty, fifty at a time into the port-side bulkheads. The crashing sound was accompanied by another sound that submariners knew well—those who'd been in combat, at any rate . . . a shrill, piercing squeal, almost like a woman's scream.

It was the death cry of a ship, the sound made by twisting, tearing steel.

As he watched, the *Innoshima Maru* shuddered, rolled suddenly, and literally fell full on her port side in a colossal cascade of white spray. The shriek of tearing metal grew suddenly sharper and louder, and then with a wrench, stern separated from bow, the rear half submerging rapidly, the bow rolling and settling a bit, still afloat, but going down fast. For a time, the blunt prow of the *Innoshima Maru* remained jutting above water like a red-and-black-painted island, almost engulfed by black smoke.

Ten minutes later, it was all over. With a final rattle of steel and cargo spilling into the depths, a final rumble of water flooding internal compartments, the last of 52,000 tons of ship and cargo vanished beneath the waves.

Shuhadaa Muqaddaseen had scored her first major seagoing kill.

Headquarters
Fleet Activities
Yokosuka, Japan
1512 hours, Zulu −9

"Thank you for coming ashore, Commander," Captain Theodore Summers said. "I know you're damned busy."

"It did catch me by surprise, Captain," Garrett replied. "My orders are quite explicit about wrapping things up here and moving on to our next waypoint with all possible speed."

Garrett was standing in Summers's office, clad in his dress white uniform, as protocol demanded.

"Quite right," Summers said. He was a heavyset man with a mustache, close-cropped hair the color of steel, and the brusque manner of a corporate CEO. Captain Summers was in fact the senior Naval Intelligence officer at Yokosuka, and a member of Admiral Montgomery's personal staff. Montgomery was the CO of Fleet Activities, and an order from his intelligence officer was as good as an order from the Man himself. "But I thought you would want to see these. . . ."

He handed Garrett a string-tied messenger envelope, marked TOP SECRET and EYES ONLY. Garrett read the security classification warning box, then looked up at Summers, questioning.

"You have the proper clearances, Commander. I arranged it."

Garrett undid the fastening and pulled out two 8×10 black-and-white photographs. Both appeared to have been shot from the air at an oblique angle. Both showed the surface of the ocean in almost crystalline detail and clarity. One showed a large cargo or container ship of some kind, partly sunk and engulfed in the stain of oil and black smoke. The other was more difficult to identify. It looked like a building—was that a heliport on one end?—or possibly a large ship of some sort, twisted, broken, and aflame.

Identifiers at the corners showed that the photos both had been taken by KH-12 reconnaissance satellites. According to the time and date stamps, one—the strange-looking structure—had been taken five days ago. The other had been taken . . . my God! Less than three *hours* ago. That was astonishingly fast work for this sort of intelligence dissemination down the ladder from NPIC and the CIA. Someone at the very top must think that it was *very* important that Garrett see these.

"That," Summers said, pointing to the first photo, "is . . . *was*, I should say, the Vietnamese oil exploration base on Amboyna Cay, in the Spratly Island Group. I gather Washington flashed you about that?"

"Yes, sir."

"Good. And *this* one was taken this afternoon about 175 miles west of Amboyna Cay, halfway between the Spratlys and the southern tip of Vietnam. It's a Japanese commercial car carrier. Panamanian flag, but it had the name 'Nissan' spelled out in giant letters down both sides, so there's no possibility that her attackers didn't know who she was. That ship was sunk deliberately and without warning. Now, look at this."

He pulled a standard marine navigational chart from its storage tube and unrolled it on his desk. The chart showed the South China Sea, from the Philippines in the east to Malaysia in the west, from the northern shore of Borneo in the south to southern China in the north. Six Xs marked the chart, each neatly labeled. Five lay clustered among the central

Spratly Islands, and another was located well out of the archipelago and off to the west, almost due south of the bulging belly of Vietnam.

"These two," Summers said, "the Vietnamese exploration rig and the *Innoshima Maru*, that Japanese cargo ship, are apparently just the last two of a number of sinkings in this region. Reports are still filtering through, and we may not have all of them yet. These first three . . . here, here, and here, represent the last reported positions of one Vietnamese and two Filipino fishing trawlers. The first went missing sometime last Saturday, 27 May."

"Somebody thinks those sinkings were connected with Amboyna Cay?" Garrett asked, one eyebrow giving a skeptical lift. "I imagine fishing boats go missing in those waters all the time."

Summers nodded. "The South China Sea is one of the most dangerous areas for boats and small craft in the world. You wouldn't think it in this day and age, but piracy is not a thing of the past."

"Yes, sir." Garrett had read reports of whole fleets of pirate vessels—mostly fishing boats and trawlers disguised to look like harmless working craft—operating out of the Philippines, Malaysia, and Indonesia. Their victims tended to be fishing boats and trawlers, small commercial craft, and the like; sometimes, though, when political shifts sent hordes of refugees fleeing their native countries in overcrowded rafts and boats, the pirates indulged in bloody orgies of robbery, rape, and murder. "But . . ." Garrett held up the photographs. "You don't think these were the work of pirates, do you? A major base and a Nissan carrier are pretty big targets. Besides, what's the payoff?"

"Correct. Pirates go after weak and defenseless targets . . . and they're only going to do it if they get something out of it. Amboyna Cay and the *Innoshima Maru* are part of something else, something bigger. Someone may be trying to disguise them as piracy. Or . . . maybe the pirates have some new players on their team."

Garrett studied the photos a moment longer. "What kind of weapons are we looking at here?"

"What's your guess?"

"Torpedoes. The car carrier looks like her back was broken. That suggests an explosion under her keel. Since when do pirates in the South China Sea use torpedoes?"

"That is why the Pentagon is assuming Chinese involvement. We know they have attack subs in the region. We also know they want the Vietnamese out of the Spratly Islands. Amboyna Cay could be a first move on their part in that direction."

"But then . . . why sink the *Maru*?"

"That is what the Pentagon *doesn't* know. There are no particularly bad tensions between Beijing and Tokyo right now. In fact, there's a Far Eastern trade conference going on in Singapore right now, and Japan and the PRC are actually working together pretty well, for a change. Beijing is supporting the Japanese Trade Ministry's call for a new East Asian trade consortium, against objections by the United States and the Europeans. So what's the motive?"

"I see you've also got the *Sea Breeze* marked," Garrett said.

"Right. Same area. It's possible it was a pirate attack, though according to Global Oil, DuPont had security people on board. They should have been enough to deal with garden-variety pirates."

"Yeah. But someone is loosing torpedoes down there. That could mean a surface warship . . ."

"Or it could mean an attack submarine," Summers said, nodding. "Exactly. And that means not your run-of-the-mill pirate outrage."

Garrett set the photographs on Summers's desk. "So . . . where does that leave the *Virginia*, sir?"

"It leaves her continuing to the Spratly Islands as ordered, with a SEAL team on board. Washington will continue to update you and feed you a list of possible targets—both ashore and afloat. We want you to do a lot of covert looking and listening—a sneak-and-peek mission. We need to have hard intel if we're going to make even a half-assed guess at what's really going on. You follow?"

"Yes, sir."

"Good. Washington is especially interested in this." He handed Garrett a second envelope, this one containing a single photograph. It showed the stern quarter of a sleek, elegant vessel, obviously a pleasure craft. The name on the transom was in Arabic and English. The English letters spelled AL QAHIR.

"What's this?"

"A yacht officially belonging to a Dhahran national named Feisel. But the Agency feels a character named Zaki Abar might just be on board her right now."

"Abar?" The name was familiar . . . an al Qaeda operative? He tried to remember the lineup of the current most-wanted list.

"Al Qaeda. One of their nastier and brighter masterminds. They think he was behind the bombing of that airliner in Greece in January, and maybe the bomb in the Tokyo nightclub that killed five sailors last year.

"We've been tracking *Al Qahir* by satellite. Apparently whoever is on board is transmitting low-wattage signals to somebody in the area, and the Agency thinks it's a submarine."

"Whose submarine?"

"Good question. Smart money backs the Chinese . . ."

"But I can't imagine the Chinese wanting to be seen associated with al Qaeda."

"Exactly. There's also the matter of that Japanese car carrier. What motive would the Chinese have for sinking her?"

Garrett shrugged. "Bringing instability to the area, maybe? Or providing an excuse to send their navy in to 'restore order?' "

"A possibility," Summers agreed. "A definite possibility."

"An attack boat couldn't operate in a vacuum, Captain. They would need a base—a place to take on supplies. I assume we're talking about a diesel boat here. That means they need fuel."

"Correct. We need to know who's deploying that submarine, and why. To that end, your orders are being amended. While you're patrolling the Spratly Islands, you will do all you can to assist the SEAL team embarked with you to investigate Chinese facilities in the region, and to locate and shadow Chinese submarines that may be operating in the area. You will also be expected to shadow the *Al Qahir*."

"That should be interesting. I take it we're going after this Abar person then?"

"Negative. Langley wants to gather intelligence. I gather they're hoping to get enough rope together to hang the bastard. No, *Virginia* will be involved in signals intercepts and tracking the *Al Qahir*'s movements. You will not reveal *Virginia*'s presence."

"Yes, sir."

"But you'll also be hunting for that submarine out there, if it exists. We want to know who's torpedoing

Vietnamese bases. If it's a rogue sub, we want to know how it's carrying out operations, who's supporting it. If it's Chinese, we want to know that, too. But when you find out, you will report the fact but not take action, not until and unless CINCPAC or the Joint Chiefs give you the word. Is that understood?"

"Yes, sir. Perfectly."

Shit. *Virginia* would be walking a political tightrope, that much was all too clear. If the Chinese weren't behind the sinkings, Garrett would need to find out who was without stepping on Chinese toes. Whether the mystery sub belonged to China or to somebody else, the Chinese were certain to be watching the Spratly area closely. There would be a Chinese sub in the area, probably more than one. It would be all too easy to sink the wrong boat, and trigger a shooting war between China and the United States.

Hell, a wrong guess on Garrett's part and the *Virginia* could end up being responsible for starting World War III. Not a career-positive move for anyone, least of all *Virginia*'s skipper.

Sunday, 4 June 2006

**Attack Submarine *Shuhadaa Muqaddaseen*
Southwest of Spratly Island
South China Sea
0730 hours, Zulu –8**

The unending hours were weighing heavily on all of
the people from the *Sea Breeze*. Days had passed,
clearly, since their capture and imprisonment in these
herring-can quarters, but how many? Their captors
had removed wristwatches, belts, and shoes, and in the
artificial enclosure of a submarine there is no distin-
guishing night from day.

Periodically, they were fed—usually bowls of rice
with dry beans and a little fish or other meat added,
which they ate with their fingers because no imple-
ments were provided.

Periodically, plastic pitchers full of tepid water were
brought in, and the empties taken away.

Periodically, they were allowed—one or two at a time—to leave the cramped compartment in the company of a pair of guards, and taken a short distance down the passageway outside to a bathroom with four toilet stalls, two metal sinks, and an open shower area. The stalls had no doors, and the lack of privacy was especially rough on Katie and Ginger, who complained that the guards and other sailors watched them relieve themselves with leering grins, commenting to one another in Arabic.

Periodically the two metal buckets left in their quarters for wastes or vomit were taken away and emptied.

The rest of the time, they were left alone.

And, *God,* how the place stank! Actually, the entire submarine stank, the air a foul miasma of sweat, fear, and unwashed bodies, the sharp ammoniac tang of urine, and the heavier odors of machine oil, diesel fuel, and wet laundry, but those odors were concentrated inside the locked compartment to a degree that made those brief trips to the head a welcome chance to draw a deep breath.

The rankness of that room grew worse day by day. Though they could wash faces and hands in the sinks, none had been allowed to use the showers, and the sweltering heat and humidity of the place had them sweating so much that the deck and bulkheads were slimy-wet to the touch. Most of them had been sick to their stomachs at one point or another in this voyage. When the submarine was running submerged, the motion transmitted through the deck was gentle, but they could always tell when the vessel had surfaced from the way the deck pitched and rolled with the action of the waves outside. The corkscrew motion—much worse at some times than others—was made infinitely worse by the oppressive heat and the stale, diesel-tainted air; the third time someone vomited on the deck, their guards had provided the buckets. That meant they no longer had to clean up the mess with rags provided by their captors, but the smell was awful.

And lately, Zubrin, Davis, and Schiffer had all come down with savage bouts of diarrhea. Sometimes the guards came to escort them to the lavatory in time . . . and sometimes they didn't. Once, when he was a kid, DuPont had found a burlap bag in his father's barn and tried pulling it over his head. The bag was empty, but once had held manure. The indescribably foul smell in that bag, as DuPont remembered the experience, was no worse than right here in this tiny compartment.

Sometimes, when the submarine was running on the surface, a vent in the passageway outside washed the corridor with a stream of cool, fresh air that tasted like pure heaven compared to the stench of their prison. Of course, after walking that passageway at such a time, the air back in their room seemed that much worse by comparison.

All the prisoners had slumped into deep depression. There was no conversation any more, no talk at all save at long, rare intervals when someone asked to be taken to the bathroom. They sat or lay huddled on the steel deck; by agreement, the women had been given an upper bunk for their sole use, but every other square foot of space was taken up by cramped and unwashed, unshaven, unmoving bodies. The fear was palpable, a constant presence. They'd all heard the sounds hours ago when the submarine had attacked another vessel. They'd heard clearly the sharp twin hisses of torpedoes sliding into the ocean and, minutes, later, the heavy thuds and crashing noises marking the death of a ship. Since then, the sub had been running submerged, judging by the lack of wave action on the hull.

Who were they attacking? The Vietnamese? Was the Vietnamese navy looking for them, trying to hunt them down?

At times, DuPont found himself praying that the submarine would be found and sunk. It would, at least, end this nightmare of fear, claustrophobia, and stink.

Across the compartment, Schiffer groaned, placed a white hand across his belly, then rose unsteadily and picked his way past sprawled legs to the door. "Hey!" he shouted, thumping on the door. "Hey, out there! I gotta go!"

There was no answer, and Schiffer pounded on the door, harder.

"Jesus, Schiffer," Kingsfield said, making a face. "Just put a cork in your ass, for cryin' out loud."

"Leave him alone, man," Carle said. "When you gotta go . . ."

"Yeah, but he's makin' a fuckin' religion out of it."

"Watch your language, people," DuPont said. "We've got women in here."

"Fuck you," Kingsfield said. "They've heard fuckin' worse."

DuPont started to make a sharp response, then sagged back against the bulkhead, too exhausted, too wrung out to continue. It was astonishing how quickly the veneer of civilization—the polite language, manners, mutual respect, and simple *caring* for other people—could all vanish after just a few days of privation.

No one answered Schiffer's increasingly frantic pounding. At last, he turned away, yanked down his swim trunks and squatted over one of the buckets. Impossibly, or so it seemed to DuPont, the fetid stink of raw sewage grew worse. DuPont gagged against the odor, leaning back, squeezing shut his watering eyes, fighting down the nausea, the depression, the sheer terror. God, how much longer could they stand this torture?

Some time later, the door banged open and, as a sailor with an AK rifle stood guard from the passageway, a young sailor came in and removed the buckets, replacing them with clean ones. Instead of locking them in again, however, the armed guard stepped back and left the door open. A moment later, one of their captors strode in.

This was the one DuPont worried about the most. Kingsfield thought the guy might be Afghani. DuPont didn't know and didn't really care; what bothered him were the man's eyes, dark and probing and . . . *arrogant* was the word that came to mind. He wore no uniform but carried himself in front of the prisoners like a general, someone who would tolerate no disrespect, no rebellion. He stood inside the open doorway, fists on hips as he surveyed the captives. Then he pointed at the upper bunk where Ginger and Katie were seated and barked something in Arabic. Grinning through his scraggly beard, the guard stepped in, reaching up for Ginger's leg, his hand closing around her bare ankle. She screamed, pulling back from the edge of the bunk, kicking blindly . . .

"Just a goddamned fucking minute!" DuPont shouted, rising suddenly with a strength he'd had no idea he possessed. *"Get your paws off of her!"*

The guard, momentarily distracted, was holding his rifle casually with one hand, muzzle-down, and DuPont caught him by surprise. His wildly hurled fist connected with the side of the man's head and slammed him back into the bulkhead. DuPont whirled on the other man, stepping between him and the bunk. "I want to talk to whoever is in charge!" he shouted, his face inches from the Afghani's face. "You understand me? You speak English? I want to talk to the captain!"

The man spat something in Arabic. The guard was back, furious, his AK raised. DuPont didn't care. "I want someone who can talk to me in goddamn English!"

The guard swung his rifle, the butt connecting with DuPont's chest. Pain exploded through his body and he collapsed in a heap, gasping to draw breath.

The other men had roused however, and were moving forward, putting themselves between the women and DuPont. Kingsfield snarled something in Arabic, and both the guard and the Afghani blanched. As DuPont struggled to get back on his feet, the Afghani and Kingsfield snapped Arabic at each other, Kingsfield defiant, the other shaking with rage.

Suddenly, the Afghani turned, pulled the AK assault rifle from the surprised guard's hands, and brought the muzzle up to Kingsfield's head. Kingsfield grappled with the man, trying to grab the weapon, but the rifle fired, the shot detonating like a bomb blast in the tiny room, and the side of the American's skull literally exploded in a spray of blood and brain and chunks of bone that splattered like hurled paint across half of the bulkhead at Kingsfield's back. The former Green Beret dropped, rag-doll limp.

In the stunned and ringing silence that followed, the guard, his eyes so wide they looked like they were starting from his face, took his weapon back and aimed it at them, sweeping it back and forth in tight, nervous arcs. The Afghani, his arm and sleeve covered with

Kingsfield's blood, screamed something unintelligible at them all before backing out of the room. The guard backed out after him, and the door slammed shut.

Carle knelt beside Kingsfield, but it was all too clear that the man was already dead.

My God, what have I done? DuPont thought. *Now they're going to kill us all. . . .*

Control Room, USS *Virginia*
South of Honshu
Japan
1015 hours, Zulu –9

Virginia was under way once more, racing southwest at thirty knots on her way to her rendezvous with the Navy SEALs. Garrett slouched in his command seat, watching the view screen on the forward bulkhead with glum distraction. While ashore conferring with Captain Summers, he'd made a slight detour by the Navy exchange and tried calling Kazuko. He'd gotten her roommate, a woman who spoke only a few words of broken English, but who managed to convey the message that Kazuko was not home. "Kazuko go work," the woman had said over and over. "Kazuko go work." That meant she was working a flight. With a lot of patience and a lot of repetition, Garrett had finally learned that Kazuko had left that morning for a flight to Singapore. *Ichi-ichi-ni-go bin*—Flight 1125 if his rocky Japanese was working right.

Well, those were usually short layovers, a quick there-and-back. She'd be back in Tokyo in a few days. Maybe he could see her on the return leg of *Virginia's* deployment.

The trouble was, he didn't know how long that deployment was going to be. No one did, and no promises could be made. *Virginia* might be stalking mystery subs and poking around Chinese bases in the South China Sea for the next week . . . or for the next three months.

And in the meantime, Jorgensen was compiling a charming list of *Virginia*'s shortcomings and problems, and that meant trouble of a less personal and far more direct nature. *Virginia* was a brand new boat two times over—newly built, and the very first of her kind. Though she'd been on a pretty thorough shakedown under Commander Fitch, everyone had expected that more problems would surface.

They had. During the run south from the Bering Strait, no fewer than ninety-three separate electrical faults had been noted and logged, and some of them were in some pretty damned inaccessible spaces, way back in the depths of *Virginia*'s belly. The big galley freezer had quit working while they were under the ice; the galley crew had had to bring a small mountain of frozen stores on board at Yokosuka to replace the ones ruined by an unexpected thaw. A set of fluorescent light tubes in the passageway aft of the torpedo room had stopped working, and replacing the tubes had not fixed the problem. There was an electrical short in there somewhere, and the ETs hadn't been able to find it yet. More worrying than that, the port side broadband sonar was out. If the sonar boys couldn't fix it, *Virginia* would be half deaf.

"Captain?" Jorgensen was at his side.

"Yes, XO."

"Thought you should see this, sir."

He handed Garrett a clipboard with a sheaf of engineering reports and an extract from the troubleshooting log. Garrett scanned the entries quickly, flipping through the pages.

It was not pretty. The ET and engineering crew had traced more than half of those electrical faults to a single component—a thumb-sized computer chip identified by a long string of alphanumerics, and referred to as the "3C" for short. The chip was, in effect, a kind of electronic valve that determined when power flow through one set of circuits was approaching the system's tolerance levels, and shunted the flow to a parallel system. The idea was to prevent power overloads that could burn out circuits, and the system was used in literally hundreds of places throughout the *Virginia*, from sonar systems to cruise missile power-up circuits to communications relays to crew-space lighting and air circulation throughout the boat.

In these reports, Lieutenant Mizell, *Virginia*'s chief engineering officer, was pointing out that those chips were failing under voltage fluctuations well within their supposed tolerance limits.

"Shit, XO," Garrett said. "What are we dealing with here . . . lowest bidder?"

"Looks that way, sir. Eng is fit to be tied. He recommends yanking all of the 3Cs and replacing them with . . . well, he told *me* chewing gum and duct tape. And he says he would recommend using a Tomahawk on the production plant in California that made these things, but that the chips in the launch circuits would probably fail and the missile wouldn't fire."

Garrett gave Jorgensen a hard glance. "He thinks our weapons circuits are compromised?"

The exec shook his head. "Not completely. The buggers fail randomly and intermittently. He's saying . . ." Jorgensen reached over Garrett's arm and flipped through several pages, to a sheet giving the engineering officer's recommendation. "There. When we went in at Yokosuka, he pulled and tested a bunch of 3Cs, and says they're running about a 12 percent failure rate, but only when the voltage fluctuates above a certain tolerance. They work fine . . ."

". . . until they're used. Shit, XO, that's flat out UA. Unacceptable. You're telling me we have a one-in-eight chance of pushing a button and nothing happening. Or worse, a fire."

Of all possible casualties, the single greatest dread on board a submarine was *fire,* the demon dreaded more than crush depth, asphyxiation, or enemy action. An overloaded chip could cause a circuit to overheat. Overheat it enough, and a circuit breaker would cut in—theoretically. If the circuit breaker failed for any reason, fire was the inevitable result.

"That's about it, Captain. Eng recommends testing all of the 3Cs in stores to identify the bad ones, then pulling all the ones already installed and replacing them. Just to make sure."

"How long?"

"Two weeks at least."

"Two *weeks*?"

Jorgensen shrugged. "They have to run regular engineering duties, too. This is essentially extra-duty grunt work."

"Just how expensive is this little gem?" Garrett asked.

Jorgensen chuckled. "Eighteen dollars."

"Jesus. A billion-dollar sub crippled by an eighteen-dollar gadget you can probably buy off the shelf at Radio Shack."

"Well, that is the COTS philosophy. Screw up more for less money."

"Right. Okay, pass on to Eng that he can get to

work pulling those chips. Just keep me informed if he wants to shut down a critical system."

"Aye aye, sir."

This promised to be a long patrol indeed.

Aft enlisted head, USS *Virginia*
South of Honshu
Japan
1345 hours, Zulu –9

EM1 Kirkpatrick was furious. He backed Wallace up against the bulkhead, his livid face inches from Wallace's, and screamed, "Wallace, you are an A-1 fuckup, you know that?"

"Yes, sir."

"Don't goddamn call me sir! I *work* for a living!"

"Yes, s—" He stopped and tried again. "Yes, Petty Officer Kirkpatrick."

"You pull another stunt like you did this morning, Wall-eye, and I will have your balls for breakfast, you understand me?"

"Yes, uh, yes, I do."

"If we had a big school chalkboard installed on this boat, I would make you write one thousand times, 'I will not be a screw-up.' But we don't have a chalkboard, so you will scrub out the shitters instead. You will use your freakin' toothbrush if necessary, but you will get them to shine *and* you will scrub the urinals *and* the sinks *and* the shower head and *then* you will swab the deck until you can eat your goddamn corn-flakes off of it! Now get to work!"

The aft head on board the *Virginia* was about the size of a typical restroom in a McDonald's, with less privacy and more stainless steel—two open stalls, two urinals on the bulkhead, and two sinks. Kirkpatrick spun on his heel and left, leaving Wallace to face his task.

"Jesus, Wall-eye," a voice called from one of the stalls. "What did you do to piss *him* off?"

"Uh . . . I forgot to log out on my fire and security watch last night."

"Oops. Bad move, son." The hiss of the toilet being flushed sounded from the stall, accompanied by the distinctive and unmistakable stink of raw sewage. A moment later, Chief Kurzweil emerged, tucking his shirt into his trousers. "At least the head is brand new. You won't have to scrub hard."

That was true enough. Most of the stainless steel in the small compartment already gleamed bright in the overhead lights, and normal shipboard routine kept the place fairly spotless.

The insides of the commodes, though, were not gleaming. The smell made him hesitate at the door to the first stall.

"Pretty bad, isn't it?" Kurzweil said. "If they're ever able to build a submarine that doesn't let the stench in from the holding tanks, I will sign on for life, and personally kiss the designer."

"Isn't there a way to seal the septic off from the commode?" Wallace asked. "You know, a double door or something?"

"Negative. You know how the thing works?"

Wallace shook his head no.

"Pretty simple, really. You got your two ball valves—a big eight-incher at the bottom that lets the water and shit out of the bowl, and a small one that closes off a one-inch pipe bringing in sea water. You do your business, then yank that big lever to open the first valve, so a positive-displacement pump can move the shit into the sanitary tank. Then you close that, and use the other level to refill the bowl. Sealing it off would be a lot more complicated, a lot noisier, and a *lot* harder to keep clean. I can tell you, though, it's a lot better than it was on the old boats."

"Yeah?" Wallace walked to the storage locker and began pulling out brush and disinfectant.

"Yup. In the old diesel boats, you had to every so often air-load the sanitary tank—pump it up to 700 psi—to vent the waste overboard. They vented the air back into the boat—had to, so they didn't show any bubbles—and that meant one hell of a stink! The charcoal filters were supposed to take care of that, but they never really did the job.

"And heaven help you if you opened the main ball valve on a crapper when they were blowing sanitary! You could get a face-full at 700 pounds per square inch!"

Wallace was on his knees, scrubbing at the first toilet. "I guess it made a mess, huh?"

"A mess? Yeah, you could say that. Thing was, there was a way you could get even with someone you didn't like. There was this one engineering chief—a real asshole. Everybody hated him. He had this habit of yanking the ball valve open while he was still sitting on the throne, y'know? So some parties unnamed one day took the 'secured' sign off the door to the head when a sanitary blow was in progress. This chief walks in, does his thing, opens the ball valve while he's still sitting down, and whoosh! They say it was like a ping-pong ball shot up out of the throat of fuckin' Old Faithful.

"Of course then, certain parties unnamed had to scrub out the head, and that was *not* pretty. But man, oh, man, was it worth it!" He chuckled. "Too bad you can't do that to old Jerkpatrick, huh?" Kurzweil turned and walked out of the head then, whistling, leaving a thoughtful Wallace to his task.

Attack Submarine *Shuhadaa Muqaddaseen*
Southwest of Spratly Island
South China Sea
1715 hours, local time

After an unknown time, they'd come and dragged Kingsfield's body out of the compartment. DuPont had expected some further repercussion, but none occurred . . . not unless you counted the fact that no one brought them food or water for a *long* time after that. DuPont had the uneasy feeling that someone on this submarine was thinking hard about his captives . . . thinking about whether or not it was worth it to keep them alive.

DuPont, once his head had cleared, pounded on the locked door to the room, shouting as loud as he could that he wanted, that he demanded to see the captain, and someone, anyone, who spoke English. He was ignored, and at last he gave in to the pleas of his fellow prisoners. "Look, Mr. DuPont," Schiffer told him. "Up until now, they haven't hurt us. They've just kept us locked in here, and they *have* to, y'know? They can't let us wander around loose on a submarine! I say we go with the program, keep a low profile, know what I mean? Jesus . . . now that they've killed one of us, they might decide to do the rest of us, too!"

At long last, a pair of guards showed up, pointed their rifles at DuPont, and ushered him out into the passageway. This time, they turned him right, not left, marching him in the opposite direction from the head. A moment later, he found himself in a crowded, narrow hole of an office, standing in front of a cold-eyed man who, he guessed, must be the captain of this submarine.

"You are DuPont?" the man demanded.

"Yes, sir." There was no need to antagonize the guy, especially if he spoke English.

"I am Commander ul Haq, the captain of this vessel. I am told you wished to speak with me."

DuPont drew a deep breath. "Yes, sir."

"I cannot tell you how long you will be held, or anything of that nature, Mr. DuPont. Essentially, this vessel is at war, and war is filled with uncertainties. I regret that you have been inconvenienced, but that is the way things are."

"I understand that. But I do wish to point out that you won't have many hostages left if you keep all of us inside that closet where you have us now. We can hardly breathe, and the heat is making us sick. Three of the men are down with diarrhea, and could be on the verge of major dehydration. And I don't know how long you'll be able to keep the lid on, either."

" 'Keep the lid on?' What do you mean?"

"It means that the people in that room can't be held responsible for their actions." DuPont was warming to the cadence of his argument now. He'd faced some tough customers over boardroom tables more than once in his career. Now his life, and the lives of those with him, depended on his ability to negotiate from a position of weakness. "If you put too many rats in too small a box, Captain, after a while they start eating one another . . . and attacking anyone who comes close. They go crazy. That's what's happening in that box right now. That's why one of my people is dead."

"Ah. Yes. What was the man's name?"

"Michael Kingsfield. He was one of my employees."

"He should not have attacked the guard."

"The guy—not the guard, the *other* guy—shot him in cold blood, Captain! Kingsfield stopped the guard from grabbing one of the women. Then the other guy started shouting, and then the *other* guy shot him."

"Ah. I had not heard that version of events," ul Haq said. "Normally, I would have no reason to believe you, of course ... but I do know Noor Khalili. I gather, from Mr. Khalili's account, that your Kingsfield admitted that he was in Afghanistan."

"I don't know. They were both speaking Arabic."

"Kingsfield, I was told, said something about ... I believe the expression was 'killing Arabs in Afghanistan.' Noor Khalili is Afghani, Mr. DuPont. He lost family when your nation invaded his. He has ... how do you say it? A sword to grind?"

"An 'ax.' An ax to grind. Okay. He doesn't like Americans. The point is, Captain, that Kingsfield was trying to protect one of the women. He got into an argument with this Khalili guy, and Khalili murdered him."

"And ... what do you expect me to do about this?"

"Captain ul Haq, we are *your* prisoners, and that makes us your responsibility. You can decide to just kill us all and be done with it ... but if you want to keep us alive for whatever reason, you're going to have to attend to certain conditions."

"What conditions?"

"That closet you have us in is too crowded. You need to put us into at least three rooms that same size."

"That closet, as it happens, is the largest private living compartment on this vessel. It was shared by four of the senior petty officers on board. They must now sleep with the regular enlisted men, to make room for you."

"I appreciate that. There's no room on a submarine, I know that. But the fact remains, you have ten . . . no, nine, now. Nine people crowded into a room barely big enough for four. We do not have adequate ventilation, and the temperature in there must be over a hundred degrees."

Ul Haq smiled. "You exaggerate. It can scarcely be the temperature of boiling water."

"Oh. I was using Fahrenheit. Celsius would be . . . I don't know. Thirty? Anyway, it's so hot we're all close to collapse in there. And three of us need medical attention. I don't know, drugs . . . salt. I don't know what would help. But they're sick and need a doctor."

"We have no doctor on board." He looked thoughtful. "I cannot promise anything, but I will see what can be done. Anything else?"

"Yes. Privacy."

"Privacy?" Ul Haq's eyebrows crept high up his forehead. "On a submarine?"

"We have two women in there. They have no clothing and they can't even go to the bathroom without guards watching everything they do. I thought your Holy Quran taught you better than that! Is this how the Quran teaches you to treat helpless women? Is this what the Quran expects of an honorable warrior?"

Ul Haq's eyes flashed dark with anger. "You will not speak of the scriptures in that way. I will not be lectured on the tenets of the Quran by an infidel. . . ."

"Why not? Do you believe what it says about the treatment of your fellow man—*or woman*?" DuPont

was skating on very thin ice now. He'd never read the
Quran himself—there'd never been a reason to—but
he'd discussed it with an Islamic roommate in college,
once, and he'd had a class in comparative religion that
same semester. He remembered arguing that Islam encouraged the mistreatment of women. Ali, his roommate, had insisted that the Prophet had been a radical
and compassionate reformer where the rights of
women were concerned. He desperately hoped the
Quran backed that bit of information dredged from a
late-night college bull session thirty years ago because,
right now, he was shooting from the hip. "I mean no
disrespect, sir," he continued. "I simply ask . . . do
you live by the Quran? Or is the Quran just . . .
words?"

"I am a servant of Allah," ul Haq began.

"Then you know what your own religion says about
hospitality to strangers. And protecting women.
And . . . isn't there something in your religion about
Christians and Jews both being 'People of the Book?'
We are *not* 'infidels,' as you put it. In Allah's name, I'm
asking you, I'm *begging* you for help! We are being
treated like animals, and if this goes on we will die!
And then you will not have hostages for ransom or
whatever else you want out of us!"

He stopped for breath. Ul Haq sat behind his narrow desk, regarding him in silence for a long and
aching minute. DuPont forced himself to remain still,
and outwardly calm. Had he pushed too hard, said too
much?

"Do you believe in God?" ul Haq said at last. "Are
you Christian?"

"Yes, I am." Well, technically. He'd not been to
church since he was a kid, and the Sunday school lessons had never taken, as he liked to say. He wondered

if he needed a quick brush-up lesson from Schiffer.

"And those with you?"

"They're Christian, yes." He hoped none of the papers and passports these pirates had grabbed listed anyone's religion as Jewish. He didn't even know if any of them were Jews, but somehow he doubted that this Muslim's tolerance for other faiths extended to them.

Ul Haq nodded. "You are correct, Mr. DuPont. We do recognize the People of the Book, not as followers of Islam, but as . . . fellow travelers. However, there is very little I can do about the conditions you find yourself in. This is a *submarine*, a steel tube seventy-three meters long and less than seven meters high, with sixty men on board crowded into a space that would be cramped for half that many. We do not have private lavatory facilities for women—"

"Well, maybe you should have thought about that before you brought us all on board!"

"Would you prefer that I had left the women behind with the two Vietnamese we found on your boat?"

DuPont felt a cold chill on his spine at that. It was the first time anyone had hinted at the fate of Phuong and Nguyen. "No . . ."

"They would be dead now if we had done so. Mr. DuPont, I do regret your discomfort, but there is very little I can do. However, since you did ask in Allah's name, I will do what I can. I promise this, by Allah who is all-merciful. Is that sufficient answer to your . . . conditions?"

"I guess it will have to do."

"Very well. Good day, Mr. DuPont." Ul Haq nodded to the guard who'd been standing just outside the open door for the entire interview, and DuPont was led back to the room to rejoin the other captives. He knew *something* had just changed, that ul Haq had made some sort of key decision about the nine of them, but he wasn't certain what.

He hoped he hadn't just convinced the submarine's captain that his prisoners were more trouble than they were worth.

Tuesday, 6 June 2006

Control Room, USS *Virginia*
South of Oluanpi
Taiwan
0858 hours, Zulu –9

"Think they're here yet?" Jorgensen asked.

"They're SEALs," Garrett replied. "They're here. The problem is finding them in an invisible needle in a very large haystack."

Virginia had made good time coming south from her too-brief stopover in Japan. After taking on board additional supplies—including fresh fruit and vegetables for the galley and more frozen food to replace that lost when the freezer had gone tits-up—they'd continued south, rounding the southern tip of Taiwan to reach the spot specified in their orders. They were cruising slowly now at one hundred feet, waiting to make contact with the SEAL element designated Trident.

"So . . . what do we do? Hang out a 'welcome' sign?"

"Much as I hate to say it, we wait another minute . . . and then we go active."

Jorgensen made a face, and Garrett could sympathize. Submariners employed two distinct forms of sonar, their principal means of sensing what was in the ocean around them. *Passive* sonar was the act of listening. Most things moving around in the ocean were noisy, to one degree or another, and *Virginia*'s sensitive electronic ears could pick up a tremendous amount of information just by paying attention.

Active sonar meant sending out a loud, sonic chirp—the sound equivalent of radar—and collecting the reflected sound waves when they bounced back from a target. Active sonar was far more informative than passive—especially when your target was another submarine designed to be as stealthily quiet as possible.

But going active also meant broadcasting your existence and your exact position to every passive listener in the area, and that was something that submariners tended to regard as a decidedly unnatural act—kind of like a burglar shouting "Anybody home?" as he crawled in through the window.

Garrett was all too aware that this region south of Taiwan had recently been a combat zone. Three years ago, he'd brought the *Seawolf* into these waters, and taken on a small fleet of hostile attack subs, courtesy of the People's Republic of China. The PRC's new and growing fleet of attack submarines had been crippled in that exchange, but there was every reason to believe they were in the process of making a comeback.

Might there be PLAN boats lurking out there, listening for an American sub to go active? It was a distinct and uncomfortable possibility.

"Sonar, Conn."

"Go ahead, Conn. Sonar."

"Heads up back there, and ears on. We're going to go active in a second, and I want to know if you get so much as a twitching octopus as a response."

"Aye aye, sir!"

He checked the control room clock, which was still set to local time. Oh-nine hundred hours. . . .

"Sonar, Conn. Give me a ping. We're looking for an ASDS in this immediate vicinity."

"Conn, Sonar. One ping, aye. . . ."

ASDS-2
South of Oluanpi
Taiwan
0900 hours, Zulu −9

The sonar pulse struck the ASDS hull like a hammer blow, loud enough to leave ears ringing. Lieutenant Mark Halstead looked up and said quietly, "Right. They've got us."

"And close, too," TM1 Diller added. "That's good. I want out of this freaking sardine can."

EM1 Arthur Nemecek chuckled. "Yeah, but we'll be trading one sardine can for another. Let's just hope we get to stretch our legs a bit during the crossover!"

"Shit, Nemmie," Halstead said. "At least we're riding in style! It could be a lot worse."

"Roger that," Chief DiMercurio said, laughing. "You ever ride in a Mark VII?"

"Sure," Nemecek said. "In training."

"Then thank your stars this isn't training. You think this is cramped? This ain't *nothin'*."

There were eight other SEALs in the ASDS passenger compartment, together with their gear, and the quarters were indeed cramped. Designated as the Advanced SEAL Delivery System, the ASDS was essentially a large, blunt-nosed torpedo—sixty-five feet long, just under seven feet wide, and just over eight feet high. On-board crew-habitable spaces consisted of three compartments—the control room forward where the pilot and copilot ran the thing, a central lockout chamber, and the aft passenger-cargo space. Designed to carry up to sixteen SEALs—a full SEAL platoon—the passenger space was still claustrophobic with half that number, especially when they'd brought rucksacks and carry bags filled with weapons, ammo, and combat gear. They sat hunched over, side by side on the narrow, thinly padded bench, wearing their wetsuits against the possibility of an unscheduled swim, with their gear at their feet or piled up aft.

The best that could be said about the vehicle was that it was *dry*. Until the introduction of the ASDS only a few years before, SEAL underwater delivery vehicles had been wet, which meant that even in enclosed SDVs, the passengers needed to be fully suited up, and breathing either from their own scuba gear or from an onboard air supply.

Halstead had been in on some of the battles over wet versus dry SDVs early in his SEAL career, shortly after the first Gulf War. Navy departments, like all bureaucracies, tended to protect their own turfs, and ever since the 1960s, the submarine service had insisted that only they should own and operate dry submarines.

The SDV—the official acronym stood for "Swimmer Delivery Vehicle," but everyone uniformly referred to the vessel as a SEAL Delivery Vehicle—had been designed to carry up to eight SEALs silently and invisibly to their target, but their range was sharply restricted, partly by the limitations of their electric batteries, but mostly by the fatigue of the operators. Riding inside an enclosed, fiberglass hull was less tiring than swimming, but it was still uncomfortable and cold. The whole idea of the SDV was to preserve the strength and stamina of the SEALs riding it, extending their range and increasing their endurance. Wet transports simply could not protect passengers from the heat-sapping effects of the sea, or the physical stress of a long haul under water.

So the SEAL community had long been angling for a dry transport. They'd evaluated a number of possible machines; the Mark VII Mod 6 had been a dry version, but it carried only four SEALs, its endurance was limited to five hours, and it could only manage about seven knots, giving it an operational range—to the target and back—of only about fifteen miles. In any case, there'd been incredible political pressures against its adoption from the Navy Department's submarine contingent. Dry submarines belonged to the submariner service, damn it, and all SEALs should take note.

For their part, the SEALs insisted that SDVs should be operated solely by the Teams' Special Boat Squadrons. SBS crews were themselves SEALs, and so could be trusted to listen to SEAL concerns about a tricky approach to a target or a mission requiring tight timing.

Slowly, though, as the SEAL presence in the Special Warfare community had expanded during the '80s and '90s, a workable compromise had been reached, and the first ASDS had gone operational in 2000. A true minisubmarine built by Northrop-Grumman Ocean Systems in Baltimore, Maryland, it displaced fifty-five tons, could manage ten knots, and had a range of over 125 nautical miles. The political compromise turned out to be a simple one. The vessel's pilot and commander was a submarine officer, while his co-pilot and navigator—Halstead, in this case—was a SEAL officer.

The whole issue of who controlled what had first amused Halstead, then frustrated him. As long as the squad got to where it was going, he didn't much care who was driving . . . or which department at the Pentagon claimed the ownership, the credit, or the budget. The important thing was that the SEALs now at long last had a minisub that could get them and their gear to the target, if not in complete comfort, at least in full fighting trim.

Another sonar ping chimed through the bulkhead, louder this time. "Heads up, back there," Lieutenant Michaels called over the 1MC from the forward compartment. "We've got a lock on the *Virginia.* We'll be docking in five minutes."

"About freakin' time," HM1 Forrester said. "This is *not* my preferred means of travel."

"What is?" DiMercurio asked. "Jumping out of airplanes?"

Nemecek looked at his diver's watch. "Hell, we've been in this glorified coffin for three hours now. Right now, I'd take being wrapped up and shipped FedEx if it was faster." They'd departed at just past 0100 hours that morning from the Taiwanese naval base at Kaohsiung. Eight hours on that narrow bench was enough to drive anyone nuts.

"Hey," RM2 Pulaski said. "Is it true what they say about chow on submarines?"

"Abso-damn-lutely," DiMercurio said. "Best chow in the Navy. Best coffee, too."

"Yeah," Halstead added. "You just have to not

mind if the guy next to you at the table has his elbow in your ribs."

He felt the ASDS roll slightly to the left and accelerate, moving to a rendezvous in the darkness.

Control Room, USS *Virginia*
South of Oluanpi
Taiwan
0905 hours, Zulu –8

"There they are. Helm . . . thruster control. Hold us steady." Garrett could see the approaching minisub now, a dark-slate shadow like a huge, squared-off torpedo looming out of the surrounding blackness from astern. The camera in the Photonics mast captured the approach, transmitting the image to the big screen in the control room. Floodlights on the aft edge of the sail illuminated the silent incoming shape of the ASDS, barely discernible against the black backdrop of the ocean one hundred feet down.

Like the docking of a smaller spaceship with a larger in some science-fiction epic, the minisub gentled down toward *Virginia*'s afterdeck, aligning itself with the circular rim of the forward escape trunk hatch. A soft thump echoed through the *Virginia*'s control room as the ASDS settled home and the docking collar sealed.

"ASDS docking complete," the dive officer said. "Docking collar secure and locked."

"Mr. Jorgensen?" Garrett said. "Perhaps you'd like to welcome our guests on board. See that they're settled in—torpedo room."

"Right, Captain."

A few moments later, Jorgensen led the SEALs in through the control room. All, Garrett saw, were big, massively muscled men—young, hard, and imbued with an almost palpable air of quiet and deadly competence.

"Welcome aboard the *Virginia*, gentlemen," Garrett said.

"Thank you, sir," one of the men replied. He appeared to be the leader of the group, though none wore emblems of rank. "Good to be aboard."

"I'm Captain Garrett."

"Lieutenant Michaels, sir," the man said. "This is my SEAL opposite number, Lieutenant Halstead."

"My XO will see that you're bunked in properly, show you where to stow your gear. If you need anything, see him."

"Yes, sir."

The line of SEALs filed through the control room, on their way down to the torpedo room. A closemouthed lot, Garrett thought . . . though the ASDS commander, Michaels, would be a submarine officer rather than a SEAL, at least so said the protocol for those odd little hybrid beasts.

Garrett had worked with SEALs before. Submariners, he'd long ago decided, had much in common with the SEALs. SEAL training was more brutal than submariner training, while submarine school was far more technical than the SEALs' BUD/S program, but both groups were as tight-lipped as clams when it came to talking about themselves or what they did, and both groups were consummate professionals.

And, like submariners, the SEALs were *very* good at what they did.

It meant some crowding, but he was glad to have them on board.

Japan Airlines Flight 1125
Above the South China Sea
1540 hours, Zulu −8

Kazuko Mitsui couldn't wait for the flight to be over. She'd been on some bad flights, but this one was the worst ever. The drunken lawyer in G-3 reached out and groped her ass. "Hey, baby! Come sit with us!"

Somehow, she maintained her plastic smile as she spun out of the lout's grasp. *Be nice to them*, she thought. *You must be* nice *to them. Bastards!* . . .

JAL ran several special flights down to Bangkok, designated informally as sex-weekend specials. They were especially popular with Japanese businessmen— men usually quite devoted as husbands and fathers back home, but who enjoyed taking a weekend "business trip" every once in a while to the fleshpots of Bangkok, where for a price you could party in nightclubs much wilder than any on the sex strips of Tokyo or Kyoto, have your choice of girls-for-an-hour or for-a-night or for-the-weekend, or even take to bed a couple of twelve-year-olds of either sex.

Flight 1125 had originated in Tokyo, flown to Singapore to pick up some more businessmen in that repressed but cosmopolitan hub of commerce, then gone north to Bangkok, carrying a raucous cargo of vacationing men all eager to sample the fleshpots over a *very* long weekend, one extending all the way through to Tuesday. Now, the flight was headed back to Tokyo, again after a stopover in Singapore. Some of the men were still sampling, and it promised to be a long and difficult flight home.

Kazuko walked to the front of the main cabin and began helping the other flight attendants with the liquor wagon—the big cart filled with drinks of various descriptions, snacks, plastic cups, and ice. She heard a yelp and turned. Miko, another stew, had just been pawed by the same man who'd grabbed her. She met Miko's gaze but the other just rolled her eyes and shrugged. Another day on the job. Together, Kazuko and Miko began passing out drinks, moving slowly down the aisle.

She was thinking of Tom. She'd been thinking about him a lot these past few days.

Kazuko was beginning to realize that she still loved the tall American submariner, that she'd loved him ever since she met him during the time he'd been stationed at Atsugi. She'd been pretty hard on him during their last phone conversation. Damn it, she still couldn't see a long-term future for the two of them when he was at sea for such long stretches of time.

Stretches that never seemed to match up with the long periods when she was working overseas flights.

Another explosion of bawdy laughter from the back of the aircraft made her shake her head. The behavior of some of the passengers embarrassed her, and reflected badly on Japan Air Lines. Some of the passengers—that sweet family in Row K, for instance—had nothing in common with these international booze-and-sex-party junkies. The flight must be a nightmare for them.

She was beginning to wonder if the answer might not be for her to quit her job, move to America, and marry Tom.

Of course, at this point she didn't even know if he would have her. She'd been pretty rough on him, after all. But he had promised to try to visit when he was in Tokyo. Maybe, on the way home from this deployment . . .

Attack Submarine *Shuhadaa Muqaddaseen*
Thirty kilometers northeast of Singapore
South China Sea
1550 hours, Zulu −8

Ul Haq leaned against the combing along the edge
of the small weather bridge atop the sail, reveling in
the cool and blessed feel of the wind against his face.
After hours breathing the stink of a submerged diesel
boat, it was good to taste the clear, clean salt air once
more.

He was glad of the chance to give the batteries a
good, long recharge, but even happier at the chance to
feel clean wind on his face again. The day was bright
and hot, the sea glassy and smooth. No other ships
were visible, no aircraft, nothing but the unvaryingly
crisp line between sea and sky in every direction.

But, because he was captain of a submarine, and because submarine captains worry about such things, he
still was anxious. *Shuhadaa* had been running on the
surface for a dangerously long time, now, and the
chance that the submarine would be spotted on the
surface was considerable.

They had come now over a thousand kilometers
from their starting point at Small Dragon Island, and
they were no longer within the Spratly Islands. Just
thirty kilometers to the southwest lay the southern tip
of Malaysia, and the city of Singapore.

After today, *Shuhadaa Muqaddaseen* would begin
making her way back to the northeast. She needed to
refuel and to replenish onboard consumables. But she
had come this far to the west in search of a particular
target. According to the Maktum, and information ra-
dioed that morning from Zaki, that target was approaching *Shuhadaa*'s position at that very moment,

and approaching fast, at a speed of nearly seven hundred kilometers per hour. But the target had yet to appear on radar.

Had Zaki been wrong about the timing? How long should he wait, risking detection on the surface in broad daylight, before submerging once more? Zaki had also reported the imminent arrival of an American aircraft carrier battlegroup, and that meant American submarines and American antisubmarine aircraft.

How long before they were within range?

"Captain!" sounded over the speaker on the weather bridge. "This is the radar room!"

"Go ahead."

"Sir, we have a target, airborne, bearing two-zero-one, range twelve kilometers! Altitude two thousand meters."

This was it. "Very well. Sound battle stations! Weapons! Stand by surface-to-air!"

This was it. . . .

Japan Airlines Flight 1125
Above the South China Sea
1551 hours, Zulu –8

"What's that?" someone screamed from the port side of the aircraft. An instant later, a savage bang rocked the cabin, and Kazuko and Miko both were thrown to the deck. The aircraft dropped into a sharp roll to the left, sending the drink cart toppling into seats and passengers caught in its path.

Things happened too quickly for Kazuko to sort them out. Something was terribly, terribly wrong with the aircraft—she knew that—but exactly what the problem was she couldn't tell. It *felt* as though the port engine had fallen off, leading to a sharp wing-drop to port. Was that possible? . . .

She tried to see out the port-side windows, now below her and behind screaming passengers and cascading drinks and ice. It looked like a fire; she could see the flicker and glare of yellow light.

Then the aircraft began tumbling wildly, and Kazuko fell into the ceiling. The drink cart followed, crashing down on top of her, along with Miko and a number of passengers who'd not been belted in.

She was fortunate to lose consciousness then. She was not aware of the burning airliner's long, long fall into the sea. . . .

**Attack Submarine *Shuhadaa Muqaddaseen*
Thirty kilometers northeast of Singapore
South China Sea
1556 hours, Zulu −8**

Ul Haq watched the pillar of smoke rising from the western horizon. The target, JAL Flight 1125, had been hit by a single surface-to-air missile fired from the single-rail vertical-tube launcher in the aft part of the submarine's sail and brought down into the sea. The Pakistan navy had paid a great deal extra for that little technological trick; most Russian Kilo-class submarines built for export didn't have a built-in SAM.

The *Shuhadaa* did, however, and the Maktum had plans for its use. Why struggle with slipping a bomb past airport security, when a Stinger anti-air missile or a SAM fired from a submarine launch tube could do the job just as well? This new SAM design, especially, was deadly—a heat-seeking missile that could strike a target at an altitude of up to five thousand meters. The original Russian design had been strictly for last-ditch and desperate defense against incoming air. The new design was considerably larger, fired from a tube inside the sail itself. No longer was the weapon strictly for self-defense. The only restriction was that the target be low enough to hit, which meant the attacking vessel needed to get close enough to the airport to engage the aircraft before it climbed above five thousand meters.

In Pakistan, ul Haq had seen plans for having a Kilo-class submarine patrol off the southern approaches to Long Island on the American East Coast, along the incoming traffic lanes for JFK International Airport. A suicide mission, perhaps, for the submarine and all on board, but the air lanes there were so busy that a skillful skipper might down four or five jetliners before other aircraft were routed away from the scene, and the American Navy closed in for the kill.

He wondered if he would volunteer for such a mission. So many civilians, men, women, children . . .

Isn't there something in your religion about Christians and Jews both being "People of the Book?" We are not "infidels."

Somehow, he could not shake DuPont's words from his mind.

"Request permission to join you on the weather bridge."

Ul Haq looked down in surprise. The Chinese attaché, Hsing, was looking up at him from the ladder below the sail's round hatch.

"Of course."

Hsing clambered the rest of the way up into the cockpit. "I watched the kill on radar," he said. "An excellent shot."

"We can thank our Russian friends for the technology," he replied. "Little skill is required with a heat-seeking missile."

"You are aware, of course, that the Americans will be far more upset by this attack than at the destruction of Amboyna Cay."

Ul Haq nodded. "The Vietnamese can be seen as provocateurs on the world stage," he said. "But the passengers on that jet . . ."

"How do you justify that, Captain? I understand Khalili and even Zaki. But you seem to be . . . more reasonable."

"I am a follower of Islam . . ."

"So am I," Hsing said. "Ah, that surprises you? There is a sizeable population of Chinese Muslims, especially in the western parts of my country."

"I knew you were Muslim," ul Haq said. "But I assumed that you had joined *Shuhadaa Muqaddaseen* because of your orders, not because of your faith."

"It was more because of the Americans. My brother was killed three years ago in a battle for our Taiwanese province."

"Ah." Ul Haq nodded. "I see. You and Noor Khalili have much in common then."

"I find the man a thoroughgoing psychotic. He is too . . . intense. A fanatic. He lets his fears and his hatreds lead him, not his head."

"I see. And you are guided by your head?"

"In part. And by a determination to see the American imperialists stopped. They seem to feel they now own the world, with the right to intervene in the internal politics of other nations any time, and anywhere, they please."

"Ah. I see." He nodded. "That, I suppose, is why I am here as well."

"It can be lonely, standing against a colossus."

"And it can be rewarding when you strike a solid blow."

"And how do you feel, Captain ul Haq, about the fact that the blow you struck just now was against several hundred innocents on board that airliner?"

He thought about it a moment. The question had been bothering him for some time, he knew, but he'd not allowed himself to face it.

"There *are* no innocents," he said at last. "We are in a war, on the side of Allah, blessed be His name, against the decadence and greed and corruption of the West. Those not actively with us are legitimate targets. Those who do not help us are the enemy."

That, at any rate, was the party line, parroted in full from one of the handbooks of the Maktum.

He thought again of DuPont using the Quran against him, and wondered if he truly believed what he'd just said.

Tuesday, 6 June 2006

Control Room, USS *Virginia*
South of Oluanpi
Taiwan
2034 hours, GMT/shipboard
1234 hours, Zulu −8

"Captain? A general flash just came in over the SAT-COM. You might want to punch it up."

"Right." Garrett pressed the message-waiting icon on his touchscreen, and read it with a dawning, pit-of-the-stomach horror.

TO: ALL US NAVAL UNITS, WESTERN PACIFIC
FROM: FLEET ACTIVITIES, YOKOSUKA
RE: TERRORIST ATTACK
WARNING ORDER.

I. BE ADVISED THAT US MILITARY RESPONSE/

READINESS LEVELS IN THE WESTPAC THEATER HAVE BEEN RAISED TO LEVEL 2.

2. AT APPROXIMATELY 0730 HOURS ZULU, JAL AIRLINES FLIGHT 1125 WENT DOWN OVER THE SOUTH CHINA SEA, WITH NO SUR-VIVORS. SATELLITE RECONNAISSANCE OF THE AREA AT THE TIME SUGGESTS THAT THE CAUSE OF THE CRASH WAS A SAM LAUNCHED FROM A KILO-CLASS SUBMARINE OF UNKNOWN ORIGIN AND NATIONALITY.

3. BECAUSE OF RECENT HOSTILE ACTS IN THE SPRATLY AO, BOTH JAPANESE AND U.S. OFFI-CIALS ARE TREATING THIS AS A TERRORIST ACT, THOUGH MILITARY ACTION BY PLAN FORCES CANNOT YET BE RULED OUT.

4. U.S. MILITARY FORCES IN THE WESTPAC THE-ATER ARE INSTRUCTED TO BE ESPECIALLY VIGILANT. THE CURRENT HOSTILE ACTIVITIES IN THE SPRATLY AO MAY BE THE FORERUN-NER OF A GENERAL TERRORIST ASSAULT AGAINST WESTERN OR JAPANESE INTERESTS THROUGHOUT THE REGION.

5. U.S. SHIPS IN PORT ARE INSTRUCTED TO MAINTAIN MAXIMUM SECURITY READINESS AGAINST THE POSSIBILITY OF TERRORIST ATTACKS VIA SMALL BOATS, TRUCK BOMBS, OR SUBMARINE ATTACK.

SIGNED
C. MONTGOMERY, ADMIRAL
CO FLEET ACTIVITIES
YOKOSUKA

. . . all of which was a cover-your-ass set of orders if Garrett had ever seen one.

Fifty-five years after Pearl Harbor, the whys and wherefores of American military preparedness in December of 1941 were still hot topics at Annapolis and other U.S. military schools. Of special interest was the fact that numerous warnings had been sent to the Hawaiian Islands shortly before the Japanese attack, but those warnings were either so vague or so badly worded that no solid preparation was possible. In fact, a warning about the hazards of sabotage by Japanese civilians living in Hawaii at the time resulted in Army aircraft being parked closely together in order to better guard them . . . which, of course, made them perfect targets for the Japanese naval air assault of December 7.

Unfortunately, the lesson learned from the incident appeared to be that warning orders such as this one were best used to shunt responsibility to the Other Guy. *Hey! I did my duty and sent out a warning! It wasn't my fault!* The order conveyed almost zero useful information in a military sense.

The news of Flight 1125's destruction, though, had an intensely personal meaning for Garrett.

Kazuko had been on that flight . . . at least that was the number her roommate had given him when he'd called her from Yokosuka. Kazuko! Had she been on that plane?

The terrible fear growing in the pit of his stomach told him that it was true, that she'd been on that flight. A part of his mind wanted to cling to hope; perhaps she'd been ill or delayed in Bangkok or Singapore, and missed her flight.

But the cold and rational part of himself could only

see the fact that Kazuko was almost fanatical in the pursuit of her duties. Once she'd refused to take sick leave and worked a Tokyo-to-Calcutta flight with a 101-degree temperature—a violation of company rules, incidentally, but a fair indication of how stubborn she could be.

And determined.

Yes, she'd been on that flight, and now she was dead. *Kazuko!* . . .

The fact that she'd told him she was leaving him meant nothing now. They would have gotten back together, he was certain of that. They would have worked something out. Hell, Garrett wasn't going to stay in the Navy forever. He had no interest in seeking flag rank, and doubted he would achieve it in any case. He didn't have the political connections. He could have retired in another few years, retired and lived anywhere in the world that suited him. And Kazuko wouldn't have stayed with JAL forever, either. They'd talked, once, about the two of them retiring one day and meeting halfway—literally—in Hawaii.

A long time later, he lay in his quarters, the door locked to keep the bustle and routine of the submarine at bay. The XO had the chair, and here there was time to lie down on his bunk, time and quiet to think.

Not, Garrett thought, that thinking was a particularly good thing to do just now.

A military man lived by plans. Op orders, sailing orders, duty rosters, plan-of-the-day, all were means by which the military life could be organized and channeled, so that individuals—from the 153 men on board the *Virginia* to the hundreds of thousands of officers and enlisted personnel Navy-wide—all could pull together, working as one.

What Garrett was now acutely aware of was the

need for a plan for his own life. Every time he started to get things squared away for himself, it seemed, someone would come along and kick him in the balls. Each time he thought he knew where he was going, it turned out he wasn't going that way at all.

Damn it, life ought to be more than reacting to what other people did. Ever since Claire had left him, he'd struggled with the idea of taking control of his own life.

He was the captain—the man in control—of the most modern attack submarine in all the arsenals of the world. Why couldn't he control his own life?

He recognized that pang of self-pity as the onset of a depressive episode, placed his hands over his face, and groaned.

He'd been dealing with moderate clinical depression for several years. Hell, depression was an occupational hazard for submariners. You had to be borderline crazy in the first place to voluntarily lock yourself away from the sun and stars in a steel sewer pipe deep beneath the surface of the ocean. Too-close quarters, too tightly regimented a life, too few outlets for normal relaxation or play, these things demanded men who could handle a lot of stress. All too often, though, stress turned to anger, and anger was turned inward, suppressed, buried, because there was no way on board a Navy submarine to release that anger when it first flared hot.

And anger suppressed in that fashion swiftly metamorphosed into a cancerous, soul-devouring depression.

The Navy handled the problem in a typically Navy way. Men with severe depression could not hold command, of course, and all command personnel were subject to periodic psych evaluations. Enlisted men were expected to report unhealthy behavior in their shipmates. Classes and awareness seminars were mandated for personnel on shoreside rotation. Garrett had never seen any figures, but he'd heard that the submariner service accounted for more doses of Prozac and other antidepressants than any other department in the Navy.

The antidepressants weren't helping now. At least, he sure didn't feel like they were. He felt as though he could barely move.

He was angry—at himself and at the service. He'd totally blown it with Claire; she'd left him because he was never home, never there when she needed him, and he'd not been able to balance his career in the Navy with the demands of a life at home.

And he'd blown it with Kazuko. He'd hoped to be able to get her to change her mind, to convince her that he could change, that he *would* change, that this time he would find a way to strike that improbable balance between husband and submarine commander.

But now, Kazuko was dead and he would never have the chance to tell her what he thought, what he wanted, what he'd dreamed for both of them. She'd died thinking he didn't care, thinking that he loved the Navy more than her.

Maybe she'd even died hating him. It was so easy to imagine that.

Damn, I'm an idiot. . . .

There was no way to release the anger he felt at himself. All he could do was hold it, control it . . . and feel it shifting to a self-loathing depression that pinned him there to his bunk.

He felt, too, as though he were balanced between two paths. Slip one way, and he would drop into an abyss of self-pity, surrendering everything he'd built in his career so far—his command, his reputation, the trust of those both below and above him in the hierarchy of rank. Go the other way, and he would suck it all up, deal with it, *suppress it*, and continue to function as he always had.

The first choice was so enchantingly easy. Hell, he could call up Jorgensen on the private internal comm channel right this moment and formally relinquish command. Hell, do it now, before Doc Colbert had to do it for him!

He reached for the microphone in its cradle on the bulkhead next to his bunk.

And stopped.

No . . .

The other choice was a lot harder. But he also knew from experience that the blackness and self-doubt were temporary. He could command an attack submarine.

He could, he *would* command himself.

Attack Submarine *Shuhadaa Muqaddaseen*
Northeast of Pulau Luat
South China Sea
2225 hours, Zulu −8

The *Shuhadaa* was racing along on the surface at twenty knots, running parallel to the northwest coast of Borneo, which lay some five hundred kilometers over the horizon to the southeast. Ul Haq was taking advantage of a heavy cloud cover that had rolled in over the area at sunset. Weather reports were calling for a storm over the entire Spratly region, and he wanted to use the cover clouds and rain would provide—protection from the all-seeing eyes of American spy satellites. Already, the wind had freshened and the sea had begun picking up. The wind was blowing out of the northeast now at twenty knots, and the waves were beginning to join one another in long, rolling swells capped by white horses and scatterings of spray.

Ul Haq stood alone on the sail's weather bridge, wrapped in a plastic hooded poncho, feeling the wind blast against the exposed skin of his face. Salt spray stung out of the darkness. *Shuhadaa* was plowing directly into the teeth of the wind, which made for rough sailing. The narrow hull of the submarine pitched and yawed and rolled with each passing swell, with waves surging across the forward deck and exploding around the narrow, upthrust barrier of the sail.

He'd considered submerging; even with a full gale blowing on the surface, at fifty meters the sea would be as calm as the inside of a fishbowl. But ul Haq had decided to stay on the surface as long as he possibly could. He wanted to give *Shuhadaa*'s batteries a chance to recharge to full, which was only possible when she was running on her diesel engine. The submarine *could* run her diesel while submerged, drawing in air and venting the poisonous exhaust gases through her snorkel, but running on the snorkel was a compromise that would not help the situation. At snorkel depth, *Shuhadaa* would still be subject to the pitching embrace of rough seas, her airway would intermittently be blocked by breaking waves, and no snorkel system was 100 percent effective. The stink of diesel fuel and exhaust fumes would fill the boat, compounding the misery of seasickness and sharply reducing the efficiency of the crew.

Better to run on the surface, with the diesel fully venting topside and fresh air freely available through the boat's deck intakes. Later, the storm might become so rough that he would *have* to submerge, and when that happened, he wanted a full battery charge to give him a minimum of ten to twelve hours at depth. In the meantime, the fresh air blowing from the bulkhead vents below helped combat the seasickness, and cleaned out the mingled stinks of diesel fuel and vomit—a little, anyway. No man lasted long as a submariner if he didn't have a *very* strong stomach.

"Captain? Captain!"

He looked down at the open sail hatch in the deck beneath his feet. The face of Lieutenant Saad al-Muhabi peered up at him through the circle of the hatch combing.

Ul Haq squatted on his haunches, sheltering his ears from the roar of spray and wind so that he could hear. "What is it?"

"The prisoners again, sir. They say they're dying, that their sickness is worse."

"They will have to make do."

Al-Muhabi looked worried. "Captain, with respect . . ."

"What?"

"Sir, there's talk among the crew. They say you're torturing the Americans. The cabin they're locked in . . . sir, it's a hellhole. It is an affront to Allah, the merciful."

"And what do they suggest that we do, Lieutenant?" he replied. "Throw them overboard?"

"Sir, that might be the kindest thing we could do."

He shook his head. "Our orders are to bring them to Zaki. The leader, DuPont, may have value for the movement."

"If there were only DuPont, there would be no problem, sir. But keeping so many locked in that compartment . . . Captain, we could at least put the women overboard. They are *only* women, after all, and their treatment is inflaming the other prisoners, and some of the crew as well."

Al-Muhabi, ul Haq remembered, was Saudi, with the conservative Saudi's belief that women were of less worth than men. As a Pakistani Muslim, ul Haq had a somewhat more liberal view. Women might not be as intelligent or as powerful as men, he believed, but they were still *people*, not things, not property.

"All have value in Allah's eyes, the men and the women both," ul Haq replied. "The Prophet himself, blessings on his name, declared that women deserve just treatment. It is our duty to keep *all* of our guests safe."

He thought for a moment. Between the diarrhea and the vomiting, the senior petty officer's quarters must indeed be a hellhole by now.

"Detail extra men to keep watch on the prisoners," he said. "See that they have access to the sanitary facilities every hour, and permit them to shower if they wish. Have someone who speaks English tell them that they will be allowed up on deck for air as soon as this storm is past. That might give them something to look forward to."

"Yes, sir."

"Maintain a guard of two men at the door."

"I do not believe our 'guests,' as you call them, are going anywhere, Captain."

"No. The guards are there to keep out members of the crew who may wish to take advantage of the women . . . or of the men, for that matter. And two guards allows one to watch the other."

"It almost sounds as though you trust the Americans more than you trust your own crew. Sir."

"I *know* my crew, Lieutenant. They are men, with men's weaknesses. And they will see the helplessness of our guests as an invitation to take advantage of them. I will not have that."

"Yes, sir."

"In any case, they will not be on board for much longer. We will be rendezvousing with Zaki on our way back to Small Dragon Island."

The other nodded. "That, of course, is the best solution, sir. There is no room for prisoners on board a submarine."

"I agree. Please check with the navigator on watch and get me an expected time of arrival at Waypoint Alif." That was the agreed-upon location, some two hundred kilometers south of Spratly Island, where they would rendezvous with Zaki's yacht.

"Yes, sir." Al-Muhabi ducked back into the hatchway, vanishing down the ladder.

Ul Haq stood up again, drawing a deep breath, savoring the sting of spray on his face.

He was eager to make that rendezvous. He'd talked personally to Zaki over the radio the night before, discussing with him the problem of the prisoners. One or two prisoners could be cared for easily enough, and might indeed have served the purpose of providing a human shield against enemy retaliation, but only if that enemy knew they were on board.

But communicating that fact to the world, enabling them to use the prisoners as an onboard deterrent to attack, was problematical in the first place. And in the second, it was clear that the presence of those prisoners—especially the women—was affecting the morale and the performance of his crew. He needed to get them off the submarine as quickly as he could.

At worst, he would take them back to Small Dragon

Island. *Shuhadaa Muqaddaseen* needed to refuel and
replenish her provisions. But the fact that Zaki was
supposed to be near Point Alif for the next several days
would let him offload them that much sooner.

"Captain?"

Al-Muhabi was back. There was an intercom
speaker on the sail's weather bridge, of course, but it
could be difficult to hear in this kind of wind. He
squatted down again, the better to hear the man.
"Yes?"

"The navigator says—if we can maintain twenty
knots—fifteen hours."

He nodded. "Excellent." By one o'clock tomorrow
afternoon, the prisoners would be someone else's
problem . . . thanks be to a merciful Allah.

Control Room, USS *Virginia*
180 kilometers northwest of Point Mayraira
Luzon, Philippines
1140 hours GMT
2340 hours, Zulu −8

"Captain?"

"Yeah."

"Weps wants permission to take the weapons systems off-line."

Garrett looked up, meeting Jorgensen's gaze. The
direct eye contact was almost more than he could
stand, and he looked back down at the touchscreen on
his board. "Why?"

"He's swapping out some of the 3Cs in the firing circuits. Remember?"

Garrett looked up again. He'd heard the worry in Jorgensen's voice. Had he done something or forgotten something to trigger the XO's concern?

This time it was Jorgensen who first broke the uncomfortable eye contact, checking something on the clipboard in his hand. "The swap-out's on the sched, sir. You approved it."

"Yes, XO. I remember." He sighed. "Sorry, Pete. Woolgathering. My mind was somewhere else."

"Not a problem, sir."

"He's sure the swap-out won't leave us toothless for more than twenty-four hours?"

"That's what he says, sir. Although there's always the unexpected."

"*That* is God's own fucking truth."

Jorgensen started at that, and Garrett realized how tightly wound the man was right now. Garrett rarely, if ever, used profanity, and his sailor's talk must have caught the exec off guard. Or had it been the intensity with which he'd said it?

It didn't matter. He was going to have to watch himself more closely, keep a tighter rein on the emotions galloping through his brain. It wouldn't do to let his officers or the crew know just how shaken he was.

"The People's Republic is still right off the starboard beam, XO," he said. "And we still don't know what their intentions are, what they're up to. I'm a bit nervous about entering the South China Sea without torps or Tomahawks."

"Same here, Captain. But we agreed that it made more sense to take both systems off-line at the same time, so that we have both when we reach the Spratlys."

"I know. Pass the word to the sonar boys, would

you? I want an extra sharp set of ears out in these waters." Jorgensen didn't answer, and Garrett pressed him. "What?"

"Sir, we're traveling at forty knots. Sonar can't hear shit at that speed."

"It is my intention, XO, for us to come to dead slow every . . . make it every two hours, so that sonar can have a good listen around and we can clear our baffles."

Jorgensen visibly relaxed. "Ah. Aye aye, sir."

Garrett had covered his slip. The truth was, just for an instant, he *had* forgotten that sonar couldn't hear a damned thing when they were moving at full-ahead.

His hastily improvised coverup actually made sense, though. If a Chinese sub did spot them and try to follow them south, a periodic clearing of the baffles—a maneuver in which *Virginia* would make a full circle in order to give sonar a chance to "see" the sonar-dead space astern of the boat—should pick it up. And by slowing to take sonar readings every couple of hours, they could create a kind of rough sketch of the water traffic around them, enough to alert them if major surface traffic was closing on their position.

But the fact of the matter, Garrett reminded himself, was that he *had* slipped up, and that was something no captain could afford. *Damn!* he thought with a white, savage fury. *What's happening to me?*

"Have Weps and his boys get on it, XO," he said.

"Aye aye, Captain."

Maybe I was right. Maybe I should step down now, Garrett thought. *Relinquish command. Jorgensen's good. He'd get the job done.*

His momentary lapse had shaken him. Everyone makes mistakes, forgets something, gets momentarily confused, has a brain fart, as he'd heard it so eloquently described . . . but when the commander of a submarine had a brain fart, people could die. He had no business remaining in command if he could not keep his mind and his heart focused on the task at hand.

There was, at the same time, a deep and very human part of Garrett that refused to give up the chance to strike back, directly, at whoever it was that was blowing up ships and aircraft in the South China Sea. Whoever it was who had killed Kazuko.

There was one thing, Garrett had discovered long ago, that could relieve the depression when he feared it might be getting out of hand. Not a cure, by any means, but a worthwhile distraction.

Work. He would concentrate on the command of the *Virginia,* and forget about Kazuko.

At least for now.

Sonar Room, *Yinbi de Gongji*
160 kilometers north of Huangyan Dao
South China Sea
2348 hours, Zulu −8

"There, sir. There it is again."

Captain Jian pressed the headphone tight against his right ear, eyes closed as he listened. It had been a few years since he'd stood a sonar watch, but the old skills never completely deserted you. He ignored the sonar screen with its cascade of green light and slanted lines, each line representing the movement of a different contact out there in the abyss around them. No, to hear, to *really* hear a faint and distant contact, was to shut out the visual, to turn one's mind inward, and to reach out with an entirely different sense altogether.

He could hear the soft rushing rumble of the ocean itself, the click and squeak and clatter of its denizens. And there . . . just at the threshold of hearing, the faintest hint of a pulsing hiss.

"What is your estimate?" he asked the sonar officer.

"This contact is not in our data banks, Comrade Captain. However, it sounds to me much like one of the American *Seawolf* submarines . . . but moving at extremely high speed."

"You would not hear it at all if it was *not* moving at high speed," Jian said. "They say a hole in the water is noisy by comparison." He listened a moment more. "I'm surprised we picked up this much. What do you think the range might be?"

The sonar officer shook his head. "Sir, we were extremely lucky to catch this. It is almost certainly a convergence zone contact."

"I see. So . . . fifty kilometers . . . or one hundred . . . or one hundred fifty."

"Or possibly two hundred. Yes, sir."

"Very well. Stay on the contact."

"Yes, sir. We have designated the target as *Ch'ien* Nine-five."

Jian left the sonar room and made his way to the main navigational table at the rear of the control room. Elsewhere, *Yinbi de Gongji*'s crew sat or stood at their stations, attentive to their duties and all too obviously trying to ignore the presence of the submarine's captain close by. He said nothing. If nervousness made them even more attentive, so much the better.

Yinbi was currently cruising northwest at a depth of three hundred meters, her position currently at approximately 16° North, 117° East, 160 kilometers north of the tiny island of Huangyan Dao, and 300 kilometers west of the Philippine island of Luzon. She was trailing her towed array, which gave her an uncannily sensitive ear on the ocean to port and to starboard. And she'd picked up that whisper of sound on her starboard side.

Convergence zones were a freakish effect of depth and pressure on sound waves. A submarine captain couldn't count on them, because often the conditions to create them simply didn't exist.

Here, though, they did. *Yinbi* was crossing the abyssal plain known as the South China Sea Basin, a tongue-shaped depression in the ocean floor between Vietnam and the northern half of the Philippine Islands with depths as great as 4,500 meters. Huangyan Dao interrupted the basin at its eastern end. To the north and to the south, like the two halves of a fish's tail, a deep trench embraced the island of Luzon just off its west coast; the northern part of the trench served as a kind of highway extending from the shallow waters of the Luzon Strait between Luzon and Taiwan, and the main part of the basin.

The point was the basin's depth. Below a couple of thousand meters, the ocean's pressure was so great that it actually served to deflect sound waves, bending them back toward the surface. In a convergence effect, the sound from, say, a fast-moving submarine would hit the high-pressure water and bend up, then hit the surface and deflect down, to be bent up again by the water pressure. The sound waves were focused at specific, clear-cut intervals—usually every fifty kilometers or so—which meant that *Yinbi* could detect the other submarine when it was fifty kilometers distant, or at any multiple of fifty kilometers out to a range of four or five times that distance. Once the target moved a little closer, *Yinbi* would lose it. But, if they were lucky, they might pick it up when it entered the next convergence zone, fifty kilometers closer. Jian suspected that the topography of the sea floor—that long, slightly curving trench running toward the north and northeast—was serving as a deep sound channel, creating the convergence-zone effect and also giving him a good idea of the other vessel's exact course.

It was Jian's intent to close with that target, and find out what it was.

Was *Ch'ien* Nine-five an American *Seawolf?* Very possible. Very possible, indeed. Chinese Naval Intelligence had already informed him that elements of the American Seventh Fleet were en route through the Luzon Strait, no doubt to provide an intervention force, if necessary, in the Spratly Islands. American attack submarines, like the *Seawolf,* would most likely precede that force.

And one of those attack submarines would be the target for this entire operation—that and one of the American supercarriers.

Tempting targets indeed, but targets that required extraordinary skill and luck to stalk and kill.

Jian knew he had the skill.

All he needed was a small bit of luck . . . and that sonar contact just might be the luck he was looking for.

Wednesday, 7 June 2006

Flying bridge, yacht *Al Qahir*
Waypoint Alif
South China Sea
1412 hours, Zulu −8

"What in the name of Allah is going on over there?"

The man who now called himself Zaki Abar lowered his binoculars and gave the young man standing next to him a sharp look. "Do not swear upon the name of Allah, glory be to Him."

Muhammad Jabarrah gave Zaki a sour look. "Not all of us share your . . . *intense* interest in religion. That does not mean we do not share the same devotion to the cause."

Zaki sighed. He'd learned long ago that a certain amount of latitude was necessary in dealing with the wildly diverse range of beliefs within the far-flung army of the Islamic jihad. There was a powerful temptation to see the alliance as monolithic, a united army of God, holy and righteous, marching together beneath His holy banner of jihad. That mistake was common enough in the West, and especially in the United States, where the activities of groups like al Qaeda and Maktum were seen as representative of Islam as a whole.

In point of fact, however, most Muslims cared little for politics, or for the struggle between the faithful and the West. One key purpose of Maktum was to educate the faithful worldwide, to show them that the decadent American giant could be brought down as the prophet Dawud had brought down the giant Goliath. America could be fought, could be *defeated* with the help of Allah, praise be unto Him. Within the ranks of the movement itself there was an astonishing array of belief and practice—Sunnis and Shi'ites, Sufis and Ismailis, puritanical Wahhabis and reform-minded Ahmadiyas—and even those individuals like Jabarrah who seemed to have no faith, no belief in Allah at all.

The unbelievers, the mere fact of them, bothered Zaki at times, but he'd long ago decided that the best course was to leave their souls in the hand of Allah, blessings upon His name. There was little Zaki himself could do to argue them into paradise, and too stringent an insistence upon observance of the *sharia* might even drive such men from the movement.

And Maktum desperately needed fighters such as Jabarrah, men with a fanatic's hatred of America and the West, but with the cold, hard, calculating minds of born killers.

So Zaki said nothing, raising his binoculars to his eyes once more, and studying the long, low shape of the submarine surfaced ahead.

There was a heavy swell running beneath a slate-gray sky—the precursor to the fast-approaching storm system. The waves were high enough to almost entirely obscure the submarine's deck, though the bluff, sharply rectangular conning tower rose above the dark water like a cliff.

It was the *Shuhadaa Muqaddaseen*, obviously enough, its hull such a dark gray as to appear almost black. There was no flag above the sail, and no number on the hull; one of the PLAN subs in the region would have been flying the bright red flag of the PRC.

Through the binoculars, he could see a number of people on the sub's forward deck. They appeared to be a ragged lot, most without shirts, some completely naked, none in anything like a uniform. They appeared to be bathing, squatting or standing on the deck and using sponges and buckets of water to wash themselves down. Several uniformed men stood nearby, armed with assault rifles, so Zaki assumed that these were the prisoners Captain ul Haq had told him about over the radio.

"It would appear," Zaki said after a moment's study, "that those are our new guests. It looks like they're having a seawater bath."

"Do you seriously think it a good idea that we take them aboard? We don't have the facilities to care for prisoners."

"And you believe a submarine does?" Zaki chuckled. "Believe me, my friend. They will think their quarters on board *Al Qahir* palatial compared to what they had on the *Shuhadaa Muqaddaseen*."

"It was not their comfort I was thinking of," Jabarrah replied. "It was the difficulty of guarding several hostages. And it was particularly the danger of holding hostages. If the Americans find out—"

"And how are they supposed to find out?" Zaki asked with a shrug. He glanced up at the solidly overcast sky. "This rendezvous was specifically arranged to take advantage of this approaching storm. The American spy satellites cannot see through a solid cloud deck."

"You underestimate their technology."

"And you fear their technology as if it were magic. It is not. Remember the lesson of Vietnam. Remember the Russians in Afghanistan."

During the war in Vietnam, a poor and tiny country, with few technological assets, had managed to hold the American tiger at bay for ten years, and ultimately to wear him down to the point that he'd given up. In Afghanistan, the Soviet giant had been defeated by a handful of the faithful, mujahedin armed with antique weapons and a few hand-me-downs from the Americans. A crafty, determined, and dedicated fighter could always outlast the giant, no matter how imposing his arsenal of military toys.

"I remember," Jabarrah said, nodding. "And I also remember the Americans in Afghanistan . . . and in Iraq. They have learned their lessons from Vietnam very well indeed, and we cannot stand up to them face-to-face and survive. They have technologies to see in the dark and to see through storms. It *is* magic, of a sort. And it is a magic that your reliance on Allah will not be able to balance."

"All things are possible for Allah, the powerful, the compassionate, the all-knowing," Zaki said. "And all things are possible for those who trust Him. All the technology in the world could not withstand His wrath."

Jabarrah turned sharply, eyes blazing. "Yes? And where was His wrath when the Americans descended upon Afghanistan? Where was His wrath when their aircraft and missiles and smart bombs found our bases and our headquarters and our training camps and our arsenals and reduced them all to flaming debris and shattered bodies? Where was His wrath when their Special Forces came, digging us out of our caves and mountain redoubts? Where was His wrath when they overthrew the Taliban and imposed the rule of their puppets on the nation?"

"Gently, my friend. I am not your enemy." Zaki was about to say something about the ways of Allah being mysterious, but decided against it. Jabarrah, he knew, had lived in Afghanistan for many years, had had two Afghani wives and a son who'd fought for the Taliban. Both wives had been killed during the bombing of Kandahar; the son had been missing since the American assault on Tora Bora, had probably been one of thousands buried alive inside one of the caves during the bombings there.

Jabarrah, Zaki thought, had every right to be bitter. What he didn't yet understand was that it was useless to blame Allah for the murders of his family, that sometimes the ways of Allah *were* beyond human comprehension. All Zaki could do with such a man was to exercise patience, and trust that Allah would bring him back to the true faith in the end.

"I have no answers for you, my friend," Zaki said simply. "I do not know the mind of Allah. But I do know that the Americans, though powerful, are *not* Allah, and do not have His power."

Jabarrah gave Zaki a scornful look. "They could have one of their Los Angeles or Seawolf submarines thirty meters away from *Al Qahir*, right *there*." He pointed at an empty path of ocean off the yacht's port side. "It could be lying in wait, lurking just beneath the surface, watching every move we make, perhaps listen-

ing to our very words, and you would never even be
aware of it!"

Zaki sighed. "If that is true, why should we even
bother to continue the fight? Why not simply give up,
assume that Allah has abandoned us, and flee while we
still have our lives?"

Jabarrah looked away, silent for a long moment. "I
suppose it comes down to wanting to take as many of
the Westerners with me as I possibly can before I am
overwhelmed. *Vengeance*. I want to kill them for what
they did to me and my family!"

"My friend, if you cannot trust Allah just yet, then
have trust in me, and in your brothers within Maktum. We have resources, and we have knowledge that
you don't know about. You *will* have your vengeance.
Believe me. But for now, you must learn trust, and you
must learn patience."

Al Qahir was drawing much closer to the submarine
now, close enough that the prisoners on her forward
deck were easily visible without binoculars. Two of
them, he saw with a small start of surprise, were extremely beautiful women wearing skimpy swimsuits.
That must have made life interesting on board the submarine.

Crewmen on the *Shuhadaa Muqaddaseen* were rig-
ging fenders—large tires tied to lengths of mooring
line and suspended from deck cleats along the curving
side of the submarine's hull. Sailors tossed lines across
the narrowing gap of water between the two vessels
and, as *Al Qahir*'s pilot briefly reversed engines, then
shut them down, they gentled the yacht up to the submarine's side and made her fast. It took a few minutes
to rig a brow—a boarding gangplank reaching from
the submarine's aft deck to the yacht, an evolution

made difficult and dangerous by the surging waves. The task was accomplished at last, however, and an armed, black-bearded man in a Pakistani naval lieutenant's uniform waved them aboard.

"You are Zaki?" the lieutenant asked as he stepped off the pitching and shifting uncertain footing of the gangplank.

"I am."

"Lieutenant Daulat," the man said. "Come with me, sir."

Zaki followed the man to the submarine's forward hatch, bracing himself to descend through the narrow tunnel down through the deck into stygian darkness, then ducking out through a stoop-through into a harshly lit world of green-painted steel, claustrophobic ceilings covered by pipes and bundled wires, and men. Ul Haq was standing by the gleaming column of the periscope tube.

"Hello, Captain."

"A pleasure to see you, sir. Be welcome on board."

"Thank you. I . . . saw the packages you have for us up there." He pointed at the overhead. "The ones you want us to take off your hands."

Ul Haq's voice dropped to a whisper. "I need them off this vessel, Zaki. They are disrupting morale and harming the efficiency of my command."

"So your report stated. Very well. We can take them back to Small Dragon Island for you, I suppose."

"Excellent. *Shuhadaa Muqaddaseen* is on her way there now for reprovisioning, but we will be much better off without the prisoners."

Zaki looked bemused. "Your submarine has a speed of . . . is it twenty knots?"

"Yes."

"And *Al Qahir* can manage perhaps twelve. You would get the prisoners to safety more quickly if you kept them with you."

"One of the prisoners has already been killed," ul Haq told him. "The conditions in which we must keep them are . . . not good. I fear more will die if they stay on board the *Shuhadaa Muqaddaseen.*"

"You show compassion for the weak, the helpless, and even for the infidel. The Prophet would approve, I suppose."

"This is not a matter of compassion, Zaki. It is a command decision I make for the good of my vessel, and for the good of my men. The prisoners all are topside at the moment, bathing and washing out their clothing. I would appreciate it if you could transfer them directly to *Al Qahir.*"

Zaki nodded. "I understand. It will be done." He stopped, blinked, and looked around the close confines of the control room. "In the name of Allah the merciful," Zaki said, his eyes watering, "why does it stink so in here?"

"If you were a submariner," ul Haq replied, "you would know, and understand."

Control Room, USS *Virginia*
200 kilometers southeast of Huangyan Dao
South China Sea
2017 hours, Zulu –8

Garrett studied the glowing screen of the chart table, scowling. According to the slowly moving line of green light across the various shades of blue on the map, *Virginia* was making good time, but as she moved into the Spratly AO, he needed to make some decisions about where to begin the mission.

His orders gave him a fair amount of latitude. He was required to check out Small Dragon Island with the help of the SEAL element on board, and he was supposed to try to track down and investigate an eighty-foot yacht wandering somewhere in all those hundreds of thousands of square miles of atoll-speckled ocean.

There was also the small matter of the renegade submarine causing so much havoc in the Spratly Islands. And beyond.

Kazuko . . .

But where to begin? The Spratly Area of Operations encompassed something like a quarter of a million square miles of mostly open ocean, an area roughly the size of the state of Texas, made treacherous by submerged reefs, coral atolls, and extensive and largely uncharted shallows.

His first inclination was to head west, probing the region around Spratly Island, and out beyond in the direction of Singapore. The renegade sub was out there somewhere, and he wanted to find that vessel with all the hunger of a desperately starving man.

But it had been over twenty-four hours since Flight 1125 had gone down; a Kilo-class sub could be anywhere within 500 miles of the shoot-down point—a tiny and hard-to-find target lost somewhere within an area of some 780,000 square miles. It would be useless to simply charge in and start looking. *Virginia*'s sonars were the best, most sensitive sub-borne arrays in the world, but the Kilo, when operating submerged and on her batteries, was one of the quietest submarines in the world.

There was an old adage in the service, however. *To*

catch a submarine, you use a submarine. Attack subs like the *Virginia* were the natural enemy of hostile subs, designed specifically to hunt them down and destroy them. And the point was not only that Virginia had the equipment for that kind of hunt, but that her skipper had that kind of mind.

A *hunter's* mind. A mind that knew how the enemy sub's skipper thought, and could use that information to hunt down the quarry.

And what Garrett's hunter mind was telling him now was that a Kilo-class submarine on an ocean deployment would most likely be at the far end of her patrol leg if she'd left Small Dragon Island and ended up at the place where Flight 1125 had gone down. Her captain would want to take on more fuel for the boat's diesels, and fresh food for the crew. What were the possibilities?

Not Vietnam, certainly. If the reports were true, this Kilo was knocking off Vietnamese targets in the Spratlys. Vietnam would be the Enemy.

Most likely would be a submarine tender . . . a large ship equipped to resupply, rearm, refuel, and reprovision a submarine at sea. There were no intelligence reports of such a vessel in the area, however. Further, if that Kilo was trying to maintain a low profile, something as big and as highly visible as a sub tender would be a definite liability.

Which left some other land port or base.

A port in Indonesia was a possibility, but the only destination that made sense was Small Dragon Island, which had featured prominently in the earlier intelligence reports on activities in the region. It was possible that one of the other Chinese-held islands was equipped to restock the Kilo . . . but the CIA reports on Small Dragon suggested there was a kind of a hangar blasted into coral rock, a garage, if you will, large enough to accommodate a couple of submarines, with channels and approaches deep enough that the subs could enter the base submerged.

Garrett was willing to bet his career that the pirate Kilo was headed toward Small Dragon Island, on the eastern fringes of the Spratly Island group close by the Palawan Passage.

That was where *Virginia* would begin her hunt. If the Kilo wasn't at Small Dragon now, she soon would be . . . and *Virginia,* and Garrett, would be ready.

A chime sounded. "Captain? Comm," a voice called over the map screen's intercom function.

"Yes?"

"Message in from Yokosuka, sir. VLF band, priority urgent."

Virginia was currently trailing an antenna from her sail that enabled her to pick up VLF signals while submerged. That limited his speed to less than twenty knots but enabled him to stay in touch with the outside world. "Let me see it."

He walked back to his command chair and sat down, pulling up his touchscreen and tapping open a message window. The message, brief and to the point, scrolled across the screen.

TO: USS VIRGINIA, SSN 774
FROM: FLEET ACTIVITIES, YOKOSUKA
RE: RENDEZVOUS

1. YOU ARE HEREBY DIRECTED TO PROCEED AT BEST SPEED TO RENDEZVOUS POINT HOTEL AT N12°56.51', E115°48.29'. VIRGINIA IS EXPECTED ON-STATION BY 1930 HOURS ZULU, 07 JUNE.

2. ONCE ON STATION AT POINT HOTEL, VIR-
GINIA IS TO SURFACE AND REMAIN SURFACED
IN ORDER TO MAKE CONTACT WITH COMPANY
PACKAGE VIA AIRBORNE EXPRESS.

3. COMPANY PACKAGE WILL BRIEF CO VIRGINIA
ON RECENT DEVELOPMENTS.

SIGNED
C. MONTGOMERY, ADMIRAL
CO FLEET ACTIVITIES
YOKOSUKA

A company package? That could only mean someone from the Agency—the CIA—and that, Garrett
thought angrily, could only mean trouble. The fancier
the electronics, the better the communications net, the
more damage some REMF back in Washington—or
Langley—could do through ass-stubborn micromanagement. *Damn!*

However, orders were orders, and *Virginia* had a
rendezvous to make. He glanced up at the control
room clock, which had been reset at Yokosuka to reg-
ister *local* time, now Zulu −8, as opposed to GMT.
The time was now 2020 hours local, but that was
1220 Zulu—Greenwich Mean Time. He had a bit
over seven hours to get to the rendezvous point which
was—thankfully—only about three hours from *Virginia*'s current position.

"Navigation Officer! Set a new course. Come right
to two-zero-zero. Comm, reel in the wire and prepare
for thirty knots."

They would keep that rendezvous, but the "company package" had damned well better stay out of the
way.

Sonar Room, *Yinbi de Gongji*
200 kilometers southeast of Huangyan Dao
South China Sea
2025 hours, Zulu –8

"*Ch'ien* Nine-five is making unusual noise, Captain."

Jian nodded, looking over the shoulder of the sonar officer. The sound trace for the target was faint, almost lost in the background noise of the ocean, but it *was* there. "What is it? What do you hear?"

"I'm not sure, sir. It might be an electric motor . . . some kind of winch. There's a kind of intermittent metallic scraping sound. It could be a cable being pulled into the target."

"Let me hear." He accepted a sonar headset and listened for a moment. Yes . . . there it was . . . a faint, almost undetectable fluttering sound, a faint whir, and the occasional clunk and scrape of metal on metal.

Jian nodded, then handed the headset back. "He's drawing in his low-frequency antenna. Perhaps he's received new orders."

VLF radio signals—those on the EM spectrum from about 3 to 30 kilohertz—could penetrate the ocean to a depth of about fifteen meters. A submarine could pick up those signals by traveling very close to the surface, or by trailing either a wire antenna or a loop antenna buoy.

It was fortunate that the target was streaming an antenna, for what Jian was attempting to do would not otherwise have been possible.

Stalking the American submarine was itself an exercise in extreme frustration. The *Yinbi* could manage a top speed of about twenty knots—perhaps a bit more. The American submarine could reach thirty easily, and once had apparently touched almost forty. That made trailing the American more than a little difficult.

Fortunately, the American wasn't running at full speed all the time and, as he entered the waters that embraced the Spratly Islands, he'd begun moving more sedately, streaming the antenna in order to receive radio signals from his headquarters.

The faster a submarine ran, the more noise it made. Even one of the ultraquiet American boats left an acoustic signature when they burst into a sprint. When this one was moving at thirty knots or better, it was difficult—but possible—to track him.

But, of course, at such speeds the American sub would swiftly leave *Yinbi* behind. Fortunately again, however, when the American streamed his VLF antenna, the cable vibrating as it moved through the water produced a unique sound—not loud, but loud enough and distinctive enough to allow *Yinbi* to track him. When *Yinbi* had first picked up the American, he was traveling deep and fast; six hours ago, he'd slowed to less than twenty knots and begun streaming his antenna.

At times, too, the American slowed even further— probably so that his sonar operators could take a careful listen around. At those times, the American appeared to simply vanish off *Yinbi*'s screens, but was then moving so slowly that Jian could close on the target's last-known position.

It was important to stay behind the American—"in his baffles," as the expression put it. The *Yinbi* was extraordinarily quiet herself, but Yankee sonar technology was capable of picking Jian's vessel up if he made the slightest mistake.

And so, *Yinbi* pursued the American in a series of alternating sprints and rests. The enemy was averaging a speed of about eighteen knots overall, which meant that *Yinbi* could stay with him if his own slowdown periods for listening were kept to a minimum. The task was made easier—a little easier, at any rate—by the fact that the American had been maintaining a more or less straight course for the past twenty hours. Each time *Yinbi*'s sonar lost him, it was easy to estimate his position with the assumption that he was still traveling south, but at reduced speed.

It was made more difficult—and deadly—by the fact that each time the American slowed, he became effectively invisible. When that happened, there was a chance that *Yinbi*, sprinting toward the last-heard position at twenty knots, would run right into the American from behind. Operating solely on passive sonar, there was no way of knowing either the target's exact depth or its range.

"Winch noise has ceased, Captain. He may be preparing to speed up."

If so, *Yinbi* might well lose him this time. Jian had been able to stay on the target's tail so far only because the American had been trailing that antenna. If he was going to sprint again, he would almost certainly get away.

"Captain!" the sonar operator snapped. "Target changing aspect!"

Jian picked up the microphone for the sub's intercom system. "Maneuvering! Come to dead slow!"

He studied the sonar screen. Sure enough, the long, straight line barely visible against the hash of background noise was now slanting toward the right—an indication that the target had changed course and was now registering on sonar receivers along *Yinbi*'s side, and not solely from dead ahead.

It was possible that the American was clearing his

baffles—moving in a large circle to allow his sonar operators a chance to listen for pursuers in his wake. At such times, all the hunter could do was go dead slow and silent.

"Target is maintaining new aspect, Captain. He appears to be coming to a new course . . . I make it between one-nine-five and two-one-zero."

So he wasn't clearing his baffles, but changing course. That made sense, if one assumed that the target had just received new orders over the VLF antenna.

However, if he was about to begin a high-speed sprint, he would swiftly leave the Chinese submarine far behind.

"Target is picking up speed," the sonar officer reported. He reached up and touched his headset, pressing it tighter against his right ear. "I'm having trouble . . . Sir, the target has disappeared."

Jian had already seen the slanting line on the screen growing fainter. Now it was gone, lost somewhere in the ocean ahead.

Yinbi's captain scowled. "Keep listening. Inform me if you pick up anything."

"Yes, sir."

Still scowling, a black and introspective expression that kept his subordinates at bay as effectively as a high stone wall, Jian returned to the control room. Which way should he go?

His orders were reasonably specific. His *first* target was any American aircraft carrier that entered these waters. Other PLAN submarines were supposed to be in the area, ready to track and kill American attack subs, to, in effect, keep American submarines away from Jian's command while he stalked and killed the supercarrier.

Jian, however, was an opportunist. American attack

submarines were notoriously difficult even to find, much less track. Picking up this one had been pure luck, thanks to the convergence zone west of the island of Luzon, and the fact that the target had been trailing a VLF antenna for the past few hours had given him an excellent opportunity both to hear the American, and to keep up with him. There were no American super-carriers within the horizon of *Yinbi*'s sonar yet, and the sub he'd been trailing represented a target almost as tempting.

So the question now was . . . did he extrapolate the American's new course and attempt to follow? Or did he break off pursuit, radio the target's last-known po-sition, course, and speed to headquarters, and hope the other PLAN subs could find it?

He'd not been able to close yet to an effective attack range; when he did, *Yinbi* would need to score a kill with her first salvo, because she would not get a sec-ond chance.

Jian, however, was confident of his own abilities, and of those of his crew. There was a good chance that he *would* be able to pick up the American again, espe-cially if he began streaming an antenna once more. The alternative was to return to his patrol area north of Huangyan Dao, and wait for a supercarrier to show up.

He thought about the choice for only a moment.

"Maneuvering," he said. "Bring us to a new head-ing . . . two-zero-three. Ahead flank."

If the American submarine presented him with the opportunity, Jian would kill it.

Thursday, 8 June 2006

SH-60H Sea Hawk Bravo Five-one
Approaching Rendezvous Point Hotel
N12°56.51', E115°48.29'
South China Sea
0350 hours, Zulu −8

" 'Next time, Jack, write a memo.' "

That line from a well-known submarine movie of a few years back, or something much like it, had lately become something of a mantra for John Stevens. The officer from the terrorism branch of the CIA's Directorate of Global Affairs said the words again to himself with a grim smile as he flew through the wind-and-rain-lashed darkness on board one of the Navy's heavy-lift transport helicopters. He'd loved that movie when he'd first seen it years ago as a young Green Beret officer. He'd never expected to *live* it, however.

264

At the moment, he was balanced more or less uncomfortably on one of the hard, fold-down seats on the Sea Hawk's cargo deck, scarcely able to move. He had traded his Washington pinstripes for a wetsuit with rubber boots and gloves, a lightweight helmet, an inflatable life jacket, and a harness securing him to a length of white line coiled carefully on the deck and secured by heavy clasps. A waterproof document case was strapped to his thigh. The wetsuit trapped his body heat so that he was sweltering in its close embrace.

The Sea Hawk's crew chief stood over him in the red-lit compartment. "Can you hear me okay?"

It was hard to hear above the roar of the massive, seven-blade rotor, but the crew chief's bellow carried. Stevens nodded.

"Okay! Skipper says we have contact!" The man held up a gloved hand, showing his widely spread fingers. "Five minutes!"

Stevens nodded again. His hand touched the document case for perhaps the hundredth time that night, reassuring himself that it was still there.

The trouble was, this adventure had begun with a memo . . . and it was not something that his superiors cared to broadcast by radio, even coded. They'd flown him first to Yokosuka, where he'd arrived after *Virginia's* departure and just before the shoot-down of Flight 1125. There'd been talk of trying to have him rendezvous with the submarine south of Taiwan, where the *Virginia* was supposed to pick up a SEAL element, but the timing had not allowed for that. Instead, he'd been put aboard a C-2 Greyhound, a COD aircraft—COD standing for Carrier On-Board Delivery—and been flown out to the deck of the USS *Franklin D. Roosevelt*. The *Roosey* currently was part of CBG-8, traveling west through the Luzon Strait north of the Philippines en route to the Spratly Islands.

And from there, two hours ago, he'd been bundled up in the wetsuit and life jacket and put on board the Sea Hawk. They were going to attempt an at-sea transfer.

Normally that wouldn't have been much of a problem, but the weather had turned foul in the past twenty-four hours. Right now, most of the Spratly AO was blanketed in a thick storm—rain and lightning and high-gusting wind—and the fact that it was still the wee hours of the morning didn't help one bit. The SH-60H was equipped with night-flying gear, Stevens knew, but even the best technology could be easily confounded by Mother Nature.

Despite the storm, they'd apparently made contact with the *Virginia*, which meant she was on the surface and waiting for him somewhere up ahead. Stevens began taking long, deep breaths, trying to quiet the panic he felt.

John Stevens had begun his career in the Army, almost twenty years earlier, and after making sergeant he'd been accepted by the Special Forces, the Green Berets of song and legend. He'd resigned after sixteen years in the service, ten of them as a Special Forces operator. The politics of peacetime conflict were tougher to face than incoming hostile fire, and in the drawdown after the Second Gulf War he'd decided to call it quits.

However, the contacts he made with the Company—the CIA—had stuck with him, and when they'd offered him a job with the agency he'd agreed. For a time, he'd trained new recruits at a secret facility outside of Williamsburg, Virginia, the "Farm," but later he'd been transferred to a desk in Langley. He'd thought he would be there for the rest of his new career.

But when the director of DGI had needed someone with specific elite military experience—the sort of experience that trained men to do crazy stunts like jump into the ocean out of a helicopter flying through a raging storm—Stevens had volunteered. He still wasn't sure why.

Maybe he'd just wanted to get back in the field, back in harness once more.

He tugged at the harness and the lifeline. Yeah, he was in harness all right. Next time, *don't* send a memo. Get someone else in the office to do it!

The crew chief jerked a gloved thumb upward. Clumsily, he got to his feet, using a handrail to stay upright as he moved toward the open side door.

Wind shrieked and shuddered beyond the door, though it was impossible to tell how much of that was the helicopter's rotor wash, and how much the storm. The rain, whirled by the prop wash into a fine mist, wet his face, and glowed a bright blue-white in the glare of the helicopter's external lights. Leaning against the side of the door and looking out and down, he was appalled at first to see nothing but glare and darkness. Only after several wind-blasted moments could he make out the vague shape of something in the water below—a long, lean shadow rolling in the swell.

Another helo crewman stood by the door, loading a weapon that looked like one of the old, Nam-era thumpers, a stubby shotgun with a barrel as long and as thick as his forearm. Instead of inserting a round at the breach, however, he was adjusting the fit of a blunt harpoon secured to the other end of the safety line attached to Stevens's harness.

The crew chief tapped his shoulder. "Your vest will

inflate when you hit the water!" the man shouted into his ear. "Just relax and let them do the work, okay?"

He nodded, not trusting himself to speak. It had been *way* too long since he'd done this sort of thing.

As a Green Beret, he'd trained for helocast missions, launching himself out of a low-flying helicopter into the ocean, sometimes at night. It was a fast, slick way to insert a squad into a coastal area.

It was also dangerous.

The SH-60 was easing its cumbersome bulk closer to the water, and Stevens could see the submarine more clearly now, a black rectangle erect in a wind- and spray-blasted sea. He thought he could see figures on the deck in front of the sail, made visible by bright orange life jackets, but he couldn't be sure.

The man with the thump gun took aim and fired, sending the harpoon arcing down through the darkness, the white safety line unraveling behind it. In more traditional maneuvers at sea, in a technique that went back six hundred years at least, a rope could be passed from one vessel to another by attaching it to a "monkey's fist," a length of heavy cable knotted into a ball that could easily be thrown from one ship across the deck of the other. The thump gun and harpoon served the same purpose here, sending the line falling through the night and across the deck of the submarine below. Closer now, Stevens could see the crewmen on deck scrambling to grab the line and begin reeling it in.

The crew chief unfastened the clips on the coil of line and tossed it into the night. Stevens now stood on the SH-60's cargo deck with the other end of the safety line in the hands of the sailors below. "Good to go!" he shouted, clapping Stevens on the back.

Stevens took a final, quick mental inventory, then launched himself into the dark.

The prop wash from the SH-60 pressed him down like a giant hand, and, despite his best efforts, he felt himself begin to tumble. If he became tangled in his safety line, he might easily drown. Training asserted itself, however. He crossed his legs, folded his arms across his chest, and tilted his head as far forward as possible, a posture designed to keep the water from blasting up his nose with explosive force when he hit. For a dizzying moment, he was suspended between glare and darkness. . . .

He hit the ocean, plunging deep, the jar of the impact hammering his body. For a moment, he thought he'd been driven too deep . . . but his life jacket, a model designed for aviators to inflate automatically in case the wearer was unconscious, popped into reassuring fullness, first slowing, then halting his descent. The impact had blasted the breath from his lungs, but only a few seconds passed before his head broke above the waves again, and he pulled down a deep and satisfying chestful of wet, salt-laden air.

Above him, the helicopter was all but invisible, a dim shadow masked by the twin suns of its landing lights illuminating the ocean below. Its prop wash actually flattened the waves around him, creating a vast circle of wind-blasted relative calm. Turning in the water, he could see the black wall of the submarine's sail perhaps thirty yards away, towering against the night. He felt a hard tug at his harness; sailors on the submarine's forward deck were pulling in the safety line now, dragging him toward the sub. He remembered the crew chief's injunction and relaxed, letting them do the work.

He guessed it would take them five or ten minutes to drag him on board.

Control Room, *Yinbi de Gongji*
N12°58.05', E115°50.86'
South China Sea
0358 hours, Zulu –8

"Up periscope!"

The gleaming tube of the main periscope rose in front of Captain Jian; he snapped down the handles and rode them to the full up position, pressing his eye to the eyepiece and walking the scope in a full-360 as it cleared the water.

Nothing. Darkness and rain, with waves periodically surging over the periscope like dark blankets. The range was still fairly long—estimated now at 6,100 meters. On a clear, sunlit day with a flat sea, he might have been able to see the target at that range, but on a night such as this—not a chance.

He wanted to confirm the sea state, however, and check for nearby ships or aircraft that sonar might have missed.

"Down scope. Weapon status."

"Tubes one, two, three, and four loaded, Captain. Tubes dry. Outer doors are closed."

"Very well. Prepare to fire tubes one, three, two, and four, in that order. Target is *Ch'ien* Nine-five. Set for acoustical homing."

"Torpedos one, three, two and four set for acoustical homing, Captain."

Jian took a deep breath. He was gambling everything here . . . but opportunities such as this one rarely presented themselves.

If the sonar evidence was to be believed, *Ch'ien* Nine-five was now on the surface six kilometers away. There were numerous unidentifiable sounds out there as well, but the sounds of waves breaking over a hull riding on the surface, the clatter of cables or ropes on a deck, and the hiss and rumble of a ship's propeller straining to keep the vessel on-station in a rough sea were unmistakable. Jian's best guess was that the target had either surfaced to rendezvous with a helicopter—possibly to take on supplies—or because of some problem on board, fire or reactor failure. It seemed madness to perform a supply operation in this weather, but *Yinbi*'s sonar had not picked up any of the characteristic sounds of an emergency, and he could think of no other reasonable explanation for the target's behavior. American attack submarines did not surface unless they had to.

In any case, *Yinbi*'s luck was holding. They'd followed *Ch'ien* Nine-five's projected course and thirty minutes ago had picked up sounds of a submarine blowing ballast. Cautiously, Jian had closed the distance, creeping forward to close to attack range. His orders to destroy an American supercarrier be damned. The American submarine was almost certainly one of the new Seawolf vessels, an incredibly valuable U.S. naval asset. Sinking that submarine would quite nicely strike the blow intended by Operation Yangshandian, a multibillion-dollar target the Americans simply could not afford to lose.

And if a supercarrier showed up, there would be time to sink her as well.

Another deep breath. *This begins it.*

"Flood tubes and open outer doors. . . ."

Sonar Room, USS *Virginia*
Rendezvous Point Hotel
N12°56.51', E115°48.29'
South China Sea
0359 hours, Zulu –8

Sonar Technician First Class Ken Queensly leaned far back in the chair at his sonar console, ears encased in headphones, his eyes closed. To the untrained ear, the noise hissing and rumbling through his headset would have been just that—noise. And, in fact, most of it was noise that could be ignored—the sounds of water breaking over *Virginia*'s bow, of booted feet on the forward deck, the stuttering clatter of the helicopter hovering above the water off the port side.

But a computer command had muted those known and catalogued sounds to a faint and manageable level, leaving Queensly free to probe the depths surrounding the *Virginia* with a sense far more acute than vision in these circumstances.

His eyes snapped open. He'd heard something, a faint sound that commanded his attention simply because it was different from all of the other background noise. He checked the trace on the waterfall, of course . . . but he was already reaching for the intercom switch that would put him in touch with Captain Garrett.

"Bridge!" he shouted, startling the sonar techs in the compartment with him. "Sonar! Probable torpedo tube flooding and tube doors opening!"

"Sonar, Bridge," Garrett's voice came back, rough with the blowing wind. "Roger that. Bearing?"

"Bearing approximately zero-nine-zero! Designating contact as Sierra One-seven-two!" He froze, hearing another, more deadly sound. "*Torpedo in the water!*"

Bridge, USS *Virginia*
Rendezvous Point Hotel
N12°56.51', E115°48.29'
South China Sea
0359 hours, Zulu −8

Garrett glanced to starboard, toward the east . . . but of course saw nothing but night. He hit the 1MC switch by his hand. "*Sound general quarters! Torpedo in the water!*"

Instantly, the hollow *Bong! Bong! Bong!* of the sub's emergency warning bell echoed through the hull.

"Sonar, Bridge! How far?"

"Estimate six thousand meters, closing at fifty-five knots. Captain! Two . . . no, *three* torpedoes in the water!"

Six thousand meters at fifty-five knots . . . very roughly a kilometer and a half per minute. *Virginia* had four minutes before disaster.

Below him, on the forward deck, half a dozen sailors in blue foul-weather gear, bright orange life jackets, and safety harnesses securing them to the deck were hauling at the line fired from the helicopter. The man at the end of that line was lost somewhere in the waves off to port. How far off was he?

Every submariner knew the score. The captain of an American submarine was expected to think *first* of the mission, then of the safety of the submarine, *then* the safety of the sub's nuclear power plant, and only after that of the safety of the crew. *The mission, the boat, the plant, the crew.* That simple, deadly equation was hammered into every sailor during his training at New London and was part of the responsibility borne by every submarine officer. Right now, that "package" out there in the water was completely expendable. To

save his command, Garrett was prepared to order the
sailors on deck to toss the safety line overboard and
immediately get below. *Virginia* needed to maneuver,
and every second of delay brought that hostile torpedo
closer, eating away at his tactical options.

"*Deck there!*" he called over the loudspeaker. "*Cast
off the line. Clear the deck!*"

He could see the stunned consternation of the
sailors below in the way they froze in midmovement.
Then the chief in charge of the working party barked
an order, and they gathered up the line on the deck and
hurled it over the side.

"Maneuvering! This is the Captain! *Dive the boat!*"

He scrambled for the inviting circle of the sail hatch
beneath his feet. . . .

Rendezvous Point Hotel
N12°56.51', E115°48.29'
South China Sea
0359 hours, Zulu −8

Stevens was less than twenty feet from the side of
the *Virginia* when he saw the sailors on board scoop
up the free coils of line they'd already gathered in and
throw it at him, casting him helplessly adrift.

What the fuck? . . .

With growing horror, he saw the sailors vanishing
down a hatch in the deck, saw the *Virginia*'s sail begin
to surge forward . . . and down.

The submarine was submerging!

He screamed in helpless fury against the storm,
against the night, against the nightmare unfairness of
being abandoned this way. . . .

Control Room, USS *Virginia*
Rendezvous Point Hotel
N12°56.51', E115°48.29'
South China Sea
0400 hours, Zulu –8

"Radio room! Flag Bravo Five-one! Tell them the package is in the water!" Maybe the hovering Sea Hawk would be able to find the CIA officer in the ocean . . . and maybe not. That was no longer Garrett's problem. The survival of the boat was.

"Come right to course two-seven-zero," Garrett barked. "Ahead flank."

"New course two-seven-zero, aye! Ahead flank, aye!"

"Make depth one hundred feet!"

"Make depth one-zero-zero feet, aye, sir!"

"Weapons status!"

"Tubes one and two warshot loaded," Lieutenant Carpenter replied from the weapons board. "Mark 48 ADCAP."

"Snapshot, two, one!"

"Snapshot two, one, aye aye!"

It would take about forty-five long seconds for the final preparations in the torpedo room, including flooding the tubes and opening the outer doors. In the meantime, though *Virginia* was swiftly submerging, he could not order a deep dive, not without complicating the flooding and pressurization of the tubes.

He could, however, begin putting some distance between *Virginia* and the unknown attacker out there. The incoming torpedoes were moving at an estimated fifty-five knots. *Virginia* could manage thirty-eight . . . maybe forty over the short haul, which meant that the enemy fish would only creep up on their target at a relative speed of fifteen knots. The course change put the torpedoes behind the sub and racing to catch up.

Meanwhile, *Virginia* was submerging to take full advantage of her natural element, the sea. The roll and bump to her hull, so pronounced when she'd been on the surface and subject to the battering of the waves, steadied almost at once as her ballast tanks filled and she slipped swiftly into the depths of the night-black abyss.

"Course now two-seven-zero," Chief Bollinger announced from his chair overlooking the steering and dive controls. "Speed coming up to thirty-five knots . . . thirty-six knots . . ."

"Sonar, Conn," Garrett called. "What's the status on those fish?"

"Now *four*, repeat, *four* torpedoes in the water, Captain. Estimate the closest at 2,500 yards. Sir, they appear to have been fired by a single hostile in a staggered spread."

"Speed now forty knots, Captain," Jorgensen said. "Eng says we can't hold this for long without busting a gut."

"Very well." Twenty-five hundred yards presented a running time of a hair over one minute at fifty-five knots. At a relative speed of fifteen knots, the running time extended to five minutes. He'd bought them that much time, at least, and there was a slender chance they could outrun the things until they ran out of juice.

The control room crew manned their stations, worked their consoles, with a grim and death-silent concentration. They would all know by now that *Virginia* had abandoned a man to the ocean topside.

Being submariners, they would also know *why*. With enemy torpedoes bearing in on the *Virginia*, they would know their survival depended on Garrett's decisions, even when those decisions were tough ones.

The mission first. Then the vessel. And then the men.

Four minutes, now.

Torpedo Room, USS *Virginia*
Rendezvous Point Hotel
South China Sea
0402 hours, Zulu −8

"Tubes one and two flooded!" Rodriguez shouted.

Wallace squeezed back out of the way. His heart was pounding, his hands slick with sweat. This was his first qual rotation in the torpedo room, and it was promising to be an exciting watch. Shit . . . ten minutes ago they'd had him swabbing the deck with a mop and bucket, and now . . .

He was watching a gauge on the fire-control panel. "Outer doors open!" he called, when two lights flashed red.

"Snapshot," Chief Giangreco yelled, bringing his palm down on the big red firing button. "Fire number two!"

Nothing happened.

"Shit!" Giangreco growled. "Hang-fire!"

Wallace stepped back, putting himself as much out of the way as possible, as Giangreco and Rodriguez bent over the fire-control panel, trying to find out what had gone wrong. Giangreco hit the intercom switch. "Conn, Torpedo Room! Hang-fire on number two!"

They were in trouble. That much he knew. A snapshot order meant that an enemy had fired torpedoes at them, and that the captain was sending a torp or two back in the direction from which the attack had come, an unaimed shot-from-the-hip that might get lucky.

But the first torpedo fired had failed to leave the tube. It would not be armed as yet—it had to travel a certain distance before its warhead went active—but the situation was still incredibly dangerous. If one thing had gone wrong, chances were a whole cluster of things had gone wrong as well. . . .

He looked aft, at the stolid, watching faces of the Navy SEALs. The torpedo room was the one compartment on board with room enough to house *Virginia*'s eight guests. Bunks had been unfolded along the bulkheads, above and below the stored, quiescent, black-and-red giants, the torpedoes waiting on their hydraulic racks, making the normally neat and hyper-efficient space of the compartment seem a lot more crowded and claustrophobic than usual. The SEALs, too, were standing back out of the way, close by the watertight door leading into the aft end of the torpedo compartment.

"Shit and double shit," Giangreco said. "The whole firing net's gone!"

"One of the fucking three-Cs?" Rodriguez asked.

"Maybe. . . ."

Wallace leaped into the central passageway and raced aft, toward the midsection of the torpedo room. Rodriguez's words had triggered something.

Two days ago, Wallace had been down here as part of an ET work detail, swapping out 3C chips from a routing station buried in the port-side bulkhead. Chief Kurzweil had told him at the time that some of the computer chips could fail when current went through them, starting a fire. . . .

The panel was hidden behind one of the SEALs' racks. He grabbed the mattress and yanked it out into the passageway. "Hey!" one of the SEALs shouted. "What the fuck? . . ."

But Wallace had exposed the sealed access panel where he and Chief Kurzweil had been swapping out one of the 3Cs. He pressed the palm of his hand against the access panel. Usually, the bulkheads were cool . . . but the panel was warm to the touch. "Fire!" he shouted. "Fire in the bulkhead, right here!"

Rodriguez, Giangreco, and two other torpedomen were with him in an instant. The access panel was locked and there was no key, but Giangreco had a pry tool in one hand. "Out of my way!"

The flat end of the tool went into the grip recess, and Giangreco strained against it.

"You sure, kid?" Rodriguez asked Wallace. "I don't smell no smoke." He sounded worried, though. Of all the possible dangers on board a submarine, none—not even a casualty in the reactor room—was as dreaded as fire.

"I helped replace one of those computer chips here the other day," Wallace said. "It's right there, behind that panel. And it feels warm. . . ."

"If you're wrong, Wall-eye," Giangreco growled, "the cost of the repairs comes outta your hide!"

Then the panel snapped open. Sparks danced and crackled, and, an instant later, smoke billowed from the opening in a thick and acrid cloud.

Rodriguez was already leaning against the 1MC. "*Fire! Fire in the boat!*"

"Secure that door!" Giangreco bellowed, and one of the SEALs aft slammed the watertight door shut and dogged it. Their first duty was to contain the fire—and the potentially deadly smoke—and keep it from spreading through the rest of the boat.

Only then could they begin to fight the fire.

Thursday, 8 June 2006

Control Room, USS *Virginia*
Rendezvous Point Hotel
South China Sea
0403 hours, Zulu –8

"Fire! Fire in the boat!"

The warning windows appearing on his touchscreen told Garrett that the alert was coming from the torpedo room. The compartment had just been sealed, containing the fire and smoke.

"Rig the boat for fire, now, rig the boat for fire" sounded over the 1MC. Both of the control room's watertight doors clanged shut hard, the dogging wheels pushed hard to the right to seal them—"righty-tighty, lefty-loosey" as the old mnemonic phrase had it.

"Ventilation systems secure, Captain," Jorgensen announced. "All compartment hatches shut and dogged. Fire party laying forward to the torpedo room."

"Very well."

"Captain," Lieutenant Carpenter, the weapons officer, reported. "I have negative signal on tube two. The
fire may have melted the fiber optics."

"Very well."

The tension on the control room deck was electric.
The men were scared, but they continued to carry out
their duties with the calm professionalism Garrett expected of them.

Three problems now complicated *Virginia*'s survival, and Garrett needed to deal with all three. The
submarine was racing away from four oncoming torpedoes now strung out astern, with four minutes more
to go before the first one caught up with the racing
Virginia. One of *Virginia*'s snapshot ADCAPs was
hung in torpedo tube two, and there was no way as yet
to tell if the fish was damaged—or if the fire casualty
had armed the ADCAP's warhead. The torpedo was
wire-guided, but Carpenter was reporting negative signal . . . meaning information wasn't getting through
in either direction. If the torpedo had armed itself, it
could explode at any moment.

And finally, there was the fire. Electrical fires were
rare on board American submarines, but they did happen from time to time. They were almost commonplace
on board Russian boats, which had older technology,
wiring that was nowhere near up to U.S. Navy spec, and
crews not nearly so well trained as American sailors.
Torpedo-room fires were especially dreaded. Those
silently ranked ton-and-a-half monsters down there
possessed both peroxide—a fuel that contained its own
oxygen supply—and 650 pounds of PBXN-103 in the
warhead. A torpedo-room fire had been responsible for
the sinking of the Russian submarine *Kursk,* K-141, in
August 2000, killing all 118 men aboard.

And a fire inside *Virginia*'s torpedo-room bulkhead could also have another disastrous effect—touching off the fuel in the Tomahawk missiles in their vertical launch tubes, nestled in between the outer hull and the bulkhead on either side of the torpedo room. If a Tomahawk engine lit off while the missile was still in the tube, the blowtorch blast from its engine would melt right through hull and bulkhead both, resulting in a swift and one-way trip to the bottom.

Yeah, as they said . . . a torpedo-room fire could ruin your whole day.

At the moment, though, there was little else Garrett could control. The hang-fire would explode or not, and there was little that could be done now save closing the outer doors and emptying the tube, tasks that would be carried out once the fire was under control. Fire-control parties were dealing with the fire.

And Garrett had done all he could about the oncoming torpedoes, at least for the moment. When they got closer, maybe . . .

He wondered if the Sea Hawk had been able to pluck the CIA "package" back from the angry sea. He didn't regret doing what he'd done; making that kind of decision was what the U.S. government paid him to do.

Yet he also had to consider what must be going through the crew's minds right now. Even knowing that *Virginia*'s survival depended on *instant* response, they would be identifying with that poor son of a bitch adrift in the storm, watching his ticket home slide away into the depths. And they would be aware that standing orders had sealed off the men in the torpedo room as soon as fire was detected. That was *survival*.

Survival meant sacrifice.

Garrett found himself thinking about one of the

great heroes of the U.S. submarine service—Commander Howard W. Gilmore. While commanding the USS *Growler* on her fourth combat patrol in the Pacific during World War II, he'd been on the conning tower when a Japanese gunboat attacked out of the darkness, spraying the bridge with machine-gun fire. Desperately wounded as the lookouts had scrambled below deck, he'd waved off the sailors who'd tried to come back for him. "Take her down!" had been his final command.

Growler had submerged out from under Gilmore, and for that act he'd been posthumously awarded the Medal of Honor.

Survival.

And more than survival. *Striking back.*

Who was it who'd just ambushed the *Virginia*? Occam's Razor—the premise that the simplest explanation was most often the correct one—suggested that that other sub out there in the darkness was the rogue submarine that had been torpedoing Vietnamese assets, taking American hostages . . .

. . . and blowing helpless civilian airliners out of the sky.

He wanted that other submarine, wanted it very badly indeed. *Curse* the damned luck that had crippled *Virginia*'s weapons system on her very first shot fired in anger! He detected the hand of the ubiquitous Murphy here. *If something* can *go wrong, it* will *go wrong.*

Garrett decided that he needed to be a bit proactive with old Murph. There had to be a way to encourage things to start going wrong for the hostile sub out there.

If he could understand the enemy, understand his *thinking,* he could kill him.

Torpedo Room, USS *Virginia*
Rendezvous Point Hotel
South China Sea
0403 hours, Zulu −8

"Don EABs!" Giangreco yelled. The compartment was swiftly filling with smoke, burning the lungs and rendering sight all but useless.

Wallace had been through the emergency drill a hundred times, first back at sub school, then later as a raw, air-breathing unqual during the trip under the ice—being forced to find EABs and overhead air source manifolds in every compartment on board— *blindfolded.*

Emergency Air-Breathing masks were full-face respirators with regulators that clipped to your belt, and air hoses that attached to manifolds in the overhead. Wallace pulled his mask into place, tightening the straps behind his head, and inhaled hard to draw his first breath. Submariners called wearing the damned things *sucking air* or, more impolitely, *sucking.* Partly that was because you had to suck hard to draw each breath, which was incredibly tiring after the first few minutes, and partly too, the sailors said who'd done it, it was because wearing the things sucked.

With the EAB on, however, he could breathe, and he could see better without the stinging smoke searing his watering eyes. The other *Virginia* men had their masks on, too. The SEALs, though, were coughing and gasping in the aft end of the compartment; there weren't enough masks for everyone.

But, then, all that was necessary was to have enough masks for the people needed to fight the fire. A CAT— an emergency Casualty Assistance Team—would be on the way by now, but if the fire could be extinguished sooner, so much the better. Giangreco had snatched a bright red CO_2 fire extinguisher off the bulkhead and was approaching the fire like a warrior prepared for battle.

It was tough to see through the boiling smoke, but to Wallace's eye it appeared that a bundle of plastic tubes and plastic-coated wires had caught fire inside the opened access, and the stuff was bubbling up into a tangled, blazing mass of molten plastic.

Something exploded inside the access panel, and a glob of flaming plastic smacked against Giangreco's visor. He stumbled back, dropping the fire extinguisher and clawing at the clinging, burning goo.

"Chief!" Rodriguez yelled, turning to catch the chief torpedoman. For an instant, all was chaos in the noisy, smoky hell of the fire-lit compartment.

The explosion, Wallace saw, had also spit a mass of burning plastic the size of his head out of the panel and onto the black-and-red steel of a Mark 48 ADCAP, just ahead of the propulsor shroud. It landed right over a peroxide intake vent, blazing furiously.

Wallace didn't think; he *couldn't* think. Somewhere, deep inside his mind, fear gibbered . . . and with it the knowledge that if the fuel supply of that torpedo ignited, it would be like loosing a three-and-a-half-ton rocket inside this tiny space. Lunging forward, he scooped up the burning mass, dragged it from the torpedo, and looked wildly about for something to do with it.

His hands were burning. *Christ* the pain! But he managed to take three swift steps aft, drop to his knees, and plunge the plastic, the flame, and his blistering hands into the bucket of mop water he'd been using just a few minutes before to swab the linoleum tiles of the deck.

He discovered he was shrieking in white agony into his EAB mask.

Control Room, USS *Virginia*
Rendezvous Point Hotel
South China Sea
0404 hours, Zulu −8

"Conn, sonar! First torpedo has just gone active! Range seven hundred yards!"

"Thank you, sonar." Acoustical homing torpedoes could follow the sounds made by the target, or, if they got close enough, they could begin using active sonar to ping the target, homing on the echoed return.

Only two strategies were really open to Garrett—using decoys or outrunning the hunters. The trouble was, that other sub skipper was *good*. Rather than firing four torpedoes all at once, he'd staggered the firing, spreading the torpedoes out from side to side and stringing them sequentially, so that the first was now seven hundred yards away, but the last was still nearly two thousand yards away.

That meant that Garrett was going to have to defeat each torpedo in turn, that the decoy he used to trick the first one would not take out the next as well.

"Captain!" sounded over his headset, the voice muffled by an EAB face mask. "This is BM1 Johnson, CAT leader!"

"Go!"

"Sir, the fire in the torpedo room is secured! We have one man down with burns."

"Get a corpsman down there on the double."

"Already on the way, sir."

"Very well. Set a reflash watch and report back to me."

"Aye aye, sir."

With any fire on a submarine, there was always a danger that hot flammable materials would rekindle themselves. The reflash watch was a sailor detailed to just sit there and watch the smoldering rubble, and to sound the alarm if the fire flashed back into life.

He would also need to deal with ventilating the smoke.

However, there was the small matter of enemy torpedoes to deal with first.

"Sonar! Conn! Give me a range countdown on the nearest fish!"

"Conn, Sonar! Range five hundred yards . . . four-seven-zero . . . four-five-zero . . . four-three zero . . ."

It felt as though the torpedo were crawling after the *Virginia,* but it came on, relentless and deadly.

He could hear the pinging now, a faint, high-pitched ringing, growing steadily louder as the torpedo probed the ocean ahead of itself, searching for *Virginia*'s hull.

"All hands. Brace for sudden maneuvering!"

"Two-five-zero . . . two-three-zero . . ."

"Release countermeasures!" he called.

Lieutenant Carpenter practically pounded on his touchscreen. "Countermeasures released, Captain!"

"Emergency dive!" Garrett said. "Make depth seven hundred feet!"

"Emergency dive, aye. Make depth seven-zero-zero feet, aye aye!"

The deck tilted sharply as *Virginia* angled sharply down and plunged into the depths.

The countermeasures—a pair of canisters designed to release a cloud of highly reflective bubbles, popped clear of *Virginia*'s hull, drifting along in her wake. *Vir-*

ginia, meanwhile, went nose-down in a steep dive, letting the expanding cloud of bubbles momentarily mask her maneuver.

Coming in two hundred yards astern, the first torpedo, its active sonar pinging, picked up the reflected echoes from the bubbles and kept coming in straight, punching straight through the bubble cloud . . .

. . . and losing the target echo.

The torpedo's idiot-level brain fell back on its list of programmed directives. Still pinging, it began to circle, searching for a target, any target.

It would continue to do so until its fuel supply ran out.

Virginia, meanwhile, continued its dive, gradually leveling off at seven hundred feet.

Of the remaining torpedoes, the fourth one, at the southernmost extreme of the spread, had traveled far enough off the line-of-sight to the *Virginia* that it had failed to acquire the target, and continued moving in a straight line off into the empty darkness of the ocean, again until its fuel gave out.

Numbers two and three, however, were close enough that both had already acquired the *Virginia* when their sonars went active, and far enough back not to be decoyed by the countermeasures. Both detected *Virginia's* dive, and both angled their propulsors to change their paths into dives that would intercept the fleeing American submarine in another few moments.

Because of the enemy sub's firing spread, the angle between the two incoming torps was almost thirty degrees. Garrett couldn't turn left or right, because to do so would sharply reduce the distance between the sub and one or the other of the torpedoes. All he could do was continue traveling straight, seeking to outrun them both.

Virginia's published dive depth was 800 feet, but in fact she was capable of a bit more . . . one thousand feet with a 10-percent safety margin. The *Seawolf* could dive deeper but certain trade-offs had been forced on the new submarine design. *Virginia*'s hull was made of HY-100–grade steel, the same as *Seawolf*, but the pressure hull was thinner to save on weight and on-board space. Her smaller power plant meant she wasn't as fast as *Seawolf*, even though she was just three-quarters of the *Seawolf*'s weight, and that meant she wasn't as easy to handle at great depth.

"Leveling off at seven-zero-zero feet, Captain," the diving officer announced.

"Very well. Sonar, Conn! Update on the closest fish."

"Torpedo two, Captain. Range now four hundred yards. Closing at a relative speed of fifteen knots. Time to impact . . . forty seconds."

He waited. The ventilation system was still off, in order to avoid spreading smoke from the torpedo room throughout the boat. That meant it was hot. Sweat was dripping from every face—partly from the lack of air circulation, partly from simple, stark *fear*. As the seconds passed, as the torpedoes drew closer, the stink of fear grew thicker and thicker.

There was also, Garrett realized, a slight haze of smoke as well. The CAT party would have opened the watertight door to the torpedo room in order to enter it, and some of the smoke would have escaped. Even though all watertight doors on board were sealed now, a little smoke seeped through every time someone went from one compartment to another, and the air was fast becoming pretty foul.

"Incoming torpedo at one-three-zero yards . . . one hundred yards . . ."

"Release countermeasures! *Full up planes!*"

"Countermeasures released, Captain."

"Full up planes, aye aye!" *Virginia*'s deck tilted sharply, bow-up. A calculator slid off a console and clattered aft across the deck, followed by the crash of a carelessly placed coffee mug.

Again, a cloud of bubbles exploded in *Virginia*'s wake. Again, the torpedo—this time coming down at an angle as it continued to pursue the sub on its dive—homed on the bubbles and not the *Virginia*. Punching through the bubble cloud, it abruptly lost its sonar lock. Still diving, it began to circle, simple-mindedly searching for the suddenly vanished submarine.

There'd been a chance, actually, that the torpedo might plunge beneath its operational depth and implode, but a torpedo was a fairly densely packed mechanism, and could generally operate at greater depths than most subs. After a few moments, the torpedo angled upward, widening its search spiral.

By that time, the third torp was closing on the fast-rising *Virginia*.

"Torpedo range now four hundred yards! Three-eight-zero. Three-five-zero . . ."

"What's our depth?"

"Depth five hundred feet, Captain. And rising."

What Garrett was counting on was that a torpedo moving through the water at fifty-five knots could not react immediately to a change in the target's bearing. The tactical trick, here, was to let the hostile torpedo get close enough that, when he pulled a sudden maneuver, it didn't have time to react.

But he couldn't wait too long. At a relative velocity of fifteen knots, that torpedo was closing at a rate of ten yards each second.

"Incoming torpedo at one-two-zero yards . . ."

"Release countermeasures!"

"Countermea—"

"Full right rudder! Emergency turn, hard right!"

Virginia slewed so sharply that the deck, already canted from her rise up through the depths, now heeled over far to starboard. A sailor standing by the helm station lost his grip, slipped, and hit the deck with a yelp of pain, sliding across the deck to thump against the starboard bulkhead forward.

"Captain! Sonar! Torpedo number two has reacquired!"

Ignore it. Right now, he was dancing with number three. . . .

"Captain! Sonar! Torpedo has not decoyed! Range one-three-zero yards . . ."

"Blow emergency ballast!"

"Blow emergency ballast, aye aye!"

Virginia's hull shuddered as bottles of compressed air blasted the water from her ballast tanks, and she began rising toward the roof. Three shrill *ooo-gah!* alarm blasts sounded, as the 1MC blared "Now, *surface! Surface! Surface! . . .*"

Her rise was spectacular—better than ten feet per second—as her nose lifted to a forty-five degree angle. Still driving forward at forty knots, she sprinted for the surface.

The third torpedo struck turbulent water and detonated. . . .

Control Room, *Yinbi de Gongji*
N12°58.05', E115°50.86'
South China Sea
0406 hours, Zulu –8

"Hit!" the sonar operator called over the intercom. "Torpedo three hit the target!"

Jian allowed himself to relax. He'd been following the chase for long minutes now, as it was relayed to him by his sonar officer. The twists, turns, and dodges of the American submarine had been spectacular, but at least one of the Chinese fish had ignored the decoys and homed in for the kill.

"Correction, Captain," the sonar officer announced. "I am not getting break-up noises." There was a hesitation. "Sir, target has blown his ballast tanks and is surfacing. He may be damaged. . . ."

Jian slammed his palm against the periscope housing. *Ancestors!*

He immediately regretted the outburst, even unspoken. The men expected him to be passionless and cool.

He knew one simple fact, however. Either the American submarine would be sunk or crippled within the next few minutes, or it would turn on its attacker with the ferocity of a wounded tiger. If the first, there was no problem. If the second, however, Jian doubted that the *Yinbi* would survive the assault. Frankly, he was surprised the American hadn't sent a torpedo back down the line of attack. That bespoke a curious confidence on his adversary's part. Confidence or foolishness.

Jian *never* underestimated an opponent. If the American was that confident of finding and killing the *Yinbi* . . .

"Maneuvering! Come to zero-three-zero! Ahead slow, silent operation!"

Control Room, USS *Virginia*
Rendezvous Point Hotel
South China Sea
0406 hours, Zulu –8

The torpedo blast slammed against *Virginia*'s aft
hull like a sledgehammer, rolling the fast-rising submarine onto her port beam. In the control room, men
were thrown from their seats—those who weren't
buckled in. Instead of the *ooh-gah* of the emergency
surface alarm, the swooping wail of the collision
alarm cut through the shouts and cries of shaken men.

Garrett hadn't fallen out of his seat, not quite, but
he'd had to cling to the arm and his touchscreen console with a grip that left his hands painful. Slowly, still
surfacing, *Virginia* righted herself, and members of the
control room watch began scrambling back to their
stations.

No leaks in the control room . . . no thunderous
blast of water exploding through the submarine like a
detonating bomb. What the hell had happened?

"We're still in one piece, Captain!" Jorgensen called
from a board where he could monitor leaks or damage
throughout the boat. "Jesus! What happened?"

Garrett had the same information coming up as a
schematic on his screen as well. "I'm not sure, XO," he
replied. "Either that torpedo had a proximity fuse, or
else it hit the turbulence from our EMBT blow." The initials were shorthand for Emergency Main Ballast Tank.

"Makes sense." Jorgensen nodded. "At this depth,
hitting the MBT outflow would've been like hitting a
solid wall. Either way . . ." He slapped the bulkhead
fondly. "The old girl held together."

Old girl? *Virginia* was scarcely that on this, her first
mission.

But Garrett knew *he* was feeling pretty old right now. . . .

"Sonar! Where's that last torpedo?"

"Sorry, sir. We lost it there for a moment." Between the roar of the EMBT blow and the explosion itself, it was a miracle Queensly could still hear anything. "Torpedo two has definitely reacquired and is closing, bearing one-seven-oh, range three hundred!"

Too close! "Helm! Come left to zero-one-zero! Maneuvering, maintain flank!"

"Come left to zero-one-zero, aye! Maintain flank speed, aye aye!"

"Depth!"

"Passing two-seven-five feet, Captain! Ascending at eighteen feet per second!"

"Release countermeasures!"

"Countermeasures away!"

"Come left four-zero degrees!"

"Come left, four-zero degrees, aye aye!"

Virginia turned while still climbing, twisting away as the last torpedo homed in for the kill. Garrett could hear the torpedo now, they *all* could hear it . . . a faint, high-pitched whine growing louder . . . louder . . . accompanied by the ping of its sonar. . . .

A scraping sound, metal grating on metal, sounded from overhead, from the sail. Garrett saw the faces of Jorgensen and several others go white . . . but then the whine faded.

"Christ! It missed us!" Queensly called over the comm link. "Correction . . . sir, I think it struck a glancing blow on the sail, but it didn't explode!"

It must have been deflected just enough by the countermeasures and *Virginia*'s half twist to the side. That had been *way* too close for comfort.

"Track it, Sonar."

"Yessir! Still tracking. It's lost us . . . it's starting to circle . . ."

They weren't out of it yet. When that torpedo circled halfway around, it would pick them up again.

"Conn! Sonar! It's coming around again!"

Fortunately, it would have to cut a pretty wide circle to come about. And in the meantime, *Virginia* was going up on the roof.

And Garrett had one final bit of physics on his side in his limited bag of tricks.

Throughout the world's oceans, at a depth that varies with conditions between one hundred and two hundred fifty feet, is a layer called the thermocline where the warm waters near the surface change rapidly to the near-freezing chill of the depths. Because the speed of sound waves decreases sharply in the colder water, the thermocline tends to isolate sounds above the layer from those below. Subs and shipborne sonar systems had a lot of trouble hearing submarines below the thermocline.

And submarines—or acoustically homing torpedoes—had a lot of trouble hearing targets above the thermocline as well.

Racing upward at a forty-five degree angle, "flanking it," as submariners would say, *Virginia* pierced the thermocline layer at a depth of 130 feet, then seconds later burst from the ocean and into the rain-swept night, hurtling so far out of the water that only her screw remained submerged. She hesitated there a moment, in an unlikely attempt to conquer the air . . . before falling forward like a breaching whale, hitting the water with a thunderous crash of spray.

The last torpedo swept by somewhere beneath her. Possibly it had been damaged by its glancing encounter with *Virginia*'s sail, or possibly its fuel supply was nearly spent. In any case, the sounds of its engine and sonar pings were masked by the thermocline. Queensly reported he was no longer hearing it.

A few long minutes later, they could assume that its engine had run out of juice.

Garrett slumped back in the command chair, his uniform drenched with sweat, the strength leached from his body.

"Jesus H. Christ!" Jorgensen said, shaking his head. "You *did* it, Skipper!"

"Never seen a performance like that in all my years in the service!" Bollinger added. "Fuckin'-*A*!"

"Sonar! Any sign of the boat that 'bushed us?"

"Negative, Captain. If he's out there, he's laying low and keeping quiet."

"Put all your ears out, Queenie. If anything so much as twitches out there, I want to know."

"Aye aye, sir."

The battle had in fact been a draw. *Virginia* had survived—barely—but the first shot she'd ever tried to fire in anger had hung in the tube, and they'd come *that* close to being sent to the bottom. The enemy sub was still out there, doing what submarines do best.

Waiting and listening.

And in the meantime, *Virginia* was an easy target, wallowing on the surface with a smoke-filled torpedo room and fumes leaking through the boat. They would have to tend their wounds before going back and hunting down that enemy submarine . . . and hope to hell the enemy didn't come looking for them first.

As the minutes stretched out, though, it became clear that the enemy sub was not pursuing its momentary advantage. If it was still out there, it was staying very quiet indeed.

Garrett knew, though, that there would be another

confrontation. As soon as *Virginia* was ready to re-sume the hunt, they were going to track the enemy submarine down, and when they caught him, they were going to nail his metaphorical hide to the meta-phorical wall.

And Garrett was going to take a great deal of per-sonal satisfaction in doing just that.

Thursday, 8 June 2006

Sick Bay, USS *Virginia*
Rendezvous Point Hotel
South China Sea
0615 hours, Zulu −8

V*irginia* continued to ride on the surface, the rough
seas giving her hull an unpleasant corkscrewing motion. Her diesel had been switched on, which added to
the discomfort; the engine had been rigged to draw air
from the smoke-filled torpedo room and vent through
the diesel exhaust port atop the sail. When the compartment was more or less clear, the boat had been
rigged for surface ventilation. The stink of diesel fuel
continued to linger, however, along with traces of
smoke. Added to the uncomfortable pitch and roll, the
combination could bring the hardiest sailor to the
point of seasickness.

Garrett met Lieutenant Halstead in the passageway

outside of *Virginia*'s sick bay. "Captain," the SEAL said, nodding.

"What's up?"

Halstead put a hand out to brace himself against the roll of the deck, and shook his head. "Just came down to see how the kid was doing. Jesus, Captain. That was the gutsiest damned thing I've ever seen."

"Coming from a SEAL, that's high praise. What happened, anyway?"

"He seemed to figure out where that fire was in the bulkhead before anyone else did. Went right to the spot. Then when they had the access panel open and were trying to fight the fire, a big glob of molten plastic spilled out onto one of the torpedoes. I guess the kid thought the fire was going to light off the torp's warhead or fuel or something. He just reaches down, scoops up the burning gunk with his bare hands, and drops it into a bucket of water, slick as you please."

"Shit. Something like that wouldn't have set off a Mark 48. It would have had to be a real conflagration."

"Maybe he was afraid it would become a conflagration, Captain. I don't know. All I know is . . . that kid's got it where it counts."

"On *that* I agree completely." He started to move past the SEAL.

"Oh . . . sir?"

"Yes?"

"I might as well ask you now. The guys've been speculating about where we go from here. Back to Japan?"

"Negative. The mission comes first."

"But . . . didn't that fire trash your weapons system?"

"I've got my best people going over the damage

now. With luck, they'll be able to jury-rig something that will let us shoot back next time . . . if there *is* a next time. Meantime, though, we have a mission and we're going to carry it out, whether we can shoot back or not."

"I understand, sir. Thank you."

"Not a problem. Tell your people that we will be in the vicinity of Small Dragon Island sometime tonight. We'll go in after dark, have a look-see by UUV, and decide how we want to play it after that."

"I'll pass that on, Captain. Thanks."

Garrett opened the sick-bay door and stepped inside. *Virginia*'s sick bay was small, with only two beds, both occupied. RM1 Padgett had fallen during *Virginia*'s spectacular ascent and broken an ankle, so he was confined to one of the racks. Wallace lay in the other one, both hands heavily swaddled in white gauze and surgical tape. Five other men had been injured in the fun and games with the torpedoes that morning, but, fortunately, only two had to stay off their feet for a while—a badly twisted knee on one, a sprained ankle on the other—and both could stay in their own racks until they could be transferred off the boat.

Virginia's doctor—Lieutenant Colbert—and HM1 Wilkins, the corpsman, were next to Wallace's rack.

"How is he?" Garrett asked.

"Doped up on drugs right now, Skipper," Colbert replied.

"Is he going to be okay?"

"Ah, sure. First- and second-degree burns on his hands? He's young. He'll heal up in no time. We do need to get him and several other men off the boat, however. I'd like to see them back at Naval Hospital Yokosuka, stat."

"I know. Some other small matters come first." *Like*

restoring Virginia *to full combat capability,* he added as an unspoken thought.

He took another look at Wallace, who appeared to be sleeping. Possibly, his sacrifice hadn't been necessary; it was pretty hard to set off a torpedo accidentally. On the other hand, though, it was possible he'd just saved the *Virginia*. How the hell did a nineteen-year-old kid rise to a challenge like that?

The same way, he decided, that teen-aged kids had been rising to challenges since the Peloponnesian War. War all too often was started by politicians, but endured and resolved by kids like Wallace.

"Keep me posted," he told the doctor. "Let me know when I can talk to him."

"Aye aye, sir."

Garrett's beeper chirped. He was wanted in the control room. He walked to an intercom speaker on the sick-bay bulkhead and hit the switch. "Garrett."

"Captain?" Jorgensen's voice replied. "Eng reports the air quality in the torpedo room is now at acceptable levels."

"Very well. Secure the diesel."

"Aye aye, sir."

"What's the status on the repairs?"

"The damage repair party has secured tube two, Captain. The fish never triggered."

"Good." As he'd thought.

"Repairs to the firing controls are under way. Weps estimates fifteen hours."

A long time. Too long to wait. He braced himself as the deck heaved again beneath his feet. "Let's get the hell off the roof," he said. "Take us down to two-zero-zero feet. Have Nav set a course for Small Dragon Island."

"Submerge to two-zero-zero feet. Set course for Small Dragon Island. Aye aye, sir."

"I'm on my way up."

He'd only just begun his trip back to the control room when he felt the deck tilt beneath his feet. Almost immediately, the rolling, pitching sensation ceased, as *Virginia* entered once again her true domain.

The hostile sub had vanished . . . a very good thing, since *Virginia* had been making enough noise during the past couple of hours to wake the dead, much less an enemy sonar operator. He was ready to bet his career that the hostile had been a Russian-built Kilo, a boat slow and limited in range compared to *Virginia*, but nearly as quiet when running on her batteries. Finding her would be a hell of a challenge, but he knew how to narrow that hunt somewhat.

Sooner or later, the hostile would show up at the Chinese base at Small Dragon Island.

And then he would take her down.

Bridge, yacht *Al Qahir*
Small Dragon Island
South China Sea
1539 hours, Zulu −8

The rain was coming down in sheets, and visibility was only intermittent and brief between each sweep of the windshield wipers. Zaki leaned forward, trying to pierce the rain. He thought he could just make out the gray loom of the Chinese sea base ahead.

"The prisoners," Muhammad Jabarrah was telling him, "will be extremely useful as shields. I suggest we keep two of them on board . . . as insurance."

Zaki straightened up, then glanced at the Maktum

fighter. "Ah. And which two did you have in mind?"

"The women, of course," Jabarrah replied without hesitation. "They are the most easily controlled."

"I see. And that choice would have nothing to do with your desire for, shall we say, the spoils of war, would it?"

"I don't know what you mean, Zaki."

Zaki sighed. "Those women have already caused trouble enough for the crew of *Shuhadaa*. I don't think it wise to tempt *this* crew as well."

"Nonsense. The trouble on the submarine was caused by trying to transport so many prisoners in so small a space. Two women will be easy to guard. Besides . . ." He shrugged. "By separating them from the men, perhaps we guarantee the men's good behavior."

Zaki considered this. "Very well," he said at last. "But transfer them to the stateroom aft of my own."

Jabarrah's face creased in an unpleasant smile. "Oh?"

"The better that I might hear if anyone violates their privacy."

Jabarrah's smile vanished. "As you wish."

The other man turned suddenly and stalked from the bridge, leaving Zaki alone with *Al Qahir*'s pilot and captain.

The bastard wants to rape the women, he thought, angry. *He will not get the chance.*

Zaki was beginning to wonder if this Maktum operation was truly worth the risk. Several Vietnamese assets had been destroyed for their Chinese associates, yes . . . and the tally now included a fifty-two-thousand-ton Japanese transport, a civilian airliner, and the hostages now under guard in *Al Qahir*'s aft lounge. What had seemed a brilliant operation on paper, however, seemed less so now. Their Chinese partners, he knew, still hoped to settle old scores with the American Navy when they entered these waters, and by all reports, that would be within the next couple of days. Intelligence reports had been relayed to the *Al Qahir*, indicating that the *Franklin D. Roosevelt* carrier battlegroup was now rounding the northern tip of Luzon.

The destruction of an American aircraft carrier, of course, would be worth almost any risk—a means of striking at the hated Americans as spectacular as the attacks against New York City and Washington, five years before. By taking the credit for the sinking—and Beijing certainly wanted to maintain a low profile in this operation—Maktum might well rally the global forces of radical Islamic jihad against the Americans, simply by proving the Americans were not omnipotent.

But right now, he was beginning to doubt that the Chinese would be able to sink the *Roosevelt*. Unarmed civilian merchant ships and freighters, yes. One of the almost legendary supercarriers . . . well, that seemed most unlikely.

At least, he thought, *the weather is cooperating now. Thank you, Allah, for your mercy.* With this storm blanketing the region, American spy satellites would be rendered all but useless. Certainly, they would be unable to track a vessel as small as the *Al Qahir*.

Then *Al Qahir* glided close enough to the Chinese base that, even through the rain, he could see the yawning cavern of Small Dragon's sheltered port, the light inside spilling into the rain in a diffuse smear of golden light. A few moments more, and the rain stopped with the abruptness of a falling blade. *Al Qahir* motored gently into the enclosure.

Ahead, at the pier, a single submarine—ul Haq's—
lay tied to the dock, as sailors worked to load supplies.

Which would be more efficient, he wondered . . . to
send the Pakistani submarine out again to raid civilian
shipping? Or have her deploy to the north, into the
path of the oncoming American fleet? The Chinese
might appreciate the extra set of torpedo tubes.

He would need to confer with ul Haq, and see what
the ex-Pakistani naval officer thought.

Behind them, with a low-voiced rumble, the sliding
steel doors closed, cutting them off from the storm.

The real storm, Zaki thought, *is yet to come. Allah,
defend us!*

Aft deck, USS *Virginia*
Rendezvous Point Juliet
South China Sea
1555 hours, Zulu –8

Here we go again, John Stevens thought, a little
wildly. He clung with aching gloved hands to the cable
secured to his safety harness and stepped out of the helicopter's side door, fighting the sudden stab of panic
as his feet dangled in midair. *Next time . . . delegate!*

He still wasn't sure how he'd survived the botched
transfer twelve hours ago. He remembered his horror
when the sailors on board the *Virginia* had tossed his
safety line overboard, remembered the fear turning to
panic as the submarine had submerged.

Fortunately, the helicopter that had ferried him out
to Rendezvous Point Hotel had continued to hover
overhead. He'd been afraid they wouldn't see him in
the rain and surging ocean swell, but a powerful

strobe beacon attached to his life jacket had triggered when he hit the water, and the helicopter, apparently warned by the submerging submarine, had swung around and come back for him, drifting slowly forward dangerously close to the waves.

A man had jumped in after him, bringing with him a rescue line. Bathed in the frosty glare of the helicopter's lights, the two men had clung together as his rescuer attached the line to his harness, then signaled for the helo's crew chief to haul them both back out of the sea. Five minutes later, he'd been back on board Sea Hawk Bravo Five-one, as someone draped him and his rescuer with blankets and the helicopter had circled toward the east and begun climbing.

They'd flown to the nearest air base, which happened to be a Filipino military facility outside of Manila. There, after breakfast and a quick checkup from a doctor, he'd been headed for a well-deserved nap when a Filipino army colonel had presented him with new orders from Yokosuka.

Once again, he'd found himself on board Bravo Five-one, edging through savage weather toward the tail end of the same submarine that had abandoned him in the wee hours of that morning.

I am definitely *going to delegate next time,* he thought. *This shit is not worth another star on the Wall.*

Back at Langley, just inside the security checkpoint for the main lobby of the CIA's headquarters, a number of gold stars inscribed with engraved names adorned a wall between the flags of the United States and of the Central Intelligence Agency . . . one star, one name, for each man or woman killed in the line of duty during the Cold War and after.

The wind and the rotor blast together blew at him

wildly, twisting at his body and threatening to tear him free. Only about fifteen feet below, sailors on the extreme aft deck of the *Virginia* were raising a pole to discharge the static electricity that had built up in the Sea Hawk during its flight through the storm. With a crack audible even above the rushing air, the static discharged, and hands began reaching for Stevens's booted feet.

Instead of dropping him into the ocean alongside the *Virginia*, the helicopter pilot had opted for the slightly more hazardous approach of attempting an at-sea personnel transfer. As before, a safety line had been hooked to his harness and tossed to the waiting submariners below. The helo crew then had lowered him on a second cable, easing him down toward the submarine's aft deck.

Last night's drop had been more dangerous for him, but safer for the helicopter. This way was risky for them both but not quite as rough for him as another dunking in the storm-stirred ocean. The chopper pilot was willing to try this approach in daylight, but not in the dark. Submarines, Stevens was told, often took on supplies at sea this way.

Swaying at the end of his cable, Stevens wafted toward the deck until he was surrounded by men in heavy rain gear. They unhooked the quick release on the cable from the winch, then freed him from the safety line.

"Welcome aboard the *Virginia*," one of the men shouted in his ear. "This way, sir!" Bravo Five-one was already clawing for altitude, circling once more back toward the north for its return to the *Roosevelt*.

Stevens just hoped the damned submarine didn't start submerging before he was safely inside.

Clutching a safety line rigged along *Virginia*'s aft

hull, he made his way forward, toward the imposing bulk of the ASDS resting on the submarine's deck aft of the sail. A circular hatch was open in the deck just aft of the tail of the ASDS, and a crewman waved him on. They helped him step into the hatch and down the ladder.

By the time he was in a fluorescent-lit passageway walking forward, the deck was tilting beneath his feet, and *Virginia* was slipping once more into the ocean's dark embrace.

Control Room, USS *Virginia*
Rendezvous Point Hotel
South China Sea
1601 hours, Zulu –8

"Ahead flank," Garrett said.

"Ahead, flank speed," came the echoed response. "Aye aye, sir."

"Captain?"

Garrett turned in his chair. Jorgensen was stripping off his foul-weather slicker. Beside him was a muscular man looking just a bit like an alien in wetsuit, harness, and life jacket.

"Stevens," the man said.

"Welcome aboard, Mr. Stevens."

"It's good to finally be aboard, Captain. I was beginning to feel damned unwanted."

"You were the guy we had to leave in the drink this morning?"

"I was."

"I'm glad you're okay. I *do* regret the necessity that forced us to cast you off that way."

"Yeah, what the hell happened, anyway?"

"We were under attack. If we'd waited another thirty seconds, we would not have been able to fight clear."

"Jesus! Who attacked you?"

"Actually, I was hoping you had that information for us. That's why someone decided to drop you on us, isn't it? To fill us in on the latest hot shit in person?" Stevens started to reply, and Garrett waved him to silence. "Later. Mr. Jorgensen will take you to the torpedo room and get you bunked in with our SEALs. You can brief me after you get dry, warm, and settled in."

"Thank you, Captain." He glanced up at the big monitor on the control room's forward bulkhead. At the moment, it showed a normal-spectrum camera view of the surface, seen through the Photonics mast—gray clouds and rain, empty gray ocean, and the impression of great *speed* as the mast sliced through the ocean swell. "May I ask . . . where are we headed now?"

"Small Dragon Island, Mr. Stevens. Based on what you people have passed on to us so far, my guess is that the rogue sub may be operating out of that base with Chinese help. It is my intention to scout that base, and see if we can find any sign of either that submarine, or the yacht you people alerted us to . . . what was the name?"

"*Al Qahir.*"

"Yes."

"We'll talk, Captain. We'll talk. . . ."

Garrett watched as the XO led Stevens aft again, toward the ladder that would take him down to the torpedo room deck.

Micromanagement again. The armchair admirals

weren't content with saddling *Virginia* with constant mission updates over the high-tech communications links, but had decided to send a human proxy. Garrett felt a great deal of resentment at this intrusion into his world, his mission. Yet he was also curious.

He wondered what Stevens would have to say.

Mess Hall, USS *Virginia*
Rendezvous Point Hotel
South China Sea
1812 hours, Zulu −8

"My God, did you see the way the Old Man handled the boat? Poetry, man! Pure poetry!"

Chief Kurzweil had been waxing enthusiastic about the day's events ever since sitting down at the table with his tray. Mark Halstead and the other SEALs had taken over one of the long tables in the mess hall as their own preserve, but there was room for more, and three of the submarine's petty officers, Kurzweil, Chief Evans, and EM1 Kirkpatrick, had joined them.

The SEALs so far had managed to keep more or less to themselves, and preferred it that way. They felt a certain kinship with the submariners, true, but long habit and the isolation imposed by the nature of their work and training tended to put up barriers that others rarely challenged.

In the wake of the battle that morning, with its wild maneuvers and the smoke-choking events in the torpedo room, the barriers had begun to wear thin.

"I dunno," Kirkpatrick said. "What I want to know is how a hostile got the jump on us, huh?" He nudged

Evans in the side. "Why didn't you guys pick the turd up?"

Halstead ate in silence, but listened with careful interest. Supper that night was sliders—hamburger patties supposedly given that name because they slid around in their own grease. In fact, sliders and their close kin—"rollers," or hot dogs—took their names from a comparison with a more scatological source. Submariners, Halstead had noticed, seemed to delight in the disgusting . . . a tendency they shared with SEALs.

"If he'd been making any noise, we would've," Evans replied. "Diesel boats are damned quiet when they're running on batteries."

"So? We're quieter."

"When we want to be," Kurzweil said. "But we're not silent running at thirty knots, or when we're banging around on the roof trying to fish a CIA spook out of the water."

"So what's your point, Kirkpatrick?" Evans asked. "Just because we're quiet doesn't mean *we* can hear *them*. My guess is that he happened to be laying low in the area and picked us up coming in to the rendezvous. He saw a chance to nail us with four fast fish and took it."

"Yeah," Kurzweil added. "And the bastard's probably still running, snatching a look over his shoulder now and again for fear we're right on his tail."

"What I want to know," Evans said, "is who the guy was."

"Chinese," Kurzweil said. "Definitely Chinese."

"Get fucked," Kirkpatrick said. "The Chinese wouldn't be playing terrorist and shooting down airliners."

"Yeah?" Evans said. "Then who was it?"

"Indonesia," Kirkpatrick said. "They have Kilo-class boats."

"Fuck," Kurzweil said. "*Everyone* has Kilo-class boats nowadays. They're Russia's numero-uno export!"

"Yeah," Evans said. "And why would Indonesia want to take *us* on?"

"They've got AQ cells in Indonesia, don't they?" Kirkpatrick asked. "Maybe some of them got hold of a submarine somehow and are using it for AQ terror missions."

Kurtzweil laughed. "Shit. There are al Qaeda cells in Malaysia, in the Philippines, in Borneo, in Thailand . . . what makes you so sure it was Indonesia?"

"It's an interesting idea, though," Evans said, thoughtful. He took a swig of coffee. "Al Qaeda couldn't build and operate a submarine themselves. They had to co-opt it from someone else."

"Yeah," Kurzweil said. "China."

"Why China?"

"They want to get back at us for what the Skipper did to 'em off Taiwan a couple years back."

Kirkpatrick laughed. "Shit, Kurz! You're saying this is *personal*?"

"It's sure as hell personal for the Old Man," Evans said. "You guys seen his face since we got the word about that airliner? I've never seen anyone so pissed."

"Just so he keeps drivin' this boat the way he did this morning!" Kurzweil said with a shake of his head. "Like I was sayin', pure poetry!"

Evans turned suddenly and addressed Halstead. "What do *you* guys say, Lieutenant? Who are we fighting?"

"The *enemy*," Halstead replied.

"Yeah, but who's the fucking enemy?" Kirkpatrick insisted.

Halstead shrugged and concentrated on a forkful of slider. "Does it matter?" he replied. "Dead is *dead*."

Which ended that particular conversation very nicely.

Thursday, 8 June 2006

Captain's Office, USS *Virginia*
80 miles northwest of Small Dragon Island
South China Sea
1845 hours, Zulu –8

Stevens punched up the data on Garrett's monitor—
several hundred meg of photographs, charts, and documents brought along in his sealed canister. Rather
than storing the data on a CD or a set of floppies, it
resided on a specially designed hard drive, one that
would in true spook fashion fry into a useless chunk
of carbonized circuits if anyone tried to access it without certain key programs running. He'd come to Garrett's closet-sized office right after he'd finished
eating, and connected the hard drive to an IEEE port
on the office computer.

"China," Garrett said, reading the first few document pages. He nodded. "I thought so."

"Why?" Stevens asked him. "The Chinese have been playing this one *very* close to the vest. It took us a good two weeks of digging to figure it out. How do you know it's the Chinese?"

"Style," Garrett replied. "That attack on us this morning . . . whoever was behind the sights on that other boat was a pro. He was well trained, and he was experienced. Somehow, he picked us up and tailed us . . . not an easy thing to do. And he caught us when we were vulnerable and took his shot." Garrett shook his head. "We were damned lucky he didn't connect. The point is, he didn't act like an amateur. The only people around this part of the world with that degree of skill—and balls—are the Chinese."

"Mmm. Keep reading."

A moment later, Garrett looked up, obviously surprised. "*Pakistan*? . . ."

Stevens nodded. "Not Pakistan *per se*, but a cabal within the Pakistani navy that supports al Qaeda. We think the rogue boat is Pakistan's latest purchase from our former playmates in Moscow, S-137, which they've named *Al Saif*. The Sword."

"Huh." Then he shook his head. "I don't buy it. Some of the Pakistani officers have a fair amount of experience, but they haven't been in a shooting war for some time, now. India is their enemy of choice, and the last war between them was, when? The early seventies?"

"In '71," Stevens said, nodding. "Though they started openly clashing again over Kashmir in 1983. But things have been a little calmer since both countries exploded test nukes in '98. Mutual assured destruction, y'know?"

"But no naval action since the seventies," Garrett said. "Mr. Stevens, *Virginia* was up against a pro this morning. I don't buy the Pakistan connection."

"We have that connection on very good authority," Stevens said.

"What authority?"

Stevens considered the question. The nature of intelligence work demanded compartmentalization and the sharing of information on a strictly need-to-know basis. The fact that the CIA had received information leaked to them by a high-ranking member of the Chinese naval bureau was not for casual dissemination.

"How much do you know about Chinese politics, Captain?" Stevens asked.

Garrett shrugged. "That it's pretty rough-and-tumble sometimes. Why?"

"Suffice to say that there is within the Chinese military hierarchy a small group of men who oppose their government's current adventurism. We call them 'the Conservatives.' Traditionally, China has been interested in keeping its own borders secure, and intervening beyond their borders only when they feel directly threatened—as they did in Korea. Some of the younger up-and-comers see China's future as a major player in the region and want her to have a military role to match. We call them the Expansionists. The Conservatives see this as the short road to hell, at least until they can match us at sea. Some of them might be helping us to help their own cause in Beijing."

"Makes sense. You're talking to some of the Conservatives, then?"

"There are times," Stevens said, sidestepping the direct question, "when a government will deliberately leak information in order to pass a message to the other guy. We're still examining this leak carefully to see if it's misinformation, a fancy bit of political backstabbing, or the real McCoy. But right now, this looks like it's either real, transmitted by an idealist, or real, transmitted by someone trying to hurt a political rival. Either way, we're taking it seriously."

Garrett kept reading. "Okay," he said after a time. "This is all very interesting, but it's not telling me what I need to know. Is my finger on the trigger, or not?"

"It's on the trigger, Captain. Washington intends to send a rather pointed message of its own. We will hunt down and destroy terrorist cells wherever we find them, and we will not tolerate any nation's support of those cells. At the same time, however, we don't want another Iraq."

"Meaning an open war?"

"Exactly. Bush took us to war against Iraq three years ago not because of those infamous weapons of mass destruction everyone was harping about—though the DOD's suspicions about that *was* a factor. It was because we had hard evidence of Iraq's support of al Qaeda . . . but it was evidence we couldn't make public without compromising our sources. So we publicly focused on the WMDs."

"Which were never found."

"Right. We took a PR hit on that one in order to deal with the terrorist issue."

Garrett snorted. "The hell with public relations."

"A warrior's response, Captain. But the decisions are made by politicians."

"And rightfully so. It doesn't make it any saner." He studied the document a moment more. "So . . . what all this is saying is that the Chinese—for reasons of their own—are covertly supplying help to a Pakistani submarine that has gone rogue, and is now operating at the behest of al Qaeda."

"That's it."

"What do the Chinese get out of this alliance? They

don't do something like this without a considerable payback."

"Plausible deniability when the rogue hits Vietnamese and Filipino interests in the Spratly Islands. The Expansionists want to make the Spratly group a solidly Chinese bastion, both as an overseas site for naval facilities and for future access to possible oil reserves in the region. The Spratlys' strategic location astride the sea lanes between Singapore and Japan is a factor too. There's also this."

Reaching across the desk, he brought up a new page on the intelligence briefing. Garrett read it. "Shit," he said. "This is hard?"

"It's hard. We were pretty sure that one Chinese submarine, one of their new Kilos, had left Darien a month ago. They tried to hide it with a decoy, but wood and fiberglass don't reflect the ultraviolet in sunlight the same way steel does. We spotted that one right off. Three days ago, the rest of these subs sailed from Hainan. They must be in the region by now."

"For what purpose? I thought you said the Chinese are letting the AQ take the heat for this one?"

Stevens sighed. "I wish we knew for sure. Intelligence work is mostly guessing, you know. But one good guess has it that Beijing is expecting us to overreact to the AQ sub's attacks. We send in the Seventh Fleet, shooting up everything in our way. And they have a fleet of *very* quiet submarines waiting to take us down a notch. Our . . . informant suggested that one of their targets might be the *Roosevelt*."

"A supercarrier would be a pretty impressive notch on their gun," Garrett agreed.

"Yup. And they could *still* plausibly deny involvement, and say the AQ did it. But the loss of an asset like the *Roosevelt* would make us think twice and maybe three times about overextending ourselves in the South China Sea. Beijing could become the preeminent power in the region almost by default."

"It would make their designs on Taiwan more realistic, that's for sure," Garrett said. "I gather then that you're saying I can take on submarines working for the AQ to my heart's content, but that I'm not supposed to go after Chinese submarines."

"That's about the size of it."

"Shit, Stevens! How the hell am I supposed to implement that as a mission order? Sonar targets do *not* advertise their nationalities!"

"You are expected to defend yourself, Captain. If you are fired upon, or have a reasonable expectation that you are about to be fired upon, you have weapons free, and can take whatever tactical action you consider appropriate."

"Those are part of an attack boat's standing orders, Mr. Stevens. If attacked, we strike back. But without knowing who is who out here, some Chinese boats might be hit."

"Part of Washington's idea here, Captain, is to use this incident to send a very strong message to Beijing. 'Do *not* provide assistance to the AQ or other terror groups.' If it takes sinking one or two of their submarines to send that message, well . . . we just expect you to be discreet about it."

Suddenly, surprisingly, Garrett laughed, long and loud. To Stevens' ear, it sounded as though a great deal of pent-up frustration and stress was behind the laugh, which stopped just short of becoming touched with hysteria.

The outburst, from a submarine skipper, was unsettling, to say the least.

Control Room, USS *Virginia*
10 miles off Small Dragon Island
South China Sea
2250 hours, Zulu −8

Garrett leaned forward in the command chair, hands clasped, studying the scene displayed on the big control room monitor. Jorgensen stood to his left, Stevens to his right. All conversation in the control room had ceased, as those not immediately focused on their duties watched the scene as well.

"Holy shit," Jorgensen said softly after a long moment. "That is one hell of a marina."

The television monitor showed an image picked out in infrared, and so was a grainy monochrome picture in various shades of green, ranging from almost yellow to dead black.

The structure was enormous, raised on pylons above the sea. It was low tide, now, so bits of the coral atoll showed above water. Most of the four-story main building was elevated above the coral, however, looking like the crew facility for a remote seabed oil rig which, in fact, it almost certainly was. Light gleamed brightly from several dozen windows, and from the off-center helipad raised above the flat top of the building.

To one side, however, was a huge structure nearly as large as the building, if not quite as high. It possessed no windows, but the western face was pierced by an enormous set of sliding doors, opening onto a cavernous, brightly lit interior that was clearly designed to shelter boats or small ships.

"Do you think we could get closer?" Stevens asked.

"Take us in closer, Weps," Garrett said. "I'd like to see inside if we can."

"Aye aye, Captain," Lieutenant Bill Carpenter said. "I'll see what I can do."

Carpenter was not conning the *Virginia*, though the view on the big control room monitor might have conveyed that impression. The weapons officer was seated at his console against the control room bulkhead to Garrett's left, using a joystick and touchscreen to control a torpedo-sized extension of the submarine, an AN/BLQ-11A LMRS Mod 4 reconnaissance/monitor platform, or "Junior," for short. The initials LMRS stood for "Long-term Mine Reconnaissance System," and referred to a remote-piloted Unmanned Underwater Vehicle, or UUV.

Junior was a torpedo without a warhead. Instead, it had an extremely sophisticated command control system and a sensor/camera suite. It was a bit shorter than a Mark 48 ADCAP, but the same width, so it could be released through a torpedo tube; a completely retractable Photonics mast let it cruise just beneath the water's surface while gathering electronic and visual data. Images, sensor data, and position information were relayed back to the *Virginia* either via a satellite relay, or directly through the water using a low-frequency coded acoustical data link. Carpenter's fly-by-wire control instructions were transmitted to the UUV the same way. *Virginia*'s torpedo tube one could be fitted with a long, telescoping arm that could literally reach out, snag Junior, and haul him back inside at the completion of his mission.

The LMRS had originally been conceived as a means of investigating minefields and strange objects on the bottom that might be mines; Junior was certainly more expendable than a billion-dollar attack submarine and crew. By the time *Virginia* had been launched, however, UUV technology had advanced to the point that Junior was capable of handling a broad range of remote reconnaissance missions. It could detect and scout mines, yes, but it could also creep close to an enemy harbor or base and return detailed images of what it saw there.

That was what the control room crew was watching now. *Virginia* was submerged at periscope depth a safe ten miles northwest of Small Dragon Island, while Carpenter used his joystick to send low-frequency acoustical data link signals—or L-FADs—to Junior, nudging the remote closer to the open hangar door on the side of the Chinese base.

Using L-FADs in these waters was a calculated risk, of course. The acoustical signals were, in fact, active sonar signals, and emitting them could call unwanted attention to either *Virginia* or Junior or both. Those signals were not conventional sonar pings, however, and they were masked by seemingly random patterns of noise that were filtered out by the computers that processed the signals at both ends. They were also transmitted in frequencies outside of the range generally monitored by antisubmarine passive sonar systems. Chances were that the occupants of that base were totally unaware of the streams of data flowing back and forth across the miles, and that they'd have no idea what they were listening to if they did hear anything.

Junior accelerated slightly, moving at less than three knots to avoid putting up a wake. It was completely submerged except for the slender Photonics mast extending above his hull, about where a sail would be on a conventional submarine. The darkness masked the UUV's approach, as did the layers of radar-absorbent materials coating the mast. Slowly, it crept closer.

"Looks like some kind of activity inside," Jorgensen said. "Hard to see, though."

Rain earlier in the day had given way to something midway between mist and drizzle. The light spilling from the open hangar tended to blur and smear the infrared image, making details fuzzy. But it did look as though something was moving inside.

Alphanumerics on the lower right-hand corner of the display gave Junior's coordinates, speed, depth, and the range to the target—determined by a tiny infrared laser mounted on the Photonics mast. When they were eighty meters from the near side of the hangar, Garrett said, "All stop on the UUV."

"Aye aye, sir," Carpenter said, tapping out a command on his touch screen. Junior drifted forward a few more yards before coming to a halt, partly on inertia, partly on the time delay as acoustical signals traveled from *Virginia* to the UUV. The sea state was considerably lower than earlier in the day, but there was enough of a swell to make the transmitted image roll and pitch slightly with the waves. Carpenter was doing an amazing job of keeping the camera platform reasonably steady.

"We definitely have a new contact, Captain," Carpenter announced. "I'm getting screw noises. Twin screws, moving dead slow."

A moment later, a shape resolved itself out of the blur of green light, a sharply curving prow, a high superstructure with an elevated flying bridge, two decks' worth of portholes above the main deck.

"Rich man's yacht," Jorgensen said, eyebrows rising. "Is that *Al Qahir*?"

"That's her," Stevens said. "We've just lucked out."

"Mr. Jorgensen," Garrett said, "alert the SEALs. We have a target for them."

"Aye aye, sir."

Al Qahir first . . . and then the Chinese base.

Friday, 9 June 2006
Bridge, yacht *Al Qahir*
Twelve miles west of Small Dragon Island
South China Sea
0035 hours, Zulu –8

The rain had stopped some time ago, but visibility was still poor—blessedly so, since Zaki wanted to be far from Small Dragon Island by the time the clouds lifted and the ocean surface was again visible to the prying eye of American spy satellites. He walked over to the circular screen of the yacht's radar display and studied the empty green sweep of the rotating cursor for a moment. *Al Qahir* was alone, for the moment, on a wide empty ocean.

Which didn't necessarily mean safety, of course. Turning, he walked toward the rear of the bridge area, to the console where a young Saudi sonar technician seemed to be puzzled about something he was hearing.

Though she looked like a typical wealthy man's yacht, *Al Qahir* had some very special appointments indeed—not the least of which was a highly advanced sonar system, a Russian-built Tamir high-frequency system capable of picking out the approach of submarines or underwater commandos from the background noise of the ocean deeps.

Zaki was extremely aware that American submarines could be operating in the area.

"What is it?" he asked.

The sonar man shook his head, then removed his earphones and handed them to Zaki. "At first I wasn't sure, sir. I was picking up a strange noise of some sort. But listen." He grinned.

Zaki held one of the earphones to his ear and listened. The far-off, eerie cry, echoing through the deeps, was at once familiar and hauntingly alien.

"Whalesong," he said.

"Yes, sir. A whale love song."

"Then perhaps we can relax," Zaki said, smiling as he handed the headphones back. "If whales are making love beneath us, that means there is nothing about to disturb them . . . like American submarines!"

"Exactly what I was thinking, sir."

Zaki returned to his usual spot behind the bridge windscreen to the right of the Saudi pilot, staring out into the empty night, giving thanks to Allah for the darkness, the clouds, and the solitude.

He would be glad when this mission was over. *Al Qahir* would remain in the area only for another five days, coordinating the activities of *Shuhadaa Muqaddaseen*. After that, with the American fleet entering the Spratly group and—in all likelihood—engaging the Chinese, they would round the western coast of Borneo and make for Jakarta. The Maktum cell in Indonesia would provide him with the papers and identity necessary to smuggle him back into Europe. He would also turn the two women over to the Maktum people in Jakarta. Let them worry about ransom, about keeping them safe from the sexual appetites of their guards . . . or about the possible repercussions that might descend out of the night sky.

ASDS-2
Twelve miles west of Small Dragon Island
South China Sea
0037 hours, Zulu −8

Lieutenant Mark Halstead leaned forward in the number-two pilot's seat of the ASDS, watching the blip representing the target grow slowly closer. "Range four hundred," he said softly. "Relative bearing still zero-zero-zero, closing at eighteen knots."

So far, so good, he thought. They were only going to get one shot at this, and it had to go down perfectly.

Once *Al Qahir* had been positively identified emerging from the sheltered base at Small Dragon Island and her westward course confirmed, *Virginia* had swung around to the southwest, putting herself directly in *Al Qahir*'s path. The SEAL detachment had climbed up the escape trunk ladder and into the ASDS. When they were a mile from the approaching *Al Qahir*, the SEAL minisub had cast off from its larger consort, heading due east, bow-on to the yacht.

The ASDS had a sixty-seven-horsepower motor that could propel the fifty-five-ton minisub at a top speed of eight knots. *Al Qahir* was currently moving at ten knots which, combined with the ASDS's speed of eight, meant the two were approaching each other at eighteen knots—about twenty miles per hour. Four hundred yards at eighteen knots . . . about forty seconds more to contact. If the yacht veered off to right or left, the ASDS would be hard pressed to match the maneuver; if they missed on their first pass, the minisub would not be able to catch up in a stern chase. *Virginia* would have to disable the yacht instead, and that would be both messy and dangerous.

The idea was to take the yacht down as swiftly and as quietly as possible, both to prevent those on board from putting out a distress call and alerting the defenders of Small Dragon Island, and just in case there were hostages on board. The passengers and crew of the *Sea Breeze* were still unaccounted for, so the SEALs would be treating this as a hostage rescue.

First, though, they needed to stop the yacht, and

they needed to stop it without alerting its crew.

He checked the sonar screen once more. One hundred fifty yards. Whalesong chirped and clicked and moaned, startlingly loud in the tiny control compartment.

The ASDS was using active sonar—they *had* to in order to get precise range and target data. But they were trying a new twist; irregular sonar pulses were masked behind a computer recording of a couple of mating humpback whales. The ASDS computer could mask out the recording in order to receive clearly the echoed sonar returns. Anyone listening on board the target, however, would hear only the whales—unless they were *very* good, or had extraordinarily sophisticated equipment.

Or unless whoever was listening on board the target happened to know that humpback whales didn't frequent these seas, or mate at this time of year.

A calculated risk.

As was this head-on approach. The ASDS didn't mount torpedoes or other weapons. In order to stop the yacht, they would have to use the minisub itself as a blunt-nosed torpedo.

One hundred yards, end zone to end zone on a football field.

Like *Virginia*, the ASDS possessed a Photonics mast. Its sensor suite included a camera that relayed the view to a large-screen monitor in the control compartment. Right now, all that Halstead and Michaels could see on the screen was the dark gray nose of the ASDS below, and above the diffuse glow of hull lights reflected from tiny particles of muck adrift in the water. Going in with the forward hull lights on was another calculated risk; the *Al Qahir*'s pilot might see the light in his path—a light that *might* be mistaken for natural phosphorescence, but which also might give the game away seconds too early.

The ASDS was traveling at a depth of fifty feet, too deep for the light to show on the surface. Michaels, at the controls, was going to have to do some fancy flying in the next few moments to avoid having the lights visible on the roof while still hitting the target.

Fifty yards. . . .

"I'm starting to bring her up," Michaels said.

"Right." Halstead picked up the intercom mike. "Listen up back there! We're on our final approach. Brace for collision!" He checked his own seat belt. He didn't know how rough the impact was going to be. The ASDS was ruggedly built. She *should* survive the collision . . . he hoped. . . .

The ASDS's active sonar continued pinging down the range, a few yards at a time, with the actual figure counting down on the main view screen. Ten yards . . .

The bottom of the yacht became visible, a dark shadow against a deeper blackness overhead, wedge-shaped, sharp-prowed, churning through the water straight toward the minisub's bow.

Rising parallel to the surface, the ASDS made contact first with its dorsal surface, scraping hard against the yacht's keel. The clang of impact rang through the minisub's interior, and Halstead felt the vessel roll sharply to the right.

Directly ahead on the monitor, he could see the yacht's twin screws churning through the dark water, illuminated by the minisub's lights.

With a second, louder clang, the ASDS's nose slammed into the yacht's starboard screw and rudder. Again they rolled hard, this time to the left, shuddering with the impact. The continuous metallic scrape of hull on keel sounded like the minisub was tearing open.

And then the sound, blessedly, ceased. Michaels tapped out commands on his touchscreen, pushing his joystick forward and to the right. The ASDS heeled hard over to starboard as it dropped into a sharp, descending turn. "Kill the lights!" he snapped, and Halstead hit the touchpoint on his own screen. Instantly, the scene on the monitor was plunged into darkness absolute.

"Are we okay?" Halstead asked.

"Never better," Michaels replied. "That *did* kind of jar the fillings in the teeth, though, huh?"

Halstead studied the sonar screen a moment. "Target has ceased movement," he said.

"Right! Time for you guys to do your SEAL thing!"

"Roger that!" Unsnapping his seatbelt, Halstead stood and, stooping to avoid hitting his head against the low overhead, began making his way aft toward the lockout chamber.

"Hoo-yah!" DiMercurio said, meeting him in the chamber and handing him an H&K MP5.

"Time to earn our pay," Halstead replied. "Let's get wet!"

**Bridge, yacht *Al Qahir*
Twelve miles west of Small Dragon Island
South China Sea
0038 hours, Zulu −8**

Zaki grabbed hold of the console in front of him to keep from being thrown down. "What was that?"

The impact, sharp as it was, went on for several seconds, dragging down the length of *Al Qahir*'s keel with a shuddering, grinding series of jolts.

"We've hit a reef!" the pilot snapped.

"Nonsense. Small Dragon Island is the closest reef around, and that's twenty kilometers behind us! . . . ."

Unless they were badly off course. Turning, he hurried back to the sonar station. "What's our depth?"

"Sir . . . I'm showing nine hundred meters! No sign of a reef or rock or anything we could have hit!"

Al Qahir possessed two types of sonar—the Tamir array for tracking submarines or other undersea noises, and a depth indicator, a simple-minded idiot by comparison. This last gave its readout as a depth in meters at the helm, and here, at the sonar console, as a visual graph showing the seabed as a contour line. Zaki peered at the display, then pointed. "What's this?"

The depth indicator showed a kind of shadow beneath and behind the yacht.

"Fish, probably," the sonar operator said. "You can use this instrument as a fish-finder, you know."

"Fish? Or something else?" The shadow was too small to be a submarine. Perhaps one of those lovestruck whales they'd been listening to?

The helmsman was turning the yacht's ignition key. The engines had stopped when they hit the thing, whatever it was, and he was trying to restart.

"What is the problem, Jabal?" he asked.

"Our right propeller is damaged, sir," the pilot said. "Both engines stalled when we hit. I think I can get the left engine going again, but the right screw is useless."

Zaki was suddenly worried . . . and not by the damage report alone. They *might* have hit a whale . . . but they might have hit something else as well.

He picked up the intercom microphone. "Attention! All hands!" he snapped. "Go to combat stations!"

Better, he thought, remembering an American expression, to be safe than sorry.

Or dead.

Friday, 9 June 2006

Stateroom, yacht *Al Qahir*
Twelve miles west of Small Dragon Island
South China Sea
0039 hours, Zulu −8

Muhammad Jabarrah had been in the yacht's large and luxuriously appointed lounge when *Al Qahir* had jolted hard, scraped noisily along something just beneath the water, then floated free, her engines dead. Several of the fighters relaxing with him in the common room leaped to their feet, looking alarmed.

"That idiot pilot!" Jabarrah snapped. "We've hit a reef!"

"Are we sinking?" one of the fighters asked. He was a teen-aged Pashtun tribesman from Afghanistan, wearing a bulky orange life jacket over his combat fatigues. The kid looked shaken. Small wonder. People from his tribe had little experience with boats and rarely found themselves venturing onto the open ocean. He was probably terrified of drowning.

"I doubt it. But it sounds like one of the propellers was damaged." He could feel the shudder as the helmsman tried to restart the engines. Before becoming one of Zaki's strong men, Jabarrah had had a fair amount of experience piloting pleasure boats in the Arabian Gulf, and knew the feel of a badly bent propeller blade. Judging by the shock, he was willing to bet that *Al Qahir*'s right propeller and rudder were either badly bent, or had even been knocked off. If the former, the yacht would need to be rigged to travel on one engine. If the latter, there would almost certainly be leaking around the damaged shaft. They would need to sound the well and determine how bad the flooding was, then take steps to seal it off.

A moment later, Zaki's voice came over the intercom. "*Attention! All hands! Go to combat stations!*"

The men scrambled to grab their weapons, and started bounding up the three short steps out of the common room and onto *Al Qahir*'s aft well deck. Jabarrah followed, stopping when he was outside to take a long, calculating look at the ocean.

The night was overcast, dark, and calm, with a low and oily swell to the sea. He looked over the side and saw only black water. Looking astern, he saw that the ocean was empty for as far as he could see. Nothing, no waves breaking, to mark the submerged reef they'd just kissed.

Yes, but he knew how easy it was to ground on a reef, and these waters were notoriously treacherous in that regard. The pilot should have been more circumspect in his choice of course, and should have been traveling more slowly.

No matter. The accident made possible a course of

action he'd been considering for some hours, now, ever since they'd left Small Dragon Island.

Turning, he retraced his steps back down into *Al Qahir*'s lounge, then made his way forward along the main central passageway to a portside stateroom guarded by two fighters. "I'll watch the prisoners," he told them. "You are needed on the aft deck."

"Yes, sir!" one of the guards said. He was another young Pashtun, and he looked scared.

"Be careful," the other guard, a Pakistani, an older man, said with a wink as he slung his AK-47 over his shoulder and handed Jabarrah the stateroom key. "They are wildcats. They might bite!"

"I think I know how to handle a couple of *women*." He sneered the word.

The Pakistani grinned, nodded, and walked away up the corridor, leaving Jabarrah alone outside the door.

Excellent. Zaki would be occupied on the bridge for quite a while. It would take time to assess the damage to the propeller and keel, and to repair any leakage around the shaft. *Al Qahir* would have no trouble reaching Jakarta with one engine, propeller, and rudder out of commission, but it would take a while—possibly several hours—to make certain the yacht was still seaworthy. That gave Jabarrah plenty of time.

He reached under his shirt and pulled his pistol out of his belt, an old but serviceable 9mm Makarov. It was quite possible that the two prisoners would have to be shot while they were trying to escape. But not just yet. . . .

With the pistol in one hand, he unlocked the door with the other and stepped swiftly inside.

Yacht *Al Qahir*
Twelve miles west of Small Dragon Island
South China Sea
0040 hours, Zulu –8

Halstead rose silently through blackness, one hand extended until he felt the smooth, solid bulk of the hull above him. Carefully, he felt his way off the keel and up the rounded slope of the yacht's hull until he reached the waterline just beneath the port bow.

Like the rest of the assault squad, he was garbed for what the Teams referred to as a VBSS subsurface assault—the initials stood for "Visit, Board, Search, and Seizure." He wore a Nomex flight suit and hood, mask and fins, both a Secumar UBA jacket connected to his Draeger oxygen rebreather and a standard inflatable UDT life jacket, and an assault vest with web gear. The assault gear and clothing made him massively bulky, and in the water it felt as if it was dragging him down, but he adjusted the pace of his kicks to hover motionless in the water.

He had to work entirely by touch in the ink-black darkness, but he could feel the tug at his combat harness as he moved that told him DiMercurio was a few feet away, attached to him by a short safety tether. With his free hand, he raised the leech and pressed it home.

"The leech" was a temporary mooring ring, an attachment point for the cable DiMercurio was trailing behind him. Halstead sealed it to the hull by pushing down two levers, one to either side of the ring, creating a powerful suction that anchored the device to the hull. As soon as it was set, Halstead tugged at the safety tether three times. DiMercurio moved closer, then, snapping a hasp over the mooring ring. The

ASDS was now secured to the yacht; the suction device wouldn't be up to towing a fifty-five-ton SEAL minisub very far, but if the yacht suddenly hared off toward the far horizon, the drag on the mooring line would certainly slow the *Al Qahir* before it gave way. The line also provided a path, by following it down hand-over-hand, back to the relative safety of the sub, should the assault squad need to make a hasty exit.

"Trident Three, in position" sounded over the headset imbedded in his Nomex hood, the voice somewhat garbled, but intelligible. The SEALs wore seaproof Motorolas, tiny radios with microphones imbedded in their flight suits at their throats. Range was sharply limited underwater, since radio waves didn't penetrate that medium well, but was good enough for the squad to maintain contact in the area immediately around the target.

"Trident Seven, ready."

"Trident Four, ready to roll!"

One by one, the other SEALs checked in, each reaching a pre-assigned position and sounding off.

"Trident One ready," Halstead said when the other seven all had spoken. "Trident Two, give us a sneak-and-peek."

"Roger that," EM1 Nemecek's voice responded. "I see four . . . five . . . make it six tangos on the aft deck. AK-47s. Looks like they have an attitude."

Meaning Nemecek thought they looked like they were on the alert. Well, they couldn't have everything.

"Assault team, stand ready. Trident Two, give 'em a show!"

Nemecek had come to the surface some fifteen to twenty yards off the *Al Qahir*'s starboard side, surfacing just enough that he could get his face above water and eyeball the target. At Halstead's order, he yanked

the lanyard on a small flare attached to its own flota-
tion collar and hurled it into the darkness; the flare
burst into intense white light, bobbing on the surface
of the ocean only a few yards off the *Al Qahir*'s starboard side.

"They see it," Nemecek announced. "Port side
clear!"

"Trident, *go!*" Halstead snapped, and the SEAL
squad surged upward.

There were nine SEALs in the water including Halstead. One—Nemecek—was providing the starboard-
side diversion. The rest worked in four buddy teams of
two. In each pair, one man carried as a part of his gear
an extensible painter's pole with a hook on the business end attached to a rolled-up caving ladder. On
Halstead's command, the four men with the painters'
poles surfaced, extended the poles, and snagged *Al
Qahir*'s gunwale at four different spots along the port
side. The other four SEALs, weapons strapped at the
ready to their sides, grabbed hold of the caving ladders
and scrambled up out of the water.

The brightly burning flare had grabbed the attention of every man on *Al Qahir*'s deck, dragging them
over to the starboard side. Four SEALs came up the
port side as one, opening fire as soon as their heads and
shoulders cleared the yacht's gunwale.

Most of the tangos—milspeak for terrorists—had
their backs to the SEALs as they leaned over the side,
staring at the flare. One tango was just turning to face
the port side as Halstead surged up the railing. Halstead grabbed the grip of his H&K, flicking on the laser
sight. When the dancing red dot jittered across the
tango's center of mass, he triggered the weapon one-
handed, putting the man down with a sound-
suppressed three-round burst.

CQB—Close Quarters Battle—is not the arena for fair play or chivalry. The man Halstead gunned down probably hadn't even seen the SEALs, not if he'd stared into the flare's light and wrecked his night vision. The other terrorists started twisting and collapsing as silenced rounds slammed into their backs close behind the dancing red dots of the laser sights, cutting them down before they even had a chance to realize they were in danger. Within three seconds, the first four SEALs were on the deck, each down on one knee, their weapons covering all directions as the next four men climbed aboard.

A tango standing on the weather bridge walked over to the ladder leading down to the superstructure; Diller hit him with a three-round burst and he tumbled down the ladder, hitting the deck with a heavy thud.

Slipping off his fins in favor of the gripping soles of his wetsuit booties, Halstead rose and jogged for the door leading down into the yacht's interior. DiMercurio took the ladder next to the door, heading up topside for the superstructure and bridge.

They'd studied the blueprints for yachts identical in design to *Al Qahir*, and had a good idea of what was where and how to get from one place to another. The assault now had three goals. First and foremost, they needed to find out if there were hostages on board and secure them. Halstead's group had that responsibility. At the same time, DiMercurio's fireteam would secure the yacht's bridge and communications center. Only after those goals were accomplished would they take down the rest of the terrorists on board.

Halstead kicked in the flimsy door to the yacht's lounge and rolled back as Forrester tossed a crash-bang through. The lounge lit up with a firecracker string of piercingly loud detonations, and then Diller and Pulaski stormed through the door and down the steps.

One tango, a scrawny, terrified-looking kid wearing a bright orange life jacket, was on his knees, hands over ears streaming blood. Diller shot the kid through the head and the SEALs kept moving. Ahead, a passageway led forward, with four closed stateroom doors.

Each SEAL took a different door, moving up beside it, slapping a breaching charge next to the lock, and yanking the fuse igniter. Almost as one, the four charges went off in a stuttering barrage of four ringing blasts that splintered wood and filled the passageway with roiling clouds of smoke.

Halstead leaped through the wreckage of the door, his H&K held shoulder high, the red beam from its laser startlingly crisp in the smoke-filled air. There was only an instant to determine that he'd hit pay dirt—a blond woman in a bikini handcuffed to a chair to the left, a red-headed woman on the bed to the right, naked, pinned down on her side by a wild-eyed, half-naked man.

The man was already dragging the woman in front of him as a shield with one arm, while his other hand brandished an automatic pistol. "*Tawaqaf!*" Halstead yelled as the laser dot jittered back and forth between the bulkhead and the woman's body. "Halt!"

"She dies!" the man shouted back in English, the muzzle of the pistol pressed hard against the woman's head. "You move, she dies!"

The woman doubled forward against the guy's arm, slamming her right elbow against the man's ribs. She probably didn't hurt him much, but the blow startled him enough to break his focus. Halstead triggered a three-round burst as the laser dot danced between the terrorist's eyes, exploding the man's head in a gory spray across the bulkhead over the bed. The pistol fell from nerveless fingers as the terrorist crumpled backward; the woman spilled onto the deck, shrieking.

"Lieutenant Halstead, U.S. Navy!" he shouted. "Stay down! Stay down!"

He checked the stateroom for other threats, then turned to cover the shattered doorway. "This is Trident One!" he called. "Room Three! One tango down! Two hostages secure! Clear!"

"Room One, all clear!" came back.

"Room Four, one tango down. Clear!"

"Room Two! Clear!"

Diller came through a moment later. "Looks like you won the prize, Skipper."

"Cut them, loose," he snapped, keeping his aim on the door. "We're not out of this yet!"

Bridge, yacht *Al Qahir*
Twelve miles west of Small Dragon Island
South China Sea
0041 hours, Zulu −8

Zaki had just been discussing *Al Qahir*'s condition with the yacht's captain when they'd heard the consternation coming from the aft deck. Leaning out of the starboard door and looking aft, he could see something burning on the water.

"What is that?" the captain asked. "A flare?"

"The men may be playing games," Zaki said, his voice dangerous. "I *will* have words with them!"

For Zaki, it was one more irritation in a *very* irritating night. According to the captain, water was coming in around the damaged propeller shaft at an alarming rate. It could be patched, and would not immediately threaten the boat, but it meant a further delay of some hours before they could get under way once more, and that news had not improved Zaki's temper.

"I don't think so," the captain said, scowling. "My crew knows better!"

"It might be my people, however. I'll go check. . . ."

But he stopped himself an instant before stepping outside, something nagging at his awareness.

That was it. During one of his rounds of training at a camp in Afghanistan, years ago, he'd studied some of the great hostage and terrorist actions of the past forty years. If one knew how the opposition had launched assaults and hostage rescues in the past, it was possible to better prepare for the future.

In particular he'd read about a classic action in Somalia in 1977. The then-West German GSG-9 antiterrorist unit had stormed an airliner hijacked by Palestinian commandos at Mogadishu, killing the terrorists and liberating the passengers and crew.

What Zaki was remembering was the diversion—a bonfire built in the night some distance in front of the aircraft's nose, a fire that drew all of the terrorists forward to the cockpit moments before the GSG-9 troops stormed aboard.

"We are under attack!" he shouted, whirling away from the door. "Arm yourselves!" He reached for an AK-47 on the chart table. A loud thump sounded from overhead.

"What was that?" the sonar man said, rising from his console.

"Probably Abdul," the captain replied. "Stay at your post!"

Something bounced onto the bridge from the open

doorway leading aft, past the radio room. Zaki spun, following the object with his eyes . . . and then the object detonated with a string of blinding flashes and ear-wracking blasts.

He dropped to the deck, the AK falling from his grasp. He couldn't see! His ears were ringing, he couldn't hear . . .

And then something unseen and unheard slammed against the side of his skull, punching Zaki into unconsciousness.

Control Room, USS *Virginia*
Twelve miles west of Small Dragon Island
South China Sea
0215 hours, Zulu −8

"Now hear this, now hear this" rang over *Virginia*'s 1MC, as Jorgensen passed the word. "Rig ship for female visitors. That is, rig ship for female visitors."

Garrett looked up from his console, met Jorgensen's eyes. The XO shrugged. *Women and submarines do not go together*, he seemed to be saying.

Women rarely came on board submarines, in fact. When a sub was in port, there were the occasional dependents' cruises, where mothers, wives, and girlfriends were taken out on a quick sortie. The boat would dive—no deeper than 400 feet—and go through some angles and dangles to impress them, and then return straight to the dock.

With "ship rigged for female visitors," nudity was secured, cursing and loud shouting were secured, and all hands wore full uniform instead of skivvies or towels. It was, in fact, the same routine as for when a visiting admiral or other dignitary came on board.

The real problem was where to put the two women just rescued from the *Al Qahir*. They would be headed for sick bay first to be fully checked out, but after that . . . where did you put two women on a sewer pipe already crowded with 150-some men?

The gallant choice—Garrett surrendering his own cabin—was not an option. The bunk in there would only sleep one, hot-bunking was not a good idea when both women needed to catch up on a lot of sleep, and the adjoining office was a high-traffic area with lots of noise and lots of coming and going. In the end, he'd talked to the denizens of the goat's locker—*Virginia*'s chief petty officers—and asked them to volunteer their quarters for the duration. The women would have their own shower, head, and some privacy. The chiefs would bunk with the enlisted men in the already crowded torpedo room and enlisted quarters.

Fortunately, Jorgensen had remembered in time to send Chief Kurzweil forward to the goat's locker with instructions to secure all salacious material—pin-ups, copies of *Playboy* and assorted skin books, posters, and Internet printouts of naked women and sex acts, and the like. Such materials were officially prohibited and vanished magically just before each shipboard inspection, but Garrett and Jorgensen both knew that those materials always reappeared magically within moments of the inspecting officer's departure.

On the control room screen forward, the monitor showed the view aft, where the *Al Qahir* had been tied up alongside the *Virginia*. Several sailors rigged with safety lines secured to the deck were helping to bring the two rescued women across to the submarine. Both wore life jackets and ill-fitting dungarees. Lieutenant

Kendall had broken the dungarees out of stores to replace the swimsuits and tattered shirts that were all they'd had with them on board the yacht. That nudity-secured rule went both ways in the cramped world of a submarine.

The women were safely on board. *Good.* Lieutenant Falk was leading them forward to the main hatch.

He was standing a moment later when Falk led them into the control room. Both had dark blue blankets draped over their shoulders and around their bodies; there was no way to transfer from a small boat to a submarine without getting at least a little bit wet.

"Welcome aboard, ladies," he said. "I'm Captain Garrett, commanding officer of the USS *Virginia.*"

"Captain Garrett!" the redhead exclaimed. "I'm Katic Milford. Thank you, *thank* you for the rescue!"

He grinned. "All I did was provide the bus service, ma'am. It was the SEALs who did the actual rescuing." He glanced at the blonde, who had a dazed expression on her face. Katie was supporting her with an arm around her shoulders. "Is your friend all right?"

"Ginger's been through a rough time, Captain. She'll be fine."

"You've both been through the wringer. Lieutenant Falk will take you down to sick bay, where Dr. Colbert can have a look at you. I'll have them send down more dry clothes."

"Thank you, Captain."

She looked as though she wanted to say something more. "Yes?"

"I told this officer already. There are seven more of us being held back at that island."

"The island. Small Dragon?"

"I think that's what they called it, yes. There's a

huge base there, covers the entire island. It has a dock inside a huge room, like a garage a couple of stories tall with sliding doors."

"You were there on the yacht, the *Sea Breeze*?"

"Yes, sir. A submarine surfaced and hijacked us first. That was . . . God. I don't know how long ago. Days, though."

"A submarine." He studied her face. "Was it Chinese?"

"I think there was at least one Chinese officer on board, but he wasn't in command. No, the crew was Arab."

"Arab." That could mean almost anything.

"They kept us locked in a tiny room. They shot poor Mr. Kingsfield when he tried to stop them from taking me and Ginger away. Then they met up with the *Al Qahir* at sea and we were sent over to the yacht. A day later, we reached that island base. They took the men off the yacht and led them into the complex, somewhere. They kept Ginger and me on the yacht. I didn't know why at the time." She made a bitter face. "I guess I do now."

"I'll want to have a talk with you later. We'll need to know everything you can tell us, everything you remember, about that base, and about your friends. But later. Have the doc check you out, and get some dry clothes, some food, and some rest first. Okay?"

She smiled. "Okay. Thank you, Captain. Again. Come on, Ginger. . . ."

Garrett watched as Falk led them out of the control room. Out of the corner of his eye, he caught the sailor at the dive plane station nudging the helmsman with a lascivious grin.

"Belay that shit, Simmons," he growled. "Eyes on your station or you're on report!"

"Aye aye, sir!" Simmons yelped, his eyes snapping back to his console so sharply Garrett could almost swear he'd heard them click.

"Our two passengers have been to hell and back. They will be treated with kindness, gentlemanly conduct, and respect, or I'll have the hide of the sorry son of a bitch in question nailed to the Photonics mast as a flag! Am I clear?"

"Clear, sir!"

The word, Garrett thought, would spread . . . and be more effective than a 1MC announcement.

He returned his attention to the control room monitor. The deck party was casting off *Al Qahir*, so that the yacht and the submarine didn't risk damage to each other in the heavy seas. The SEALs, all but their CO, would remain on the terrorist yacht for the time being—along with five prisoners taken out of the eighteen men on board, and with Chief Vance and a working party of the *Virginia*. *Al Qahir* was taking on water, and the idea was to plug the leak around her starboard shaft and keep her from going to the bottom. As soon as a Navy Sea Stallion could reach them from the *Roosevelt*, terrorist experts and computer technicians would begin sorting through the small mountain of data stored in the computers on board. At that time, a special boarding party would try to take *Al Qahir* to port—probably to Manila, which was closest—and begin disassembling her, looking for any useful scrap of data.

Virginia would have to remain in the area until then. The evaluation team would relieve the SEAL VBSS party, which would then return to the *Virginia*. At the same time, the two rescued women would be transferred to the helicopter and flown back to the *Roosevelt*. Current ETA for the Sea Stallion was no sooner than 1030 hours—about eight hours from now—and the met boys already were making doubtful noises about that estimate. For this kind of at-sea transfer, the helicopter pilot needed daylight, low winds, and a calm sea. According to the most recent satellite weather report for the region, they would be looking at more rain by dawn, and that might mean Katie and Ginger would be guests on board the *Virginia* longer than expected.

Garrett decided he would worry about that when the time came. In the meantime, *Virginia* could submerge in order to take the ASDS back on board. The minisub had limited battery life, and needed to be docked in order to recharge. That maneuver was next on the list, just as soon as *Al Qahir* was clear, and the last of the deck party on her afterdeck had come below.

Lieutenant Falk returned to the control room. "The ladies have been escorted to sick bay, Captain. Request permission to return to my station."

"Granted, Mr. Falk." Falk was currently standing as JOOD—the junior officer of the deck—which meant partly that he was learning the duties of the OOD, or officer of the deck, and partly that he was on hand to run errands like escorting visitors below to sick bay.

Lieutenant Lanesky was the diving officer of the watch. "Mr. Lanesky. Make all preparations to submerge."

"Make all preparations to submerge, aye aye, sir!"

As the control room crew went back to work, Garrett took another look at the *Al Qahir,* wallowing uncomfortably in the seas off the Virginia's port stern quarter. The report he'd heard from Halstead mentioned that one of the captured men was Zaki—the al

Qaeda kingpin who might well be in charge of the terrorist operation in the Spratlys. Garrett was going to be *very* interested in hearing what that debrief had to say.

Garrett needed that last bit of information—plus an interview with the women, if it could be managed—and then he could begin planning the final leg of this op: taking down the Chinese base supporting terror activities in the region, and hunting down and killing a terrorist submarine.

"Skipper?" Jorgensen said, approaching the command chair. "Eng and Weps say the firing system is good to go. All circuits tested out okay."

"It'd better be," Garrett said. "We're going to need it."

It wouldn't be long now.

Saturday, 10 June 2006

Mess Hall, USS *Virginia*
Twelve miles west of Small Dragon Island
South China Sea
1345 hours, Zulu –8

The last shift for the midday meal was over, and, except for the five of them, only the mess crew was left, cleaning up and getting ready for the first supper dogwatch. Because it was the roomiest compartment on board, Garrett had commandeered the area, chasing out a half-dozen off-duty sailors using it as a lounge and posting a sentry at each door.

Katie Milford was present, along with the CIA officer, Jorgensen, and Lieutenant Halstead. Doc Colbert had given Ginger, the other woman, a sedative and was letting her sleep it off in sick bay. Katie's observations on board the terrorist submarine and yacht, however, would be invaluable.

"So the submarine that picked you up was crewed by Arabs," Stevens was saying. "Is that right?"

"Yes, sir," she replied.

"How did you know they were Arabs?"

She shrugged. "I don't know. The language, and the accent of the ones who spoke English kind of sounded like it, you know? Some wore turbans. Most were dark skinned, with beards or at least mustaches. Eyes like Omar Sharif. They *looked* Arab."

" 'Arab' takes on a lot of territory, Miss Milford. What kind of Arab? Saudi? Egyptian? Iraqi?"

"I don't know. Iranian, maybe? Or from Afghanistan?"

"Iranians and Afghani aren't Arabs. Damn it, miss, don't you have *any* clues about who these people are?"

"Take it easy, Stevens," Garrett warned. He understood that Stevens was trying to get information from the woman without leading her, but enough was enough. "Not everybody knows their geography like the crowd at Langley."

Stevens shot Garrett a dark, stay-out-of-my-business look, but changed the direction of his questioning. "What do you remember, Miss Milford? About the submarine. About your captors. Any little detail might help."

"I know Mr. DuPont thought they were Muslims. One of them got mad when he quoted something at him out of the Koran."

"That's *Quran*," Stevens said absently, correcting her pronunciation. "Did they stop to pray five times a day?"

"Mr. Stevens," Katie said with a tired sag to her shoulders, "you have to understand that we spent just about every minute crammed inside that tiny little room. All I saw was the other people from the *Sea*

Breeze, and mostly they were too seasick to talk much. Poor Mr. Schiffer was raving Bible verses at the end, and Mr. Kingsfeld was killed. They took us out one or two at a time when we asked to go to the bathroom, and then stood over us the whole time, watching and making jokes about what we were doing with each other. Once, just once, they took us up on deck to wash ourselves and our clothing in the ocean, and to get some fresh air. That was when the yacht arrived, and we were taken off the sub. After that, things were a little better. We had more room, and better food. We still didn't have privacy, though . . . and when we got to that island, they took the men off and left us there. That's when things started getting *really* bad. . . ."

She gave a shudder, and Garrett interrupted. "Stevens, I don't think badgering Ms. Milford further is going to get us anywhere. We know what we need to know . . . terrorist forces have a submarine in the area, and the Chinese are helping them keep it armed and fueled. Her description sounds to me like a Kilo-class boat. That certainly tallies with your information about a Pakistani boat gone rogue."

"Yes. Yes, it does. But what we still don't know is how committed the Chinese are to this operation. Why are they helping terrorists? What's in it for them?"

"Control of the Spratly Island Group, perhaps," Jorgensen put in. "They don't want an open war with Vietnam, so they get proxies to knock off Vietnamese assets in the region."

"Seems reasonable," Stevens said.

"And it explains the downing of a civilian jetliner," Garrett said. His fists clenched before him on the mess table. He struggled to control his voice. "If the terrorist sub was a Kilo with a surface-to-air missile, they could take on aircraft." He ticked the points off on his fingers. "An American yacht engaged in commercial negotiations with Vietnam. A Nissan car carrier. A Japanese airliner. It looks like they're waging war against Asian nations that are benefiting from Western commercial interests."

"Is that a political statement?" Jorgensen wondered. "Or an economic one?"

"In this day and age, the two are often the same," Stevens pointed out. "Economic power translates as political power."

"Leave it to the CIA to expose the cynical underbelly of terrorism," Halstead said, laughing.

"It's true, though," Garrett said. "When the AQ attacked Manhattan on 9-11, what did they go for? The World Trade Center. The living, breathing image of Western capitalism, and an economy bent on dominating the world. At least, that's the way al Qaeda would see it."

"Are those terrorists al Qaeda, then?" Katie asked. "Like the ones who blew up the Trade Center?"

"Quite possibly . . . or they're a closely related group," Stevens told her. "We've had reports for several years now about another shadowy terror group—called Maktum. The name means 'silent' or 'hidden.' They were a Pakistani offshoot of al Qaeda during the American operation in Afghanistan, and may have been organized to help some Taliban and AQ leaders escape the country. One of their leaders is a Saudi named Mahmud Salah Zahid. Nowadays he goes by the name Zaki Abar."

Garrett nodded. "Zaki."

"We have him in custody now on the yacht," Stevens added, "shaken up but alive. When that helicopter from the *Roosevelt* arrives, he'll be going on a little ride. I expect that when they interrogate the bastard back at Langley, we'll learn all sorts of interesting things about al Qaeda and the Maktum."

"All well and good," Garrett said. "But where does that leave us with the terrorist sub?"

"One thing . . ." Katie said.

"Yes?" Stevens said.

"There was one guy on board that submarine. I think he was an officer. He wasn't Arab. He was Chinese."

"Yes, that confirms that China is helping those bastards," Garrett said.

"Great," Jorgensen added. He made a face. "This could get real nasty, real fast."

Stevens scowled. "Your exec is right, Captain. We need to move on this fast. By now the Chinese on Small Dragon must know something's happened to the *Al Qahir*. They'll be making contingency plans."

"So . . . will the Chinese fight to help their AQ allies?" Jorgensen wondered. "Or stand back and watch us mop the deck with them?"

"They'll fight," Garrett said.

Stevens looked at him, questioning. "And how do you figure that, Captain? The best analysts at Langley have been going crazy for the past few weeks trying to determine the answer to that question. As far as they know, it's an even toss of the coin."

"They'll fight because they've already fought us," Garrett said. "That torpedo attack on the *Virginia* two days ago? I'm betting that that was a Chinese boat."

"What makes you think so?"

"Sun-tzu—a very wise philosopher of things martial—pointed out once that if you know the enemy *and* know yourself, you will always be victorious. Whoever the guy was that popped four fish at us the other day was good. He picked up a Virginia-class submarine, the quietest sub in the ocean, and managed to get into a firing position without us picking him up. I know how good my crew is, Stevens. I know how good—or how lucky—that guy had to be."

"Fine so far. Why couldn't it have been the terrorist sub?"

"Because no Islamic states have been engaged in a naval war since . . . well, the last one I know of was Pakistan and India thirty years ago. You need a shooting war to stay in practice."

"But—"

"There's more. Ms. Milford here has made a point of telling us that the crew of the submarine that picked her up was a pretty ragged and undisciplined bunch. Some in uniform, others in dirty civilian stuff, almost rags in some cases. Her description of what happened—the shooting of one of *Sea Breeze*'s crewmen, the way the women were treated—it all speaks of a lack of discipline that you will not find on an efficient, well-run boat with a well-trained crew.

"But the Chinese *have* been in a shooting naval war recently . . . with us, a couple of years ago. They're still licking their wounds, I imagine, and some of their officers must be thinking pretty dark thoughts about us. Whoever ambushed the *Virginia* Thursday was a pro. That means the Chinese, not a damned mob."

Stevens nodded slowly. "That does make sense."

"Damned right it does. And here's some more sense. If you were the Chinese, sitting here in the Spratlys encouraging your new Muslim allies to take on the whole world, what would you expect would happen next?"

"Well . . . I don't know. I guess I'd expect the United States to strike back somehow."

"Right. How?"

"A naval task force . . ." Stevens's eyes widened. "The Seventh Fleet. The *Roosevelt* carrier battle-group."

"Does it strike you as interesting that the Chinese would arrange things to get the U.S. Navy involved in these waters? Imagine. We come stomping in with a battlegroup, looking for terrorists. And if a couple of torpedoes took out our carrier . . . would we blame the Chinese? Or the terrorists?"

"You're saying it's a trap."

"I'm saying I'm damned suspicious of this whole setup. The Chinese may be political opportunists, but they are not stupid, and they do not engage in foreign military adventurism without *very* good, very practical, very pragmatic reasons behind it. Right now, they're nursing a grudge because of the Taiwan incident a couple of years ago. Maybe some of them see this as a way to strike back without getting themselves involved in another open war. Or maybe the idea is to get us to abandon our support for Taiwan."

"I'm afraid that makes entirely too much sense," Stevens said, thoughtful. "I'm going to want you to write something up to that effect for me to transmit."

Garrett nodded, keeping his thoughts to himself. The report would present yet another opportunity for the Rear-Echelon Micromanagement Freaks to engage in their favorite pastime.

Still, given that they would find a way to microman-age no matter what he did, Garrett thought it better that they do so being fully informed. If the revolution in computer technology and communications made it easier for the REMFs to run things in real time from the comfort of a Pentagon basement, at least they also made it possible for them to do it knowing what the front-line people knew about the situation.

"Captain Garrett" sounded over the 1MC speaker on the mess hall overhead. "Captain Garrett to the control room."

"Damn." He stood. "Katie, you let these people grill you for another ten minutes, max, and then tell them where to get off. Do you read me?"

She smiled. "Aye *aye*, Captain, sir!"

He caught Stevens's eye. "Ten minutes."

"I think we're almost done here, Captain," Stevens said with a shrug.

Moments later, Garrett walked into the control room. Falk, the OOD, wore a worried look. "Whatcha got?"

"Sonar reports a new target, Captain. Sounds like a diesel boat running on its snorkel. Bearing zero-three-zero. It may be making for Small Dragon Island."

"Hot damn!" He swung into his command seat, swiveling to check the big navigation plot board on the control room's aft bulkhead. Zero-three-zero. Northeast, close enough.

Katie Milford had reported that the Muslim-crewed submarine was currently at Small Dragon. She'd seen it at the dock as the men were being led ashore from the *Al Qahir*.

If this contact was coming from the north, there was an excellent chance that it was the one that had taken a shot at *Virginia* two days earlier.

And Garrett *wanted* that sub, wanted it almost as badly as he wanted the Muslim-crewed sub at Small Dragon.

He was in a difficult place. His current task was to keep station with the *Al Qahir* until that Sea Stallion could arrive—an event that would not happen for at least another five hours, might not even happen until tomorrow.

His heart wanted to go after the submarine inside

the enclosed pen at Small Dragon. That would be the Pakistani sub.

That was the boat that had shot down a civilian aircraft, the passenger plane with Kazuko on board.

But Garrett the tactician knew that chance had just handed him a golden opportunity. That diesel boat—probably a Chinese Kilo—was coming into Small Dragon on her snorkel, doing so to recharge her batteries. Snorkeling was an appallingly noisy procedure, one easily tracked by a good sonar crew. This was his chance to nail the bastard that had taken a potshot at *Virginia*, and, just maybe, to even the odds against them a little bit.

The down side: They were not officially at war with China yet, and while *Virginia*'s orders allowed her to fire back if fired upon, Garrett could not prove, incontestably, that the Kilo out there was the same sub that had fired at him. Besides, firing back when fired upon didn't usually include a forty-eight-hour delay between the two salvos.

But in combat, victory generally goes to the side that makes the fewest mistakes, and that other sub skipper out there had just made a big one.

"Mr. Falk, sound battle stations," Garrett announced.

He was going to take that bastard down.

**Control Room, *Yinbi de Gongji*
Eight miles north of Small Dragon Island
South China Sea
1402 hours, Zulu –8**

"Captain! A message from Small Dragon Island!" The messenger handed Jian a printout. He accepted it and scanned down the columns of computer-printed ideo-grams.

Zaki's yacht, *Al Qahir*, appeared to be in trouble. The boat had left the Small Dragon enclosure before midnight the night before last. At a point just twenty kilometers west of the island, *Al Qahir*, as tracked by radar from Small Dragon, appeared to have gone dead in the water. There'd been a confused radio broadcast—something about hitting a reef . . . and then silence for thirty-seven hours.

The presumption was that the yacht had struck a reef, and damaged her radio in the process. *Yinbi*'s orders, signed by General Han, were to proceed west to the yacht's radar-plotted position and investigate. If the yacht was damaged, he was to provide assistance. If the craft could not be repaired, he was to bring Zaki and any of Zaki's key personnel back to base.

Jian did not like the orders. Had he been submerged, of course, he would not have had to acknowledge them, since *Yinbi* couldn't even receive radio signals once she submerged. However, with the snorkel above water, the UHF and broadband radio antennas were as well. The problem with technology, he decided, was that the chair-bound self-declared strategists back at a safe, cozy headquarters office somewhere could decide what the people on the front lines needed to do, directing them like so many expendable pieces in a game of chess.

Jian walked to the navigational chart table and studied the depth soundings west of Small Dragon.

No . . . no . . . no. It didn't fit. Much of the Spratly Island region was poorly charted, true, and there were indeed areas made deadly by reefs and shoal water. But the general area around Small Dragon had been fairly well surveyed when the base there was constructed. If submarines were going to be coming and going to the island, the waters had to be well charted.

And his charts showed open water to the west, with the bottom plunging sharply to a depth ranging between eight hundred and twelve hundred meters. There was no way they could have missed a coral reef that close to the construction site. It just wasn't possible.

If *Al Qahir* had not hit a reef, then, the only reasonable explanations were either some sort of fire and explosion, or enemy action. That fragmentary message hadn't mentioned an explosion. What they'd thought was a reef in otherwise comfortably deep water might well have been some sort of snare designed to stop them preparatory to a boarding action.

At least Jian had to assume that to be the case.

And then something else occurred to him.

Consider. The *Al Qahir* had gone dead in an otherwise empty ocean. If the terrorist yacht had been boarded by enemy commandos, those commandos must have come from somewhere . . . and, since no other radar targets had been detected, no ships or small craft, no aircraft, that somewhere must be an American submarine.

Quite probably the same Seawolf-class submarine he'd engaged two days ago.

So just possibly this encounter would provide Jian and the *Yinbi de Gongji* with a spectacular tactical opportunity. He could approach Zaki's yacht on battery power, silent as death. If the other submarine made a single noise, Jian would be ready with another spread of torpedoes, fired this time from such close range the American would not have time to outrun them.

"Engineer!" he snapped. "What is the charge on our batteries?"

"We've recharged by two-thirds, Captain. I recommend another six hours to bring the charge up to full."

Two-thirds battery power would allow *Yinbi* to maneuver silently for at least six hours, more if they moved slowly.

"Two-thirds will suffice," he replied. "Secure from snorkeling. Secure the diesel. Engage electric motor."

"Yes, Captain!"

"Helm! Come right to new heading, two-six-zero. Make depth one hundred meters, speed eight knots."

"New course two-six-zero! Depth one hundred meters, at speed eight knots! Yes, sir!"

"Sonar!"

"Sonar here, Captain!"

"We will be entering an area almost certainly occupied by an American submarine. I want to know the instant you hear *anything* out of the ordinary!"

"Yes, sir!"

The other submarine captain had the very luck of the devil, as Americans liked to say, evading or surviving a spread of four torpedoes.

That luck, however, was just about to run out.

Control Room, USS *Virginia*
Twelve miles west of Small Dragon Island
South China Sea
1405 hours, Zulu –8

"Target has gone silent, Captain," Queensly reported. "He's secured snorkeling and gone deep."

Damn! Garrett considered the navigational screen for a moment. The other guy was getting cagey.

Why did he choose to go silent now? Garrett closed

his eyes, trying to get inside the mind of his opponent. It *could* be chance, true. The Chinese captain might be under orders to run silent when he was within a certain distance of Small Dragon Island, in order to mask Chinese submarine activities in the area from American sonar.

But there could be a slightly more paranoid explanation. While snorkeling, the other sub's radio antennas, some of them, were above the water. And, as Stevens had pointed out a few minutes ago, the Chinese base must realize that something was wrong with the *Al Qahir*—unmoving and out of communication.

It was entirely possible that the Chinese skipper had just been ordered to investigate the terrorist yacht.

"Weps?" he said.

"Yes, sir," Lieutenant Carpenter replied, turning from his board.

"Warshot status."

"Tubes two and four loaded, sir. Junior is loaded in number one."

"Prepare Junior for EVA."

"Prepare LMRS for EVA, aye aye."

He pressed the switch opening his 1MC mike. "Mr. Stevens, Mr. Jorgensen, Mr. Halstead, Mr. Michaels to the control room."

He checked the status readouts on his console. *Virginia* was currently station-keeping at eighty feet.

Lieutenant Michaels, the command and helm officer for the ASDS, reached the control room first. "You called for me, Captain?"

"Yes, I did. How long will it take to ready the ASDS for launch?"

"Her batteries should be charged up by now, sir. And the go-over for damage after the collision checked out okay. But we'll still need to run through the prelaunch checklist. I'd say . . . twenty minutes? Thirty at the outside."

Garrett scowled. That was not the answer he'd hoped for, though it had been what he'd expected.

As always, working off sonar data alone, the range to the other submarine was unknown. Just working off the nav chart, and assuming the Chinese boat had been on a course to Small Dragon from somewhere north, it *could* be as far away as twenty miles . . . or as close as five.

A Kilo had a top speed of twenty knots. That meant it *could* be moving into firing position within an hour . . . or as soon as fifteen minutes. The other skipper, if he was opting for a silent approach, would probably cut his speed back to twelve knots or less, both to avoid making noise and to allow his sonar operators to hear. That extended the time, but the other boat could still be in the area well inside of half an hour.

And preparing the ASDS for launch, and releasing it from the hatch, were fairly noisy operations. Hell, even if the SEAL minisub was ready to release *now,* there was a good chance the noise would be picked up by the Kilo, if it were as close as five or even ten miles away.

Stevens, Jorgensen, and Halstead entered the control room. "Reporting as ordered, Captain," the exec said.

"Sonar contact, XO. That Chinese boat was snorkeling toward the island, and just went silent. She may be maneuvering to close."

"I should get back aboard the yacht, Captain," Stevens said. "I'll take the women with me, so they'll be safe."

"Negative," Garrett rasped. "There's not enough

time to clear the ASDS for launch. The other guy has his ears on."

"What about surfacing, Captain?" asked Halstead. "Or let me go up with a scuba tank. I want to be with my men."

"Sorry, Lieutenant. Those options are all way too noisy. You're with us for the duration, I'm afraid."

"Damn!"

"I must protest, Captain," Stevens said. "Your priority is to protect the yacht, the hostages, and our prisoners."

"Didn't you hear the man?" Jorgensen snapped. "That hostile is coming *here,* and he's likely coming to have a look at that yacht. Protecting the yacht is exactly what he's trying to do!"

The mission, the boat, the plant, the crew. . . .

"I regret the inconvenience, gentlemen," Garrett said. "You're all four welcome to stay in the control room. Just stay out of the way, and hang on if we have to do some sudden maneuvering. Mr. Jorgensen? I wonder if you would escort Ms. Milford to her quarters, and see to it that she's in a rack, or at least hanging on. This could be a rough ride."

"Like the other day?" Jorgensen grinned. "Yes, sir!"

"I'd like to at least alert my team, on board the yacht," Halstead said.

"Negative, Mr. Halstead. That means coming to periscope depth to raise a mast, and that means noise. Diving Officer!"

"Diving Officer, aye, sir!"

"Rig for ultraquiet!"

"Rig boat for ultraquiet, aye aye, sir!"

"Where's the thermocline?"

"Thermocline is at two hundred eighty feet, Captain."

"Take us down to three hundred ten feet. Helm, bring us to course one-eight-zero."

"Set depth to three-one-zero feet, aye, sir."

"Come to course one-eight-zero, aye, sir!"

Virginia slid into the black silence of the depths.

Saturday, 10 June 2006

Control Room, USS *Virginia*
Twelve miles west of Small Dragon Island
South China Sea
1450 hours, Zulu −8

Ultraquiet running had been developed during the bad old days of the Cold War, a form of silent running specially designed for American attack boats trailing Russian boomers. Each sub skipper set his own preferences from a basic list of possibilities. For *Virginia*, ultraquiet meant the main coolant pumps were switched off in favor of natural circulation; all fans were switched to slow; the fresh water evaporator, laundry, showers, and all maintenance work were secured; and red lamps were switched on and white switched off throughout the boat in order to remind the crew that silent running was in force. The galley was secured except for uncooked meals—peanut butter, cold cuts, and the like—and all hands not on watch were required to be in their bunks. Reading was permitted for off-duty personnel, but no movies, card playing, excessive talking, or exercising were allowed.

During the Cold War, some boats had slipped along in stealthy pursuit of an unsuspecting Russian ballistic missile sub for a week at a time, until the unnatural quiet—the hushed voices and careful movements; the conversations carried out with eyebrows, shrugs, and grimaces—became what passed for normal, and the din that resulted when ultraquiet was secured seemed like a shocking violation of the natural order of things.

The control room was eerie in red light, like a scene out of some Dantean hell. The tension was palpable. The enemy submarine must be out there, not very far away.

Silently, Garrett went over a mental checklist for at least the fiftieth time. Tubes two and four were loaded, and the outer doors already open. Junior had been launched half an hour ago and steered to a point nearly half a mile northeast of *Virginia*'s position, where the UUV was circling slowly, saving its batteries. The boat was rigged for ultraquiet and the crew were at their stations or in their racks.

What had he forgotten? Nothing he could think of. He would have liked to have been able to go ahead and load tube three as well, but reloading was a noisy procedure that could take twenty minutes, and he didn't want to risk being heard by the other boat.

On the control room monitor, dust motes, brilliantly illuminated like stars in deep space, drifted past. Carpenter had switched on the UUV's powerful external lights, bathing the water around the mobile device with illumination. Visibility was limited to perhaps twenty or thirty yards; beyond that range, the light was swallowed by the ocean. The chance of actually being able to see the enemy sub was slim, but there *was* a chance. The Kilo wouldn't be able to see the UUV's lights; that gave them an advantage unheard of in submarine warfare . . . the slender chance of actually spotting the other sub visually.

So far, though, there was nothing but drifting motes within a vast and empty ocean.

A tiny clicking from his chair console attracted Garrett's attention. On the console monitor, a window had opened, and words were typing themselves out in the window.

CAPTAIN, QUEENSLY. POSSIBLE CONTACT, BEARING ZERO-ONE-ZERO. DESIGNATE SIERRA-103.

Garrett opened his touchscreen keyboard and typed out a reply.

DEGREE OF CONFIDENCE?

And Queensly's reply came back seconds later.

LOW. MORE A FEELING THAN ANYTHING ELSE.

Still, for someone of Queensly's skill, a feeling was a damned good thing to go by. When it came to listening to the sounds emerging from the surrounding ocean depths, Garrett put more credence in Queensly's feelings than he did in most men's presentation of solid fact.

The electronic postings of messages back and forth saved having a messenger go back and forth, and was quieter than intercom connections or the 1MC. The silence continued to drag out for another long minute.

The tactical situation was fascinating. Two attack submarines, both among the quietest vehicles ever to slip beneath the surface of the ocean, seeking one another in a game of double blindman's bluff, two opponents each trying simultaneously to hear the other while remaining completely silent. The first one to make a mistake was dead.

The control room monitor continued to show lighted motes of crud streaming past the camera lens, with empty blackness beyond. Garrett had taken a long shot launching the UUV. Without knowing the other submarine's exact course or depth, the chance of acquiring the target visually was remote.

However, he thought suddenly, leaning forward in his chair, there was *another* way to use the UUV.

Typing again, he posted a message to both the weapons console and to sonar.

WEPS. KEY SONAR'S POSSIBLE CONTACT INTO JUNIOR'S NAVIGATIONAL STORAGE.

The reply came back a moment later. DONE.

SEND JUNIOR TOWARD THE CONTACT AT HIGH SPEED. AFTER A FEW MINUTES, HAVE IT GO ACTIVE ON SONAR.

Carpenter didn't respond immediately. When he did, it was to say,

PLEASE CONFIRM ORDER.

SEND JUNIOR TOWARD THE CONTACT AT HIGH SPEED. AFTER THREE MINUTES, SWITCH ON THE UUV'S ACTIVE SONAR. PRETEND TO BE A TORPEDO.

PRETEND TO BE TORPEDO, ROGER THAT!

Junior, the sensor-laden reconnaissance/monitor platform, was still, essentially, an ADCAP torpedo. It could not reach the fifty-knot-plus speed of a Mark 48 ADCAP, but it could hump along at a respectable thirty knots.

And when it moved that fast, it would sound *exactly* like a torpedo in the water.

Control Room, *Yinbi de Gongji*
Twelve miles west of Small Dragon Island
South China Sea
1455 hours, Zulu –8

"Captain! Torpedo! Torpedo in the water!"

"Where?"

"Bearing three-five-eight, speed thirty knots, range eight hundred meters!"

"Helm! Come hard left rudder! Increase speed to twenty knots!"

An ambush! But how had the enemy detected them?

He would worry about that later. Right now, all that mattered was evading the other submarine's torpedo.

Unfortunately, with a maximum speed of twenty knots, a Kilo-class submarine wasn't much of a competitor in a footrace with a torpedo, but Jian could extend the time to impact by moving away from the incoming shot, and it would give him an opportunity to use countermeasures.

The problem was that eight hundred meters was damned close . . . maybe *too* close for a successful evasion.

"Control room, sonar! We're cavitating!"

When a submarine attempted to accelerate too quickly, bubbles could form on the blades of the propeller, and the collapse of those bubbles was both noisy and distinctive.

Yinbi's cavitation was unimportant for the moment. Obviously, the enemy had already spotted them somehow, and some extra noise would not make things worse. . . .

Control Room, USS *Virginia*
Twelve miles west of Small Dragon Island
South China Sea
1456 hours, Zulu −8

"Captain!" Queensly called over Garrett's headphone. "I have a contact, close aboard! Sierra One-zero-three, bearing three-five-five, estimated range two hundred yards! She's a probable Kilo-class boat, and definitely close!"

"Thank you. Update me on the target's movements." *Damn!* Two hundred yards was point-blank range for submarine combat. In fact, the target might be too close for *Virginia*'s torpedoes to arm before they hit the target. This was *not* a good situation!

"I'm picking up cavitation, Captain. Sounds like he's really putting the pedal to the metal! He's at fifteen knots . . . make that eighteen knots . . . still accelerating. Changing aspect too. Looks like he's turning away from our UUV!"

The good news was that at twenty knots, the Kilo's sonar operators wouldn't be able to hear a thing.

"Maneuvering!" he called. "Bring us ahead slow. Come left to bearing two-seven-zero."

"Ahead slow, aye aye. Come left to two-seven-zero, aye aye, sir!"

Virginia had been hovering motionless as she waited, her bow pointed toward the northeast. She needed a bit of way, however—some forward speed—in order to turn. Garrett intended to pivot *Virginia* as sharply as possible, bringing her around until she was heading west. By that time, perhaps, Sierra-103 would have passed *Virginia* traveling south, opening the distance between the two.

At least, that was the tactical idea. . . .

Control Room, *Yinbi de Gongji*
Twelve miles west of Small Dragon Island
South China Sea
1456 hours, Zulu –8

"Speed twenty knots, Captain! Heading now one-eight-zero!"

"Sonar! Range to torpedo?"

"Sir . . . estimate range . . . four hundred meters! Time to impact . . . one minute, twenty seconds!"

"Continue to give me range data."

"Yes, sir! Torpedo range now three hundred seventy meters . . . three hundred fifty meters . . ."

Jian closed his eyes, forming a mental image of the tactical situation. *Yinbi* was running south at flank, the enemy torpedo close behind. The American submarine must be somewhere farther north . . . how far north was unknown. American ADCAP torpedoes had a range of at least thirty-five kilometers.

He would have to be a lot closer than that, however. He could not possibly have detected *Yinbi*'s movements at a range greater than, say two kilometers, and that was giving him a great deal of the benefit of the doubt.

"Range to torpedo now three hundred twenty meters . . . three hundred meters . . ."

No homing sonar yet. That meant the enemy torpedo was being wire-guided, which, in turn, meant the American had a sonar fix on them.

Damn it . . . *how?*

Control Room, USS *Virginia*
Twelve miles west of Small Dragon Island
South China Sea
1457 hours, Zulu −8

"We're closing the range between Junior and Sierra One-oh-three, Captain," Carpenter announced. "Three hundred yards!"

"Sonar! Position on Sierra One-oh-three?"

"He's due west of us now, Skipper. Bearing two-seven-zero, range one hundred eighty yards!"

It was tempting to fire a snapshot now, with the enemy's position so firmly locked in. Torpedoes armed themselves, however, after a set passage of time, a safeguard to prevent a torpedo from acquiring a target lock on the firing submarine, and circling back for what was euphemistically referred to as an own goal. *Virginia's* ADCAPs were set with a thirty-second delay, which translated to about eight hundred yards of travel. The time delay could be reduced, but that was not seen as a healthy tactic. Blowing your own submarine out of the water was not a move calculated to enhance a naval officer's career.

And so, Garrett waited.

On the control room monitor, a dark gray shadow was slowly taking shape, all but hidden in the murk. Garrett found himself fascinated. There'd been times during the Cold War when American subs had passed close enough to a Russian sub to be able to photograph the other vessel's hull through the periscope, but never had this level of detail been possible. He was actually *seeing* the enemy sub, not less than a hundred yards ahead of the remote UUV.

Control Room, *Yinbi de Gongji*
Twelve miles west of Small Dragon Island
South China Sea
1457 hours, Zulu –8

"Torpedo now at one hundred meters, Captain, closing at ten knots!"

Close enough. "Release countermeasures!"

"Countermeasures released, sir!"

"Down planes! Submerge to three hundred meters!"

"Submerge to three hundred meters, yes, sir!"

Jian grabbed hold of a handhold on the periscope housing as the deck tilted sharply beneath his feet. With just a little luck, the American guiding that torpedo would lose his lock on the *Yinbi* as the vessel vanished behind an expanding cloud of bubbles. In that brief moment of invisibility, *Yinbi* would dive, dropping beneath the thermocline and disappearing from the enemy's sonar screens.

Down . . . down . . . and down further still. Would the American torpedo follow?

If they could break the enemy's targeting lock, *Yinbi*

could go deep, then circle back around toward the north.

Toward the enemy. . . .

Control Room, USS *Virginia*
Twelve miles west of Small Dragon Island
South China Sea
1458 hours, Zulu –8

On the monitor, a cloud of silver bubbles exploded across the screen as Junior's lights cast weirdly shifting vistas of shadow and rainbow. For a moment, nothing was visible but the rushing bubbles; then the UUV burst into the clear. The ocean ahead was empty and dark.

"Lost him!" Carpenter exclaimed.

Once behind its countermeasures screen, the Kilo could have turned right or left, gone up or down. "Take Junior down," he ordered. "I'm betting the bastard is going deep."

That, after all, was what Garrett would have done, plunging beneath the thermocline to evade enemy sonar detection.

At first, nothing was visible but darkness. Then, as the UUV continued to descend, once again a dark shadow loomed ahead, barely visible against the even darker night of the ocean depths.

"Got him!" Carpenter exclaimed. "You were right, Skipper!"

"Switch on Junior's active sonar," Garrett ordered. "Let's shake this guy up."

Faintly, the chirp of a sonar pulse sounded through *Virginia*'s bulkhead.

"Captain! Sonar," Queensly said over his headset. "We're below the thermocline, too. We may be illuminating ourselves!"

"Noted, Queenie. But our friend has other things on his mind right now. Keep tracking him!"

The Kilo was diving fast, still moving at a good twenty knots. The rush of water past his hull would drown out any sonar echo bouncing back from the *Virginia*. In any case, the Kilo's sonar people were probably completely focused on the UUV right now.

"Helm," he said. "Continue coming left . . . but open it up a bit. I want to swing around very gently and come in right on the bad guy's tail."

"Aye aye, sir. Continue turn to put us on Sierra One-oh-three's six."

"Diving Officer, take us down to eight hundred feet. But *slowly*. I want him to pull out ahead of us. Make revolutions for five knots."

"Yes, sir. Make depth eight hundred feet. Make revolutions for five knots, aye aye, sir!"

Gently, the deck tilted forward, canted slightly to port as *Virginia* continued her wide turn. The faint chirp of sonar continued to ring and echo in the distance.

"Captain?" Carpenter said. "We're going to have contact with Sierra One-oh-three in another few seconds."

Garrett glanced at the forward monitor. Junior's lights were illuminating the deck and the aft part of the Kilo's sail, now. The UUV was shuddering slightly as it passed through the Kilo's wake; the image steadied as it left the cone of disturbed water astern the Chinese sub, and passed slowly along the afterdeck.

"Slow the UUV, Weps. Have it keep pace with the target, if you can."

"Aye, Skipper. I'll do my best."

"And keep pinging him. I want to keep driving the bastard."

The range between hunter and hunted continued to widen. . . .

Control Room, *Yinbi de Gongji*
Twelve miles west of Small Dragon Island
South China Sea
1459 hours, Zulu −8

PING! . . .

The sonar pulse hammered through the control room bulkhead, a shrill ring assaulting the ears . . . and the mind.

"Captain?" The sonar operator sounded unsure of himself . . . a bad sign.

"What is it?"

"Sir . . . the enemy torpedo. It's slowed to match our speed."

"*What?*"

"I read it as *very* close . . . less than fifty meters, still astern . . . but it has reduced speed to twenty knots. Sir, it appears to be simply following us in our dive."

Impossible! Torpedoes didn't act that way!

PING! . . .

At least, *known* torpedo weapons such as the American Mark 48 ADCAP did not.

Jian wrestled for a moment with the thought that *Yinbi* was being pursued by a new weapon of some kind. If so, it could have one of two possible effects. Either it was intended to give warning that the target could be destroyed at any moment—presumably by the flip of a switch on the enemy submarine's weapons panel—or the device was actually a homing beacon of some sort, a remote vehicle that found and locked on to the target submarine, broadcasting sonar pulses that would very quickly draw *real* torpedoes. If the first, then part of the weapon's purpose was psychological warfare, a means of shaking the target's crew. If the second, the device might be designed to patrol a designated area and lock on to any submarine that entered its homing range, at which point it would begin broadcasting a "here I am" homing message for American submarines or ASW ships or aircraft.

PING! . . .

The question was how much fuel or battery power the device had—how long could it track the *Yinbi* before running out of juice?

And the answer was . . . unknown. American technological prowess certainly suggested that it would have a considerable loiter time depending on its speed and range—as much as an hour, perhaps?

PING! . . .

Several of the men in the control room were looking panicky now, eyes wide as they stared toward the overhead, as if trying to see *Yinbi*'s noisy pursuer. The men remained at their posts, but the tension, the sheer *fear*, was increasing. How much longer before that fear passed out of their control?

"Diving Officer! What is our depth?"

"Passing two hundred twelve meters, sir."

"Level off at two hundred fifty meters."

"Leveling off at two hundred fifty meters, sir." Gently, the deck began rising.

"Slow to ten knots." How closely would the American weapon pursue them?

"Slowing to ten knots, yes, sir!"

PING! . . .

Control Room, USS *Virginia*
Twelve miles west of Small Dragon Island
South China Sea
1458 hours, Zulu –8

"Captain! Sonar! Target is slowing . . . and appears to be leveling off at 775 feet. Speed now fifteen knots . . . still slowing . . . sir, the target is making revolutions for about ten knots."

On the control room monitor, the televised image from Junior showed the aft edge of the Kilo's sail looming huge just ahead, a titanic, oddly tilted cliff partly illuminated by an oval of harsh white light from one of the UUV's lamps. Carpenter hauled the joystick controller over, and, after a delay that was very nearly too long, the remote vehicle yawed sharply to the left, narrowly missing the Kilo's sail. The monitor went black as the UUV twisted away from the target, its cameras again peering out into the empty black of the ocean depths.

"Damn!" Carpenter exclaimed. "He pulled up on me and hit the brakes!"

"That's okay, Weps. Bring Junior around again. Slow to match the target's speed, but stay with him."

"Yes, sir."

Moments passed. Again, the enemy Kilo appeared ahead, a dark and murky shadow moving through the night.

"Mr. Carpenter . . . let's pick up on the pinging. I want to rattle that guy's cage."

Garrett steepled his fingers as he leaned forward in the command chair, watching the display with intent fascination.

Control Room, *Yinbi de Gongji*
Twelve miles west of Small Dragon Island
South China Sea
1459 hours, Zulu −8

PING! . . . PING! . . . PING! . . . PING! . . .

The American weapon's sonar probing had increased sharply, the pings coming very close together now. When the sonar operator gave his next report, it was difficult to hear his words because of the racket.

"Sir! Enemy torpedo now circling around behind us. It appears to have slowed to match our course and speed!"

Jian sagged, eyes closed, fist clenched at his side. The situation was impossible. A submarine lived by remaining unheard, unseen, unnoticed. For any submarine commander, this constant and unrelenting acoustical scrutiny was a kind of hell. Enemy torpedoes, *real* torpedoes, might be on the way already, homing on the acoustical signature of the echoed sonar pulses.

Yinbi de Gongji would die . . . and for what? Operation Yangshandian, a madman's attempt at geopolitical adventurism.

"Diving Officer!"

"Yes, sir!" The man's face was ashen, drenched with sweat.

"Blow main ballast, if you please. Emergency surface."

"Yes, *sir!*"

And *Yinbi* began rising from the depths.

Saturday, 10 June 2006

Control Room, USS *Virginia*
Twelve miles west of Small Dragon Island
South China Sea
1500 hours, Zulu −8

"Captain, Sonar! Target is blowing ballast. Damn, sir, he's *surfacing*!"

Garrett sagged back in his seat, shaky with relief. He'd played a long shot, and won.

During the Cold War, there'd been numerous incidents where Soviet submarines had wandered closer than American commanders liked to key naval targets—an aircraft carrier, say, or a U.S. boomer. With live fire not an option—the two giants had not actually been at war, after all—it was tough to enforce a "back off" order when the other fellow had decided to play hardball. One of the few weapons American attack boat skippers had possessed—short of ramming a too-persistent Soviet sub—was to ping him, relentlessly and unceasingly, letting him know he was smack in the crosshairs of American antisubmarine forces until he either fled or surfaced.

By showing the Chinese sub skipper that he was in *Virginia*'s sights and that he would not be able to get away, Garrett had delivered an ultimatum. Depending on his orders, the Chinese commander might have responded with a torpedo . . . but Garrett had been hoping that the man had more of an instinct for survival than that.

After all, China was not at war with the United States now, either.

"Captain! Sonar! *Torpedoes in the water!*"

"Where? Sierra One-oh-three?" Had the bastard popped a couple of fish as he blew ballast?

"Negative, sir! These are coming from our stern quarter starboard . . . bearing zero-eight-eight, closing at forty-five knots! Estimate range to be . . . thirty-five hundred yards!"

That Chinese sub ahead might not be at war with the United States . . . but *someone* was!

Control Room, *Shuhadaa Muqaddaseen*
Twelve miles west of Small Dragon Island
South China Sea
1501 hours, Zulu –8

"Fire three!"

"Tube three fired electrically, Captain! Torpedo running hot, straight, and normal!"

Ul Haq clung to the periscope housing, feeling the exultation surge through his body. *Shuhadaa Muqad-*

daseen had left Small Dragon Island moments after
General Han had ordered the *Yinbi de Gongji* to investigate the silence of *Al Qahir*. Moving swiftly but
silently, the Pakistani Kilo had approached the battle
zone from the east in time to acoustically "see" the
American submarine banging on Jian's vessel with
sonar . . . apparently from some sort of small remote
weapon or device. The sonar served to illuminate both
vessels from *Shuhadaa Muqaddaseen*'s vantage point.
It hadn't taken long to distinguish the two targets, one
from the other. A Kilo-class boat had an exposed
screw which, though very quiet, still made a distinctive
noise. The American submarine—presumably a
Seawolf-class boat—possessed an eight-bladed propulsor mounted inside a shroud. It too was very quiet . . .
but the noise it made was distinctive as well.

Besides, the Chinese, as far as ul Haq knew, possessed nothing like that small, remote sonar device
that was hammering at Jian's vessel.

The American was in a broad, slow turn away from
the oncoming *Shuhadaa Muqaddaseen*, providing ul
Haq with a nearly ideal shot right up the Yankee sub's
ass. *Perfect!* . . .

Both Khalili and the sub's exec, Muhammad Hassan
Fitaihi, stood with him, waiting expectantly, Fitaihi
with an expression of almost bored self-control,
Khalili with the fanatic's flame of impatience. "How
long?" Khalili demanded.

"Three and a half kilometers, at fifty knots?" the
exec said. "Do the math."

"It depends on what the target does, my friend," ul
Haq said gently. "But at fifty knots, a torpedo travels
roughly a kilometer and a half in one minute."

"So, about two minutes and twenty seconds,"
Khalili observed.

"More," ul Haq said, "if the American tries to out-run our torpedoes."

Which he would do, running being the only viable strategy.

But it would do him no good. The outcome, ul Haq told himself, was assured.

Control Room, USS *Virginia*
Twelve miles west of Small Dragon Island
South China Sea
1501 hours, Zulu −8

"Now three, repeat *three* torpedoes in the water, Captain," Queensly said. "Estimate speed at fifty knots. Time to impact . . . I make it two minutes, fif-teen seconds!"

"Ahead flank!" Garrett ordered. It would take time for *Virginia* to claw her way up to forty knots.

"Sir, new contact . . . designated Sierra One-oh-four! Probable Kilo-class boat at zero-eight-eight, range approximately thirty-five hundred yards, mak-ing revs for twelve knots!"

"Snapshot, two, four, target Sierra One-zero-four!"

"Snapshot, two, four," Carpenter acknowledged. "Target Sierra One-zero-four!"

A snapshot was shooting from the hip, loosing a tor-pedoe without lining up the shot ahead of time. If those incoming fish were wire-guided, it *might* make the other fellow blink and break off before the torpe-does had acquired their own targeting lock.

Chances were, though, that the incoming torpedoes were the usual old Soviet design, free-swimming 533-mm fish that were completely fire-and-forget. If so, the snapshot was more an attempt to extract revenge than anything else, a way of possibly destroying the hostile after *Virginia* had already been hit.

"Torpedo room! Reload tube three, on the double!"

"Torpedo room, aye aye!"

Now, more than ever, Garrett was feeling the essential difference between a Virginia–class submarine and the *Seawolf* he'd last commanded. *Virginia* possessed four torpedo tubes, while a Seawolf–class packed eight. At the moment, *Virginia*'s tube one was out of commission, since it was currently occupied by the retractable arm used to recover the LMRS. Tubes two and four were unavailable as well, since the guidance wires for those two torpedoes would be cut if the tube doors were closed. Until those torps acquired the enemy sub on their own, he couldn't cast them off without essentially throwing them away.

Tube three alone was empty and ready to receive a new fish. He'd held off on loading it because of the noise reloading made, but that was no longer important.

Damn the penny-pinchers in the budget office! Right now, Garrett would have been willing to do just about anything in exchange for a Seawolf's eight-tube salvo capability.

"Speed now thirty knots, Captain! Thirty-two knots . . ."

Those hostile torpedoes would be catching up fast, still incoming at a relative speed of twenty knots or a bit less. Once *Virginia* reached flank speed—about forty knots—they would be catching up at a relatively slow-paced five to ten knots.

Soviet 533-mm torpedoes had a listed range of about ten miles at forty-five knots. If these had been goosed up to fifty, the range would be a bit less. How much less? The answer might determine whether *Virginia* lived or died as she tried to outrun those high-speed fish.

"Speed now at forty knots, Captain."

"Sonar! How are we doing?"

"Estimate range to the nearest torpedo, Captain . . . I make it fifteen hundred yards. Estimate time to impact now at five minutes, ten seconds."

Not enough. If those fish had a range of ten miles at 45 knots, they could run for at least ten to twelve minutes before expiring. *Not fucking enough . . .*

Control Room, *Shuhadaa Muqaddaseen*
Twelve miles west of Small Dragon Island
South China Sea
1502 hours, Zulu –8

"Enemy torpedoes in the water!" the sonar officer announced over ul Haq's headset. "I make it two torpedoes on opposite tacks, north and south."

"Have they acquired us yet?"

"No, sir. They appear to be swinging wide, so as to close on us from opposite directions."

Trying to hem us in, ul Haq thought, *to make it so we can't evade.* "How long before our torpedo hits them?"

"Target is now traveling at an estimated forty knots, Captain," the sonar officer replied. "Time to impact on torpedo one . . . five minutes."

Five minutes. An eternity in combat. He was beginning to have the uncomfortable feeling that he'd fired too soon. If he'd waited, if he'd gotten closer, close enough that the enemy *couldn't* run . . .

"We should close with them, Captain," Khalili said. "We must be certain of the kill!"

"I don't think so," ul Haq replied. "If we do that, we guarantee our own destruction."

"A martyr's death! And we assure the destruction of one of the American supersubs!"

"It is not yet time to speak of martyrdom." Ul Haq shook his head. "Maneuvering! Hard right rudder! Bring us to new course zero-nine-zero!"

Shuhadaa might yet survive this. . . .

Control Room, USS *Virginia*
Twelve miles west of Small Dragon Island
South China Sea
1502 hours, Zulu −8

"Up planes two-zero degrees," Garrett said. "Bring us up to three hundred ten feet."

"Up planes two-zero degrees, aye aye, sir. Make depth three hundred ten feet."

Virginia tilted nose-up as the planesman pulled back on the joystick. The thermocline was at 280 feet, and he wanted to be just beneath it.

Minutes crawled past . . . an intolerable agony of waiting and growing tension. The oncoming torpedoes changed aspect slightly, rising to meet *Virginia* as she moved toward the surface.

"Captain? Sonar."

"Go ahead, Queenie."

"Sir, Sierra One-zero-three just broke through the roof. The noises are faint through the thermocline and at this speed, but it sounds like he's firing up his diesels."

"Very well. Keep half an eye on the bastard, just in case he wants back in the ring."

Possibly the Chinese boat's skipper had opted out of the fight . . . or possibly he would rejoin the battle when he realized *Virginia* was under attack. Either way, there wasn't much *Virginia* could do about it at the moment.

More minutes crawled past. *Virginia* continued racing through the ocean at forty knots, now just beneath that magical interface between the warm waters of the surface, and the frigid waters of the deep.

"Torpedo one is closing, sir. Range two hundred meters . . ."

"Range to torpedo two and torpedo three."

"Two is at approximately two hundred fifty meters. Three is at about two hundred eighty meters."

It would have to do. "Weps! Release countermeasures!"

"Countermeasures released, Captain."

"Maneuvering! Up planes, four-zero degrees! Hard right rudder! Stand us on our tail, Mr. Falk!"

"Up planes forty degrees, aye aye! Hard right rudder, aye aye!"

"Hold on to your stomachs," Master Chief Bollinger called from his post behind the helm station.

The deck tilted wildly, both nose high and canting sharply to starboard. Coffee mugs crashed and clattered across the deck. Nearby, a microphone dangled from its cord at an impossible angle out into the middle of the control room. The men were all strapped in, however, and stayed at their posts. Garrett heard a crash from forward, however, followed by a yell of surprise and pain. *Another one for the Doc*, he thought. He hoped it wasn't serious.

But the order was the mission, the boat, the plant, the crew. Right now the crew had to look after themselves.

Garrett had been wishing the *Virginia* was a Seawolf-class boat, and the extra four torpedo tubes would have been a nice asset. Now, though, he was able to bring *Virginia*'s big strength into play . . . her maneuverability. With a third less the mass of the bulky Seawolf, Garrett could fly the *Virginia* like an aircraft.

At least, that was what he was going to try. . . .

Control Room, *Shuhadaa Muqaddaseen*
Twelve miles west of Small Dragon Island
South China Sea
1506 hours, Zulu −8

"I've lost him!" the sonar officer called, his voice nearly a wail. "I've lost him!"

"What? How?"

"I believe the target has punched up through the thermocline, sir. I'm not picking up his plant noises any longer!"

"Damn!" But there was nothing to be done about that now. *Shuhadaa* was fleeing for her life, trying to slip out from between the two American torpedoes fired five minutes earlier.

The good news was that both American ADCAPS were almost certainly being guided by wire—connected to their torpedo tubes by miles of thin filament. As soon as the enemy sub engaged in a violent maneuver, however, those wires would be cut. If the torpedoes hadn't acquired the *Shuhadaa* yet, there was a good chance the Pakistani boat would be able to run clear.

He hoped. *Allah, the merciful, the compassionate! Protect us now from our enemy's wrath! Keep us unseen, unheard, protect us . . .*

"What did you say?" Khalili asked.

He hadn't realized he'd spoken aloud.

"Nothing."

The waiting was becoming intolerable.

Control Room, USS *Virginia*
Twelve miles west of Small Dragon Island
South China Sea
1506 hours, Zulu −8

"We're above the thermocline, Captain! Torpedoes have lost us!"

"Stay with it, Queenie." If the torpedoes popped above the thermocline and started circling, they might yet reacquire. By sharply turning *Virginia* and doubling back on her track, Garrett was closing the range on the torpedoes before they could reacquire, closing . . . then passing over them, leaving them hunting the *Virginia* off to the west.

They would also start to close the range on the enemy submarine.

"Torpedo room! Reload tubes two and four! Sonar! Have our fish acquired the target?"

"Sir, I can't hear a damned thing at this point. Nothing but splash." Of course. At forty knots, only the loudest noises would make themselves known to *Virginia*'s sonar crew—that Kilo on the surface running on diesels, for example. Or the howl of an incoming torpedo a few hundred yards astern.

Damn. Garrett was willing to bet that the second Kilo out there was the terrorist sub out of Small Dragon. *Kazuko's murderers.*

And they were on the point of getting away again.

An idea . . .

"Weps!"

"Yes, sir."

"Do you still have a lock on Junior?"

Carpenter looked surprised. "Uh . . . yes, sir! Junior is above the thermocline . . . and about four miles away. He went into idle mode when things got exciting."

"That's one way to put it. Okay . . . does he still have enough juice for another mission?"

"I'll see what I can manage, sir," Carpenter said, grinning.

"Drop him below the thermocline. I want to try to track the other boat."

"We'll lose contact with him if we do, Captain."

"I know. But we'll reacquire in a moment."

More minutes passed. Finally, Carpenter announced, "Junior is below the thermocline, sir. We've lost contact."

"Very well. Mr. Falk! Take us to three hundred fifty feet!"

"Make depth three-five-zero feet, aye, sir!"

"Sonar! I want you to keep your ears sharp and polished . . . both for the enemy sub and for those torpedoes astern. I don't want them coming back to bite us!"

"Aye aye, sir!"

Moments later, as *Virginia* slid deeper, Queensly announced, "I hear two enemy torpedoes, Captain.

They're circling . . . trying to reacquire. Range approximately two thousand yards. I don't hear the third fish. It may have gone above the thermocline."

"Or run out of juice." *I hope. . . .*

"We've reacquired Junior, Captain. He's responding to signals."

"Patch the visual from the UUV to the control room monitor."

"Done, Captain." There was a jump, but no marked change on the screen. Both sets of cameras were showing empty ocean.

"Captain, Sonar. I've picked up both of our fish, sir. Bearing zero-two-one and one-two-five. Sierra One-zero-three is right between them, at zero-nine-eight."

"Very well. Weps, steer Junior toward the target. Active pinging."

"Aye aye, sir!"

"Mr. Falk, make depth two-five-zero feet. Take us back up above the thermocline."

"Make depth two-five-zero feet, aye, sir."

"Playing tag, Skipper?" Jorgensen asked.

The exec's quiet voice startled Garrett. He'd not known the man was standing behind him and to his right.

"That's the idea. I don't want Junior to illuminate us for the bad guys. But maybe he can light up the target for our torpedoes."

"Maybe. . . ."

ADCAP torpedoes, for all their sophistication, still possessed idiot-grade brains. Their wires to *Virginia*'s weapons console cut, they would circle until they acquired a sonar target to home on, or until they ran out of fuel. At the moment, they were too far from the enemy submarine to pick up its noise signature, too far to go active and home on the target for themselves.

But they were close enough to the LMRS to pick up its sonar pulse, close enough to hear the pulse and begin following it, Pied-Piperlike.

And the LMRS had been aimed at the enemy by a *human* brain, not the simple-minded yes-no, on-off literalness of a computer chip, however high-tech.

If Junior's batteries could hold out just a little longer. . . .

Control Room, *Shuhadaa Muqaddaseen*
Twelve miles west of Small Dragon Island
South China Sea
1509 hours, Zulu –8

"Another torpedo, Captain! It's gone active!"

"Where?"

"Almost directly astern, sir. Speed thirty knots, range estimated at twelve hundred meters!"

"So close!"

"I couldn't hear him until he went active, Captain. Our speed. . . ."

"Never mind that. What of the other enemy torpedoes?"

"They . . . sir! They appear to have broken off circling and are tracking the third torpedo. Sir! It's leading them to us!"

"I don't believe it!" Khalili snarled.

Ul Haq sighed. "Believe it." There was one chance left . . . to lose the enemy torpedoes above the thermocline. "Diving Officer! Take us up! Make depth ninety meters!"

The deck tipped. They rose. . . .

"Torpedoes appear to be following us, sir! Range one thousand meters!"

Too far for countermeasures to be effective. What was that third American torpedo, anyway? They weren't supposed to be able to *do* that.

A little longer, now. He still had two torpedo tubes loaded and ready to fire. If he could evade this American salvo, he would be able to close for the kill. . . .

Control Room, USS *Virginia*
Twelve miles west of Small Dragon Island
South China Sea
1510 hours, Zulu −8

"Take us below the thermocline, Mr. Falk. Let's see how we stand."

"Aye aye, sir. Depth?"

"Make depth three hundred fifty feet."

"Three hundred fifty feet, aye, sir."

"Captain, Junior is just about dead. He's losing speed."

"Have the torpedoes acquired the target?"

A pause. "Torpedoes have acquired! Yes, sir!"

"Recall Junior, then. Cease active pinging and bring him back in."

"Yes, *sir*!"

"I think Bill is getting attached to that machine," Jorgensen commented.

"If I could give it a medal, XO, I would. Sonar! What's the target doing?"

"I think he may be trying to evade, Skipper. I'm hearing sounds of blowing ballast."

"Is he going up to the roof?"

"It's not a full emergency blow, sir. Sounds like he's just trying to get above the temperature gradient."

Exactly what I would do. "Stay with him." *But he's doing it too little, too late.*

"Both torpedoes are closing fast, now, sir. Time to target now . . . twenty seconds."

Wait for it . . .

"Fifteen seconds . . ."

Control Room, *Shuhadaa Muqaddaseen*
Twelve miles west of Small Dragon Island
South China Sea
1511 hours, Zulu –8

"Range to incoming torpedo . . . three hundred meters! Two hundred fifty! Two hundred! . . ."

"Release countermeasures!" ul Haq barked. "Emergency surface!"

"Countermeasures released!"

"Blow main ballast! Emergency surface!"

Shuhadaa Muqaddaseen shuddered as high-pressure air blasted into her ballast tanks, tanks already partially emptied during her attempt to get above the thermocline. The submarine rose, but sluggishly . . . sluggishly . . .

"One hundred meters! . . . Fifty meters! . . ."

"Hard right rudder!" Maybe he could still twist them aside. The American ADCAPs *must* be nearly out of fuel by now . . .

The nearest ADCAP went dead, its fuel supply exhausted. Automatically, its active sonar switched off and, slowed by friction with the water, it began to sink, having missed the *Shuhadaa* by scant meters.

The second ADCAP still had another twenty seconds of fuel left when it punched through the cloud of countermeasure bubbles and, rising sharply, reacquired the target and drove itself home.

The torpedo struck just forward of the aft diving planes and exploded.

Saturday, 10 June 2006

Control Room, USS _Virginia_
Twelve miles west of Small Dragon Island
South China Sea
1511 hours, Zulu –8

"Hit!"

The sound of the distant explosion rang through _Virginia_'s hull.

Garrett's fist came down on the arm of his command chair. "*Got the bastard!*"

Only much later did another thought arise.

Kazuko. . . .

He felt a wetness on his cheeks. _Not tears,_ he told himself. _Sweat._

And in the red-lit control room, no one would notice.

"Good shot, Captain!" Stevens said, but Garrett ignored him.

Control Room, *Shuhadaa Muqaddaseen*
Twelve miles west of Small Dragon Island
South China Sea
1511 hours, Zulu –8

The explosion aft hammered at the hull, threw men to the deck, and plunged the submarine's interior into darkness. After a moment, emergency generators kicked in and the battle lanterns switched on, but the light was dim and uncertain.

The control room had been tipped almost ninety degrees, so that the aft bulkhead was now the deck, the forward bulkhead the ceiling. Ul Haq struggled to sit up, shoving the chart table off of a painfully injured leg. Around him, pandemonium reigned—men screaming, cursing, praying, shouting, some trying to crowd their way to an escape hatch, others sitting down where they were amid wreckage and debris and injured men and waiting to die.

I had hoped, he thought, *to accomplish more. Merciful Allah . . . we commend ourselves into Your hands. . . .*

Khalili was at his side, eyes wide with terror. "Do something!" the man screamed, his face a hands' breadth from ul Haq's. "*Do something!* Save the ship! Save *us!*"

"There is nothing to be done, my friend. *Shuhadaa* is doomed, as are we." Not even their vaunted Chinese allies could help them now.

Shuhadaa Muqaddaseen was sinking slowly, tail first. A gaping hole blown into the aft machinery spaces had already flooded the shaft and motor compartments, and was swiftly flooding the engineering room. As more and more water flooded the aft compartments and the half-empty trim and ballast tanks, the Kilo's rate of descent increased.

Ul Haq could hear the water shriek as it entered the vessel somewhere beneath him. With every meter of descent, the water pressure outside grew greater. They'd been hit at one hundred meters, more or less. How deep were they now? Four hundred? Four hundred fifty? Too deep, at any rate, to attempt to use the escape trunk and make for the surface. Too deep for anything, in fact, but prayer.

His eardrums popped, the pain sharp and stabbing. With the submarine in this tail-down attitude, the air was trapped in the forward compartments by water boiling in from the open stern. As the water pressure outside increased, so, too, did the air pressure inside. The water would continue to force its way up from engineering as the air was crowded into a smaller and smaller space. The watertight doors had been secured when *Shuhadaa* went to action stations, but evidently the shock of the explosion had sprung enough of them badly enough that they no longer held the pressure.

It didn't matter, of course. One way or another, the immense pressure of the abyss would crush them like a titan's closing fist. Only minutes remained, if that.

The emergency generators failed, again plunging the control room into a darkness so absolute ul Haq could not see his own hand. Around him, the pleading, the cursing, the screaming seemed louder, more frantic. Somehow, the unrelieved darkness made the descent that much more horrific. It was the *knowing* you would never see light again. . . .

A new sound shuddered through the straining bulkheads, high-pitched, grating, and terrible, like a woman's scream, the piercing shriek of a dying ship.

Hands grabbed ul Haq's arm with a fearful intensity. "What's that?" Khalili's voice screamed close by his ear. "*What's happening?*"

The PLAN officer, Hsing was there, part of the tangle of bodies. "It is the martyrdom you wished for," Hsing said quietly.

"Yes," ul Haq added. "Welcome to paradise. . . ."

The titan's hand closed and *Shuhadaa Muqaddaseen* imploded.

Control Room, USS *Virginia*
Twelve miles west of Small Dragon Island
South China Sea
1512 hours, Zulu −8

"I'm getting breakup noises, Captain," Queensly told him over the headset. "I think he's going down fast. He must be almost past his crush depth by—"

A dull, faint *pop* sounded through the bulkhead.

"Okay," Queensly added. "Kill confirmed. Sierra One-zero-four has imploded."

The sea bottom here lay deep—almost three thousand feet. For some reason, Garrett thought about the crossing-the-line ceremony of a couple of weeks ago, of the COB as King Neptune, and Chief Kurzweil as Davy Jones. Gods of the Abyss . . .

Garrett had done some research a few months ago, curious about the origin of the ancient sailor's patron, Davy Jones. What he'd learned had surprised him.

Two thousand years and more ago, one source said, the Celts of northern Europe and the British Isles had worshiped a god of springs and water they called *Dewi* . . . a name derived from the Indo-European *deu*, which simply meant god. For the Welsh, at least according to the article he'd read, Dewi was the ancient Lord of the Abyss . . . and so popular that when Christianity came to those realms, he was reborn as St. David, the patron saint of Wales. And from Saint David, possibly, came Davy Jones, patron of sailors and fishermen and all who risked their lives on—or under—the sea.

Dewi—Lord of the Abyss—at times implacably cruel, at times demanding sacrifice.

This day, the ancient sea king had claimed another sixty souls.

"Mr. Falk," he said. "Take us to periscope depth, if you please."

Sail, *Yinbi de Gongji*
Twelve miles west of Small Dragon Island
South China Sea
1518 hours, Zulu −8

Captain Jian leaned against the side of the sail's weather bridge, drinking in the glorious luxury of the sea air. The tropical summer sun, high in the sky, blazed hot, but the breeze was cool and fresh. After hours locked up beneath the surface with the nauseating stink of diesel fumes imperfectly venting through the snorkel, followed by that hour of deep, stark terror as they'd dueled with the American submarine, emerging into the open air and sunlight was a kind of rebirth.

We're alive. . . .

Yinbi was not alone on the surface. On the northern horizon, the yacht *Al Qahir* wallowed in the gentle swell. Binoculars showed the American flag flying from the jackstaff, and heavily armed men in black vests on her deck. American naval commandos, no doubt. Zaki and his bid to spread terror from the sea were finished.

And finished, too, was the insanity of Operation Yangshandian. "Ocean Lightning" indeed. But the lightning had struck the wrong target.

Beijing had aligned itself with the wrong allies.

By surfacing and switching to diesel power, Jian had demonstrated his desire to end the deadly conflict below. *Yinbi*, pursued relentlessly by that damnable Yankee drone or whatever it had been, would not have had a chance if he'd stayed submerged and tried to slug it out. Moments after surfacing, his sonar officer had reported sounds of another battle raging in the depths . . . a battle ending abruptly with an explosion, followed moments later by the unmistakable sounds of a submarine hull being crushed by the relentless pressure of the deep.

Which contestant had won? Which had died? Jian had his own suspicions, based on what he'd learned about the American commander, simply by having faced him in battle twice. He might never know for sure.

"Captain! Radar! We have multiple airborne contacts approaching from the northeast! Range five kilometers!"

"Very well."

The advance guard of the American fleet, then.

If the American submarine had won the battle, as Jian expected he had, the enemy captain might very well have *Yinbi* in his sights already. Certainly, if *Yinbi* submerged now, Jian risked sending exactly the wrong message to that other commander, and *Yinbi* and all on board would swiftly follow that other submarine into the unrelenting abyss.

Members of al Qaeda and Maktum might welcome martyrdom. Jian, however, was a career naval officer of the naval arm of the People's Liberation Army. As an officer, he followed orders even when he disagreed with them, but he did not needlessly squander the precious assets of his vessel or of his crew. To do so was criminal foolishness.

And so, *Yinbi* remained on the surface, red flag of the People's Republic flying proudly from the mast abaft the periscope array.

What was the identity of the submarine just sunk? Jian believed it must have been the Maktum sub—the *Shuhadaa Muqaddaseen*—but there should have been other PLAN submarines in the region. It could have been another Chinese boat.

But he doubted that. He'd had no confirmation that other Chinese subs were in the region, had begun to believe, in fact, that he'd been hung out to dry, as the American idiom had it. Besides, none of his brother officers would have so intemperately attacked an American submarine. He'd attempted it two days ago only because he'd recognized at that time a perfect tactical opportunity, and a means to achieve the mission's goal. To simply charge into a battle between the *Yinbi* and an alerted American attack submarine was to plead for an early martyrdom.

He wondered if his superiors in Beijing would see it that way . . . for his family's sake, if not for his.

Minutes later, the first of the aircraft came into view, low on the horizon . . . great, gray bug shapes approaching with the clatter of turning rotors. Seahawks, the Americans called them—multirole helicopters arriving as the vanguard of the U.S. fleet. Through his binoculars, he saw the men on board the *Al Qahir* waving.

Yinbi continued motoring along the surface at a placid ten knots, heading east. His first thought had been to return to Small Dragon Island, his original destination, but this display of American air and naval power was making him reconsider. The Americans must know the part the base at Small Dragon had played in this affair, must know, or at least have guessed. It might be best to proceed with great caution, until he saw how this was going to play out.

One of the helicopters flew low across *Yinbi*'s bow, so close he could see the helmeted and black-goggled heads of pilot and copilot in the cockpit as they looked him over. He recognized the aircraft's configuration from his recognition training—an SH-60B Seahawk in its primary role as an ASW helicopter. Slung beneath its gray bulk to either side were a pair of Mark 46 antisubmarine torpedoes—smaller and shorter-ranged than the big submarine-borne AD-CAPs, but deadly nonetheless. The Seahawk banked, circling the *Yinbi* now, making no demands or overtly hostile moves, but maintaining a disquieting presence nonetheless.

If the Americans tried to board or force *Yinbi*'s surrender, he would fight. If they did not . . . all he could do was wait and watch.

"Radio room!" he said over the intercom. "Raise Small Dragon Island. Report that we have been forced to surface, and that we are in visual contact with elements of the American carrier battlegroup."

"Yes, sir!" The voice carried the sharp edge of fear. And well it should. *Yinbi* was still in terrible danger.

"Captain! This is sonar! We're picking up sounds of

a submarine surfacing. Close aboard—one hundred meters or less to starboard."

Jian turned, looking toward the south. Yes . . . perhaps seventy meters away, something was breaking the surface.

Odd. A pair of slender, rounded heads not at all like any periscope Jian had seen were rising from their wake. They were followed moments later by the submarine's sail, black and forbidding.

Jian found those periscope heads fascinating. The whole sail was of an unusual design, much farther forward on the deck, so far as he could see it, and with a sloped, curving step at the sail's foot. What *was* it?

Throughout this operation, Jian had assumed he was facing one of the new American Seawolf-class submarines, but this vessel—while it shared some outward features of a Seawolf—was considerably smaller, and showed some key differences. He'd read reports of a brand new American design, a sub they'd named *Virginia*. Intelligence reports suggested it was as stealthy as the Seawolf, not as well armed, not as capable in some respects, not able to dive as deeply . . . but quite probably more maneuverable and more advanced technologically.

Jian had seen evidence of that maneuverability, and the technology—that sonar-pinging drone—had ended the contest between them.

Technology and maneuverability, however, were not the whole story.

He found himself wondering about the man who commanded that vessel.

He raised his binoculars, studying the other vessel's weather bridge. A man had just appeared there, wearing a khaki shirt, a billed cap, and sunglasses. His opposite number was staring back at him now through his own set of binoculars.

Slowly, Jian lowered his own binoculars, faced the other submarine, and saluted.

Even without the binoculars, he saw the figure on the *Virginia*'s sail return his salute.

Control Room, USS *Virginia*
Thirty miles northwest of Small Dragon Island
South China Sea
2328 hours, Zulu −8

"Open VLS tube one," Garrett said. "Stand by to fire."

"Open VLS tube one," Carpenter replied. "Tube ready to fire."

Virginia cruised at periscope depth. The control room monitor showed the view above the surface—a night-shrouded ocean brightly lit by an almost-full moon high in the sky. Moonlight sparkled and danced from a calm sea.

Not the best night for this type of operation, but it would have to do.

Garrett wasn't worried so much about *Virginia* as he was for the ASDS, released with its full complement of SEALs some six hours ago. SEALs, Lieutenant Halstead had explained, didn't like moonlight. It cramped their style.

Which was why *Virginia* was preparing to launch a Tomahawk.

"Confirm targeting data and GPS link," Garrett said.

"Targeting data uploaded and confirmed," Carpenter said ftom the CCS-2 console. "GPS link confirmed. We're ready to shoot."

"Two more minutes," he said.

The BGM-109 Tomahawk was a submarine-launched cruise missile. Twenty-one feet long and just twenty-one inches in diameter, it could be fired from a submarine's torpedo tube. The preferred launch mode, however, was vertically, through one of *Virginia*'s sixteen Vertical Launch System tubes.

The missile now being prepared for launch was one of the new "TACTOM" birds, a "Tactical Tomahawk" designed expressly for the land-attack role, and supplementing the older TLAM, or Tomahawk Land-Attack Missile. The TACTOM had an improved loiter capability, and a new twist—an on-board camera with a satellite link back to the firing vessel.

The two minutes passed swiftly as the control room crew waited in tense silence. The first Tomahawk to be fired from a submarine during wartime had been launched from a Los Angeles boat operating in the Red Sea, the opening salvo of the 1991 air war against Iraq. Since then, they'd been used in numerous wars and military operations, a means by which a submarine's tactical reach could be extended far, far inland.

This was the first operational launch of the TACTOM variant. Satellite data links were feeding a complete picture of everything that was happening back to the Pentagon. A lot of people back there were *very* interested in the new weapon's performance.

"Ten seconds," Carpenter announced. "Eight . . . seven . . . six . . . five . . . four . . . three . . . two . . . one . . ."

"Fire!" Garrett said.

With a hiss and a slight shudder through the hull, the Tomahawk rose from the submerged submarine. On the control room monitor, a moonlit patch of foam exploded suddenly as the encapsulated weapon broke the surface. The protective shroud fell away, the solid-fuel boosters kicked in, and the Tomahawk rose on a dazzling flare of white light from the tortured surface of the sea.

Automatically, stubby wings deployed as the weapon's on-board brain dropped it into its flight configuration.

The booster burned out, but the missile's air-breathing turbojet engine kicked in. Flying level ten meters above the water, the Tomahawk banked right and vanished toward the southwest.

The TACTOM variant had a range of 1,500 miles, which meant the *Virginia* could have hit a target in Japan—or deep inside China—from its firing point off the Philippine island of Palawan. Its programmed flight path, however, was only eighty miles or so, a vast loop going southwest, then southeast, and finally east, approaching the target from the west. At Mach 7, just under 550 miles per hour, the flight would take eight minutes, thirty seconds.

SEAL Force Trident
Small Dragon Island
South China Sea
2330 hours, Zulu −8

Mark Halstead checked the luminous dial of his watch, then cautiously raised his head above the surface. He was in the shadows here; the ocean was bathed in moonlight, but he was clinging at the moment to one of the massive support pylons that held the Chinese naval base above the partly submerged reef of Small Dragon Island. Here, deep in the shadows beneath the south end of the elevated four-story building, he remained effectively invisible.

The base, however, was on full alert. Several small boats and one of the Hainan-class patrol craft were circling the base constantly, obviously on the alert for any incursion from the sea. He could hear voices in singsong Chinese coming from an external railed walkway some yards above his head.

Yeah, the submarine dogfight that afternoon had stirred these guys up like a stick in a hornet's nest. That didn't matter, however. In a very short while, *Virginia* was going to provide the SEALs with one hell of a spectacular diversion.

He checked his watch again. Eight minutes to go, if the *Virginia* was sticking to schedule. He submerged again to join the other SEALs, hovering in the darkness above the submerged ASDS.

Eight more minutes, and the SEALs—with some help—would demonstrate just how the United States felt about people who aided and sheltered the agents of global terror.

Control Room, USS *Virginia*
Thirty miles northwest of Small Dragon Island
South China Sea
2337 hours, Zulu −8

Carpenter had switched the monitor view to the satellite feed from the Tomahawk's on-board camera. There was nothing more to be done now, save maintaining combat vigilance. That there were other Chinese submarines in the area, Garrett had no doubt, and launching a Tomahawk was a damned noisy business.

But except for that Kilo that had surfaced earlier after the battle, there'd been no sign of them. The Kilo, dogged now by relays of ASW Seahawks off the *Roosevelt*, was still motoring slowly toward the north on the surface, away from the AO.

As for the cruise missile, its course was completely controlled by its programming, its on-board computer taking constant sightings off of three or more GPS satellites at a time and comparing them with stored navigational data. Steered by the GPS system, a Tomahawk had an absolute targeting precision of ten feet or less.

Moonlight flashed and sparkled below as the missile's camera relayed the scene back to *Virginia*—and to the *Roosevelt*, to Yokosuka, and to offices in the Pentagon and at General Dynamics, the TACTOM's builder.

Something, a black rectangle, was visible against the brightly lit sea, far ahead on the horizon. The object grew swiftly as the missile closed the range. The men watching in *Virginia*'s control room and on monitors elsewhere throughout the boat had an instant's glimpse of the structure—a kind of apartment building four stories tall, raised above the sea on stubby pylons, its roof forested with antennas.

Tracer fire—like bright yellow baseballs of light—floated toward the camera as antiaircraft batteries tried to lock in on the hurtling missile. An oncoming Tomahawk, however, presented an extraordinarily difficult target.

The scene shifted slightly as the TACTOM made a final course adjustment; the objective was in two parts—the apartment building to the south, the enclosed docking area to the north topped by a helicopter landing pad. The latter was the target.

In that final instant's glimpse, the watchers saw that the sliding doors to the dock area were open, the interior brightly lit. Within, a Kilo submarine lay alongside the pier, as workers, like tiny black ants, scurried for cover along the dock.

Flying through the open doors, the Tomahawk skimmed above the moored Kilo and slammed into a stack of crated supplies in the warehouse storage beyond. Half a ton of high explosives detonated, and the camera view from the missile abruptly went dead.

Control room personnel erupted with cheers. Garrett let them yell and congratulate for a moment, before saying, "As you were!" They needed the release.

There would be time for celebrating later. Now they needed to see to *Virginia*'s security.

He wondered about that Kilo glimpsed inside the hangar. A second Chinese boat? Probably. What had Stevens said about delivering a message to Beijing? *Message delivered.* . . .

"Take us deep, Mr. Falk. Set depth at five hundred feet. Rig for ultraquiet." Until Garrett was certain that other Chinese attack subs in the area weren't going to try to find *Virginia* and retaliate, he was going to maintain a *very* low profile.

SEAL Force Trident
Small Dragon Island
South China Sea
2338 hours, Zulu −8

The SEALs felt the explosion more than they heard it, a solid *thud* transmitted through the water. Again, Halstead surfaced, raising his head above the oily water, lifting his mask so that he could better see.

The north end of the Chinese base appeared to be in flames. A siren was wailing, and he could hear the clatter of booted feet running on the walkway overhead. Out to sea, the cordon of patrol boats was moving now, circling around to the north end of the structure, presumably to conduct rescue and firefighting operations. The base had been hit hard; they would need all their assets to preserve what was left.

Submerging only long enough to signal the other members of the team, Halstead then emerged from the water, pulling himself up hand over hand along a caving ladder attached to the pylon when they'd first reached the base. A shadow among shadows, he slipped up the pylon and onto the walkway—deserted now by guards who'd rushed off toward the damaged end of the structure.

The other SEALs emerged one at a time, dripping. Rebreathers, fins, masks, and other diving equipment were abandoned. Armed now with H&K MP3 SD5 submachine guns, they moved north a few yards to a ladder set into the side of the structure, an access point discovered earlier during their preliminary reconnaissance from the ASDS.

The ladder took them up four stories, to the flat roof of the building. Two PLA guards died there without even seeing the threat, and then the SEALs were racing toward a wide set of windows set near the center of the building.

They didn't have floor plans of the base, and it was far too large for nine SEALs to conduct a random search. However, careful observation from the LRMS earlier in the evening had identified those brightly lit windows on the north end of the main building as the probable office of the base commander. Monitored signals appeared to be originating in that area of the structure, and careful observation using the zoom capability of the LMRS's Photonic mast had spotted Chinese officers moving around inside or standing at the window. Rank hath its privileges even in the PLA, and the logical conclusion was that the base commander had his office there.

Even if they were wrong, it was obviously an electronic nerve center of some sort. And that was their target.

General Han's Office
PLA Base, Small Dragon Island
Spratly Islands
South China Sea
2345 hours, Zulu −8

General Han Do Liu was talking angrily on the radio telephone. "No, you fools!" he shouted. "I tell you we are under attack! The Americans are bombing us!"

Sirens wailed and swooped in the background, making it difficult to hear the reply. "We have been tracking the American fleet, General. There has been helicopter activity west of you, but we have seen no sign of an air strike. We need to confirm."

"The submarine pen is in flames! What more confirmation do you need? More bombs could be on the way! I tell you, we need—"

The broad windows overlooking the moonlit ocean exploded in a shower of glass. Some were already broken, shattered by the blast a moment ago, but the remaining panes disintegrated with a splintering crash.

At first, Han thought another bomb had gone off . . . but then he saw the commandos, four of them, swinging through the smashed windows on ropes.

American SEALs or Delta Force, he thought. They'd somehow reached the base's roof, rappelled down the side, and blown open the windows. Instinctively, he reached for his sidearm, then froze as the four commandos raised their weapons.

Two covered other areas of the room; the other two trained their weapons on Han. When he looked down, he saw a pair of bright red laser-aiming dots dancing on his chest.

"Drop the weapon!" one of the invaders snapped in badly accented but intelligible Mandarin.

"I speak English," he said, his voice resigned, putting the phone handset down. Could they hear what was happening in Beijing? It hardly mattered. What could they do? Carefully, using thumb and forefinger only, he drew his sidearm from its holster, then dropped it with a clatter to the floor. "Don't shoot."

"The hostages," the American demanded, still speaking Chinese. "Where?"

"The floor beneath this one. They are safe. . . ."

"They'd better be, mister," the other SEAL covering Han growled, speaking English, like him. "Order them brought to this room. All of them. And if your people so much as give any of them a harsh look, you are dead!"

Han nodded, reaching for the intercom microphone. He paused, though, before giving the order. "I am curious," he said, "how you plan to get them off of this base. I assume you arrived by submarine, since we saw no aircraft."

"Never you mind," the SEAL said. "Give the goddamn order!"

Han nodded again and gave the order, emphasizing carefully the need not to harm the prisoners. Two more SEALs, meanwhile, were lowering themselves on ropes down the outside of the building and swinging themselves inside, landing on the glass-covered carpet. How many of them *were* there?

And then he heard the far-off clatter of approaching helicopters, a clatter that swelled rapidly to full-blown aerial thunder. Looking through the shattered windows toward the west, he could see a flight of bulky helicopters silhouetted against the moonlit sky, flying toward the base.

An antiaircraft gun up on the roof opened fire, the burst cut short an instant later by an answering burst from a high-speed rotary cannon on one of the helicopters.

"I suggest you tell your men to stand down," the SEAL group's leader told him. "There's no need for further loss of life."

Han hesitated, then nodded, suddenly tired. He felt . . . broken.

But at least he was still alive. He gave the necessary orders.

Sunday, 11 June 2006
Control Room, USS *Virginia*
Thirty miles northwest of Small Dragon Island
South China Sea
0230 hours, Zulu −8

When *Virginia* returned to periscope depth several hours later, they learned that the brief skirmish for the Chinese base was over. Elements of the U.S. Army

Delta Force had gone in on board MH-60K Black-hawk helicopters belonging to the 160th SOAR(A), the Special Operations Aviation Regiment (Airborne), better known as the Nighthawks. They'd deployed off the *Roosevelt* to a loiter area above the *Al Qahir* in order to present themselves to Chinese radar as more Navy choppers operating around the captured yacht. As soon as the Tomahawk had struck, however, they were on their way, serving as backup and reinforcement for the SEAL element that had already boarded the Chinese base.

The hostages, according to the latest intelligence report from the *Roosevelt*, were safe and en route back to the carrier on a pair of Blackhawks. Delta Force personnel were swarming through the captured base, disarming prisoners and assisting with damage control. According to the last report, the fire was under control. The base commanding officer was also en route to the *Roosevelt*. There might well be diplomatic fallout over this raid, but a PLA general officer in custody would be a valuable playing piece in this insane game of military threat and counterthreat. Beijing would be forced to acknowledge that the hostages had been at their base. Most likely, they would be given a face-saving way out, by way of General Han. He would explain that the PLA had, in fact, *rescued* the hostages from terrorist forces, and that the brief skirmish between Chinese and U.S. units had actually been conducted jointly against the terrorists.

Such a shame about that accidental explosion at the Chinese base, and the loss of one of their Kilo-class attack boats. . . .

And if Beijing didn't care to save face, well, the might of the U.S. Navy now dominated the Spratly Islands. Eventually, they *would* see reason.

"Okay, Nav," he said. "Set course for Small Dragon Island. We have some SEALs to pick up."

"Set course for Small Dragon Island, aye aye, sir," Lieutenant DeKalb replied. "I make our course one-one-zero."

"Ahead one-third."

"Ahead one-third, aye."

Garrett leaned back in the command chair, allowing himself a small measure of relief. Kazuko was avenged . . .

There was not much comfort in the fact. But the people who'd killed her and hundreds of others would not kill again.

"Quite a show, Captain," Stevens, the CIA officer, had said before boarding the helicopter. "Almost makes that swim in the ocean worth it." And he'd grinned as he'd shaken Garrett's hand.

Stevens wasn't a bad sort, Garrett decided. He'd brought in key information when he could have delegated a dangerous mission to someone else, and he hadn't been the micromanaging monster Garrett had half expected him to be.

Even so, Garrett was glad to see him leave the boat.

Just as glad, in fact, as he'd been to see the two women bundled into harnesses and hoisted aboard a hovering Blackhawk. Some among *Virginia*'s crew had loudly mourned the departure of the "honorary Waves," as they'd called them, but even the most vocal of the complainers had swiftly settled back into blissful male-only routine.

It was a relief to have them gone. Garrett considered himself to be reasonably enlightened where feminist issues were concerned . . . but, whatever the words of his written apology back at New London might have said, the reality was that there would be no women on board submarines until the submarines were built with female crew members in mind . . . or until the mores of both the American public and of the naval community changed substantially. A couple of centuries might do it. . . .

He'd had a brief opportunity to talk to both women about it before their departure. Katie had insisted on saying goodbye to him moments before going topside to be strapped into a harness and plucked from *Virginia*'s afterdeck to a waiting helicopter. "Tell me the truth, Captain," she'd said, looking around the control room. "Do you think there'll ever be women on board these things?"

"Katie!" Ginger had said, shocked. "What are you saying?"

"Why?" Garrett had asked. "Are you thinking of volunteering?"

Katie had made a face. "I think I've had enough of submarines," she'd told him.

"Yeah," Ginger had added. "If we get nostalgic, we'll try locking ourselves inside a closet for a week or two! Submarines!" She'd shuddered. "*Ugh!*"

Ginger seemed to have recovered from her ordeal. It sounded, though, like she was going to have a lifelong hatred of small, enclosed spaces.

"Don't worry, Ginger," he'd told her. "We won't have women on submarines for a long time to come." He'd glanced at Katie. "Does that make me a male chauvinist pig?"

"No," she'd told him. "It makes you very male." She'd stood on tiptoe and given him a quick kiss. "Thank you, Captain. For everything."

"And . . . will you thank the SEALs, too?" Ginger had asked. "We never got a chance to talk to them."

"SEALs never hang around to talk to anyone," he

told her. "They're more silent than the Silent Service."

"And . . . Captain," Katie said. "If you get back to Hawaii, look me up, okay? I'm in the Honolulu directory."

He studied her a moment. Katie Milford was smart, sweet, and incredibly sharp despite what she'd gone through. But he was thinking at the moment about Kazuko, and he was feeling terribly old.

"I don't think that would be a good idea, Ms. Milford. I mean . . . don't get me wrong. I'm flattered. But, well, it's not like a submarine captain has anything like a *life,* right?"

"Ms. Milford?" Jorgensen had called from the aft passageway, holding out a bright orange life jacket for her to don. "We're ready for you!"

"Thanks again," she told Garrett. "For everything."

He'd put the women out of his mind almost immediately. *Kazuko.* He still had some grieving to do. And some healing.

In the meantime, though, *Virginia* had a mission to complete.

The mission, the vessel, the plant, the crew. . . .

And only after all of that, the captain. He'd found he was eager to get back to work.

Because, he'd found, and despite what he'd told Katie, he did have a life after all.

A life of command, of duty . . . and of the sea.

EPILOGUE

Friday, 16 June 2006

Passageway, USS *Virginia*
At sea
1530 hours, EST

"Hey, Wall-eye!"

Wallace turned, facing EM1 Kirkpatrick. "Yeah?"

His hands still hurt, still swathed in gauze. The Doc had tried to ship him off the *Virginia* Saturday, evacuating him with several other injured men and the two rescued women, but he'd pleaded his case to the exec and been allowed to stay. His fingers were free of the gauze, and the pain was getting less each day. Jorgensen had discussed his case with the Doc, then ordered him on light duty.

After all that had happened, Wallace was not about to leave his boat, or his shipmates.

This one shipmate, though . . .

"Listen," Kirkpatrick said, towering over him, "I been meaning to talk to you."

"I'm listening."

"About what you did last week . . . down in the torpedo room. Man, that was the gutsiest thing I ever heard of. You're all right, kid. You're really all right!" He looked embarrassed. "That's all I wanted to say."

"Um . . . thank you." He scarcely knew what to say. Jerkpatrick's praise was so completely unexpected.

Wallace watched as Kirkpatrick turned, walking down the passageway toward the enlisted men's forward head. The guy *always* went in there to take a crap about this time of day. Always.

"Hey, Kirkpatrick!"

"What? Make it snappy. I gotta take a dump."

"Better not flush. The head's secured for a sanitary blow."

"What?" He looked at the door to the head. "Since when? There ain't no sign!"

Sheepish, Wallace reached behind him and pulled the sheet of manila tucked into the waistband of his trousers out from under his dungaree shirt. Printed in black marker were the words HEAD SECURED. SANITARY BLOW IN PROCESS.

Sanitary blows weren't as spectacular nowadays as they'd been on the old diesel boats, but heads were still cleaned by pumping air through them to force the waste overboard, and flushing during that operation could have very unpleasant consequences.

He handed the sign to Kirkpatrick. "I, uh, guess this fell off the door, Kirkpatrick."

Kirkpatrick took the sign, glared at it, glared at Wallace . . . and then, unexpectedly, he began to laugh. He laughed loud and he laughed long, holding his belly when the guffaws started to hurt.

"Jesus, kid!" he said, still laughing. "I guess maybe you're one of us after all!"

"Damn straight, Kirkpatrick." Okay, it might be another year or so before he won the coveted dolphins that marked him as a submariner, a breed distinct from no-qual airbreather landlubber *targets*. But after what they'd been through together over the past few days, well, he even felt that in-the-trenches bond of brotherhood with Jerkpatrick here.

"Don't get me wrong, No-qual," Kirkpatrick continued. "You're *still* fuckin' newbie-wet behind the ears . . ."

"Not as wet behind the ears as *you* were just about to be," Wallace replied evenly.

Kirkpatrick laughed again. "Welcome aboard, kid," he said, pounding him on the back. "You just might make a submariner yet!"

Wallace grinned. "It's fuckin' good to be aboard, man."